Hang My Head
and Cry

Also by Elena Santangelo

By Blood Possessed

Hang My Head and Cry

Elena Santangelo

ST. MARTIN'S MINOTAUR
NEW YORK

AUTHOR'S NOTE: All versions of historical events, persons, and places in this novel are either fiction or used fictitiously, as are all other names, characters, incidents, and locales. Any similarity to actual events, places, or persons, living or dead, is entirely coincidental.

HANG MY HEAD AND CRY. Copyright © 2001 by Elena Santangelo. All rights reserved. Printed in the United States of America. No part of this book may be used or reproduced in any manner whatsoever without written permission except in the case of brief quotations embodied in critical articles or reviews. For information, address St. Martin's Press, 175 Fifth Avenue, New York, N.Y. 10010.

www.minotaurbooks.com

ISBN 0-312-26939-0

First Edition: April 2001

10 9 8 7 6 5 4 3 2 1

To my parents

Acknowledgments

Too many people answered my endless research questions, or gave me encouragement, for me to list them all here—you know who you are and I thank you. However, I do need to mention two key players: Linda Hanson, my Charlottesville spy, and Gretchen Hall, who knows her flash points and inspired me to play with matches. I'd also like to acknowledge the University of Virginia's amazing Freedman's Bureau website, which is chock full of post–Civil War documents, and the University of Arizona's History of Pharmacy website. If I got anything wrong, it's my own fault.

As always, huge thanks to Tom Santangelo and Linda Gagliardi for their eyes, ears, and countless nudges in the right direction, and to Kelley Ragland for her superhuman patience.

Hang My Head
and Cry

Who'll Be a Witness?

I have been forty years a slave and forty years free and would be here forty years more to have equal rights for all.

—Sojourner Truth

July 2, 1871—Church Hill, east of Stoke, Virginia

Demon Fire. That's how I describe it to Preacher Moses. Wasn't all yellow like a regular blaze, not at first. The belly of these flames be glowing eerie blue, and they dance atop the church floor without consuming, like that bush in the Bible what Preacher tell us 'bout. I heared a fierce wind, too, but didn't feel more than the summer breeze where I stood, and I smelled the breath of the devil hisself, sweet and tempting as the candy sticks Mama sometimes bring me from Fletcher's Drug Store.

By the time I wake up everybody and we all come running back up the hill, the night was lit up brighter than noon and the church be already half gone. No hearth fire ever burned that fast or fierce.

This morning Preacher stand listening to me and surveying the smoldering mound that only yesterday served as our church, supper hall, schoolhouse, and general gathering place. In the first light of day, the charred wood be shiny as the satiny coat on Colonel Gilbert's black mare.

"You've never seen a whole building burn, Mance,"

Preacher say. "They all go up that quickly. This church was built of old boards, already dried out. Good tinder."

"But I seen the horseman," I told him. "The one from Pockalisp."

"The Apocalypse," he corrected. "And what you *saw*, not seen, was one of those same white men who always ride out here to cause trouble."

Preacher Moses ain't often wrong, so I questioned my own eyes first. True, I seen only one horseman, not four like in the Bible. Also true, both horse and rider be covered with plain white sheets, like the five men what rode out here the night 'fore the last election and gave old Uncle Henry such a whipping as he ain't walked right since. We all knew four of those men be the three Harris brothers and Jack Soyers, on account we recognized their voices, though the sheriff say he can't accuse them since none of us actually seen their faces.

But last night's rider never spoke and, fact was, nobody but me seen him close up this time, so Preacher Moses was just assuming. I shut my eyes, picturing the horseman again as he tossed his torch through the church doorway, and I felt sure something be different about that man.

"Go home, Mance," the preacher say to me. "Get some sleep."

My eyes felt heavy from being up all night, and scratchy from all the smoke—like a pair of rusty horseshoes was weighing down my lids—but I didn't want to miss anything important. "You calling a meeting tonight, like you did last time?"

Preacher Moses faced me then, and I can tell he weren't pleased. "How do you know about that?"

"I seen you and some of the menfolk late that night, walking out toward where them Rebel graves sit looking

2

over the river. Heard you tell everybody they had to go vote, and not let white trash scare them away."

The preacher's jaw got stiff as the statue of George Washington in front of the courthouse down in Stoke. "The laws are on our side, Mance. The Fifteenth Amendment. The two Force Acts. The Ku Klux Klan Act only last April. President Grant'll send the army down here if it keeps up. Voting's the only way we're going to stay free, the only way we can put colored men in the legislature to vote for more laws to help us. You know that."

"Yessuh, I do." I also knew that laws didn't seem to mean much where us dark folk were concerned. True, them first horsemen didn't make good their threats after our men voted, but that was only 'cause the very next night, their ringleader, Jack Soyers, met his Maker. They say he was throwed by his horse down on the Orange Turnpike, where it passes by what's left of the battle trenches. Uncle Henry say Yankee ghosts spooked his mount.

Preacher Moses hunkered down to look me in the eye, then reached up and touched his warm, moist fingers to the skin above my left eyebrow, where I got a birthmark the size and shape of a robin's egg. "The Lord placed His thumbprint on you, Emancipation Jackson, so I know I can trust you. I need you to stay with your mama tonight, to protect her, in case those riders come back. Will you do that, Mance?"

I promised I would. Them Yankee ghosts might not be so obliging this time.

1

July 1, Present-Day

I sat on the brick foundation of Miss Maggie's outside cellar door, swatting at the mosquitos feasting on various parts of my anatomy. My scalp, still wet from a quick shower, was the only cool part of me. The night was so hot I might as well have been standing in front of the ovens at my cousin Angelo's pizza parlor. At least there, the heady aroma of pepperoni was a perk.

Out in front of the house, one of two patrol cars the color of milk chocolate still had its lights on, twin beams of red and white pulsing across the edge of Bell Run's forest every half second, giving me that queasy feeling my stomach always gets when I look at strobe lights.

I tried gazing up at the sky instead, which was violet-blue in the last glow of twilight. Stars were trying to cut through the haze, their light flickering like fluorescent lamps in need of new starters. A solitary bat fluttered by, headed for the river and supper. The dope. All the mosquitos were right here, eating me alive.

Across the side yard, Deputy Dwight Pearson turned on a portable floodlight, washing out sky and stars and attracting an instant cloud of moths. The beam silhouetted the sheriff's precise but ineffectual-looking posture and Miss Maggie's bent-over but dynamic one. Dynamic even in baggy shorts with her bony knees showing.

"Use your head, Dennis," she was saying. "This ground hasn't been disturbed for as long as I can remember." She jabbed an arthritic forefinger at the small strip of churned-up dirt between them—churned up nearly three hours earlier by me, using only a gardening fork and visions of juicy homegrown tomatoes. The two-foot-deep hole at one end of the strip was my doing, too, after unearthing what I'd thought was a piece of odd-shaped tree root. Until I noticed that it had teeth.

"That skull belongs to a life lived at least nine decades ago," Miss Maggie concluded, her estimate based on the fact that she'd called this piece of real estate home all of her ninety-one years and she had a black hole of a memory. "Considering all the action Bell Run saw during the Civil War, we've probably got a soldier here. I'm not going to let you ruin a possible archaeological site."

"We'll wait to hear what the M.E. says, Miz Shelby," Brackin replied, being above all a man who liked to form his own opinions. I'll allow that's not a bad trait for the guru of local law enforcement, but Stoke County had a low crime rate and Brackin didn't get to form opinions often enough to stay in practice. His stubbornness tended to be less motivated by objectivity than by a desire to stall, so as not to resume his Maytag-repairmanlike existence any sooner than he had to.

I stood up, hoping the mosquitos wouldn't be able to find the part of me farthest from the ground, which worked for all of five seconds. From my new vantage point, I surveyed the county's two deputies, now leaning against the side rail of our front porch, shovels in their hands, waiting for the go-ahead. From this distance, Dwight Pearson and Brenda Owens looked like twins—both tall, blond and big-boned, wearing identical uniforms, which tonight were equally wilted with the heat, though Brenda had come on duty for the night shift less than fifteen minutes ago. Neither deputy appeared terribly anxious to do hard labor in this weather.

During Miss Maggie's lifetime, she'd taught eighth-grade history to just about every native of this part of Virginia, including Brackin, and now she gave him one of her teacher glares, guaranteed to make any kid admit to throwing spitballs. Brackin didn't admit to anything, but he did shut up. And luckily, the cell phone hanging on his belt let out an electronic cackle at that moment. He walked a dozen steps away from her as he answered.

Miss Maggie turned her attention back to the hole, grinning down into it like a proud parent. "This is *so* cool, Pat." I'd lost count of how many times she'd said that in the last two-plus hours. If I'd struck gold, I couldn't have made her happier. Historians are odd that way. I should explain that Miss Maggie had spent the past thirty years researching the history of her estate and tracking down the last descendant of the Bell family, who'd lived here until the Civil War left Bell Run in ruins. I was that last descendant. Long story short: Miss Maggie had brought me here in May. I stayed.

Anyway, tonight, when I'd spotted the teeth on the jawbone—after dropping it in horror, then gingerly scooping it into my little trowel and holding it at arm's length—I'd taken it inside to show Miss Maggie. She'd hauled me back outside and had me show her the exact position of the bone as I'd found it, which probably wasn't as accurate as I could have been because I wasn't willing to touch the thing with more than two fingertips. Then she'd made me help her get down on her knees—not an easy movement given her arthritis—where she took up the trowel and gently scraped the dirt away until a bony face seemed to float to the surface. That's when she'd said it was time to bring in experts.

"I still don't understand why you called the sheriff," I said, inching closer. My Italian superstitions were warring with my curiosity and my superstitions were the odds-on favorite, so I stopped inching when I could see the raised eye ridges of the skull. They were almost the same shade of gray-beige as the surrounding soil.

"Law says you have to file a police report if you find human remains. Figured I'd get the formalities out of the way before Emmy shows up."

Emmy was Dr. Emmaline Brewster, an anthropologist from the University of Virginia and another former student of Miss Maggie's. She'd phoned Emmy first to give her the details, and within the half hour we'd gotten a call back from her that everything was arranged. She and one of her lab assistants would be here later tonight.

I glanced up at Brackin, but he, still on the phone, was heading over to his deputies. "You didn't tell the sheriff you already contacted the university, did you?"

"No use complicating the matter. I'll tell Elwood when he shows up." Elwood was the doctor the sheriff summoned whenever he needed a medical examiner. For Miss Maggie, everyone in the county was on a first-name basis.

Miss Maggie let a spontaneous giggle bubble up out of her insides, a pretty scary sound coming through her raspy old vocal cords. "This is the first historic find for the Julia Bell Foundation, Pat. Aren't you excited?"

I hadn't thought of it that way. The whole concept of the Foundation—that is, setting aside the majority of Bell Run's acreage as a historical and environmental classroom—was only six weeks old. The ink had barely dried on the preliminary paperwork. Yet here we were with our first project. It *was* exciting, but I wished I'd found something more along the lines of a lost city. Finding bones *had* to be a bad omen.

"Once word gets out," Miss Maggie was saying, "this is bound to bring in donations—"

My ears pricked up. Bad omen or not, the Bell Foundation needed bucks. I wondered if Yorick would take offense at being a poster child.

"I can't get over it," she continued, a regular motormouth in her enthusiasm. "All the years I've lived in this house and never knew this was here. Then you come along and—what made you dig here, Pat? Weren't you going to put your garden on the other side of the house?"

I nodded. "I thought I wanted a spot that gets sun most of the day." And, I didn't say aloud, the lazy couch-potato inside me wanted a bare piece of ground, where I wouldn't have to chop up sod now or fight weeds later on. "But I couldn't get my fork more than a few inches down into the soil over there."

"Well, what with the drought we've been having these last three weeks, the ground's probably baked into adobe."

Too true. When I'd come here to Bell Run in May, wildflowers had been at high tide, filling every inch of clearing between the house and the surrounding forest. Now only tidal pools of white clover and buttercups remained in the shadier areas, like here on the east side of the house. Everywhere else was matted brown straw.

Miss Maggie had been tolerant of my gardening whim. After living in an apartment all my adult life, I'd felt almost obligated to plant a few tomatoes and peppers, though it was way late in the season to expect much of a crop, even down here in Virginia where the first frost might hold off an extra week or two.

A cynical little inner voice kept whispering that I was really marking my territory.

I justified it by telling myself I was honoring my Italian heritage by continuing one of my family's traditions. Thing was, where Dad put his veggies had never been decided by soil or sun or drainage. No, Mom said he had to plant down at the end of our small yard because the garden attracted sparrows—they nibbled the lettuce and took daily dust baths between the rows of basil sprouts. And Mom didn't want birds pooping anywhere near her clotheslines.

This, I explained to Miss Maggie, was the extent of my landscaping knowledge. "Then this morning I realized that if the wildflowers had dried up and died out back, my plants probably would, too. Actually, I had this recurring dream about it the past few nights: I'm trying to loosen up the hard ground when one of the local farm boys comes up the path from the creek and tells me I should dig over here instead. So I decided to see if my subconscious knew more about gardening than I did."

Miss Maggie raised her eyebrows. "Good thing it was *your* dream. I wouldn't take farming advice from any of the local kids. Football advice maybe. Or drinking and girls."

I shook my head. "No, he wasn't anyone I've met. He was young—eight, ten maybe. A black kid. Real skinny, light complexion. Big mole over one eyebrow."

"Mole?" Magnolia Shelby wasn't easy to shock, but that made her jaw go slack. She grabbed at my forearm, but our combined sweat made her hand slip to my wrist. "This boy in your dream, what was his name?"

Her reaction spooked me and my stomach rolled from more than the strobe effect of the siren lights. "I don't know. He didn't say."

She let go my arm, but now *I* got her teacher look. "I guess Beth Ann must have told you."

Beth Ann Lee and her father, Hugh, were our closest neighbors, over on the other side of the creek. Even though I was nearly three times her thirteen years, Beth Ann and I had a sort of big and little sis relationship. "Told me what?"

Miss Maggie shifted her eyes from me back to Yorick. "Told you about Mance. Because if she didn't, it means Bell Run has itself another ghost."

2

"Ghost?" I exclaimed. "What are you talking about?"

"Hush, Pat. Dennis is coming back." So Miss Maggie got out of an explanation for the time being.

The strobe lights, I noticed, were no longer doing the wave across the wall of trees. Dwight and Brenda had taken one patrol car and vamoosed.

"Traffic accident down off Route 20," Brackin told us. "The state's calling in backup, so I had to let the deputies go." His voice sounded wistful but, being sheriff, he was required to mind the store. Must have been some pileup if the state troopers couldn't handle it alone.

We heard two engines and lots of gravel crunch on the drive through the woods. A new-looking red pickup appeared in the side glare of the floodlight, followed by an Olds sedan that hadn't rolled off a dealer's lot new since the Reagan years. From the latter vehicle emerged Dr. Elwood Walsh, a bald elf of a man who captured my heart with a twinkle of his impish blue eyes. Or maybe it was that the black socks and sandals he wore with his Bermuda shorts reminded me of my dad.

The pickup's driver was a fiftyish woman whose features were all long: height, black hair, even the fingers wrapped around the Minolta that hung from her long neck. Sort of a small-town-America version of Cher. She wore a sleeveless V-neck, the hem of which ended a quarter inch above the frayed edge of very short denim cutoffs.

"Lynn Casey," she said in a voice scratchy and low like Lauren Bacall's. "Official Crime Scene Photographer." Unmasked sarcasm and a deadpan expression. My kind of attitude, so I decided not to begrudge her shapely legs.

"You opened that new studio in town, didn't you?" Miss Maggie asked. "Phreestyle Photo?" Getting a nod for a reply, she went on to do the introductions, including herself. Lynn, I figured, must be a relative newbie in the area.

As the photographer moved around the hole, looking for the best angle, Miss Maggie said, "I want copies of whatever pictures you take now. And I may want you to come back tomorrow or the next day and take some more."

"This for your family album, Ms. Shelby?" Lynn asked, placing the camera to her eye and tapping the shutter button. The machine whirred as the film forwarded. She twisted the camera to vertical and clicked the shutter twice more. "I can take a picture of you and this dude together and do up a Christmas card. Cheaper if you get it done before the fall rush."

"Call me Magnolia." Miss Maggie grinned as she shook her head. "And no, he can't be kin. All the Shelbys and Fletchers are present and accounted for at the Baptist cemetery down the road."

"What about the Bells and Shacklefords?" I asked, meaning the original British settlers on this land, who were responsible for the few drops of non-Italian blood running through my veins. As the only living descendent, I supposed keeping track of the family skeletons fell to me.

"Rest easy, Pat," Miss Maggie said. "The only Bells who ever lived here are buried over in the family plot. The rest are planted in the Presbyterian churchyard down in Orange. And the Shacklefords have a nice spot by the east wall of St. Anne's Episcopal in Stoke. So this fellow can't have anything to do with your ancestors, either."

We watched Lynn's photo shoot, which only took about a minute more. "All yours, Doc," she said as the camera automatically began to rewind. "I'll go develop these now and bring you a set tomorrow, Magnolia."

By the time she drove off down the hill in her pickup, Dr. Walsh had poked around inside the hole and surfaced with the jawbone fragment. Frowning in concentration and making faint humming noises, he turned it over and over in his hands.

"Well, Elwood?" Brackin said impatiently. "What do you think?"

Dr. Walsh looked up, surprised, as if he'd forgotten we were all standing there. "I can say with fair certainty that these bones are at least forty years old."

"How do you know?" Brackin asked.

"Easy. That's how long the missus and I've been coming to Magnolia's Labor Day barbecue. I lost a lot of games of horseshoes right on this spot and I can't say I ever saw evidence of digging here, let alone something like a new grave."

With an irritated sigh, Brackin gave up hope of a moderately fresh corpse. "All right, at least forty years old, but there's no statute of limitations on murder. You can't rule out foul play, can you?"

Dr. Walsh shook his head. "Can't rule it in yet either, unless we're lucky enough to find, say, a bullet inside the skull. Want me to call in a bone expert?"

Brackin's spine stiffened at that, but he said, "If we need to. Once we dig it up—"

This was where Miss Maggie piped in, giving a rundown of Emmy Brewster's credentials. "She'd do it as a favor to me, but she'd want to run the excavation herself, in case she finds anything historically significant."

Dr. Walsh shrugged as he handed Miss Maggie the jawbone

fragment. "Fine by me if she's available. We don't need to be in a big hurry, and Dr. Brewster knows her stuff. I read one of her papers on bone histomorphometry applied to paleohistological analyses. Very impressive."

I was impressed by the big words alone, but Brackin was still stuck back on "run the excavation herself."

"I can authorize putting her up for a night," he said firmly, "and pay her standard travel expenses for a day or two—or better yet, we can bring the bones down to her at the University of Virginia, but the sheriff's office is *not* going to fund a summer-long archaeological dig."

"Nobody's asking you to, Dennis," Miss Maggie said. "She'll stay here and we'll provide her meals. The Bell Foundation will handle any excavation expenses."

With what money? I was tempted to ask, but I held my tongue.

Dr. Walsh volunteered the use of his equipment. "And I can get reimbursement on any forensic testing within the county's budget. Though you might want to warn her that the medical-examiner account gives the phrase 'petty cash' new meaning."

Brackin finally got it through his head that Miss Maggie was going to have her way, but he refused to leave until he'd strung yellow crime-scene tape between the front porch and forest. We finally managed to shoo the both of them away so we could go get beds ready for Dr. Brewster and her assistant.

Miss Maggie used the middle room upstairs for storage. The bed there was the off-season nesting ground for winter blankets and quilts, plus any acrylic sweaters that wouldn't fit in bureau draw-ers. As we toted everything back to my room, to stack atop a clean towel on the floor beside my dresser, I once again asked her what she'd meant about a ghost.

Miss Maggie waited for me to set my load down first before handing me hers so she wouldn't have to bend over. "Beth Ann was only four years old when she and Hugh moved here. She wasn't allowed to roam the forest by herself yet, of course. Her father was working second shift at the Locust Grove Post Office, so I baby-sat Beth Ann at my place. Once the time changed that spring, I started letting her play outside after supper—she stayed on the back porch or on the grass around the house. But after about a week, she started telling me and Hugh about a little boy who came to play with her sometimes."

On the way back to the middle room, Miss Maggie stopped at the hall closet for a set of fresh sheets. "She said his name was Mance and that he had a big brown spot over one eyebrow. Here, Pat, take this last armful. I'll strip the bed."

When I returned, she was already pulling the fitted bottom sheet over the second corner. I tucked it in on the side of the bed closest to the door.

"I started watching Beth Ann out the kitchen window," Miss Maggie continued as she snapped the top sheet open. "She'd talk to herself, but all kids do that when they play alone. I never saw the little boy myself and neither did Hugh."

"So you thought she had an imaginary friend?"

"Exactly. Beth Ann was the right age for that and didn't have kids her age to play with at home. I told Hugh it was just a phase and sure enough, about halfway through the summer—she stopped talking about Mance." Miss Maggie came around my side of the bed to fetch the blue summer-weight spread from a chair near the door. "My, Pat, you do make crisp hospital corners."

"My dad's mentoring. He was a medic in World War Two, stationed at Walter Reed. What makes you think Beth Ann's playmate was a ghost?"

"Nothing else explains how he got into your dream last night."

We finished up that bed and moved to the back room to change the sheets on mine while I mulled over the Mance story. Miss Maggie loved the idea of ghosts. As a historian, they represented eyewitnesses. No more peculiar, I supposed, than an astronomer hoping to find intelligent life on other planets.

As for me, well, besides my inborn superstitions, I'd experienced enough since coming to Virginia not to scoff at the concept of ghosts. At the same time, I wasn't ready to blame the supernatural for every bizarre coincidence. Beth Ann probably *had* mentioned Mance to me. Or maybe Hugh had.

As I was stuffing a pillow into a flowered pillowcase, the grinding sound of tires on gravel floated up through the open windows. "Go on, Miss Maggie. I'll finish up here and come right down."

By the time I pushed through the front screen door—pausing only to flip on the porch light—Miss Maggie was out in the turnaround beside a huge, dark green conversion van, hugging a sixtyish woman who'd apparently just stepped out of the passenger side. Emmaline Brewster was thin and wiry, with a short crop of straight white hair, and leathery skin, already rampant with age spots. Her smile, though, was still as youthful as a college student's. She wore hiking shorts, aged work boots, and her beige T-shirt sported the word "Bonehead" over the profile of a skull.

Miss Maggie was about to start the introductions when another person came around the front of the van. He was African-American, built like Sidney Poitier in his early movies, but with a pinch of Billy Dee Williams's elegance. His black pants, white shirt, and ID card clipped to one belt loop gave the impression he'd been at an office job all day, but the shirt was unbuttoned to his sternum, showing a passel of chest hair, and the cuffs were rolled to his elbows, showing impressive forearm muscles.

The aesthetics of the view were enough to bring a grin to my lips, though there was no smile with the return volley. I had to wonder if his mouth muscles ever engaged in that particular exercise. Or any exercise. In the porch light, what I could see of his expression seemed permanently frozen, except for an occasional shift of his eyes.

Dr. Brewster waved him closer. "This is Theo Clayborne, one of my students."

Student? This was no tender college kid. He didn't look that much younger than my thirty-six years. Like I said: chest hair.

"He volunteered to do the grunt work, at least through this weekend," she continued. "It's his first dig, but since he had access to a vehicle big enough to haul my equipment up here on short notice, his application was cheerfully accepted."

"Meaning she drafted you." Miss Maggie offered him her hand. "No problem—we have plenty of room. Nice to have you aboard." With the same hand, she clapped me on the shoulder. "This is Pat Montella, who found the skull."

"Great," Dr. Brewster said. "Good to have another strong back, too. Hard to get students this time of the summer—most of them are already working digs down in Williamsburg or Jamestown."

Strong back? I smiled meekly, imagining what I was in for, still achy from my half hour of soil chopping earlier in the evening. Then I reminded myself that the Bell Foundation would need to do more of this sort of research in the future and the more I learned now the better. "Glad to help any way I can, Dr. Brewster."

"Emmy. No formality on a dig. Now let's have a look at your bones."

Brackin had taken his floodlight with him, so I fetched a flashlight from the house and met them at the pit. The sideways circle of illumination I cast into the hole made the face truly spooky. On the back of my neck, the sweat suddenly felt chilly and I murmured an awestruck, *"Madonne!"*

Even our veteran anthropologist seemed subdued by the sight. Her voice was almost reverent when she spoke. "You say you found a jawbone first?"

"Part of one," Miss Maggie replied. "After the sheriff left, I put it in the house for safekeeping. Didn't want some animal running off with it overnight."

Emmy nodded. "Good thinking. We'll put some tarp over this hole, too, for the same reason. Let's get what we need out of the van."

Theo had been silent through all this. I'd met shy people in my time, but that label didn't seem to fit him. He had no trouble looking anyone in the eye. He was anything but awkward, moving with graceful assurance, as if he knew exactly what he was doing, first dig or not. But *something*—a hint of caution in his eyes perhaps—made me try to guess what he was thinking.

Turned out all he was thinking was that he should back the van along the side of the house, so as to clear our drive and keep the equipment handy to the excavation site. He told Emmy this in an absolutely kneecap-melting-gorgeous baritone. Even if his proposal hadn't made sense, I don't think any of us could have said no to that voice.

So I got scissors and cut the crime-scene tape, and with the three of us yelling guidance to him, Theo maneuvered the vehicle backwards to within ten yards of the hole.

He switched on the dome light and opened the cargo doors. Inside the van were shovels, five-gallon buckets, short-handled picks, frames with screens stretched over them, probably enough heavy black plastic to cover half the side yard, and a dozen bricks or so, which Emmy said were to hold the ends of the plastic down. Add to that a surveyor's pole and tripod, and a few items that looked like props for *Star Trek* away missions. These last we put inside the house, lined up against the wall of the downstairs hall, because Emmy didn't want them sitting in the van under the heat of the sun tomorrow.

After we tucked Yorick in under a sheet of plastic secured by four bricks, Emmy said, "It's nearly eleven and we'll want to get an early start tomorrow. Time to hit the hay."

We all turned toward the house except Theo, who kept his gaze on the now-covered pit a moment, then scanned the sky above him. "Anyone mind if I sleep on the back porch? Be cooler and it's a beautiful night."

I tilted my head back for the same view. One thing I loved about Bell Run: even on hazy nights, and even without much of a horizon because of the forest, I could see more stars here than anywhere else I'd ever been.

"Skeeters'll suck you dry," Miss Maggie warned him, "but if you're set on it, I have an air mattress you can put under you."

Just as glad not to have to give up my room, I volunteered my non-noxious bug repellent and brought him a couple of citronella candles.

During the heat wave, we'd been leaving all the upstairs doors open and keeping the ceiling fan above the stairwell going to encourage the house's natural cross-ventilation. Tonight, since the only male was camped outside and modesty wasn't an issue, the doors were all open once again. An intermittent tropical breeze wafted in, its stuffy molecules scattered around by a blue-bladed table fan oscillating back and forth on one corner of my dresser.

Loathe to add the heat of a light bulb, or lower the window blinds and interrupt that breeze, I got ready for bed in the dark.

I have a weird nightly routine. Some people read until they're sleepy, some watch TV, some pray, some have sex. Me? I sit beside the window until my eyelids start to droop.

I got hooked doing this the very first night I came to Bell Run. The forest smells, the absence of lights and traffic sounds—the serenity of this place—is the best lullaby I've found. I can wind down and let my mind empty out.

I settled into the wooden chair I keep by one window and leaned my forearms on the sill. The air smelled of honeysuckle and ozone. The crickets had taken over the concert opened last month by spring peepers, and I could hear a few cicadas already auditioning for their coming July gig.

Then I heard faint crackling followed by a series of loud bangs. Our local idiot was setting off his firecrackers again. The sounds came from the development across the road—one of those ugly landscape scabs of upscale, way-too-big, all-look-alike houses built too close together. (To Miss Maggie's and my eternal dismay, the place also bears the name "Bell Run," proclaimed in brass letters on a black, *2001*-like monolith beside the gated entrance.) For the last week, the Idiot had annoyed the neighborhood this way for twenty minutes or so every night. His/her idea of patriotic foreplay, I supposed, to get the rest of us in the mood for the Fourth.

Now that the serene night was ruined completely, I found myself wishing the morning would come sooner. I was anxious to start the dig, wanting proof that those bones belonged to a Civil War soldier. Maybe we'd even find other soldiers buried nearby—a forgotten interment site after Chancellorsville or Wilderness. That way, me happening upon one grave wouldn't seem so coincidental and the dream that led me to dig in that particular spot would be nothing more than a dream.

How did I explain Mance? I couldn't. I also couldn't do anything about finding an explanation until Beth Ann and her father returned home from their week's vacation. When they did, I'd mention Mance to Beth Ann, who'd say, "Oh, you remember—I told you about him," and my overactive imagination could be put to rest.

Thinking about Beth Ann led me to speculate what they'd been up to all week. They were at the shore house Hugh's brother owned down on the Chesapeake, so one could safely surmise swimming and boating. Beth Ann, junior botanist that she was, had probably filled an entire notebook with meticulous sketches of every unusual wildflower she'd come across.

They'd asked me to go with them, but I didn't have the bucks to spare and refused to let Hugh pay my way, even if it was only for groceries and gas, plus there was something a tad too awkward about me tagging along. Not that I minded being a big sis to Beth Ann when she needed one. Big sis, I told myself, not mom. I wasn't ready to feel old enough to be a mom to a teenager.

But Beth Ann wasn't the complication.

Hugh and I tend to butt heads. We've done this from the moment we met two months ago. He can be as stubborn as any of my relatives, which made me feel right at home. Before long our spats became sport, with a little flirting on the sidelines.

Problem was, Hugh was postmaster and sole employee at our local post-office annex, which meant a six-day workweek. The free time he had, he—admirably—spent with his daughter. Granted, half the time they were at our place—Hugh did Miss Maggie's general handiwork and grass mowing, and maintained the trails through Bell Run's forest. But usually the only chances I got to talk to him alone were those days when I walked down the hill to pick up our mail and found no other customer in the post office.

Not that I was complaining. I thoroughly enjoyed our exchanges and felt they'd evolve naturally into *amore* provided I kept my Italian impatience in check and didn't push. Bell Run's mood helped with that—I was learning to slow down and savor the good stuff. Plus I didn't want to rush Hugh, knowing he'd been through hell in his marriage. I also didn't want to rush me.

For the first time in my life, I didn't have to kowtow to anyone on the planet. No inept corporate manager telling me when I had to be at work in the morning and how much unpaid overtime I was expected to put in before I could go home at night. No landlord telling me I had to pay for cigarette burns the last tenant had left on the toilet seat cover. I was my own boss. I was *free*.

Free? The Giamo side of me (my maternal grandfather's Sicilian clan), which defined freedom as financial security, reminded me that my severance would run out on July eighth. After that I expected to be dependent on the State of Pennsylvania while collecting Unemployment for six months, or at least until one of the job applications I'd sown within a five-county area germinated. And no way would the Bell Foundation pull in enough money anytime soon to provide its Executive Director (me) a salary.

Okay, so this feeling of freedom was more of a quality-of-life thing. I knew it couldn't last—I'd have to sell myself into office slavery again—which was exactly why I wanted to relish the moment. And I was relishing it way too much to want to change any aspect of my life merely because a certain man kept popping into my thoughts a lot lately.

Of course, now that Hugh had popped into my thoughts once more, I figured it wouldn't hurt to take a quick peek at my mental snapshot of him. He was still a towering, burly, red-haired hunk, but with each mental scan, I swear he got even better looking. My hyper imagination again, no doubt.

At any rate, he and his daughter would be back Saturday afternoon, and we'd all celebrate Independence Day by eating burgers and tuna steaks (the latter for Miss Maggie's low-cholesterol diet) grilled over charcoal, then go into Stoke to see the fireworks. Something to look forward to while I dug up Yorick.

As the echoes of the last cherry bomb faded, I heard a murmur floating up from below—a wonderfully sonorous voice, though it was little more than undertones. Theo was singing, I realized. I strained to make out the lyrics.

> *". . . Sometimes I feel like a mourning dove,*
> *Hang my head and cry, cry, cry,*
> *Hang my head and cry, cry."*

He breathed incredible emotion out with the words: melancholy, bitterness, despair. Emotions I was sure he never allowed on his face.

I'd felt uneasy around Theo, though I couldn't say why. Was this it? Had I sensed all those hidden feelings?

My inner heckler put forth the notion that the "why" might simply be the color of Theo's skin.

That was silly, I told myself. I wasn't prejudiced. I'd grown up in a racially diverse school district. Hadn't I gotten along fine with the black kids who sat next to me in class and rode my bus? Hadn't we worked side by side decorating the Senior Class float for Homecoming and doing car washes for Student Council?

But none of those kids had been close friends. I'd never gone to their houses, they'd never come to mine. Not because my parents or theirs objected—unless, of course, we're talking boyfriends, because in my house a dream date was defined as Italian Catholic and Mom scared off everyone else. No, the main obstacle was that school integration never trickled down to clique level. And you *always* hung out with your clique. That was an unwritten law. Still is, from what Beth Ann's told me.

So, was my apprehension toward Theo a result of subliminal discrimination? I hoped not, but I wasn't so secure that I could definitely say no. My mind was as full of TV-generated stereotypes as anyone elses.

I couldn't help musing about Theo. Oddly enough, though, his singing reassured me. He had an outlet and knew how to use it. But, thinking about him out there, with no one except Yorick to sing to, the word "vigil" came to mind.

I Gotta Lie Down

The bogus Tennessee Legislature has voted to "abolish all distinctions of color." The question now is, whether the blacks are to be bleached, or the whites to be painted.
—FROM *STAUNTON SPECTATOR*, VIRGINIA, 1868

July 2, 1871—Freedom Holler

Downhill from the church and up the creek a mite, where the west bank was near flat, our six dwellings were arranged in a wide crescent so's all the doors faced the middle. The cabins weren't much to look on, made from whatever lumber could be scavenged after the war. Folks in Stoke called the place Darkieville or the Republic of Nigger, or other such names. Mama say that's 'cause we choose to live separate and not down near Stoke where white folk can keep a watch on us.

Preacher Moses say our place ought rightly to be named Promised Land since we be like the slaves what come out of Egypt. Uncle Henry named it Freedom Holler and everybody like that best. Most the time, though, we all just call it "home."

The doors was wide open this morning to welcome in the breeze, which smelled fresh since it be blowing the church's smoldering away northward. On the creek side of the cabin arc, on t'other side of the path leading up from the town road, was our shared garden. A moanin' dove was pecking between rows of young collards.

Not a body was stirring as I walked across the common yard toward the tiny one-room cabin I lived in with Mama. Most everybody be sleeping after fighting the fire all night, or gone to the work they do for white folk each day.

I stopped to look inside the fenced-in circle that we called the *kraal*, though Uncle Henry say back in Africa that word meant a whole village. Our few scrawny chickens was scratching in the dirt for any of yesterday's seed they might'a missed, and the old she-goat moseyed over to me, hoping it was feeding time. I gave her neck a good rub.

" 'Mancipation Jackson," Mama hissed at me from our doorway, "you get in here."

She was dressed in her white blouse and brown skirt, ready to go cook Sunday dinner for the Nortons. What with the cleaning up after, it like to take her most all day, but she still be coming home earlier than usual. The rest of the week, she out washing clothes and scrubbing floors 'til dark, and two of those days she work late at Caleb Fletcher's store. That's why she wasn't yet back last night, and why, when I climbed up the hill to watch for her on the road, I seen that horseman.

"Where in heaven's name you been, Mance?" she asked, settling her hands on my shoulders soon as I got over the doorsill. Small as Mama be—less'n a head taller'n me and lean as a new calf—she had a sturdy grip. 'Specially when she was asking me questions.

"Helping Preacher Moses, Mama."

She didn't look like she disbelieved me exactly, but I could see her pondering how far that truth went. If I told her what the preacher and me been discussing, I'd have to mention being out late without her say-so—which

24

didn't seem a good idea—so I just added, "I *was*, Mama."

Sighing, she give me a gentle shove toward my pallet of straw under our one window. "You best get some sleep now. I told Ida Putnam you'd help Noah fix their roof after your chores are done."

"Today? But it be Sunday."

"Yes, today." Out of the larder, she took a half loaf of bread that she must've brung home last night. "With the church gone, we'll be meeting tonight 'round the Putnams' hearth, like we used to. They got the biggest cabin."

"We met down at the river, too." I was young at the time, but I remember watching the bullfrogs peeping from the mud along the bank while everybody was praying.

"Only when the weather suited. We'll be meeting close to home from now on." She cut a thin slice of bread and give it to me. "I don't want you heading anywhere alone, Mance. Not for a while. Make sure you do all your chores where somebody can see you and don't go fetching water or firewood by yourself, hear?"

"Yes'm." I nibbled at my morsel, to make it last, as I thought about the cause behind her words. "Mama? Do you recollect the story 'bout Ananse and his wife making people out of clay?"

" 'Course I do." She went over to the row of pegs near the door to fetch her kerchief. "I ain't told you that story in ages. You remember it all?"

I nodded and settled myself down on top of my pallet. "Ananse and his wife, Aso, got put down in a forest on the new-made earth by the god in the sky." I paused, recalling what Preacher Moses say about it—how their names was actually Adam and Eve and they was put in a garden instead. I liked Mama's story better, 'cause Ananse's a spider. Ain't no spiders in the Bible story.

25

Mama must've thought I forgot, 'cause she say, "Then Ananse and Aso got lonely, so they made children out of clay and—"

"I know. They baked them like pots in their fire, only the god in the sky kept interrupting them. So some of them clay children got baked too long and turned dark, and some of them didn't bake long enough and they stayed light. But Ananse and his wife make all them come alive. That's why there's both white and dark folk on the earth now."

"That's right, Mance," she said as she wound the kerchief 'round her hair.

"So how come, if we all made of the same clay, white folk's so mean?"

Mama sighed again—she always be sighing, but this time it sound all weary. "Seems like that, don't it? They's some good white folk, Mance. President Lincoln was good."

I don't remember much of Mr. Lincoln, on account of I was a baby at the time. That was back when Mama be a slave to Travis Jackson, down on t'other side of Stoke. I never was a slave, Mama say, 'cause I was born the week after President Lincoln freed us, which is how I got my name. But to keep me safe those two years 'til the war ended, Mama called me William, the name Mr. Travis pick for me. I don't recall that either.

"Preacher Moses say President Grant be passing laws to help us," I said, "so I reckon he's good, too. Are all the good white folk up north, Mama? Don't seem to be a one here'bouts."

Mama took a clean apron off the shelf beside the hearth and tied it 'round her middle. "I know, Mance. Even those that ain't mean outright—well, they think white folk be better than us. Think we shouldn't even nod a greeting to them on the street 'cause they so blessed.

Boasting and bragging and think they know all. But some ain't so bad. Missus Reynolds, now, she been helping me try to find your brother, ain't she?"

"She married to a black man, Mama, and he be in Congress." Hattie Darden say Missus Reynolds once be so poor that only white trash was courting her, so she marry a black man what owned some land instead, to improve her station. "She *supposed* to help us."

"All right. What about Caleb Fletcher then?"

"You never liked Mr. Fletcher, Mama. You didn't want to go work for him. You told me so."

"That was—" She tucked her apron corners up at her waist to make a big pocket. "Back before the war, Mr. Fletcher be like most other whites. Worse, in fact."

"Worse'n the Harris boys, Mama?"

"Worse'n even them. The war changed folks, Mance. I don't mean just them losing their land and money, I mean they change inside. In their souls. Some got more evil, like Charlie Harris. Caleb Fletcher, well, he give me a job washing his clothes and cleaning up the room back of his drugstore, though he ain't got as much money as most. And sometime he give me food to bring home for you." She glanced at the larder so I knew where the bread come from.

"Preacher Moses say Mr. Fletcher's one of them what don't think colored men ought to vote."

"And Moses don't think women ought to vote. I ain't calling *him* a bad man for it, am I?"

"Women voting?" I exclaimed. "Where'd you get such a notion, Mama?"

"Never you mind." She knelt down by my bed. "Men like Charlie Harris and the one what burned the church last night—think of them like pots where somebody stored fish. Once that smell gets into the clay, you can't get it out. Best thing to do, Mance, is never let bad smells touch your own clay. Understand?"

I was nodding when a big yawn caught up to me. I shut my eyes and must've gone right off to sleep, 'cause I didn't hear Mama leave.

3

For the first time since leaving Pennsylvania, I set my clock radio to wake me up. Less than six weeks had gone by since I'd last tortured myself this way, but that apparently had been time enough for my internal clock to return to its natural circadian rhythms. The sudden blare of the radio, rather than yanking me into consciousness, tricked my brain into believing I was back in my old apartment, with nothing to rise and shine for but nine-to-nine office drudgery. Or rather, for the meager pay earned by that drudgery. All the more depressing because the radio offered not soothing music, but a newscast.

"—in the brutal slaying of a Charlottesville store manager—"

Charlottesville? Since when was that a 'burb of Philly?

Then I remembered where I was. And I smiled. No Dilbert-esque boss to face today. No mission statements. No inane meetings. No butt-kissing or mind poker. No rush-hour traffic. Life was good.

"—No one has been charged in what police are calling a case of road rage. The shooting took place last evening around eight o'clock, on 811 southeast of Route 20 in—"

I'd only been half-listening, but "road rage" and "Route 20" caught my attention. Was this the "traffic accident" Brackin had sent his deputies off to?

"—victim has been identified as thirty-four-year-old Wyatt

Avery of Rock Hill. The state police would like to question the driver of a black Toyota SUV in connection with the incident—"

"Thought I heard your radio on." Miss Maggie stood in my doorway, dressed in a pale yellow T-shirt and tan shorts, looking, as usual, like she'd already been up for hours. "Any more dreams last night?"

"None with Mance in them. Or any other ghosts, for that matter. Sorry."

"Too bad. Guess we'll have to rely on hard work. Wear comfortable old clothes today. You'll get real dirty and real sore."

Lovely. This morning my spine was stiff from digging and the backs of my thighs felt like taut rubber bands from bending over to yank out sod.

"Theo just went into the bathroom," Miss Maggie continued, "so you may want to come down and get breakfast while you wait."

The house had only one full bath—a roomy ex-bedroom with one-inch hexagonal floor tiles, a huge claw-and-ball tub with a pull-around curtain for showering, and a pedestal sink that was so art deco it could have been a set piece in an early Fred Astaire movie. Miss Maggie had added a powder room downstairs in the '50s but, plumbing-wise, it was the sort of arrangement where flushing the powder-room toilet while someone was upstairs in the shower was an act of terrorism.

I'd grown up in a one-bath household, so this kind of choreography was nothing new to me. In fact, I'd often wondered if the lack of communication skills in some my former co-workers could be traced back to them never having had to share a bathroom. Still, I felt grungy as I slipped a pair of shorts under the T-shirt I'd slept in and headed for the kitchen.

I paused at the top of the stairs. Barely audible over the sound of the shower, I could hear Theo singing again. Tiptoeing over to the closed door, I put my ear to the wood. No spirituals this morning. The words sounded like German and the tune like opera.

Down in the kitchen, Miss Maggie had settled herself at the table across from Emmy, who was busy sketching a still life in a spiral-bound notebook. The model for Emmy's artwork—the jawbone fragment—made a whimsical, though spartan, centerpiece between the two women. I felt sure Martha Stewart would have added a garland of belladonna.

"Eat a good breakfast today, Pat," Miss Maggie said as I walked through the doorway. "More than your usual toast."

I opened the fridge and extracted a can of Diet Pepsi for my morning caffeine. With that priority checked off, I grabbed the quart container of plain nonfat yogurt and a plastic basket of fresh blueberries. Two food groups. I could sprinkle bran cereal on top for a third.

Emmy picked up the jawbone to examine the underside. "Looks like this jaw was partially broken before death. Then the weight of the ground finished the job."

A sympathetic twinge hit my own jaw, followed by a sagging in my stomach. All of a sudden the yogurt didn't look so appetizing. Nevertheless, I brought the food over to the sink so I could wash the berries, using a trickle of tepid water so as not to give Theo second-degree burns.

"And," Emmy continued, "the jaw's not from a full-grown man—not a large man anyway."

I turned from the sink to see Miss Maggie grinning like she'd won the lottery, thinking this proof I'd dug up a certain boy with a mole on his head. I perversely asked, "Could it be a woman?"

"Sure," Emmy replied. "I'll be able to determine gender once we dig up more bones. That is, if the whole skeleton's present."

And if it wasn't? Was I ready to hear the body had been decapitated before death, too? Ick.

"But we're getting ahead of ourselves," she continued. "We

need a game plan. Our number one priority is to excavate the bones first, Magnolia, to keep your sheriff happy. Once that's done, and depending what we find, I recommend we do at least two remote sensing surveys to help you two determine where to dig next. Maybe proton magnetometry and ground-penetrating radar."

Sounded more like military reconnaissance to me, but Miss Maggie agreed. "Eventually, I'd love to do remote surveys of the whole property."

Here's where I interrupted. "Uh, the very names of those things sound expensive. The Bell Foundation doesn't—"

"So we'll raise funds." Miss Maggie waved away my misgivings. "I'll put up the front money for the first excavation, then we'll sit and plan."

"Don't worry, Pat," Emmy added. "We'll keep the initial work as bare bones as possible." She cackled at her own joke.

Dribbling a teaspoon of honey over my yogurt, I mixed in the berries. As I fetched the cereal from the pantry shelf, Emmy spread a map over the table and Miss Maggie leaned on her elbows for a closer look. En route back to the sink, I took a gander at it myself. The map was topographical and said "United States Geological Survey" top left and "Stoke County Quadrangle" top right. The detail was such that I had no trouble picking out our house.

"Lookee here," Emmy said, slapping her finger down on a "BM" which seemed to be right where our gravel drive met the parking lot of an abandoned office complex on the other side of the woods to the west. "We'll start there."

"Digging?" I asked incredulously.

"No, surveying," Miss Maggie replied. "That 'BM' stands for 'bench mark.' In other words, there should be a Geological Survey marker on that spot. We need to know the exact map coordinates and elevation where we excavate, Pat. That way if we come back in five years to do another dig, we don't have to guess where we stopped. And if some archaeologist a hundred years hence decides to use our research, he won't curse us for leaving incomplete records."

Emmy stood. "Let's go outside, Magnolia, and figure out where we want our datums."

They bustled out before I could ask what a "datum" was. I finished mixing my yogurt glop and donned a pair of slip-on tennis shoes that I'd kicked off under the kitchen table the day before (I tend to abandon footwear in odd places). Then I carried my bowl and soda can onto the back porch so I could see what Miss Maggie and Emmy were up to—mainly because I didn't want to sit at the table where my only companion was a jaw that had probably eaten its last breakfast more than a century ago.

The sun hadn't found the back of the house yet. As I stepped off of the porch, I heard birds twittering, not close by, but deep under the cool forest canopy. The breeze smelled sweeter this morning, earthy, and felt less humid on my skin.

I made my way around the side of the house, thinking I'd sit on the cellar foundation like I had last night, but Emmy and Miss Maggie had commandeered that position for their own purposes. The corner of the foundation, I was told, was to be our *alpha datum*—"Our own homemade geological marker," Miss Maggie explained. "That way, once we establish the coordinates, we'll be able to take measurements from here."

So I sat on the grass and watched them while I picnicked, deducing from their techno-speak that the idea was to pinpoint two more datums, one due south up near the drive and one due east over near the forest edge, and to use those lines to lay out a grid of five-foot squares. Then, finally, we'd be able to start digging.

Seeing how much nitpicky preliminary work was involved in doing this thing up right, I now fully understood Miss Maggie's fight with the sheriff last night. I also understood that we wouldn't be getting that skull out of the ground this morning. Probably not even today.

I studied the tarp-covered hole, feeling oddly anxious, as if we needed to hurry. *Why?* I wondered. All right, yes, I did want to get this over and done—for my own peace of mind—but it wasn't like Yorick was going anywhere.

And yet, the feeling was strong enough that I retreated back into the house to finish eating (and kick my shoes off again), making the excuse to Miss Maggie that I ought to be in the kitchen when Theo came down so I could get him breakfast.

I was putting my bowl in the dishwasher—and giving myself a lecture about reining in my imagination—when Theo entered the kitchen carrying a large gym bag. He had on gray shorts and a blue button-down shirt whose sleeves had been detached at the shoulders, worn untucked and unbuttoned, so I could see his naval. An innie. And a sexy one at that.

I gave him a rundown of the breakfast options. He chose cereal, which he insisted on getting for himself. A man who didn't need to be waited on—another point in his favor. I told him where everything was before heading upstairs, but at the kitchen doorway, I turned and asked, "I heard you singing in the shower. Um, was that opera?"

He opened the fridge and brought out the milk. "No, *lieder.* Schubert's 'Erlkönig' to be exact."

I nodded as if I knew what he was talking about.

His lips offered a hint of a grin to show he knew I didn't. "I take requests. But, please, not 'Old Man River.' Everyone asks for that."

Show tunes were something I understood. Before I came to Virginia, my idea of a wild weekend was watching a cable TV marathon of movie musicals. And before cable, UHF. I'd seen all the *That's Entertainment* flicks four times apiece. I couldn't resist trying to stump him. "Know anything from *Flower Drum Song?*"

Theo's grin grew into a fully developed, not to mention mischievous, smile. "*No one* asks me for that." He set the milk on the table and belted out the first verse of "I Enjoy Being A Girl," complete with gestures.

Miss Maggie came back in through the screen door as he was punctuating the last line with a dainty curtsy and I was laughing so hard my cheekbones hurt. Applauding, she said, "Much as I'd love to see the encore, we're wasting the coolest part of the day. Pat, soon as you're done in the bathroom, yell down. I want to fill some jugs with drinking water. We'll put 'em outside in the ice chest with one of those cold packs from the freezer."

"Yes'm." Saluting, I dashed upstairs to brush my teeth and take a sponge bath—the real shower would come later, after the day's work on the chain gang.

When I hollered down to Miss Maggie, she called back up, "If you have any shoes more heavy-duty than sneakers, Pat, better put 'em on."

"All I've got are the flats I used to wear to work."

"They'll do."

So I had to decide between black loafers—Thom McCann's so old they qualified as antiques, though they were boy's rather than women's shoes, so they'd probably last through Armageddon—or brown ankle boots—Hush Puppies knockoffs, bought at a bargain store for eight bucks. Either pair would be unbearably hot. I settled on the boots because they looked less nerdy with my shorts, sort of vaguely L. L. Bean-ish. I swiped on a layer of sunblock followed by a layer of bug repellent and decided I was ready for the trenches.

By the time I returned to the kitchen, Theo and Emmy and the surveying equipment had gone off to find the "BM." Miss Maggie was at the sink, centering a clean gallon milk jug under a stream of water from the tap. Another jug was on the counter beside her, already topped off.

"Wait, there's something in that bottle you're filling," I said, coming to stand by her side. Something white was swirling around in the water.

She shut off the tap and held up the jug against the window light. "Where?"

Now the water in the container looked perfectly clear. "I thought I saw a piece of paper or . . . or more like cloth. About the size of—I don't know—maybe a small hankie."

Miss Maggie lowered the container back into the sink and looked into it through the opening, then held the jug up to the light again. Whatever I'd seen wasn't there now.

"Must have been a trick of the light, Miss Maggie."

She shrugged and continued filling the bottle. "While I do this, Pat, you go downstairs and open up the outside cellar door. Take out the big ice chest and get the old wheelbarrow that's back in the corner by the recycling bins."

The latter proved heavy, and I was lugging it backwards up the outer stairs, one step at a time, when I heard wheels coming up the drive. From my perch two steps from the top, I saw a brown sheriff's car come to a stop in our drive a few lengths short of our pull-out. I imagined Brackin chose that spot so he'd have the best view of the cut crime-scene tape, which now that the breeze was dying down, was flat on the ground like a dead snake, right in front of the grille of Theo's van.

Miss Maggie—bedecked in one of her wide-brimmed straw hats—had brought the water outside. Seeing the car, she set the two jugs and cold pack in the cooler, shut it, and headed out front. I got the wheelbarrow over the lip of the stairs, set it down, and followed her.

The driver emerged—not Brackin after all, but Dwight Pearson, who looked like he hadn't gotten much sleep. Must have been out late helping with that road-rage incident. " 'Morning, Mrs. Shelby, Miss Montella," he said distractedly, his attention riveted on Theo's van as if it had driven right out of his fantasies. As he put on his hat, he let out a low, appreciative whistle. "What a beaut. When'd you get that?"

"Not ours," Miss Maggie said. "Belongs to Dr. Brewster's assistant. What brings you out so early, Dwight?"

He kept his eyes on the big Chevy another moment, probably seeing himself behind the wheel, or in back with a woman—his wife, one would hope. Reluctantly, he bumped back down to earth. "Sheriff sent me to observe the excavation."

Miss Maggie grinned at that. "Heck, we'll even let you help out. Wouldn't want you to get bored."

Dwight's expression said he'd rather be down on Route 3 using speeders for radar gun target practice, but his reply was, "Yes, ma'am, be glad to."

"You've got time to go change out of that hot uniform, Dwight. We're still doing the surveying." She gestured to the west side of the clearing, to where the gravel drive reentered the forest. There, right where the road curved around an ancient oak tree, Emmy and Theo were setting up their tripod in the low brush on the opposite shoulder.

As if Emmy heard us, she yelled across the clearing, "Pat, got a job for you," and signaled me to join her.

I left Miss Maggie talking to Dwight and jogged over. Theo was down on his knees, copying coordinates from Emmy's notebook onto what looked like a metal canning lid insert that had been nailed into the ground.

Emmy pointed at the long four-sided pole stretched out on the side of the road. "Take the rod over to Magnolia. She'll show you what to do with it. I want to teach Theo how to read the transit here."

I did as asked—the pole was awkward but lightweight—and Miss Maggie excused herself from her conversation with the deputy. Dwight got back in his car and started it, but he didn't leave to go change. As I walked by, I could see him holding his shoulder radio mike to his mouth, probably checking with Brackin to see if he ought to observe this part, too.

Miss Maggie beckoned me to a spot about ten yards in from the road and closer to the forest, where another canning lid had been nailed down. "This is our 'B' datum—lined up along magnetic north with the corner of the cellar foundation. We'll put something more permanent here eventually. Set the rod so the numbered side's facing Emmy and make it flush with that nail in the center of the datum." She showed me how to stand behind the shaft with my hands flat on either side, so as not to block the numbers, and how to use the built-in level to make sure the pole was plumb.

I stood like a statue until Emmy waved that they were done. Theo hoisted the tripod onto his shoulder and they walked over to us.

"Same routine," Emmy said as Theo set up the tripod and took her notebook so he could copy the "B" coordinates onto the canning lid. "Pat, take the rod up to the cellar foundation and we'll take the reading from here—"

"Just a minute." Dwight Pearson had come up behind us, right hand resting on his belt behind his gun. The last time I'd seen a cop in that posture was the one time I'd been stopped for speeding. Official police mode. The next thing out of his mouth confirmed it. "Sir, I need to ask you some questions."

The only "sir" among us was Theo. He stood warily.

"That your van?" Dwight asked, jerking his chin in the general direction of the Chevy.

"Belongs to a buddy of mine," Theo replied. "He let me borrow it for the weekend."

"I need to see the vehicle registration and your driver's license, please."

"What for?" Emmy asked, and Miss Maggie tacked on, "Something wrong with the van, Dwight? The plates expired?"

"No, ma'am, nothing like that. Your ID, sir?"

Theo reached into his back pocket for his wallet, his face immobile, muscles tense around his mouth. Same look I'd seen on every worker in my old office whenever the boss blamed us for his own mistakes.

Dwight took the cards Theo handed over. " 'Clayborne,' " he read, his eyebrows rising so much I thought his hat might fall off. "Now, don't that beat all. Must be my lucky day." He drew himself up with new authority. "You know the state troopers are looking for you?"

Theo blinked—which I interpreted as a "no"—but he said nothing. Miss Maggie, Emmy, and I all asked a version of, "Why? What'd he do?"

"Don't know that he *did* anything." Dwight tapped the registration card with the back of his forefinger. "But his buddy here—the Wyatt Avery who owns that van—got himself shot and killed last night. The Honda Civic that Avery was found in is registered to Mr. Clayborne here. Yessir, the state police are *real* anxious to talk to you."

WADE IN THE WATER

They said I must quit preaching, and put a card in the
newspaper renouncing republicanism . . . if I did not
they would come back the next week and kill me.
—Black minister Elias Hill, testifying before a
Congressional committee about the Ku Klux Klan,
1871

July 2, 1871—along Sweetwater Creek

The water was carrying it along so quick, at first I figured
it for some kind of white fish. As it swirled around the
deep pool upcreek where Lilla Putnam and me was fetching water, I tried to scoop up the fish with my bucket.
The white form disappeared, sucked under the surface.
The next moment, though, down where the stream got
shallow again, I saw the object bob up and snag between
two mossy rocks.

Curious, I walked along the bank and waded out to
the spot.

"What'ya find, Mance?" Lilla called after she'd hauled
up the last bucket we been filling. She was older'n me and
wont to boss me some, so I was surprised she asked 'stead
of yelling 'bout me leaving her to the work.

I plucked the thing out of the water, wrung it out, and
brought it back to her.

"Jes' an old white glove," she said, disappointed.

"Not so old." The only wear I could see was that the seam along the thumb was strained nearly apart. Must've been a big hand that pushed at it like that, 'cause I could get both my hands inside easy. And suddenly I recollected where I seen big hands wearing white gloves. "The rider last night—he was wearing gloves just like this."

"You jes' saying that to spook me." She made her voice mad, but her eyes got round and she glanced over her shoulder back into the woods.

The cabins were in sight downstream, so I wasn't scared like her, and anyway, this was our last load of water. I pulled on the glove so's not to lose it, and hefted two of the wood buckets, careful not to let the water splash over the brims.

"Don't make sense, Mance," Lilla say on the walk back, her mind still turning my words over. "Riders don't wear gloves like that. They's for rich folk being rode around in a fancy carriage, not for holding horse reins. 'Member last time? Them Harris brothers and Jack Soyers—they was all wearing leather gloves. 'Member?"

"Last night be too hot for wearing leather." Seem to me, though, no man what burns a church be the type to consider his comfort that way. 'Least, not when he be planning on carrying a flaming torch.

I followed Lilla down the path back to our cabins while I considered the problem.

4

Dwight recounted his luck to Brackin via his shoulder radio, prefacing his official report with, "Hey, Sheriff, you know that shooting last night? That black boy in Orange County?" Apparently, Stoke County had no budget for political-correctness training.

Brackin told Dwight to bring Theo in for questioning.

Miss Maggie stood on tiptoes, grabbed the mike and shouted at Dwight's shoulder, "Dennis, you can just haul your butt up here. Theo's not going anywhere."

"Now, Miz Shelby," his voice came back, "I've got to call in the state troopers and—"

"I don't care who else you bring along, Dennis. See you when you get here. Over and out." She walked away—leaving Dwight to do the play-by-play. To the rest of us, she said, "Might as well go sit on the porch and wait like civilized folk."

"If it's all the same to everyone else," Theo said, "I'd as soon get back to work. Like you said, Ms. Shelby, the day won't be getting any cooler." It sounded callous—he'd just heard of the death of a friend. Probably a close friend. You don't swap cars with anybody.

Then again, when I lost my dad, and a few years later, my mom—both times I'd gone back to my apartment and cleaned, baked, polished, and sorted whatever I could get my hands on. After a week or so, I began to let grief in a little at a time, in increments small enough that I could stand it. For me, busywork takes the place of a primal scream.

For Theo, too? Or, remembering his song last night, I wondered if he might be postponing his grief, until he could sneak off by himself to sing dirges.

But he was right—the day wasn't getting any cooler. The sun was now high enough that only half the side yard was still in the shade, and I'd swear we'd gained ten degrees in the last fifteen minutes. My boots were foot ovens and my dark hair was beginning to feel like a thermal blanket. I envied Miss Maggie her straw hat.

Her reply to Theo was a shrug. "Fine by me. Emmy?"

Emmy shook off the stunned look in her eyes. "Sure. Pat, take the rod back to the cellar foundation."

Miss Maggie came with me to show me where to set the pole. Once I was situated and in statue mode once more, she asked, "What do you think of Theo, Pat? Gut feeling."

Since he was behind the transit and I had to look at him anyway, I gave him a once-over. Emmy, I noted, was doing the same thing just out of Theo's line of vision. So was Dwight, standing beside his car, thumbs hooked over his belt. Emmy's attitude was supportive, Dwight's was watchful. Theo's body language was no help—he might as well have been carved from marble. "I don't know, Miss Maggie. He doesn't give away anything. All my guts have to go on is that he knows the words to uncommon show tunes."

"I'll assume that's a point in his favor. Emmy said he has a music degree. Sings in churches. In fact, he's scheduled to sing at a wedding a week from Saturday. But she said he can't make a good living with his voice. Too much of an introvert to really promote himself."

Theo waved his arm, indicating that I could relax. "So he's going into anthropology instead?"

"Actually, he's majoring in computer science—his employer's paying his tuition. This past semester he took one of Emmy's courses as an elective. She said he not only aced it, he started spending most of his free time helping out in the lab, cleaning and sorting artifacts, asking questions, learning everything he could. Emmy thinks he'd switch majors if he could afford to lose his job and pay the tuition himself." Miss Maggie shooed a gnat away from her nose. "Of course, Theo's at an age where he's getting antsy about the parts of his life that aren't satisfying. Perfectly normal."

I was glad she thought so, seeing as I was in the same age bracket, and probably even more antsy. I opened my mouth to ask her what she thought about his friend's murder when we both heard the muted gurgle of the phone ringing inside the house.

"Get it, Pat," she said. "If it's for me, I'll call back."

I ran for the back door and made it to the kitchen before the next ring. The two phones in the house—one on each floor—are both cordless. Problem is, I swear, the handsets must hear us coming and hide. On ring three I was at the threshold of the war room, the name Miss Maggie gives her combination office and living room. I murmured a word of thanks as I spied the handset where she'd left it last night: on her desk, paperweighting a mound of Internet printouts about the wounds of Civil War generals.

Before I could say hello, a low voice said, "This is Lynn Casey. I just heard on my police scanner that you've got a man named Theo Clayborne out there. That true?"

I said it was. "Do you know Theo?"

"Was his father the Reverend Beatitudes Clayborne?"

"Beatitudes? Someone actually named a kid that?"

"You never heard of him? No, you're probably too young to remember much about the Civil Rights Movement. And he never gets mentioned in Black History courses."

I didn't appreciate her "they don't teach you young 'uns anything nowadays" tone. "Theo's father was a civil rights leader?"

"That's what I'm asking you. Never mind, do you know what Theo's full first name is?"

"Theodore, I imagine."

"What's he look like? Is he black? Say, mid-thirties?"

I painted her the portrait of my own first impression, though now that I'd heard Theo sing and seen him be silly, I added Lou Rawls and Sinbad to the Poitier/Dee Williams mix, then asked again if she knew him.

"What's he doing at your place?" she said, in lieu of an answer. "And what's Dennis want him for?"

I gave the newsbite version of both explanations and got such a span of silence for my trouble, I asked if she was still on the line.

"Tell Magnolia," Lynn said at last, "I can't come out there. If she's in a hurry for her photos, she can pick them up at my studio." Then the line went dead.

A full moment passed before I realized she'd hung up on me. I set the handset back atop its mound, on a picture of General Sickles's amputated legbone, as I wondered what exactly our conversation had been about. Then, hearing more cars on the drive, I went out the front door.

The first car was a beige Caddy so big it looked like it required a tugboat to park. Then came Brackin in another brown sheriff's sedan. The Caddy stopped behind Dwight's car and the driver got out. Despite his expensive-looking dress pants, conservative tie and short-sleeved white shirt, he gave off an aura of used-car salesman. Might have been his less expensive-looking toupee, which didn't quite match the dye job on the fringe of hair below. Or his concerned expression, stuck on like a Post-it Note. Or the piece of paper he held like someone about to make you sign your paycheck away. This guy couldn't possibly be the state police detective, could he?

He called back to Brackin as I approached. "Sorry, Dennis. If I'd known you were turning in Magnolia's drive, I'd have let you go first. Thought I was getting out of your way. Is there a problem here?"

Brackin hitched up his gun belt. "No need to apologize, Congressman. You hear about the shooting down on 811 last night?"

"Yes, I did. Tragic. Fact is, I know the man who witnessed it. He told me about it this morning."

Brackin nodded in Theo's direction. "We're here to interview that fella over there—he knew the victim. But what brings you out this way, Congressman?"

"Heard I've got a new constituent." He swung around to greet me, hand extended like a metal detector that's found a gold ring. "I'm J. Dudley Apperson, your United States Congressional Representative." He liked the sound of that so much, I could tell he wanted to repeat it, but he merely added, "You must be Patricia Montallo."

I didn't have the heart to correct him, not when he was so obviously proud of himself for taking the time to learn my name, even though he hadn't. Instead, I let out a meek "hi," squirmed my fingers free and stuck them in my shorts pocket to render that hand unshakable.

Unfortunately, leaving my left hand exposed gave him a void to fill. He pressed into it the paper he was holding. "Here's a voter registration form. Now, you make sure you get that in on time to vote in the fall election."

"Well, if it isn't J. D. Apperson." Miss Maggie was suddenly standing beside me. "I'll bet you've come to discuss all the letters and e-mail I've sent you the last two years, haven't you?"

A blank look back behind J. D.'s blue irises said he'd never laid eyes on any of those communications. That's what his staff got paid for. But he put on a plus-sized smile and replied, "Why, Magnolia, I'd be delighted to sit down and hash out the issues with you any time."

"Yeah?" She looked like she wished she had a classroom pointer in her fist, to poke at him. "Then how come when I wrote you about the need for national health care, you sent a note back about how you were sponsoring an update to the Clean Water Act. So I sent you a letter saying you should start with banning those gas additives that're already polluting the Rapidan, and by association, the Rappahannock and Chesapeake, and your response was that you were supporting legislation to keep logging trucks out of the national parks. I wrote back and said that's great as long as you also quash the bill to sell off parts of Richmond Battlefield. That's when you sent me an information sheet on labor issues. I've been getting the distinct impression, J. D., that you aren't paying attention. Come to think of it, you never paid attention in my class either."

"Now, Magnolia—" he spread his hands, hoping the blame would drip off of them, "—there must have been a mix-up at my office with your correspondence. I promise we'll sit and talk someday real soon. Right now, I understand the sheriff has business here."

Brackin didn't get that he was part of a diversion. "Take your time, Congressman. I can't do any questioning until the state investigator gets here anyway."

"Well, Dennis, if he's going to have a place to park," Miss Maggie said, surveying our drive, "hadn't you ought to tell Dwight to move his car? If he pulls up past the turnaround, the congressman here would be able to leave."

She must have put a little too much emphasis on the word "leave." J. D. took it as a challenge instead of the hint she intended. "It's my duty to stay and help in any way I can, Magnolia."

Brackin decided to use the opportunity to strengthen his good-ol'-boy network ties with a little butt-kissing. "Your help is always appreciated, Congressman."

Miss Maggie rolled her eyes. "Let's take it into the shade, boys.

Pat, go fetch some folding chairs and bring them out to the front porch."

Inside, I put the voter form on the hall table and retrieved two lawn chairs from what in any normal house would have been the dining room. An antique chandelier still hung in the middle of the room, but Miss Maggie had sold the dining table and other furniture years ago, after she'd retired from teaching and before she'd published enough history books and articles to adequately supplement her pension and Social Security. Now the room was lined with bookshelves and filing cabinets holding her research and reference materials. This time of year, she kept things like lawn chairs in there so they'd be handy. In the winter, this was probably where I'd find the rock salt and snow shovels.

When I elbowed back through the front screen door, the cars were parading forward into our turnaround. After waving Emmy and Theo into the rockers and me into one of the chairs I set up, Miss Maggie took up a position behind Emmy and Theo, clutching one wicker rocker back in each of her bony hands. I knew she wouldn't sit—she never did when she was wound up. Neither, apparently, did men possessed of their own importance because, once the drivers joined us, the last folding chair remained empty.

A few heartbeats of sticky silence went by, which J. D. broke with, "This shade sure feels good." He threw in a glance toward the old cucumber magnolia in front of the porch rail, as if to acknowledge its role in our comfort and show Magnolia he was tree-friendly.

I, for one, was thinking the total shade experience would be complete only if I could kick off my boots and socks, prop my feet up on the rail, and feel the cold slick condensation from a glass of iced tea under my fingers. I was getting to the part of the fantasy where all the stress-causing visitors evaporated in the heat when a fourth car appeared.

This one was a sedan and the essence of nondescript—square, American, four-door, maroon. The kind of car my Uncle Mario always bought after gazing wistfully at red two-door sport coupes.

The driver disembarked, looking nothing like my short rotund uncle. For one thing, he wore a suit and tie instead of a bowling shirt and polyester pants. As he walked toward us, he yanked a hanky from his breast pocket to wipe the cap of sweat from his bald and sunburned head. He was a big man, the kind who'd always look hot, even in the middle of an ice storm, so you'd think he'd have the sense to lose the suit jacket on a day like today. But he was also the kind of man who lined up his belt buckle with his shirt placket and who believed that the road to enlightenment began with a perfectly knotted tie.

He took a moment to fold the hanky and slip it back into its sheath before showing Brackin his ID and, in an unexpectedly quiet voice—think Jack Nicholson with a Virginia accent—introduced himself as Sergeant Ross of the state police.

In exchange, Brackin did the introductions, ending with, "And of course, you know Congressman Apperson," in a tone that implied everyone should, and that he and J. D. were best buds, which therefore made Brackin a force to be reckoned with.

Not to be outschmoozed, the sergeant replied, "Sure I do," and for good measure tacked on, "Great to see you again, J. D. How's the wife?"

J. D. did his part in the charade by pretending he remembered Sergeant Ross, though apparently he didn't.

Emmy lost her patience at this point. "Can we get this over with? Theo came right back to the university last night after swapping cars with his friend. I met him there and we loaded the van, then drove straight here."

Ross gave her about as much attention as he did the bird droppings on the porch rail. He turned to Brackin. "Is there someplace I can interview Mr. Clayborne in private?"

"Not while I've got breath inside me," Miss Maggie retorted. "You'll either talk to him here in front of us, or you'll talk to him in the presence of a lawyer."

Ross smiled congenially, as if humoring a dotty old lady who couldn't possibly understand the situation. "No need for that, Ms. Shelby. Mr. Clayborne hasn't been charged with anything. We simply want to know about this car-switching business."

Surprisingly, J. D. came in on the side of the angels. "Then you might as well question him here, Sergeant." I surmised that he was just as nosey as the rest of us.

"The congressman's right," Brackin said, going for more political brownie points.

Ross decided Emmy might come in handy after all. "This woman claims she can vouch for Mr. Clayborne. I'll need to interview them separately, to see if their information jibes."

"Fine," Emmy said, standing. "I'll go do some work until you want me. The deputy can come along to make sure I don't sneak back and eavesdrop. Excuse me, gentlemen?"

Since real men don't sit in porch chairs, the four of them were blocking the stairs. J. D. flattened himself against the door and Brackin shuffled to one side so she could squeeze past. Dwight, looking unhappy to be left out, followed her around the side of the house.

Ross might have insisted if J. D. hadn't been there, but he gave in, taking a notebook and mechanical pencil from his inside jacket pocket. "All right, Mr. Clayborne, how did you know Wyatt Avery?"

Theo had been silent through the whole procedure, his gaze shifting warily from one lawman to the next. Now, when he spoke, I thought I detected a tiny hint of that same sadness I'd heard in his singing last night, mixed with a dollop of defiance. "He was a friend. We grew up together in Rock Hill. Known him all my life."

"How did you come to be in possession of his van last night?"

"I went over to the University after work like I do most—"

"The University of Virginia? Charlottesville?"

Theo nodded. "I work in the anthropology lab. When I got there, Dr. Brewster was on the phone trying to get hold of the department head. Ms. Shelby had called about the bones they found and Dr. Brewster needed authorization so she could rent a U-Haul to transport her equipment out here. She wasn't having any luck, so I phoned Wyatt to ask if I could borrow his van overnight."

"What time was that?"

"Right around seven, I guess." Theo leaned forward, clasping his hands in front of him. "I tried his home number first, but he wasn't there. Then I remembered he was pulling extra hours all week because he wanted to take Friday off, so I called him at work. He said he'd only be there another half hour before heading out to his girl's place. If I wanted the van, I had to go right over."

"Over where?"

"Fashion Square Mall. Wyatt was the manager at RBI Sporting Goods." He inserted a microsecond hesitation before the word "was."

Ross took out his hanky and wiped off his head again. "What time did you arrive at the mall?"

"Around seven-thirty. Maybe a few minutes later. Stopped for gas on the way."

"Describe what happened when you got to the store."

"Wyatt was ready to leave. We stood in front of RBI and talked a few minutes—"

"About?"

"He said I could keep the van for the weekend if I wanted. He and his girl were going up the mountains—Peaks of Otter. Taking her car. We exchanged keys and registrations. That was the last time I saw him."

"You didn't walk out to your cars together?"

Theo shook his head. "I'd parked in front of Penney's. Wyatt's van was on the other side, near Sears. So we split up."

"You drove the van straight back to the university?"

Theo tapped his foot nervously. "No, I drove back to my apartment to pack some clothes first."

"Anybody see you?"

"Didn't meet up with any of my neighbors. Someone might have seen me from a window—I don't know."

"What time did you leave?"

"Maybe eight-fifteen. Got back to the lab about eight-thirty."

"Which is when Dr. Brewster says she met you?"

"Not right away. She'd gone home to pack, too. She came back, I guess, ten minutes after I did. That's when we loaded the van and came here."

With a distinctly smug frown, Ross made note of the time-table. I remembered hearing on the radio broadcast that Wyatt had been killed between seven-thirty and eight-thirty. Theo was possibly the last person to see the victim alive. Besides the murderer.

Unless, of course, he *was* the murderer.

5

I admit, I can be dense. Or at least simpleminded. The radio newscaster had said "road rage," so I pictured the police in search of your basic macadam bully, who'd be a stranger to the victim and therefore not Theo. It didn't occur to me that the cops had deemed the car swap suspicious until Miss Maggie mentioned the word "lawyer."

From this new perspective, I gave Theo a second appraisal, draping a murderer's cape around his shoulders to see how it fit. Oh, he could pull off Jud Fry in *Oklahoma*. Sweeney Todd, maybe, if he got past his shyness. Or one of those opera villains. But a real killer? I kept coming back to the man who'd sung to me in the kitchen earlier.

Obviously, though, Brackin didn't share my opinion, because when Emmy and Theo switched places, he made Theo and Dwight wait over in the side yard in sight of the porch, to discourage any escape attempt. Catching Theo's eye as he descended the porch steps, I smiled. He didn't smile back, but his expression softened.

Emmy's statement didn't help Theo any, but it didn't hurt him either. All she could confirm was that he was with her from quarter to nine on, and that his manner didn't seem unusual except that he might have been a little excited about helping with the dig.

Theo excited? How could she tell?

"Hold on a sec," Miss Maggie said as Ross closed his notebook and replaced it in his pocket. "Got a few questions of my own, Sergeant."

"Ma'am?" Ross put on a polite face that said, "Tell me why I should care?"

"J. D. here said there were witnesses." She must have heard him when he and the sheriff were trading howdy-do's earlier.

"One witness," Ross corrected.

"Okay, one. A man, I think he said. Did he get a good-enough look at the killer to know whether or not Theo fit the bill?"

"The witness didn't actually see the shooting," Ross replied, shifting his bulk as if he were about to leave.

So I piped in, "On the radio this morning, they said the police were looking for a black Toyota SUV. Was that what the witness saw?"

Ross only scowled at me. Oddly enough, J. D. answered the question. "That's what the witness told me. The SUV tailgated him down Route 20, then passed and cut him off. He slowed down and backed off, then when he turned onto 811 and rounded a corner, he saw what looked like the same SUV stopped beside a car sitting on the shoulder. The SUV took off down the road, and he found the driver of the other car slumped back in his seat with blood all over him."

What was Ross thinking? That the witness somehow mistook a dark green Chevy Van for a black Toyota SUV? Or possibly the SUV driver was a witness, too, but chose to leave the scene and not get involved?

Miss Maggie hit on the essential point. "What time was this?"

Ross held up his hands as if fending her off. "Mrs. Shelby, while this is under investigation—"

"The radio," I chimed in again, "said Wyatt was killed around eight." But if Wyatt had made it out to that spot in the half hour after he left work, Theo could have made it back in about the same amount of time. No alibi there.

"Ladies," Ross said, giving me a look that said I'd better not interrupt him again, "like I said, Mr. Clayborne isn't being charged with anything, so you can quit worrying." He turned to Theo. "I'm sure you're as anxious as we are to get to the truth in this matter."

He left it hanging like a question, so Theo nodded.

"Now, Mr. Clayborne, will you be here at Mrs. Shelby's the next few days, in case I have more questions for you?"

That sounded predatory to me, and I'm sure the "don't leave town" implication wasn't lost on Theo, but he only gave another nod and a curt, "Through the weekend."

"Of course," Ross went on, reaching into his back pocket for his wallet, and sliding a business card out, "I'll have to impound the victim's vehicle. If you need a ride back to Charlottesville, Mr. Clayborne, you make sure to give me a call."

I wondered if he really did need to impound the van, or if that was simply a smooth way to control Theo's coming and going.

Emmy had jumped to her feet. "You aren't impounding anything with my equipment still in it."

Miss Maggie agreed. "We're working on a county case here, if you've forgotten, Dennis. We need what's in that van."

I could tell Ross was about to once more turn up the volume on his "I'm in control of the situation" personality, but before he could get his mouth open, still another car ground its way up the gravel of our drive. This time, a state police cruiser pulled up with two troopers inside. Rather than evaporating, the visitors were multiplying like bunnies. Maybe the heat was acting as an incubator.

Ross smiled as if he'd said "Presto!" to make the troopers appear. In a way, I supposed he had—their showing up had obviously been prearranged. "My men and I will personally unload the van for you, Dr. Brewster."

Translated, that meant they intended to search every cubic millimeter of Emmy's buckets and shovels in the process.

Ross asked for the keys and Theo reluctantly handed them over. J. D., meantime, had expressed interest in the county case Miss Maggie had mentioned. Brackin explained and J. D. wanted to view the skull.

So, for our various purposes, we all traipsed around to the side yard, back out under the now-sweltering sun. Ross and his two minions tackled the van, and Dwight was pressed into service by Emmy to carry everything they unloaded to the back porch. Theo stood by her with as glum an expression as his stony countenance allowed.

The rest of us huddled around Yorick's lair and I folded back the tarp. Surprisingly, the ground beneath was a damp, dark brown.

Miss Maggie answered the look on my face. "Emmy and I wet down the soil early this morning. We'll do it again tonight. Once the water soaks in, the dirt'll move easier. Less chance of damaging the bones as we dig."

The shower had washed the loose dirt from Yorick's eyebrows and cheekbones, so they appeared smoother now, except for a rough, greenish, crescent-shaped growth between what used to be his eye and the side of his nose.

I pointed out the blemish to Miss Maggie. "Is that part of the bone?" My thinking: here was proof that Yorick couldn't be the boy from my dream. Even a small abnormality like that would show above the skin.

The contrary part of my brain argued that if *I* were a ghost, and coming all the way from the Great Beyond to star in someone's dream, wouldn't I also alter my appearance to look my best?

Miss Maggie put her hands on her thighs and squinted at where my forefinger indicated, but apparently her nine-decade-old eyes couldn't handle the details at that distance. "Dennis, J. D., help an old lady get down on her knees."

They each supported an arm as she lowered herself. I knelt beside her, so I could show her exactly where I meant. Down on all fours, leaning out over the pit, we looked like a couple of terriers over a rabbit hole.

Miss Maggie must have thought the growth was fascinating, because she yelled, "Emmy, come take a look."

The excitement in her voice brought Theo over as well, and made a third terrier out of Emmy. Then she flopped down on her stomach and stuck her whole upper torso into the hole. "Theo fetch my toolbox."

The box she meant was of the Rubbermaid ilk—clear with a purple lid—and unfortunately hadn't yet been taken out of the van. We had to wait while Ross rummaged through its contents.

When Theo at last set the box beside Emmy, I could see that the top tray contained an assortment of dental picks. She took one and gently peeled soil away from each side of the crescent, reminding me that I ought to find a local dentist and schedule a checkup soon.

Abruptly, Emmy sat back on her heels. "Bronze. A button or a coin."

My stomach gave a little leap. "Wouldn't that give us a way to date the skeleton? Even if it's just a button—"

"*Maybe*. All depends." Miss Maggie put her arms up as a signal to Brackin and J. D. that she was ready to stand again. We waited until they helped her straighten up—a slow, painful process for her arthritic knees. "Scenario number one: Let's say I finally get fed up with J. D. here and kill him. I dig him a grave and toss a '65 Kennedy half dollar on his chest before I shovel the dirt over him. Fifty years hence, somebody digs him up, finds the coin and decides he was buried in 1965. See the problem, Pat? Scenario two—"

"Wait," I said, "I can come up with one. Someone like me, planting a garden, churns up the soil but doesn't notice the bones. A button falls off my shirt, gets mixed up in the dirt and ends up right over the skull. Fifty years later, somebody finds the skull with my button and—"

"Exactly," Emmy said, standing. "But in this case, just possibly, coins may have been placed on the deceased's eyelids to keep them closed. Then we'd at least have ourselves a 'no earlier than' date."

Brackin was getting impatient. "So let's pull it out of the dirt and see what it is."

Emmy shook her head. "Not yet. We have to set up our grid, then chart out coordinates and depth before we remove anything. Right where the object and skull touch might be where two different soil levels meet, meaning we're talking about two separate events in time. We won't find that out if we disturb the evidence too soon."

Miss Maggie took the cue to drop a hint. "If we hadn't had all these interruptions this morning, Dennis, we might already have an answer for you."

Brackin, for once, got the drift. "All right, I'll let you get to it. Dwight, come move your car so J. D. and I can get out."

I deduced two things from that: Dwight wasn't going anywhere and we were once again stuck with an official "observer," and "observer" translated to "spy" and Brackin was making use of the car-moving opportunity to give the deputy a last-minute briefing.

Two hitches. Our turnaround only accommodates about three and a half cars—three if one of them's the Queen Mary of Cadillacs. The two state police vehicles were blocking the drive, so Brackin wasn't going anywhere until the van was empty. The other snag was that J. D. didn't seem in a big hurry to leave.

Still, the sheriff and his deputy retired to their cars to discuss strategies and were therefore out of our hair. Ross and the Trooperettes were nearing the end of their gig and no longer required supervision. So Miss Maggie, Emmy, Theo and I decided to ignore J. D. and get back to work.

J. D. didn't ignore that easily. "Y'all are going to get sunstroke.

I have an open-air tent back home that I'd be glad to go get you, Magnolia. You could set it up right here, shade your excavation."

"Generous of you, J. D.," Miss Maggie replied. "No need, though—Elwood Walsh already said we could use his. Fact is, Pat was supposed to have picked it up this morning, but with all these delays . . ."

First I heard of it, though that didn't stop me from playing along. "I haven't been able to get my car out since Dwight arrived." Which was true—we kept it parked on the grass between the magnolia and the drive.

Miss Maggie waved her arm vaguely toward the parking mess out front. "Soon as y'all move, she'll be able to go fetch it."

J. D. was in an especially beneficent mood. "I'd be happy to get it for you."

"Thanks, but Pat's got to run other errands in town anyway."

I jumped into the fray again. "That reminds me, Miss Maggie—Lynn Casey called and said I could pick up your photos at her studio."

"Oh, good." She purposefully turned her back on J. D. "Come inside and I'll give you the list of excavation supplies we need."

We moved off toward the back door. J. D. didn't try to follow but instead leeched himself onto Emmy as she and Theo resumed surveying.

"Any reason you don't want J. D.'s tent, Miss Maggie?" I asked. "Doesn't seem like a bad idea."

"Which is why I'm going to call Elwood and say you'll be down for his. I should have thought of it last night while he was here." She flung open the screen door and we entered the kitchen. "All J. D.'s looking for is a photo-op. Sure, he'd bring us his tent, along with all the reporters he could round up."

More nonevaporating visitors, but I could see a plus side. "If we need to raise funds, wouldn't a little publicity be a good thing?"

"Not with our name linked to J. D.'s, Pat. Oh, he's no worse than any other politician," she continued as she headed down the hall, "probably better than some—but when he was reelected two years ago, he barely squeezed by with a majority. We'd stand to alienate all the folks who voted against him. The Bell Foundation can't afford that."

I followed her into the war room. Here, because the room had open windows that faced out to the side yard, she lowered her voice. "Plus, we don't want any negative publicity because of that shooting last night, if we can help it. There's still a fair amount of prejudice floating around this county, Pat. A front-page photo of Theo, with a mention of his connection to Wyatt Avery in the caption, would undoubtedly discourage a few rich white folks from reaching for their checkbooks." That said, she reached for her own checkbook, in the drawer of her computer desk.

Having run headlong into some of the local biases myself, I saw her point, and it made me wonder about other things. "Miss Maggie, do you think the police are suspicious of Theo simply because he's black?"

"Not *simply*, Pat. If it were that uncomplicated, I'd have thrown them all off my property first thing. Theo's a *convenient* suspect for them—he's got a proven connection to the victim and he's not from around here. But it sure doesn't help any that he's black. Humans have a basic need for scapegoats, and outsiders who look or act different are easiest to blame."

"So when you asked me for my gut feeling about him earlier—"

"All right, yes, I was wondering myself if he might be guilty. But only because he's a guest in my house." Then she regarded me with the same maternal expression I'd seen on my mom's face when she'd put a plate of homemade ravioli in front of me for my birthday dinner each year. Miss Maggie didn't say it aloud, but she was afraid of exposing me to danger. "Emmy's got a high opinion of Theo—and I respect her judgment."

"I don't think he did it either, Miss Maggie."

"Good, we're agreed." She turned back to her checkbook. "I'll give you a blank check for Lynn. You can fill in the amount when you pay for the photos. Also, ask Lynn if she's got some time this afternoon to come take some publicity shots. That way we can control who sees what. We'll send our own press release in to the papers."

"Great idea, Miss Maggie, but I doubt she'll come up here. On the phone, she sounded like she wanted to avoid Theo."

"She knows him?"

I recounted the details of the call.

Miss Maggie pursed her lips in thought. "Beatitudes Clayborne. I remember him. Not so much a civil rights leader as a follower. Never had the right kind of charisma to be a Dr. King or a Jesse Jackson. And his church was in a small town—Rock Hill. He concentrated his efforts there and around the Charlottesville area. The riots further south were more dramatic, so the press pretty much ignored him. Then, seems to me, there was some kind of scandal and he faded out of public life before he became well-known."

"What kind of scandal?"

But she shrugged and shook her head. "Too much else happening back then. Besides civil rights riots we had Vietnam, Apollo missions, the assassinations of Martin Luther King and Bobby Kennedy. . . . The goings-on of a minister in the backwoods of Virginia must not have been worth remembering, because I don't. Ask Lynn to come anyway, Pat." She rummaged through the papers and books on her messy computer desk. "Now where did I put the phone book?"

Although it sometimes seemed like Miss Maggie had everyone in the free world programmed into her speed dial, Elwood Walsh wasn't. This being another corner of the Virginia backwoods, our phone book was only a little thicker than your average *People* magazine. If it hadn't had a yellow cover, I never would have noticed it stuffed beside the seat cushion of one of the room's four recliners.

While Miss Maggie was dialing the good doctor, I heard a car start up. Looking out of the side window, I saw the van pull up onto the drive with one of the troopers behind the wheel. Ross and the other trooper got into their cars and backed down the drive until they could turn around on the grass. Then the little procession drove off into the woods.

Over at the "C" datum, Theo was holding the pole, but he watched after the van, even after it was out of sight.

"Elwood says you can stop by and get the tent any time this morning," Miss Maggie said, punching the hang-up button and setting the handset on the mantel. "And maybe while you're out, you'd better pick us up something for lunch."

The battery light on the phone was blinking so I moved the handset back to the base on the desk. "And I'll get extra groceries—two more mouths to feed. What do you want for supper?" I was chief chef. That way I could make sure Miss Maggie stuck to a heart-healthy diet.

"Anything, long as it doesn't have to be cooked. Too hot for that. Get plenty of salad fixings and fruit." We went back into the hall where she kept her handbag. From it she took her wallet and a piece of notebook paper. "Here are the things Emmy says we need."

I scanned the list: a pack of heavy-duty paper bags, a box of plastic snack bags, four soft-bristle toothbrushes, and black Sharpie pens—four regular, two fine point.

"Get whatever brands are cheap," Miss Maggie said, "except the Sharpies—don't skimp on those. And we'll need a separate receipt for that stuff, so we can keep track of Foundation expenses."

In theory, she meant. The money she handed me was her own. I was used to that. She paid for groceries. I was a kept woman.

"I wish you'd let me pay you room and board," I mumbled, "at least until my Unemployment runs out." My standard appeal whenever the subject of money came up.

"Pat, you more than earn your keep. You're my secretary, cook, chauffeur, gardener, and laundress. And as much as I'd love to believe I can fully take care of myself, at my age, having a housemate is plain common sense. I'm just grateful you don't mind living here with an old lady."

Since she usually swatted anyone who brought up the subject of her age, this admission stopped the discussion cold. But I couldn't help feeling funny about the arrangement. This new freedom of mine came with a price: guilt. Still, if I had to be anyone's housewife, Miss Maggie was easy to please.

I grabbed my own pocketbook from beside hers and another cold soda from the fridge—root beer this time—and went outside to try to free my Neon from the car-mob in front of the house.

Keep Your Hand on That Plow

I have borne thirteen children, and seen them most all
sold off to slavery, and when I cried out with my mother's
grief, none but Jesus heard me! And ain't I a woman?
—Sojourner Truth

July 2, 1871—In the shared garden

Colonel Gilbert sent word that one of his fences got broke
and a filly went missing overnight. Claimed he'd pay a
half dollar if a man would come help round up his horse
and mend the fence. Noah went, so I got out of roof
fixing.

Instead, I helped Jordana Light like I did most days.
Jordana be a slave for Mr. Travis back when Mama was,
like most all the folk living in Freedom Holler. Jordana
say her name be Jackson then, too—Alice Jackson, she
say—but soon as she got free, she give herself another
name 'cause she say she feel all new again, though she be
almost old as Uncle Henry.

Jordana know all 'bout growing things. She tend the
garden and oversee our one planting field up on the hill
across from the church. She mind the corn, taters, and
beans there like they was her own young'uns. Mama
say Jordana get that way after Mr. Travis sell off all her
chil'un to other masters and left her nobody to love and

be mama to. Like he sell off my brother, Mama say—sell him off soon as he be walking and talking.

Late that afternoon, after I helped Jordana pick a bushel of sweet corn for our own Sunday supper, we come back down to the garden so she could thin out the collards and turnips while I churn up the dirt alongside each row.

"Hoe it up good, Mance," she say. "Can't wait 'til tomorrow. Gonna rain tonight. We want all that water to soak right down to those roots."

The sky above be pure blue and the sun still hot on my head, but I didn't doubt rain was coming. Jordana say her old bones talk to her about the weather. I don't know who her bones be listening to—I just know she most always right.

I was starting in to hoe the last row when I hear Hattie Darden talking as she come up the path from the town road. Hattie and her husband Amos work as fieldhands for the Nortons. Come Sundays, though, Amos drive them to and from church, and Hattie help Mama put the meal on the table and clean up after. Then they all walk back home together. I look up from my hoeing to see, but Mama ain't with them.

"Mance," Hattie call to me as she stop by the garden fence, "your mama be coming along in a bit. She gone to the Reynolds' place to see if they found the wash she hung out for them yesterday afternoon."

"Found?" Jordana ask. "What it do, blow away during the night?"

Amos grunted. "Growed feet and run off, more like."

He kept walking on up to their cabin, but Hattie say, "All's I know is, Miz Reynolds sent her oldest running over the Nortons' this morning, asking Alma where she hung their wash 'fore she left yesterday. She tell him she hung it where she always do and he say ain't no wash there this morning."

I tugged my hoe out of the dirt and set it up straight by me. The handle was a good foot over my head. "Somebody stole the Reynolds' wash?"

"Clean off the line." Hattie laughed. " 'Clean off the line.' Ain't that funny?"

"Don't make sense," Jordana say, not meaning Hattie's joke, but still pondering her news. "If this was winter and cold out, and a body need covering, I could understand that kind of stealing."

Hattie nodded. "Ask me, them Norton boys be playing one of their pranks."

"Mama coming home by herself?" I asked. After last night, I didn't much like that idea. Mama told me not to head anywheres alone, so I reckoned that went for her, too.

"She ask Noah's eldest to wait for her."

Joe Putnam be not hardly fifteen years of age, but he strong and nearly tall as his father, so Mama be fine, I supposed. I went back to chopping up the dirt, thinking instead on what Jordana say 'bout a body needing covering.

6

I don't drink when I'm driving. After the initial guzzle, my soda can was placed firmly into the cup holder beside my knee and would stay there until I came to a stop sign or red light. I also don't eat, style my hair, paint my nails, read a newspaper, or talk on a cell phone—not that I'd ever been able to afford one to talk on. No, you won't catch me doing any of those scary things I used to see other drivers doing when I had to drive to and from work each day.

One thing I will admit to, though, is communing with nature each time I negotiate the drive though the woods. Windows open, I glance from side to side, trying for a glimpse of deer, chipmunks, birds, maybe even a new wildflower. Sometimes I stop on the plank bridge over Bell Run just to listen to the water as it plays among the moss-carpeted rocks. If I put the air-conditioning on at all—only on the hottest of days and only long enough to cool the car down—I wait until I'm out on Route 3. I don't want a totally enclosed car between me and this forest if I can help it.

Today I was on a mission, so I didn't intend to stop, but as the car's front tires bumped up onto the bridge, I thought I heard a voice calling. As the sound hit my ears, the smell of wood smoke hit my nose.

I stepped on the brake. Out of the corner of my right eye, the sunlight seemed to break through the trees and I could have sworn I saw buildings.

When I turned my head upstream, the forest looked as it always did there: shady and cool, with no manmade structure in sight. The flat ground where the creek arched away to the east was chock full of trees, vines, brambles, brilliant green ferns and, perched on the creek bank, a gang of orange day lilies.

I shifted into park, switched off the engine, and listened. No birds chirped now—the day had grown too hot for them. All I heard was the scanty trickle of Bell Run, low within its banks for want of rain. The smell in the air wasn't of smoke but of pond scum.

Normal people having similar experiences assume their brains are playing tricks on them. Little more than six weeks earlier, I would have done the same—blamed it on a blot of yogurt, a crumb of bran cereal, a bit of undigested strawberry.

I took a gulp of my root beer. My throat was dry all of a sudden, but I never thought to blame the incident on dehydration. No, the most likely explanation to me was that the Other Side's server was back online and a certain ghost I knew was sending me e-mail once more.

I didn't have time for this. Dreams were one thing—I could watch them and sleep at the same time.

"Two minutes," I said aloud as I yanked on the parking brake. "That's all I can spare. And only because you caught me on my way out. If I was coming home with groceries, no way would I stop and let the ice cream melt."

The empty forest seemed to absorb my voice like fresh Italian bread sops up tomato sauce. What had I expected? I swear this ghost business is custom-designed to make me feel like an idiot.

Turning my head so the part of the creek bank where I thought I'd seen those buildings was in the center of my field of vision, I took a deep breath and closed my eyes.

At first, I saw nothing. In the past, images sent from Great Beyond Broadcasting had always snapped into sharp focus, as if relayed via cable TV. This time the picture formed gradually, like a developing Polaroid, but seriously underexposed. What I saw was a cluster of rough wooden houses—more like sheds actually.

My other senses kicked in and I heard indistinct voices, the braying of a goat, the clucking of chickens. The air felt different—cooler. A soft breeze, smelling of stale smoke, brushed the sweat-soaked hairs on the back of my neck.

Everything faded in a rush. The two-minute warning had been heeded, with time left for station identification and two commercials, though no supernatural sponsors took advantage of the opportunity.

Opening my eyes, I studied the modern landscape. If, like my visions past, I'd been shown a moment in history, when had those houses been here? Miss Maggie had done research on this land and had versed me thoroughly, pop quizzes and all. The Bells had been tenants of the Shacklefords, but they'd originally lived beside the grist mill—along the creek, yes, but much closer to the river. Neither family had ever owned slaves.

So who would have lived here? Did the Shacklefords have other tenants? Had the mill employed something akin to migrant workers during harvest season?

Jotting myself a mental note to ask Miss Maggie on my return, I took another swig of soda and revved up the car. Not a moment too soon. The beige Caddy appeared in my rearview mirror.

The thought of driving all the way into Stoke with J. D. right behind me inspired a spur-of-the-moment decision to pick up the mail first. Save me a trip later. Not that I ever minded that short hike through the woods, even on drizzly days, as long as it wasn't raining so hard the creek flooded.

I hung a left at the end of our drive and saw J. D. turn right, so it was with a feeling of triumphant evasion that I pulled onto the strip of macadam in front of the post office trailer down the road. No other cars. Either Hugh's sub hadn't arrived yet, or was off delivering mail in the development across the road.

Inside, the place felt like a mausoleum (with smaller boxes).

Hugh always left the lights on over the counter and, when he went out, put a placard up saying when he expected to return. When he was in the back sorting mail or took a break in the other half of the trailer where he lived with Beth Ann, you could ring the bell on the counter and he'd come out. Either way, a hint of his aftershave always lingered in the air.

Today the air smelled musty and the package-mailing, stamp-buying end of the room was dark. The sign on the counter was a simple "Closed."

I unlocked the P.O. box I shared with Miss Maggie and slid out a bill—my very first independent health plan invoice—and an envelope with bold orange print that read "Pat Montella, Beazley Insurance Associates welcomes you to Stoke County." My first personalized piece of junk mail. But no Social Security or severance checks, no "you may have already won" notices, no postcards from Hugh and Beth Ann.

I realized how much I *wanted* a postcard. Any picture would do as long as it said my name had come up in a "wouldn't it be great if Pat were here" kind of way. You'd think they'd have at least sent a card to Miss Maggie, with "and Pat" tagged on as an afterthought.

I caught myself pouting, closed the box, and left.

Elwood's combination home and office wasn't hard to find, only two blocks off Route 3, right outside the town limits. The house was a fifties split-level, surrounded by blue and pink hydrangeas, and where the garage should have been was a small bay window and office door. That's where I went in, per Miss Maggie's instructions, and a bell rang as I pushed open the door.

Inside was a tiny, wood-paneled waiting room, comfortably air-conditioned, with seating for five in wide, thickly padded chairs, upholstered in leather that smelled as old as the practice. An elderly woman, bundled up in a black cardigan sweater, sat in the far corner reading a *Smithsonian* magazine. She nodded a greeting to me as I took the seat by the door. On a low table beside me was another *Smithsonian*, two *National Geographics*, and a *Ranger Rick*. I thumbed through the latter, looking at close-up photos of tree frogs sticking their tongues out.

Before I'd gone two pages, Elwood poked his head into the room. Today he had on another pair of Bermudas. A short white lab coat over a thin cotton shirt completed the ensemble.

The elderly woman began to stand, but Elwood waved her back into the chair. "Pat's just here to pick up something, Sarah. Finish up that article you're reading. I'll be right back."

"Been waiting more than an hour already, Elwood. I've got things to do at home, you know."

"Five more minutes. I promise." He beckoned to me and I followed him past an examining room, office, and powder room—all unoccupied—through another door which led into the front hall of the house. There, along one wall, was the dis-assembled tent—a bundle of metal poles, a mesh bag containing stakes and cord, and a short, thick roll of gray nylon with an old belt fastened around the middle.

"Got it down out of the attic when Magnolia called." He took off his lab coat and hung it neatly on the knob of the door behind us. "Everything's lightweight, but I'll help you load it in your car."

"I could have waited until you were done with your patient," I said, bending down for the poles.

"Sarah?" Elwood lifted the roll of nylon. "Nothing wrong with her that staying out of the heat won't cure. Sitting quietly in my air-conditioning is the best therapy for her." He hung the bag of stakes on the end of the poles, then held open the front door for me. "Soon as I let her go home, she'll be running around, clean-ing, hanging clothes out in the hot sun, and she'll end up back here anyway, or in the hospital. I'm just keeping her here 'til her daughter can drive up from Orange and take her someplace cool."

As I set the poles on the grass so I could open my trunk, he asked, "How's Magnolia doing in this heat?"

"She doesn't seem to mind it." I opened my back door so I could tilt down my rear seat, turning the trunk into a hatchback.

"Old people don't. That's the danger. Their internal thermostats get rusty and they can't tell when they're overheated. Sarah even insists on wearing a sweater. That's why I'm glad you're taking this tent. I know, what with that skull you found last night, nothing'll keep Magnolia inside today. At least this'll give her some shade."

I shoved the poles into the car. Their ends were crammed between the two front seats, but they fit. Thank you, Chrysler engineering. "I'll do my best to keep her out of the sun."

"Don't let her do anything strenuous either." He set the nylon roll and bag in the trunk beside the poles. "And make her drink lots of fluids. That's good advice for you, too, and anyone else you've got working up there. Don't want any of you getting heat stroke."

Slamming my trunk lid, I thanked him, said my good-byes, and headed off to my next stop.

Lynn Casey's studio was on Route 3, which was called Jefferson Street inside Stoke. Each Monday, the circuit judge came through town and held court, but the place never quite rose to the level of "bustling county seat." Today—a Thursday and too hot even for tourists to take the scenic route between the Civil War sites and the Shenandoahs—Stoke was downright comatose. I had my choice of parking, so I claimed a space right in front of Phreestyle Photo, between Lynn's red truck and one of the ornamental pear tree peninsulas that jutted out into the street every four parking spots. The shade from that tree was so welcome today, parallel parking was worth the trouble.

According to Miss Maggie, the shop facades in Stoke had been redone during the seventies in what she called Williamsburg Revival—sort of Colonial in flavor if you let your eye get past the aluminum siding, brickface, and energy-efficient windows. The town wasn't founded until 1839, so the Colonial look is historically inaccurate, but Miss Maggie says she likes it better than the dreary Industrial Age/Depression Era store fronts that used to line Jefferson Street.

Phreestyle Photo was one of the brickface shops, with the door on the left and two nine-over-nine-pane windows on the right. For a window display, five-by-seven photos—all portraits, half of them dogs and cats—filled three panes of each bottom window in a diagonal tic-tac-toe. A folding billboard beside the door enticed tourists to come inside and have their pictures taken in Civil War dress.

On opening the door, the first thing I noticed was a blast of frigid air that hit me squarely in the sinuses and brought on an instant headache at the bridge of my nose. The second thing was Lynn herself, bundled up in a leather jacket, and sitting behind a glossy black desk not far in front of the door. The short end of the desk was pushed against the side wall and it gave the impression of a receptionist's station. Atop the desk was a mustard yellow phone, a bright purple mug serving as a pencil and pen holder, a large lime green notepad, a small cash register painted red, and a gray police scanner, looking washed-out and forlorn amid all those other colors.

The police scanner was on low, but all I could hear was the buzz of white noise. Slow crime day. Lynn had the phone receiver to her ear and was scribbling on the notepad. As I walked in, she was saying the name "Billy Johnson" as she wrote it, but was so startled at having a customer she broke her pencil point. Recognizing me, her shock morphed into a scowl of annoyance and she told the caller to hold on as she reached into a desk drawer and brought out a photo envelope.

"I'll wait 'til you're done," I said. "I have a request from Miss Maggie to discuss with you."

She nodded with open curiosity, and waved me over to her

73

waiting area, which consisted of three red director's chairs lined up before the windows. I decided I'd get colder faster if I sat, so instead I walked around, surveying the studio. The walls, floor, and ceiling were all painted black. Light poles and reflector screens took up the most room—the actual subject area was smaller than I expected. No fancy backdrops that I could see, but along the other side wall were different kinds of chairs and stools, a variety of props on shelves over them, a portable clothes rack with maybe a half dozen costumes, and a full-length floor mirror.

"Do you have an address?" Lynn said into the phone. I glanced at her. She had a pen in her hand now and seemed to forget I was there, so I went over to the props and helped myself to a Confederate kepi hat, then checked out the look in the mirror.

No good. My hair is pure Italian mind-of-its-own wavy, which is why I keep it short. Even so, the kepi only encouraged its waywardness. Had Rebel soldiers carried around the Montella gene for chronic bad hair, they'd have locked themselves in their bedrooms instead of going off to war.

"I'm not asking for anything but public information, am I?" A dash of impatience had crept into Lynn's usually laid-back voice. Her reflection in the mirror showed an uncharacteristic tension in her tall frame.

"No," she said flatly, repeating the word twice more as I exchanged the kepi for a short gray uniform jacket with butternut trim.

I set my handbag on the floor by the mirror and slipped my arms into the coat. It was made for someone a foot taller with arms proportionally longer than mine, but still, I checked the fit in the mirror. The last button was even with my hips and, depressingly, wouldn't quite reach its designated buttonhole. But the wool felt warm, which was my main motivation for trying the thing on.

"Never mind," Lynn mumbled, her tone reminding me of my

cousin Angela those times she'd ask her mom if she could go to the mall and Aunt Sophie would give her a lecture on responsibility for her trouble.

Lynn hung up abruptly—apparently she never said "goodbye" on the phone—then leaned back in her chair to cast a speculative eye at me. I started to take off the jacket, but she said, "Leave it on. It'll keep you from getting frostbite."

I turned from the mirror to face her. "Why do you keep this place so cold?"

"Because if I didn't and I put you in one of those costumes under these lights, even for the short time it'd take to shoot your picture, you'd pass out from the heat." Putting her hands into her jacket pockets, she stood and ambled toward me. Under the leather coat, she was wearing cargo shorts, a khaki blouse, and ankle boots, much more expensive-looking than mine. Add a pith helmet and she'd be ready for a safari. "And because tourists expect it to be cold in the summertime. They rave about how wonderful it feels, even though half of them get goosebumps inside a minute. And because my landlord installed an air conditioner with two settings: on and off. Turn around."

Once I was facing the mirror again, she grasped the extra bulk of material between my shoulder blades and pulled it tight, so circumference-wise, the coat almost looked like it fit. The effect was about the same as I'd gotten with the kepi, except, instead of blaming Montella hair, I cursed my Sicilian blood for blessing me with the contours of a Bosc pear.

"You don't make a very believable Rebel," Lynn observed, "but then, you look better in this uniform than most tourists. And I suspect it fits your disposition better than a Scarlett O'Hara costume. Want me to shoot you?"

"Uh, no." Even if Lynn did mean "photograph," I (a) hated getting my picture taken, (b) couldn't afford to anyway, and (c) was here on a mission. Besides, the way she was holding the coat made me feel like I had on a straight jacket. I slid out of it and retrieved my pocketbook from beside the mirror. "How much do we owe you for the photos?"

Lynn named her price, then retraced her steps to her desk to fetch a pen, tossing the uniform jacket in a heap on the chair as she reached for the purple mug.

Once the transaction was complete and I had the photo envelope in hand, I went on to explain our need for publicity shots.

She hit a button on the register and the drawer popped open. "I can do better than that. I'll write up the article, too. Sometimes, when things get slow around here—and as you can see, things are currently at full stop—"

"No June weddings?"

"I don't *do* weddings." Her tone oozed cynicism as she lifted the till, shoved the check beneath, and slammed the drawer. Sounded like she'd said those very words to one too many gushy brides this last month. Maybe just this last week. "When things get slow, I do freelance work for the *Stoke Register*. Might even be able to get a mention into the Richmond and Charlottesville papers for you. I'll call around."

"You're a reporter?" Warning signals went off in my brain as I remembered our phone conversation, and how naïvely I'd answered all her questions. "Is that why you were asking about Theo this morning? For an article?"

Lynn produced a self-satisfied smile as she leaned her butt against the edge of the table. "Wyatt Avery's murder *is* news."

"I wish you'd told me. Could you please not write anything about the Bell Foundation in connection with the shooting?"

Her smile broadened. "I see your problem." She slid her hands into her jacket pockets. "Okay, no allusions to the Foundation, or even to Bell Run, Magnolia, or yourself. I give you my word. *If* you'll tell me what happened with the police out at your place this morning."

Swell. Blackmail. "What do you want to know?"

76

"They suspect Theo, don't they, but didn't arrest him or I'd have heard."

A flat statement. I was supposed to fill in the blanks like I had on Miss Maggie's check. "He was apparently the last person to see his friend alive."

"Does he have an alibi?"

"No—unless one of his neighbors saw him last night when he stopped by his apartment."

Lynn's eyebrows—the perfectly sculpted variety—rose a half inch. Then she stood, pushing the sleeve of her jacket up until she could see her watch. "Listen, I have a load of work back in my darkroom. Don't take it personally if I kick you out."

Being frozen down to my bones, I didn't mind at all, though I didn't believe her darkroom excuse for one moment. Like she said, her business was currently at full stop.

I welcomed the swaddling heat as I stepped out of her door. That is, until my blood pressure rose because, despite all the parking spots on the street, someone had double-parked me in. Someone who drove a humongous beige Caddy. Then again, perhaps a mere two or three parking spaces wouldn't do—that beast needed a battleship dock.

I looked up and down the block. No J. D. No anyone, for that matter—like a Gary Cooper Western just before the high-noon shootout, except no Gary Cooper or bad guy, either.

Across the street, though, between two of the second floor windows, hung a big RE-ELECT APPERSON sign. The windows flanking it were framed in red, white, and blue streamers. Campaign Central? Wouldn't be hard to find out.

STEAL AWAY

"Modern Astronomy," as studied by some of the Freedmen, is defined by a citizen of Staunton, "as looking
around in the day to see what can be stolen at night."
— FROM *THE VALLEY VIRGINIAN*, 1866

July 2, 1871—Freedom Holler

Any time there's stealing in Stoke County, all the white
folk, and even some of us black, start looking around
for the darkie what done it. But stealing ain't solely a
colored profession. What it be is work for a poor man,
and the war took plenty of white folk and made trash
out of them.

For certain, none of us living in Freedom Holler was
among the well-to-do, but Preacher Moses say there's different breeds of poor, depending what they got and ain't
got. Since we got roofs for our heads and food for our
bellies, he say we better than most black folk, and even
some white trash. Preacher say some of them whites ain't
allowed to vote neither, on account they fought as Rebels
and flat refuse to take an oath of loyalty to the United
States. He say that make us better, too, which is why the
white trash hate us so.

Mama say voting don't make a man good or bad. She
say most often it got to do with how much whiskey they
drunk. Which be why she and the other womenfolk all

make the menfolk promise not to bring liquor into the Holler.

I pondered over the stealing of the Reynolds' wash until Jordana told me to quick run and put my hoe away inside her cabin, then come right back. She'd been setting her turnip and collard trimmings in a small cast-iron pot. Now she needed my help carrying that pot upstream, so's we could wash the dirt off the leaves at the pool where we fetch water.

"Ain't hardly enough to be worth eating, I know," she say when we kneeling beside the creek. "Gonna cook down to where we all be blessed to get one bite. But good greens can't be wasted, Mance. 'Specially these tender young 'uns."

I wasn't much for greens eating myself, and I knew Lilla weren't either, so I reckoned there'd be two bites extra for whoever craved them.

"That Jordana sure is one smart colored woman!" The voice was Mama's. I turned to see her and Joe Putnam coming up the path. She look all done in from working, but her mouth was laughing. "That Jordana knows the only way to get Mance Jackson to wash his hands 'fore supper is to let him rinse off her greens." Mama stop behind me and folded her arms 'crossed her small bosom. "Now how we gonna trick him into washing his face?"

"No trick at all," Joe say, kneeling down beside me, smelling of the Nortons' stables, where he spent his day. Now he stick his hands out in the creek water, then dunk his face in. When he come up, he shakes his head like a wet dog and water go flying all over.

I was laughing at him when he took both hands out of the creek, his palms cupped together, and throwed the water right in my face. He was on his feet and back to the path 'fore I could return the kindness.

Jordana stood. "Don't you be running off, Joe. Here. Carry this pot for me. I'll come along and show you where to put it on the cooking fire."

He circled wide around Mama, so's I couldn't splash him as he reached for the pot handle. After him and Jordana left, Mama knelt in the dry spot where Jordana'd been and cleaned her own self in a more civilized manner.

"You find the Reynolds' wash, Mama?"

She wiped her face, and then mine, with her apron. "Missuh Reynolds's driver spotted the shirts and petticoats under that tall hedge what runs along the road in front of their place. I promised Missus Reynolds to go early tomorrow and wash those clothes over again."

"Hattie say the Norton boys done it."

She got to her feet, smoothing the damp wrinkles out of her apron. "Most like. No thief be leaving Missuh Reynolds's shirts behind. One of them's worth more than everything else that's still missing put together."

"Like what, Mama? Bedsheets? And a pair of Missuh Reynolds's fine white gloves?"

She'd got up on the path and she stop to look at me. "Now, how'd you know that, Emancipation Jackson?"

"That what the horseman be wearing last night, Mama— the man what burned our church. I reckon *he* done the stealing."

"Mance, just 'cause men like that always wear sheets and pillowcases when they do mischief, don't mean—"

"The gloves, Mama. The gloves is how I *know*." I told her how I found one in the creek earlier—pointed out the spot where I fished it out of the water. "I got it back in our cabin. Come on, I'll show you." I tugged at her arm to move her along.

Mama planted her feet firm and set her hands to her

hips. "First you tell me how you know that rider was wearing dress gloves."

That's when I recalled that I was s'posed to be keeping from her the fact I been out late. "I heard the commotion, Mama, and I run up to the church in time to see him ride away." True enough. She didn't have to know where I heard the commotion *from*. Then, before she could ask me more, I quick told her about Colonel Gilbert's filly. "I figure a white man poor enough to steal bedsheets probably don't have a horse neither."

Mama took my hand and walked me toward the cabins. "Last time, the Harrises rode their own horses and, like as not, used their own bedsheets." But she was frowning doubtful-like as she say it.

"Yes'm. They had riding gloves, too. That's why I think the man what burned our church was a poorer breed of white trash from the Harrises."

"Or maybe one o' the Harris brothers took the wash and the filly," Mama say, not to me exactly, but just to get the idea out in the air. "Took 'em so nobody'd recognize him or his horse. Or . . . I wonder who that fifth man was with 'em last time? We never did find that out." She gripped my hand tighter and stepped up her gait. "Show me that glove, Mance. I'll know if it come from Missuh Reynolds."

7

Across the street, mid-block, three steps above street level, was a raised-panel door brandishing the number 345 and three classy brass plaques: two law firms and a dentist's office. Inside the door was a stairwell. At the top of the stairs, I turned right and found two doors across from each other. One sported a large poster of a jovial molar holding (yes, it had arms) a toothbrush, as if all set to shepherd the teeth of Israel. As much as I hate going to the dentist's, I get a kick out of the "happy teeth" paraphernalia they always have adorning their offices. I wondered fleetingly why I've never seen happy hearts or stomachs in a doctor's office.

The door opposite had a comparatively modest APPERSON FOR CONGRESS sign, so I let myself in. The office seemed spacious, mainly because furniture was sparse: a long folding table— PC on one end, stacks of papers in the middle, three wire bins half-filled with more papers on the other end—and behind the table, a double-wide two-drawer filing cabinet with phone and fax machine on top. The only wall hanging was a small American flag, hung vertically. Not even a campaign poster. Though why waste propaganda on your own supporters?

Speaking of which, the place seemed deserted. I could see two other rooms off the main one on the right wall. The door to the first was closed and no light shown beneath. The second door was open, the room lit, and I could hear the hum of some kind of machine running. The sound stopped abruptly, followed by four beeps. I knew a microwave oven when I heard one.

"Hello?" I called out.

"In here," came the reply, female, mature and composed.

The microwave went back on, so I walked over to the room, a walk-in closet turned kitchenette. The occupant, fork in hand, was a black woman who looked younger than her voice—late twenties, I guessed—or maybe she only seemed young because of her hair, a magnificent array of cornrows which, at the base of her hairline, turned into beaded braids that cascaded down her back. She wore khakis, sandals, and a Hawaiian shirt. My kind of office casual. In the oven, I could see a Weight Watcher's entree box. Fettucine Alfredo, if my nose didn't deceive me.

She gave me a cursory glance over her shoulder. "You the temp?"

"No, I—"

"No? Guess I can write another one off. You'd think they'd at least call." Her eyes returned to her lunch as if she expected it to bubble over, but she didn't stop talking. "Well, if you're here about the job, it's ten hours a week—probably more in the fall. You can work out your own schedule as long as you're here when I am. Computer work and filing. I answer the phones, so you don't have to worry about dealing with dimwits." She went on to quote a per-hour rate that was a dollar above the industry standard for PC-skilled office work.

"No, I—" This time I stopped myself. Did she really think I'd come in to apply for a job wearing shorts and a T-shirt? Then again, maybe I'd finally found someone who didn't make hiring decisions based on the jewelry I wore with my navy suit and white blouse.

Ten hours a week, she'd said. Even with the dig, two hours a day might be doable.

Work for J. D.? What was I thinking?

I was thinking that I was actually standing here, face-to-face with someone who had a job to offer, instead of mailing my resumé to P.O. boxes listed in the classifieds. And I was thinking that Pennsylvania Unemployment would allow me to earn a limited wage and still collect, so I could rake in some extra bucks without totally giving up my feeling of freedom, especially if I could write my own work schedule.

"Just computer and filing?" I repeated, because no way would I harass people with solicitation calls.

"Right. No campaigning, no stuffing envelopes, no phoning. None of that gets into full gear for at least another month anyway, and then J. D.'ll call in his volunteers." The oven beeped and she took out her food. Not fettucine Alfredo, but linguini with clam sauce. She peeled the lid halfway back and stirred the concoction with her fork. "You'd be inputting contributions, keeping the mailing list current—stuff like that. And nobody's going to make you take an oath to vote for J. D., if that worries you. This is strictly a job."

She pulled the fork between her lips to test for doneness, then popped the meal back into the oven for two more minutes. "He's out schmoozing most of the time—doesn't hang around here much. Stays out of my way, which I like. Paycheck's always on time, though. There are worse bosses."

"I know. I've worked for them."

"Got experience? How much?"

"Twelve years with Dawkins-Greenway Corporation. Laid off in May."

"Computer skills?"

I listed the software I knew.

"If it were up to me, you could start today and name your price, but J. D. likes to pretend he does the interviewing. Let me try to raise him on his cell phone." She brushed past me into the main office, still holding her fork.

"He's not here?" I asked, following her. "His car's out front.

That's actually why I came in, not for the job. He's blocking me in."

She confirmed my story with a peek out of the window. "Probably just stopped to grab a sandwich downstairs. Once he starts talking, he forgets he's double-parked. That your Neon? The truck in front of it's pulling out."

By the time I got close enough to look, Lynn Casey's pickup was gone.

"Want me to call J. D. anyway, about hiring you?"

Asked straight out, I hesitated. Should I talk it over with Miss Maggie first? After all, I *was* living in her house, mooching off her. True, she wouldn't let me pay room and board, but maybe because she expected I'd find a regular job and be supporting myself before the summer was out.

The office manager misinterpreted my qualms. "You could ask J. D. for more money, with your skills. He can afford another buck an hour."

"I really do need to get going," I replied. "Let me see if I can catch J. D. downstairs and I'll talk to him myself. If not, I'll call."

"Okay, but we're closed tomorrow and Monday for the holiday weekend." She took my name and number and I left her to her pasta.

Downstairs, outside the door, I turned right and glanced through the window of the County Cafe, an overpriced luncheonette and lawyer hangout. Like the rest of the town, the cafe was nearly deserted, but J. D. had decided the counter waitress would do for an audience. Poor woman looked like she needed rescuing, so it was with a feeling of benevolence that I pushed through the door and started to say, "J. D.—"

That's when the odor hit me: a cross between wintergreen Lifesavers and Ben-Gay. Not an unpleasant scent, but not exactly appetite-inducing either. I figured there must be a plate of mints in the vicinity, but I didn't see one, nor anything to set such a plate on.

"Miss Montallo," J. D. exclaimed, putting an aw-shucks inflection in his tone. "My car's in front of yours, isn't it? I'll come right now and move it. Sorry about that—thought I'd be in and out of here quick."

The smell had disconcerted me enough that I'd momentarily forgotten about both his car and the job, especially since, the instant he spoke, the odor was gone. *Completely* gone. Instead of answering J. D., I dumbly stood by the door, sniffing. My olfactory cells now detected only the aroma of pork barbecue, and my salivary glands reminded me that I still had to get to the supermarket to pick up lunch for the troops.

J. D. reached past me to open the door, then gestured me through it ahead of him with the Styrofoam take-out box he held. "Now you be sure to tell Magnolia," he said as we crossed the street, "that if she needs any help with her archaeological dig to just pick up the phone. Be glad to drum up some volunteers."

I wished I could accept his offer—while supplies like tents might be borrowed or begged from around the community, volunteer diggers would be harder to come by in this heat. But like Miss Maggie had said, we didn't need politics messing up the Bell Foundation before it got started. Still, I'd run his suggestion by her. Maybe we could find a way to acquire volunteers without acquiring the congressman. So I merely nodded and changed the subject. "Your campaign office manager said you were looking to hire a part-time clerk."

"You talked to Kiesha?" He showed his surprise by raising his eyebrows as he unlocked his driver's door. "It's a temporary job, through the election. You interested?"

"Depends." I didn't allow any shrewdness into my voice. J. D. could out-slick me any day, so "uninformed" seemed the better approach. "What's it pay?"

"Well now . . ." He leaned on his open door as if he'd never considered the matter. "How much did you have in mind?"

I tacked three extra bucks onto the hourly rate his manager

had quoted, figuring J. D. would ask me about my skills, then talk me down accordingly.

That's when he floored me by saying, "Sounds fair enough. Go tell Kiesha I said to let you fill out all the papers. You can work out your schedule with her." He got into his Caddy and pulled away with a friendly wave before I could pick my jaw up off the double yellow line at my feet.

They were either desperate to hire someone or, more likely, J. D. had no idea of the particulars of the job, including the pay rate, and agreed to whatever sounded close. I mentally kicked myself for not asking for more money as I shoved my car key into the lock. Even if I went over the weekly limit allowed by Unemployment, they'd deduct the difference, then extend my coverage a few extra weeks.

But I'd definitely go home and talk it over with Miss Maggie first before signing the W-4. Besides wanting to extend that simple courtesy to my benefactor, my Italian blood makes me leery of anything fortuitous that falls into my lap this way. There *had* to be a catch I wasn't seeing.

By the time I got home, Theo was busy with a sod shovel, removing what remained of the wildflower cover right around Yorick's pit. He'd donned one of Miss Maggie's straw hats and even that looked sexy on him, especially since he'd taken off his shirt. Dwight—very nonsexy in his sweat-soaked uniform—was troweling the sod into a five-gallon bucket. Emmy, now wearing a tan baseball cap, was supervising. All of them looked about ready for a break.

Miss Maggie was sitting—yes, sitting—on a camp stool in the shade of the magnolia. Her work station was our wheelbarrow with one of Emmy's screen frames laid across the top. At her feet was another bucket of sod—the first batch apparently—and she was sifting the soil from it through the screen.

"Pat, come look," she exclaimed as I parked on the other side of the tree.

I came around the car, but stopped by the trunk. "I've got to get these groceries inside, Miss Maggie. The frozen yogurt's probably soup by now."

"One second. Let me show you our first artifact." She picked up a brown paper lunch bag from beside her feet and brought it over to me. Reaching in, she pulled out a one-inch, reddish crescent of what seemed to be stuck-together dirt. "It's a nail," she explained, seeing that I was clueless. "What's left of one anyway."

My imagination ran with that. "From Yorick's coffin?"

That got me a tolerant grin. "More likely my husband Jake dropped it when he was fixing the clapboards after Hurricane Hazel ripped through here back in '54."

"Then why are you keeping it?" Miss Maggie could be as sentimental as anyone, but not over an old nail.

"We'll save *everything*, Pat. All manmade objects and everything placed here by humans—even coal, if we find it. Never can tell what'll end up being important." Setting the artifact in her bag, she put it back by her stool. "I'll help you get the groceries inside."

I let her carry two fairly light plastic bags while I made four trips, the last of which was to tote a large watermelon.

By then, she already had the frozen yogurt put away and was inspecting the fridge-bound items, squinting at the deli parcels because she didn't have her reading glasses handy. "What'd you bring for lunch? I'm starving." After history, eating is Miss Maggie's great passion in life. Or maybe before history.

"Turkey zeps," I replied, laughing as she rolled her eyes in ecstacy.

About when Philadelphia adopted the hoagie as its very own version of the submarine sandwich, a genius upriver in my hometown stacked cooked salami, provolone cheese, tomatoes, and big, sweet onions on a long roll, and called it a "zep" after the zeppelins drifting overhead at the time. Like a good Italian hoagie, the roll isn't slathered with mayo, but sprinkled with oil and oregano. Unlike a hoagie, it's sacrilege to put lettuce in a zep. Anyway, for the sake of Miss Maggie's arteries, I make zeps without the traditional salami, substituting sliced turkey breast.

But I didn't want to talk food just then—I had too much else on my mind, from ghost cabins to job possibilities—though I decided not to mention J. D. before lunch and ruin her appetite. As I made room in the fridge for two cantaloupes, I asked, "Were there ever other tenants on this land, besides the Bells?"

"Tenants? Nothing that was ever put on paper and filed at the courthouse, no. You didn't get eggplants? The paper said they were on special."

"They didn't look so good." Actually, they looked great and I make a mean steamed eggplant with basil and oregano, but every time Miss Maggie eats the stuff her arthritis flares up, so I quit buying them. "You mean there might have been a more informal tenant arrangement? Something with no legal paperwork?"

"Anything's possible." She delved into the next bag and took out two bottles of nonfat salad dressing. "Remember what I told you, Pat: History is only our interpretation of what little evidence is left. We have to assume we don't know everything. All I can tell you about Bell Run is that no document I've seen—legal or personal—mentions tenants besides the Bells. Why're you asking?"

I hesitated long enough that she looked up from the nutritional info on the bottle to add, "Out with it, missy."

"I saw something by the creek."

Miss Maggie knew darn well what I meant by "something." She plunked the bottles down on the table and came over to me. "Describe what you saw. Exactly."

I did my best, but explained, "It wasn't clear this time. Like a bad cellular connection."

Even that fascinated her. "Interference? Psychic interference, I mean. I doubt they have short-wave radios over yonder."

I shrugged. I wouldn't know psychic interference if it walked up and handed me a pamphlet. Neither would Miss Maggie, for that matter. "You have no idea when there might have been cabins on that spot? If they were ever there at all?"

Miss Maggie returned to the grocery bags, shaking her head. "Two things interest me about this. One is that you seem certain someone was living there. If it weren't for that I'd say they could easily be outbuildings—stables, a springhouse, something like that. Though probably not a privy. Not so close to the crickbank."

"I *did* hear barnyard animals." I folded one of the big paper bags as I weighed the idea. "No, you're right. For some reason, I feel that someone lived there."

She took four long Italian rolls from the freezer to thaw. You can't get good Italian bread in Stoke, so every Wednesday when I drive Miss Maggie to visit her son at the VA Hospital in Richmond, we stop at an Italian bakery there and stock up for the week. Today's zeps would have normally used up most of our roll stash, but we'd bought a dozen extra for our July Fourth cookout.

"The second thing," she was saying, "is that you didn't simply assume you were seeing May 1864. Think about it. All your previous visions revolved around that specific week when the Battle of the Wilderness was fought near here. The natural conclusion then, given everything I've ever read about typical ghosts, would be that Bell Run is haunted by those events, or by how those events affected one person who in turn haunts the place. The logical deduction? That this latest glimpse is just another part of that same haunting."

Strange as it sounded to hear the words "logical" and "ghosts" in the same paragraph, I saw her point. "I don't know, Miss Maggie. This doesn't feel connected to that particular Bell Run."

"Still, you'd better make sure. Go on. I'll finish here and start lunch. Don't forget to wear a hat."

I wasn't sure if Miss Maggie knew exactly where she was shooing me off to, but she probably figured it out when I filled two more gallon jugs with water. This time, nothing white floated inside.

Not far northwest of Miss Maggie's house, through the forest, was the heap of bricks that marked where the Bell family made their home before the fires from the Chancellorsville battle burned the house in 1863. My destination wasn't far beyond that—the family burial plot, overlooking the Rapidan.

Usually the woods were a cool place on a hot day. Today the humidity carried the heat into the shade. Not a hint of breeze rustled the leaves above. I felt sweat running down my face before I'd gone far, and I lifted a cool jug occasionally to touch one cheek or the other. Once I reached the clearing around the Bell House ruin, I hurried through the patch of sunlight to the shade on the far side and was rewarded a bit further on with a faint stir of air rising from the river.

No squirrels or chipmunks sat on the hip-high cemetery wall today. They seem to like eating there—apparently there were primo nuts nearby and the wall provided pleasant alfresco dining. In heat like this, I imagined the little critters all back in their nests, fanning themselves languidly with oak leaves.

I surveyed the six graves of my ancestors. For Memorial Day, I'd planted a geranium in front of each stone—two where my triple-great-grandmother was buried. Now the plants looked so dried out, I wasn't sure they'd survive the week. When I emptied my jugs around their roots, the ground sucked the water in like a vacuum and, I could swear, begged for more. Made me wonder if Aunt Sophie was watering the flowers on my parents' and brother's graves back in Norristown. At least there, the water pump was only a short walk.

An inner voice told me to quit stalling and get to the business at hand. Leaving the empty jugs on the ground, I sat on the rear wall, the only place still in the shade now that the sun was almost directly overhead.

Taking a deep breath, blowing it out slowly, I closed my eyes. On the back of my lids, the typical color negative of the scene flashed on. In the next breath, though, I was bowled over by the strong smell of bread baking.

This was good—sort of a prearranged signal from Beyond. It meant everything was hunky-dory and none of the Bells were planning to disturb their eternal rest for so much as a midnight snack.

But before I could open my eyes again, another image tuned in, as fuzzy as what I'd seen down by the creek, and dimly lit, sporadically, as if by lightning. The cemetery was there, with wooden crosses instead of stones and no wall, as it looked in 1864. No, not *exactly* as it was then. The crosses were weathered to a light gray and tilted every which way. Overgrown grass and weedy shrubs carpeted the entire clearing. Enough thicket spread beyond that I couldn't see the river. The air felt damp and smelled fresh, rain-washed.

I heard a voice but, again, couldn't make out the words. As I let the vision play out, the figures of black men came into view beside the crosses. Some stood, others sat on rotting logs, while a man paced before them, talking, persuading. All were dressed poorly, though the speaker's clothes were tidier than the others. I felt myself squint, trying to fine-tune the connection, but the men disappeared completely. In that instant, I could have sworn I heard one of them say, ". . . want no more killing. . . ."

Before I could open my eyes, the bread-baking aroma came back stronger, as if to say, "Don't lay this one at my door."

"I won't," I said aloud as my eyes welcomed the sight of short, drought-browned grass and granite stones. If the condition of the graves in the vision was any indication, the Bells had all been long dead when those men met here.

Don't Be Weary, Traveler

Colored women . . . go out washing, which is about as high as a colored women gets, and their men go about idle, strutting up and down; . . . and then scold because there is no food.

—Sojourner Truth

July 2, 1871—Freedom Holler

Mama got thoughtful as she look at the glove. "I'm gonna hold onto this for you, Mance."

That meant she didn't think I ought to have it, I reckoned 'cause it didn't belong to me. "You giving it back to Mr. Reynolds, Mama?"

She nodded, but like she didn't really hear me talking.

"Don't you tell a soul you found this, Mance. Promise me?"

"What about Lilla? She know already."

"Don't you worry 'bout what Lilla knows. Promise me no one else gonna know from your mouth."

"I promise."

She put the glove away in the pouch where she keep her sewing thread. "Now let's go have our supper."

'Til today, supper and lessons and Sunday meetings be up on the hill at the church, inside or out, depending how the weather suit. Preacher say by eating together we be like Christ and his disciples at the Last Supper. He say it make us a community.

Mama say we eat supper together 'cause most all our womanfolk be off in town or in the fields working all day. Only ones left be Ida Putnam and Jordana, so they cook for everybody for a share of the money the working folk bring home. Some of the men didn't think Ida and Jordana ought to take money jes' for cooking supper, but Mama stand up and say she sure ain't gonna be a slaveholder. Ain't a one present could argue with that, so the matter be settled.

Mama tell me later that if Jordana and Ida didn't cook, those same menfolk plain wouldn't eat 'cause they think cooking be strictly a woman's chore.

While Lilla and me was fetching water today, Ida made up her cooking fire outside her cabin. Preacher didn't like it—he say we ought to meet up on Church Hill as usual—but Ida tell him nobody want to eat beside a pile of bad-smelling burnt wood.

I was as glad not to go up the hill. Didn't have to help tote water for one thing. For another, it was cooler down by the creek. Cooler and darker, so the flies was tolerable. Ida had a pot of beans simmering all afternoon, and when me and Jordana brought her the sweet corn, she soaked the ears in water 'til the husks was wet through, then roasted them on the fire. Jordana boiled up her greens with a bit of fatback borrowed from the bean pot. Might not have been a feast, but we had plenty.

Only bad thing was how Uncle Henry's leg be bothering him so that Joe and Amos had to carry him out of the little room he kept in the Dardens' cabin. Hattie brung out his chair, too, so's he could rest his back while he sat.

"Good thing we eating down here tonight," Mama say.

"Uncle Henry couldn't have made that climb and I can't imagine eating supper without him."

Everyone agreed with that, even Preacher Moses. Uncle Henry gave us all a toothless grin and say in his shaky old-man voice that he can't 'magine it either.

"Rain's coming," Jordana say. "That's why your leg hurt so, Henry. You try out that liniment we got you?"

"Made my old bones feel nice and warm," he told her as Ida handed him a little plate of beans. "I used it all up."

"Used it up?" Hattie say. "I didn't mix but a little bit of it in lard for you, Uncle Henry. You wasn't s'posed to put it on straight from the bottle."

"Guess I did, 'cause the bottle be empty." He look 'round at us with that fear he gets in his eyes when he can't remember. Which be more often than not these days.

"Don't you be worrying, Henry," Jordana say, like she talking to a young'un. She start shaving the corn off one ear to give him. "We can get you more. And I'll mix you up some each night, so you won't use it so fast."

Since Noah come home right about then, everybody forget the liniment and want to hear about Colonel Gilbert.

"We found the filly grazing this side of Flat Run." Noah helped himself to a hot ear and sat on the ground to peel the husk off. "Something must've spooked her good to send her that far. A wasp sting maybe."

"In the middle of the night?" Hattie shook her head, wise-like. "You ask me, I'd bet those Norton boys be setting off their Fourth of July firecrackers early."

"Colonel didn't say nothing 'bout hearing no fireworks," Noah told her.

Everybody else offered a notion, but Mama and me kept silent.

8

"Had to be after 1864."

How odd to hear my own thoughts echoed by Miss Maggie before I'd told her what I'd seen. Odder still that her voice was coming from the direction of the cellar.

I'd found the side yard deserted, though the tent had been set up over the hole. Emmy's grid was now distinct—four squares delineated by white string tied around thick nails at each corner. The sod had been removed not only from Yorick's square, but from the one next to it where the middle of the skeleton ought to be. I was just wondering where everyone was when I heard Miss Maggie's voice.

The cellar door was open, so I descended the steps. Two straw hats and a tan baseball cap were lined up on a shelf just inside the door. I shed my own hat and left it there. As my eyes adjusted to the light of the bare bulb hanging over the washbasin, I saw Emmy, Theo, and Miss Maggie seated around a card table loaded with sandwich fixings, cookies, and a pitcher of iced tea. Theo had donned his shirt for the occasion. Miss Maggie had on her reading glasses and a large book was open on her lap. I noticed her own zep was already history.

Miss Maggie waved me over. "Pat, sit down. I bet you could use something cold to drink."

A place was set for me, with a huge glass of iced tea to one side of a paper plate which held a proportionally huge sandwich.

The smell of onions and oregano reached my nostrils. All of a sudden I was famished, but I gulped down a third of the tea first. Miss Maggie always made it decaf, so no need to worry about caffeine making me more dehydrated.

"Where's Dwight?" I asked.

"He'll be back," Miss Maggie replied. "After a couple hours under the sun he finally begged Brackin to let him go change out of his uniform. We decided to eat in peace while he was gone. Down here it's ten degrees cooler than in the kitchen."

I felt a breeze, too. On the floor over by the washing machine, the little fan from my bedroom was oscillating back and forth.

Emmy, sandwich in hand, nodded her approval. "Down here might be a good place to set up our field lab, though we'll need more light. Magnolia, you're going to go blind squinting at that book."

"Want me to read something for you?" I muttered around a bite of my zep.

Miss Maggie shook her head, patting her book like it was a well-behaved lap dog. "Already got the info we needed. Been looking up old coins."

Emmy broke off a corner of her roll, popping it into her mouth as she explained. "Before we put up the tent, while we had room to maneuver the stadia rod, we took elevation readings for the skull and that object you found—"

"Emmy here," Miss Maggie broke in, "brushed some more dirt away to get an accurate reading, then looked at the thing with a magnifying glass." She turned to Emmy to let her continue, as if they were tossing a ball back and forth.

"I'm now certain it's a coin. In fact, if you look close, you can just make out the word 'we' on it." She slapped her hand on the table beside her plate, as if she'd reached the punch line.

I glanced at Miss Maggie for an explanation, which she was happy to provide. " 'In God *We* Trust.' The first coins to carry that motto were minted in 1864, Pat."

"And," Emmy continued, "we can narrow it down even further. The coin's bronze—I've seen that same type of corrosion on old Lincoln pennies—"

"Wait—pennies are made of bronze?" I asked. "I thought they were copper."

"Used to be," Miss Maggie replied, reaching for an oatmeal cookie. "Before 1857, they were all copper. Then they started mixing nickel in, but the war came along and nickel got scarce, so in 1864 they officially changed the mix from copper-nickel to copper-tin-zinc, which is bronze. They didn't change it again until 1982, when they started making 'em out of zinc with copper plating."

"Pennies are made of zinc?" I felt cheated somehow. How soon would they switch to plastic?

Emmy broke another tidbit off her sandwich. "Our coin is bigger than a modern cent—just a tad wider than a nickel, in fact. And the only bronze coin of that size with the 'In God We Trust' motto was the two-cent piece."

"Minted between 1864 and 1873," Miss Maggie read aloud. "So we've narrowed down the date."

"The date of the coin, that is." Emmy pulled a long strip of onion from her sandwich, tilting her head back to eat it, like she was swallowing a worm. "If the coin was buried with the body, then the burial was the date on the coin or later. If the coin is in the soil layer above the bones, then the bones are older than the coin."

I traced the logic in that as I ate another bite. Theo had been silent, listening but without much interest. I noticed he hadn't eaten much.

" '1864 to 1873,' " I echoed after a moment. "What year did your grandfather settle here, Miss Maggie?"

She downed her last nip of tea. "Can't pin down the exact year. Dummy me never thought to ask him while he was living. He bought the land in 1871, for the price of one dollar, paid to the county, but he didn't begin building this house until 1875, when Granny said she wouldn't marry him unless they had a decent home to raise a family in. Don't know if he lived out here in the meantime, or possibly even earlier. The 1870 census lists his residence as 343 Jefferson in Stoke. That's where he had his drugstore."

I recognized the number from my morning jaunt. "Is that one of the buildings across from Lynn Casey's studio?"

She nodded. "The middle one of the five that now have those ugly vinyl clapboards on the front."

"Where the County Cafe is now?"

"Right—underneath the siding are 1840-ish brick rowhouses that survived the Civil War. In 1870, they were all owned by a man named James Madison Gilbert, who operated a horse farm between here and Stoke, but apparently had business stakes all over town, too. He kept the corner building as his townhouse and rented out the others as stores and tenements. Granddaddy rented the first floor of 343. I remember him saying he was dirt poor at first and lived in one room in the back. Again, I don't know for how long."

"Did *he* ever have tenants out here?"

Now Miss Maggie understood why I was asking, and I could tell she was itching to grill me about what I'd found out at the cemetery, but she forced herself to keep her seat and look academic. "No record of tenants. But, you know, until this moment, it never occurred to me to wonder if anyone else was living on this land when he moved out here."

"Must have been," Emmy said, dabbing a napkin at a dribble of tomato juice on her chin. "This hill's flat enough to cultivate, and there's two sources of fresh water nearby. Can't imagine anyone wasting good land like this. A wonder your grandfather got hold of so many acres when he did."

Miss Maggie shook her head. "You have to factor in human nature. Everyone in Stoke had known the Bells—respected them, too—and everyone knew of at least some of the tragedies that'd wiped out the family. People don't rush to live somewhere bad things happened. Too superstitious."

"They thought this place was haunted?" That question came from Theo. I already knew Bell Run was haunted. But the idea seemed to bring him out of his own problems.

Miss Maggie shrugged as she picked up the iced-tea pitcher to pour herself another glass. "Not so much haunted as jinxed, I'd say. Mind you, this chunk of geography has its share of formal ghost stories. Every self-respecting square foot of Virginia does, you know."

Everyone laughed but me, so Emmy explained, "Virginia has the dubious distinction of being host to more ghost legends than any other state in the union."

"Only because," Miss Maggie added, "the Europeans started poking around these woods, causing trouble, at least a century before they did in most other states. The Chesapeake counties even have ghosts from Spanish galleons."

"Tell us about Bell Run's ghosts," Theo asked, his curiosity now fully awake. I wanted to know, too, wondering why Miss Maggie hadn't mentioned the tales when I began bumping into spooks here.

She let out a "pshaw" to dismiss their worth. "The legends connected to this place are more the tried-and-true type—not at all original. One tells of a headless Yankee cavalryman who's almost an exact twin of Washington Irving's horseman. Another makes Dark Hollow—that's what they called the valley along Bell Run after the Civil War—into another Dismal Swamp."

"Which is?" I prompted.

Miss Maggie raised her glass to her lips, but didn't drink. "Great Dismal Swamp's just southwest of Virginia Beach. Sort of an inland Bermuda Triangle. If you enter it, at the very least, you'll get lost. At most, you see strange lights, and eerie, awful things happen to you." She let some tea down her gullet.

"Why 'Dark Hollow'?" I asked. "The name, I mean. The woods are dark now, but back then, weren't a lot of the trees either burned during the Chancellorsville battle or clear-cut by both armies? There must have been more sunlight getting down to the creek." I was thinking of what I'd seen today—the bright clearing along the west bank.

"Ghost stories don't happen in places called Sunny Grove," Emmy reasoned.

Miss Maggie agreed. "Like I said, Bell Run had some kind of stigma in the years after the war. Granddaddy used to call the stream Bloodwater Creek and up here was Graveyard Hill." Suddenly, she was on her feet, catching her book just in time. "Holy smokes, I've been stupid!" She clapped a hand to her brow with the air of someone who's found her lost eyeglasses propped on top of her head. "I always thought that name came from the Bell family plot being here. Never occurred to me to look for a *second* cemetery. See, Pat, you can never assume."

"Now hold on, Magnolia," Emmy said. "Lots of loopholes in that theory. First off, while that coin may indicate a formal burial and a certain amount of respect for the dead, the rest of the evidence—and there's precious little of it yet—suggests that our bony friend didn't rate a coffin or the standard six feet of earth. Second, had such a cemetery existed here after the Civil War, your grandfather obviously knew about it. Would he have built his house so close?"

Miss Maggie sat down again with a frustrated pout. "Rats."

"Then again," Emmy continued, barely missing a beat, "if this was a mass grave after one of the battles—Wilderness or Spotsylvania, say, since we're talking 1864—maybe by the time your granddaddy got home from the war, the grass was grown and he couldn't tell exactly where the grave was. Might have thought he chose the spot farthest away from it to build." She squirreled another bit of bread from her sandwich, ate it, and licked the oregano slime off her fingers.

"Or if this was a black cemetery," Theo murmured, "he might not have cared."

We all looked at him, me because I hadn't expected him to jump onto the brainstorming bandwagon. He struck me as more of an observer—at least today, when his mind was crowded with other matters.

Miss Maggie caught my eye. "Well, now, *that* could explain a few things." She meant Mance, of course.

I was thinking about those black men I'd seen. Assuming my imagination hadn't been playing tricks on me—no more than usual, anyway—was that scene at the Bell family plot one of Mance's memories? Or were those men all ghosts in their own right? And, either way, why were they bothering *me*? Was someone roaming among the dead, listening to their tales of heartache, and saying, "Go see Pat Montella. She'll help you out."

My mother came to mind. Dad used to tell her she should have been a bartender. Difference was, when she was commiserating with someone, instead of Michelob and popcorn, she'd serve up coffee and pizzelles.

Miss Maggie went into an orgy of musing. "A black cemetery might not have shown up on county records. Nor had permanent headstones for that matter. Even so, Theo's right, no one would stop a white man from building right in the middle of it if he wanted. I don't remember Granddaddy talking politics or race issues much, but his family owned slaves before the war and he did join the army to preserve that way of life. Far as I know, he was as much a product of his times as anyone."

"No use speculating until we have more evidence," Emmy said. "At this point, anything's possible."

The mischievous green twinkle blinked on in Miss Maggie's eyes as she reached for another cookie. "Isn't that the truth? Who knows? Maybe Granddaddy dug that grave himself. He never did like door-to-door salesmen."

We lingered over lunch, no one anxious to go back out into the heat. Miss Maggie got the idea to put my fan on the cellar foundation, so at least the dig site would feel a tiny breeze. While Theo helped her unravel the fifteen-foot extension cord, I decided to check our drinking-water supply.

One jug was empty already, the other a third down. I took the first to refill it, plus the cold pack to swap with a fresh one from the freezer. Miss Maggie always kept two in there in case of power failures which, I'd learned, visited us with almost every thunderstorm. And during this heat wave we'd had at least one brownout per evening.

I was in the kitchen, about to turn on the tap, when I heard music coming from the hallway—an electronic melody, like I'd heard in musical greeting cards. Walking over to the doorway, I spied Theo's gym bag on the hall floor and peeking out of the front pocket was the performer: a mini cell phone.

Scooping up the compact square of plastic, I flipped it open, yanked out the antenna, hit the talk button, and said in a quasi-alluring receptionist voice, "You've reached the phone of Theo Clayborne. How may I direct your call?"

Static squawked back at me, along with a very unalluring female voice saying, "Is he there?"

"One moment, puh-lee-ase." Crossing the kitchen, I yelled down the cellar stairs and Theo emerged from the depths. "For you. A woman. And I like the tune this thing plays."

"Bach's 'Minuet in G,' " he said with a small smile before putting the phone to his ear.

I returned to my chore, not meaning to eavesdrop—I mean, he could have taken that call anywhere, but he chose to pace back and forth in front of the kitchen table as he talked. His resonant voice and singer's diction carried easily over the sound of the water running.

"Vicky? How'd you get my cell phone number?" Theo sounded none too pleased. I figured Vicky was either an un-wanted admirer/stalker or a relative asking for money. Or maybe an MCI salesperson. "Never mind. Just tell me what you want. . . . What? No, a simple mail-merge wouldn't have corrupted the new baby database. Maybe a power surge of some kind. . . . A brownout? Yeah, that could've zapped it. . . ." A longer pause followed.

Work, I deduced. I remembered calls like this on my days off, as if they couldn't do without me for one minute. Since my salary hadn't been much above burger-flipper range, and since every one of my nonwork minutes had been more precious than choc-olate to me, I used to let my machine pick up such calls. I was sorry now that I'd answered Theo's.

"Look, quit worrying who's to blame. Just get Jim to run a restore. I backed up the server before I left last night, so . . . What do you mean there's no tape? . . . Look on my desk. . . . Try next to the printers. Maybe I set it there by mistake. . . . No, I can't come in. I still have that rash I left you a message about this morning . . . no, the doctor isn't sure what it is yet but he's pretty sure it's contagious. . . ."

He stopped pacing in front of the fridge and I grinned en-couragement at him. A mysterious contagious rash. This was a man after my own heart.

"Get Jim to do a backup of what you have now, then restore using Monday night's tape . . ." He prattled off instructions while I screwed the lid on the jug. I gestured that I needed to get into the freezer. He moved, still talking.

I toted the jug and the cold pack out to the cooler, then descended into the cellar once more to clear off the table. Miss Maggie had already tossed the paper plates into a trash bag. The iced-tea pitcher had no more than a cup in it, so I left it and the glasses. At Miss Maggie's request, I left the cookies, too. Every-thing else I carried up to the kitchen.

Theo was still prattling. As I put the leftover tomato slices and onion slivers into Ziploc bags, he started repeating himself, talking slower, conveying the impatience of someone trying to potty train a cow. "No, Vicky, for the thousandth time, *I can't come in.* Jim knows how to run the jobs and . . . So ask him when he gets *back* from lunch. . . . If he has any problems, he can give me a call. . . ."

He obviously needed an out. I shoved the plastic bags into the fridge and gestured him into the hall. Crossing to the front door, I leaned out of the screen door and rang the doorbell a few times. The chime was right over Theo's head—Vicky had to have heard it.

"I have to go," Theo said. "Someone's at the door." He snapped the phone shut so fast he couldn't have waited for her to say good-bye. To me he said, "I owe you."

I latched the screen door. "Is she your boss?"

"As of two weeks ago. My last boss was a meeting junkie. Vicky hates meetings, so I thought she'd be a refreshing change." Theo looked at the phone in his hand as if it'd turned traitor on him.

"What's your company do? I heard you mention a new baby database. Does 'baby' refer to size or do you work for an adoption agency? Or maybe a cloning factory?"

That earned me a smile. "None of the above. They do direct-mail marketing. The new baby database is a mailing list of every kid under three months old from Charlottesville to Richmond, north to Fredericksburg."

"You send junk mail to babies?"

Theo slipped his phone into his front shorts pocket. "Vee-Tack will send junk mail to anyone. If you've drawn more than three breaths in this part of Virginia, odds are you're on one of their mailing lists."

"I think you're right." My handbag rested on the hall table and today's mail still stuck out of the middle compartment. I extracted the envelopes and showed Theo the insurance come-on.

"Yeah, that's one of theirs." He pointed to the return address. "Virginia Targeted Audience Communications. We call it V-TAC. You're in the 'new residents' database. Want me to delete you?"

"Can you?"

"Sure. I'll remove you from all our lists. Can't guarantee your name won't show up again next week, though. Every time you buy something on credit or pay a bill or fill out any kind of form, there's a chance someone'll sell that information to us or one of our sources. Is this another one?" Theo put a finger on the form J. D. had given me, a corner of which was visible under my purse.

"Voter registration," I explained, slipping the paper out so he could see it. "Will filling that out put me in a 'voters' database?"

He smiled sympathetically. "Mass mailings for politicians are our specialty. Just last summer, one candidate had us send out these registration forms to every adult not on the voting rolls in his district. We printed them up already filled in, except for Social Security number and signature. I told my boss I thought it tacky, if not illegal, for us to print 'Republican' under 'Choice of Party' but I was ignored."

I moved closer to see where Theo was pointing on the form, but he was so tall, I had to rise on tiptoe for an unobstructed view over his forearm. Off balance, I swayed toward his biceps. I clapped a hand to his shoulder to steady myself. The cloth of his shirt was still damp from the sweat of the morning's work.

Out of the corner of my eye, I spied movement at the kitchen end of the hall, so I craned my neck around Theo's chest for an unimpeded view. Standing beside the doorway, filling up the space magnificently, white tee and stonewashed cutoffs showing off sun-tinted skin, was a red-haired, mustachioed goliath. Hugh.

You Read the Bible and You Understand

Any person having one-fourth or more of negro blood, shall be deemed a colored person.

—1866 amendment to Chapter 103
of the Code of Virginia

July 2, 1871—Freedom Holler

After we cleaned up from supper, since it be Sunday, Preacher led us in prayer some. Then, like every other night, we commenced our lesson of the day. Preacher been teaching us all reading, writing and numbers, and sometimes history and geography. Tonight, it already be too dark in the Holler to read, so he tell us about how, long time ago, people called Greeks built a big horse out of wood—big enough to hide a whole army inside—and that's how they win a war.

"Now, why did they sail off to Troy to fight this war?" he asked, not wanting an answer, just setting up the rest of the tale. Preacher was standing in the center of our circle as he talked, but he moved with every thought that come out of his mouth, almost like he was dancing the story, which was his way. Even though his face be already shadowed by the gathering dark, his words seem to breathe like a living animal. "The Trojans had come to Greece first, and they'd carried away a woman named Helen. That's why the Greeks fought that war. For one Greek woman! Imagine a whole African nation coming here to America and waging war to free one slave."

"Why jes' that lady?" Lilla asked. "Why didn't them Trojans take all them Greeks for slaves? Then nobody be left to fight wars and build wood horses."

"Why, indeed." Preacher raise his head like he be counting the stars popping out above.

From where I sat, though, not one pinpoint of light come into view yet. The tops of the trees was swaying, rustled by a fresh breeze, sounding like old ladies whispering.

"Perhaps," Preacher say at last, "those Trojans weren't as greedy as our white slavetraders. Perhaps they were content to push their own plows and haul their own loads."

"I bet they jes' had a mess of clothes to wash," Mama say, chortling as she jostled her elbow into Ida's arm, "so they 'spect that one woman's all they need."

We all laugh with her, even Preacher. Then he say, "What if those Trojans knew that when you steal an entire people away from their homeland, the first chance those Greeks got, they'd turn against their captors? Take one woman and you only have to guard one prisoner. One woman can mother a new race of slaves—slaves with just enough Greek blood that those Trojans could point their fingers and shout 'inferior!' But with enough Trojan blood that this new race wouldn't be welcomed in Greece, or anywhere else on earth, for that matter. Slaves with no place they can escape to."

"Yup, that's real smart," Hattie agreed. "So how comes them smart Trojans get fooled by a big ol' wooden horse?"

"Because, Sister Hattie," Preacher reply, "the Trojans only saw what they wanted to see."

"Jes' like my ol' master," say Uncle Henry.

Most everybody laugh at that, too, 'cause all us know the stories 'bout slaves outsmarting the white folk.

"But we *all* able to be fooled like that, Moses," Mama say. "Black folk and white. Ain't a matter of color."

"Isn't it, Sister Alma? Who here can say what those first men stolen from Africa were like? That noble race no longer exists in America. We've all been diluted by white blood. The very weaknesses that brought white masters and their sons to our women time and again—those weaknesses were passed on to the breed of mulattos they begot. All of us here, even Uncle Henry, have at least one drop of that weak blood in us—"

The breeze picked up sudden, and a flash of faint lightning bleached the sky.

Uncle Henry sniffed the air. "Jordana's storm be coming. Coming fast."

Even as he said it, a fat drop of rain landed square on the back of my neck. We all pick up and run for our cabins, and just in time.

9

"Hugh!" I exclaimed, then cursed myself for sounding so daunted at the very sight of him, even though I was. "Why are you home early? Is Beth Ann all right?"

Hugh seemed at a loss for words. That's when I realized I was still up on tiptoes, still clutching Theo's shoulder. I came down to earth and Theo stepped away from me so hastily I expected to hear a sonic boom.

Another realization: I'd said "home," as if Hugh lived here. For all Theo knew, he'd been caught with another man's woman hanging on him, and the sheer size of the man doing the catching could scare the bejesus out of anyone.

One thing wrong with that scenario: Hugh only *looks* intimidating. He's not the honor-defending type. Now, if my cousin Chenzo had done the catching, we'd have a whole different ballgame. Not that Chenzo would get violent—our family isn't that kind of Italian—but he'd tell Aunt Lydia who'd tell Aunt Floss who'd tell Aunt Sophie. They'd offer up a novena because I'd finally found a man (alas, not an Italian-Catholic, but at least he wasn't Sicilian). Wedding plans would be laid, trays of fancy butter cookies ordered, and names chosen for my children.

Anyway, my honor was not only safe but bored silly because it hadn't seen action in ages, especially from someone who couldn't even bother to send me a postcard this week.

I decided to show these mere men just who was the civilized

one present by doing introductions. "Theo, this is our neighbor, Fitzhugh Lee. Hugh, Theo Clayborne, Dr. Brewster's assistant."

They shook hands and mumbled pleased-to-meet-yous at each other. Then Theo excused himself, pulling his phone from his pocket and saying, "I ought to call Wyatt's sister." He dropped the voter form back on the table and made a beeline for the front door.

"Where's Beth Ann?" I asked Hugh, heading off any smart remark he might make.

"She's still in Poquoson with Rich's family. They'll bring her home Saturday."

"You didn't say your brother was going to be there." Or had Hugh mentioned it and I'd been too busy imagining that he wanted to get me alone for the week? That is, alone as two people could be with a teenager in tow.

"Not Rich. Only his wife and kids. They're there most of the summer. He goes down on weekends."

Worse yet. A house full of family. "Why'd you come home then?"

He hesitated just long enough that his reply was disappointing. "Sunburn."

"Sunburn?" I took a step toward him, for a closer look at his skin. His legs and arms were tan, as they had been before he left on vacation. He *was* a mailman, after all, and spent a few hours of each day toting a mail pouch around the development. And this past month he'd been wearing those cute Postal Service uniform shorts.

Seeing my skepticism, he added, "On my back," though he made no move to turn around and lift his shirt. Darn.

"You never heard of sunblock?"

"I *used* sunblock. All I can figure is that I was sweating with this heat and the sunblock must have come off on the lounge chair I was sitting on." He inched sideways into the kitchen. "I came in to get a piece of Miss Maggie's aloe."

"The plant's still over there on the sill." I nodded toward the window over the sink, all ready to point out that he'd walked right by his objective. Before I could open my big mouth, though, my brain saw an opportunity not to be missed. "Want me to smear the aloe on your back for you?"

"No." You'd think by the tone of his voice I'd offered to spread poison-ivy sap on him. "Thanks, but I can manage it."

"Yeah? How?"

That stumped him, so I assumed he hadn't grown an extra arm out of his spine in the last week. Still, despite his protests, he made no move to turn and fetch the aloe himself. If he sent out any more mixed signals, I'd need a traffic controller to sort them out.

Time to take the initiative. "Sit down and take your shirt off." Squeezing past him, I went over to the sink to break a frond off the plant.

"Miss Maggie showed me your bones outside." Hugh had quietly followed right behind, making me jump when he spoke.

"They aren't *my* bones and you're supposed to be sitting with your shirt off." I wasn't about to let him cheat me out of this by changing the subject.

"I can't sit. The sunburn's on the back of my legs, too."

"Didn't you have to sit on the drive back from the shore?"

"Yes, and it hurt like hell."

"So you're going to stand the rest of the day?"

"Something wrong with that?"

His excuses were beginning to sound suspicious. I tried for a peek at the back of his thighs. He backed away, facing me the whole time. The only red skin I saw was on his cheekbones.

Modesty? Hugh?

"Okay, so I'll stand on a chair to do your back." Frond in hand, I pulled one of the wooden chairs free of the table, flipped back the padding, and climbed up on the seat. "Come on, before my vertigo kicks in."

Hugh let out a resigned sigh. "All right, but you have to promise you won't laugh."

Laugh? "*Madonne!* You have a tattoo, don't you?" My imagination went to town with that, conjuring up a naked seductress who writhed erotically when he so much as hiccuped.

"No!" He sounded exactly like his daughter in one of her "Ooh, gross" reactions.

"Well, if it's back hair you're ashamed of, half my cousins can beat anything you've got. Rocco had hair on his shoulders the day he was born and—"

He shut me up with another sigh, less resigned, more irritable, passing along the impression that the next sigh would be homicidal.

"Okay, okay, swear to God, not so much as a smirk."

Stepping up to my perch, he turned and lifted his shirt over his head. Expecting to be moved by the sight of one of the wonders of the natural world, I sucked in my breath in expectation. That's what stopped a full-blown guffaw from escaping.

Oh, he had sunburn, nasty in spots, already peeling. But he'd been right about the chair taking off his sunblock. From about the middle of his shoulder blades, disappearing beneath the waistband of his shorts, was the woven pattern of lawn-chair webbing, perfectly imprinted in sunburn with little white squares every two inches.

I peeked down at his legs below his shorts. Same pattern, though faded below the knee where he already had some tan. That's why he hadn't turned his back to me at first. He looked like he was wearing one of those gaudy spandex suits you see on Olympic speed skaters.

Sunblock, that great leveler of men. The pain hadn't brought him home. Mortification had.

He swung his head around to glare at me, as if disapproving of the little mewing noises my throat was making as I struggled to keep my mirth bottled up.

"I'm not laughing," I tried to assure him. Mistake. Opening my mouth let it out. To distract him, I squeezed the frond like a toothpaste tube and dribbled the sap down his spine. Then I gently spread the goo around with my fingertips. The aloe felt cool; Hugh's skin, hot.

His turn to suck in his breath, his massive ribs expanding under my touch. I stopped laughing, thinking I'd hurt him, but he let out a soft "mmm" of gratification.

But was his "mmm" for the aloe or my fingers?

I never got the chance to find out because Miss Maggie banged through the screen door. "Pat, there you are. I decided to make some sun tea for supper. Did you tell Hugh about Mance?"

You'd think someone of Miss Maggie's long-lived experience would realize that a woman alone with a half-naked man isn't going to have ghosts on the brain. I tried to convey this to her via my eyebrows, but she was too busy reaching up on top of the fridge for our sun tea jar.

"Mance?" Hugh turned, curious, but also to keep Miss Maggie from seeing his back. "You mean Beth Ann's imaginary friend?"

"Pat dreamt about him the night before last." Miss Maggie carried the jar over to the sink to fill it.

Hugh pivoted again as she moved, but his first question was for me. "How do you know about Mance? Miss Maggie, did you—"

"I didn't tell her. I thought maybe Beth Ann had."

"I thought so, too," I murmured. Since Hugh's back was to me once more, I squeezed the aloe frond some more and began coating his horizontal burns. My mind, though, was rerunning today's visions of shanties along the creek and men in the cemetery, knowing the boy in my dreams somehow belonged to that world. But how, and why? And why now? Why me?

Suddenly the skin beneath my hands was the color of a paper grocery bag and long, ugly scars crisscrossed every inch of it.

A glimpse, no more. Gone in the blink of an eye, which was

what I'd done to bring it on. I must have gasped because Hugh spun around, dropping his shirt on the floor as he grabbed my waist, thinking I was about to fall. Too bad I wasn't.

"Vertigo?" he asked.

I shook my head dumbly as my brain ran a quick analysis of what I'd seen. "Lash marks."

Miss Maggie abruptly forgot both the sun tea jar under the tap and the giggle she'd been valiantly holding in since getting an eyeful of Hugh's back. "Details, Pat. And tell me what you saw before lunch, too."

"Saw?" said Hugh, wide-eyed, swiveling his head from Miss Maggie up to me on the chair. "Not again." He knew about my first ghost experiences, and at one point he'd even seen me go into one of what Miss Maggie likes to call my "trances" (which makes me sound like some crackpot who stages séances and up-chucks ectoplasm), but I never could tell how much Hugh actually believed. His tone now implied that he'd made up his mind to accept my last yarn, but only as one of those stranger-than-fiction incidents that you relate to grandkids on snowy winter nights a couple decades down the road. The kind of thing you can sooner or later convince yourself really didn't happen.

Pretty much the way I wanted to believe it, too.

I told myself to be thankful for small favors—his hands were still around my waist. Hoping my reply to Miss Maggie wouldn't discourage him, I gave them both a quick rundown of the cemetery episode. "It happened fast, Miss Maggie, like the glimpse I got of the cabins. The lash marks were the same way. More so. Like a snapshot." And, I remembered suddenly, that the whiff of wintergreen I'd gotten in the cafe earlier was like that, too—a sniffbite from the past. If so, did Miss Maggie's grandfather's drugstore have anything to do with . . .

With what?

I was about to relate the cafe installment when Emmy came through the door, pausing to study our tableau, which I imagined resembled a scene from a *Mad* magazine comic—me still up on the chair and the sun tea jar now overflowing. All she said was, "What happened to his back?"

Letting go of me, Hugh grumbled, "It's sunburn." He scooped his shirt up and tried to slip it on, but his sweat made it stick up around his armpits, right where the burns began, and he grunted in pain. I reached out to pull the cloth free of his skin.

"Could be clown makeup for all I care," Emmy said, "long as you're here to help dig."

"Sure, he'll help," Miss Maggie volunteered as she shut off the tap. "That way he'll get invited to dinner."

Hugh grinned. "Depends what you're having."

"Like it matters," I said, knowing that he didn't have anything but dry cereal in his trailer at the moment and that he wouldn't go into town for a meal without putting on long, hot pants to cover the madras design on his legs because Stoke had no drive-thrus on their fast-food restaurants, thanks to a 1950s town ordinance designed to discourage drive-up burger joints and the supposedly delinquent teens they attracted. Besides, would Hugh choose an uninspired burger and fries over my potluck? Don't bet on it.

But I didn't have a chance to voice my brilliant reasoning because at that moment we all heard a car out front. "That must be Dwight coming back," Miss Maggie said as she reached for the tea canister.

"Great." Emmy rubbed her hands together. "Time to get back to work. Where's Theo?"

I hopped down from my roost. "Out front. I'll get him."

As I pushed through the front screen door, I saw Miss Maggie was wrong—Dwight wasn't here. A white pickup blocked the drive instead, the kind of truck men drive as an extension of their (usually imagined) virility: jumbo-sized, with fat tires and a full complement of shiny chrome accessories—grille guard, fog lights, running boards, even a flying-eagle hood ornament.

Through the windshield, I spied a gun rack mounted against the rear window.

Theo stood in front of the truck with, presumably, the driver, a fiftyish man wearing a plaid short-sleeved shirt, jeans, John Deere cap, and a belt with an enormous silver oval for a buckle. The latter was custom-made to go with the truck, no doubt. Or vice versa. The man had his hands on his hips and was doing all the talking.

I took my eyes off them for a second as I began to descend the steps. That's when the first shot rang out.

The blast came from behind the house, to my left, and I ducked instinctively, even though the logic center in my brain made the snap deduction that the neighborhood Idiot must be setting off his firecrackers over in the woods.

Over at the truck, though, I saw the stranger go down, blood and God knows what else gushing from under his cap. Theo dove behind the truck's fender just as a second shot exploded.

I dropped to the steps, flattening myself against them, my brain now saying, "Not firecrackers. Some loony's shooting people—get inside, warn the others, call 911." But my limbs and voice had other ideas, namely total paralysis. The only thing on me still moving was my heart, which was trying to thump its way up into my sinus cavities.

Then came a siren and Dwight's cruiser burst out of the forest drive. I vowed never to make fun of him again.

He took so long getting out of the car, though, that I vowed to rethink my vow, as soon as my thudding heart was done playing pinball inside my throat. When Dwight did appear, he was dressed in a muscle shirt and jogging shorts, so I gave him the benefit of the doubt, figuring he'd had to retrieve his gun from the glove compartment. He didn't exactly run to the rescue either, but crouched behind his car door, yelling questions to Theo—who, thank God, answered—and yelling requests for backup into the radio receiver clutched in his nongun hand.

Okay, okay, running to the rescue alone would have been stupid. One couldn't expect real law enforcement people to act like Mel Gibson in the *Lethal Weapon* movies. Dwight, at least, had called for help and—no, dammit, I didn't want to be trapped here for however long it took the cops to show up, my back exposed to the other side of the house. Was Mel Gibson too much to ask?

"Pat!" Hugh banged through the screen door.

"Go back," I hissed. "Get Miss Maggie and Emmy into the hallway."

"Already there. You aren't hurt?"

"No, I—"

He scooped his arm around my waist and hoisted me up like an overinflated football. Next thing I knew I was being plunked down on my feet inside the door. Hugh put both his arms around me then, coaxing me to lean back against him, somehow sensing that my knees had no intention of holding me up.

I closed my eyes and drew a deep calming breath, savoring the motion of his panting ribcage on my back. Now *this* was how a rescue should be done. Even Mel could take notes.

I heard Miss Maggie's voice and opened my eyes. She and Emmy were sitting on the stairs. Miss Maggie was on the phone, eyeing me with worry. I gave her an assuring thumbs-up, but my hand was trembling and ruined the effect. Still, she got the message and went back to talking. "We think the shooter's gone, Dennis. Hugh saw someone running back through the woods, toward the post office . . ."

"You *saw* him?" I turned my head to look up at my back support. "Tell me you didn't go outside."

"Do I look crazy? I spotted him from the hall, through the powder-room window. And actually, all I saw was movement. The guy might have had camouflage on."

"Is Theo? . . ." Emmy's voice was shaky.

"I heard him talking to Dwight," I said quickly. "I think he's okay. But there's another man . . ." The memory of the gore erupting from under the John Deere cap almost brought my lunch up. I gulped to keep it in place.

"What man, Pat?" Miss Maggie held the phone away from her ear, as if not wanting to be distracted by whatever Brackin was saying.

"I don't know who he is, but—but he was shot in the head." I felt panic down in my gut, dribbling my stomach, prepping for a lay-up. Hugh squeezed me tighter and the panic subsided.

Or maybe the squeeze was only his own muscles reacting to what he'd seen, because he said, "It's Billy Johnson. At least, that's his truck out there."

"Billy Johnson?" Miss Maggie and I repeated in unison, hers the loud exclamation of recognition, mine the muttered musing of someone who'd just heard the name that morning—coming out of Lynn Casey's mouth.

"Why would Billy come here?" Miss Maggie murmured, balancing the phone on her lap, Brackin forgotten.

"He was talking to Theo," I volunteered.

"Theo's the *last* person he'd come to see," Hugh said. "Billy heads up a local organization called America's Sovereign Protectors. They're an armchair militia—all talk and no action—but they don't hide their bigotry."

10

"That's all he said to me: 'Just came out to have a look at you, boy, before I tell the police you did it.'" Theo recited Johnson's last words slowly, without inflection, as if analyzing each syllable for hidden meaning.

This was only the second time Theo quoted the words solely for our benefit—"our" meaning Miss Maggie, Emmy, Hugh, and myself—but off and on in the last three hours, I imagine Ross had Theo repeat the sentence ad nauseam in an attempt to trip him up. I didn't know for sure because we'd all been interviewed separately this time.

Why was Ross our interrogator and not the sheriff? Oh, Brackin was at the crime scene, gut sucked in, looking about as useful as a toothbrush made of Silly Putty, but Billy Johnson, it turned out, had been the witness in the Avery case. Which at least explained Lynn Casey's interest in Billy.

The good news? Theo couldn't possibly be the murderer this time. All six of us on the scene, including Dwight, claimed that the blasts seemed to come from the woods to the north. Plus Elwood, when he examined the body, said Johnson wasn't shot at close range, let alone by a right-handed man who would have had to use his left hand to hold the weapon—a weapon which wasn't found on Theo or anywhere within a gun's throw of the white pickup.

After hearing Theo out, Miss Maggie pursed her lips in thought. "Sounds like Billy was about to change his story. I wonder why."

We'd been told we could resume work on the dig. All we were doing so far was sitting on the grass under the tent, comparing notes as we watched the show around us. Miss Maggie had wanted to pace around like a caged lion, but we fetched her camp stool and convinced her to place her backside on it so she wouldn't get heat stroke. Theo had his shirt off again, though not because of the heat this time. The garment had been commandeered by Ross as crime-scene evidence, so they could analyze the blood splatter pattern.

The woods were crawling with troopers. They'd found no assassin, nor even so much as an empty shell casing. The ground was too hard to pick up a footprint. Out front, the drive and the grass on either side were clogged with cruisers and vehicles. Johnson's truck was still in place, his body where he fell, though they'd tastefully covered him with a blue plastic tarp. A couple of forensics guys were working on the pickup.

Miss Maggie continued to voice her musings aloud. "No, come to think of it, 'why' is easy. Billy was jumping at the chance to get a black man thrown in jail. And he was too dense to realize that any defense attorney would have a field day with his Protector ties—his whole testimony would be discredited."

Hugh—I'd brought him up to speed on the Avery murder after we'd both been questioned—agreed. "Never would occur to him that the judge and jury might not share his view of the world."

"Here comes Ross," I warned. Another cruiser had joined the swarm out front and the trooper who emerged had handed the sergeant a paper. He now brought that paper over to us.

"I have a warrant here to search your house, Mrs. Shelby."

"*My* house?" She punctuated that by springing to her feet. I always winced when she did that, knowing it must hurt. Problem was, her brain still reacted as it did when she was eighteen. "What fool judge signed that thing?"

Ross tried to hold in his smirk, but he couldn't. "You aren't above the law, Mrs. Shelby."

"She isn't below it either," I said, rising to stand beside her. What my five-foot-two frame lacked in imposing stature I made up in attitude.

Miss Maggie snatched the warrant out of Ross's hand. "Hugh, look this over. I don't have my reading glasses."

Hugh was the logical interpreter—he was the local notary and could translate legalese. He remained seated on the ground as he examined the document, fighting his natural manly instinct to stand and look down on Ross. But, so far, he'd managed to keep the multitudes of cops from seeing his sunburn and he wasn't going to give them a gander now. Poor guy—the strain of indignity was beginning to take its toll.

"Andy Skinner signed it, but he was careful to specify that the only items to be removed from your house are 'twenty-two caliber firearms, incontrovertible evidence of a crime, or those possessions of Theo Clayborne exhibiting physical signs consistent with his involvement in a crime—' "

"I can save you a lot of trouble, Sergeant," Theo said morosely. "All my possessions are in a gym bag at the back of the downstairs hall, right outside the kitchen. I'd be grateful if you left me a change of clean underwear."

"We'll still have to search the whole house, in case evidence was hidden elsewhere." Nice of Ross not to directly accuse Theo of doing the hiding. As the sergeant spoke, he turned and gestured to four troopers who were waiting under the magnolia tree. They went inside.

"Why are you looking for firearms?" I asked. "Doesn't it follow that the psycho in the woods would have the murder weapon on him?"

"Not a twenty-two," Hugh said thoughtfully. "Billy was shot with something bigger."

I was about to ask how he knew that, but Miss Maggie said, "Of course. The shots were too loud for a twenty-two. The sergeant here must be looking for the weapon that killed Theo's friend. Which is why Theo's still a suspect: two different guns were used. And on top of that, there's the accusation in Billy's last words."

Ross confirmed her reasoning with a wider smirk as he turned toward the house.

"What a shame," Miss Maggie said in a stage murmur loud enough for Ross to hear. "The sergeant's gonna be all broken up when he doesn't find anything. Emmy? What'd'ya say we talk about plow layers? Seems to be the only safe subject without a lawyer present."

A plow layer, I found out, was fairly self-descriptive—the layer of soil, about the depth of a plow blade, that had been worked by farmers over the centuries. Because of old crops decaying and being plowed back under again and again, the earth took on a grayish tint.

Yorick apparently had been buried in a field where plowing had been done either at the time, or previously, or both. "However," Emmy explained, using the point of her flat trowel to etch a horizontal line in the wall of Yorick's hole where the dirt turned subtly grayer, "here we seem to have a second plow layer. In other words, after this fellow was buried, someone did some planting on top of him. It's not all that deep a layer—less than half the width of the main plow layer—so either there's been erosion, or someone tilled the ground just far enough down for something like a flower garden."

"My grandparents had a tulip garden here on the side," Miss Maggie volunteered. "Granddaddy used to holler at us young'uns every time a ball landed in it."

I tried to imagine Miss Maggie as a young'un. Wasn't that difficult actually. A big chunk of her had never grown up.

"Okay," Emmy said, "that explains it. What we need to do is remove this newer plow layer first, down to where we can make out the outline of the grave. Pat and I can work on test pit number one."

By her gestures, I guessed that "test pit" meant each square of the grid. "One" was where Yorick's head was.

"Theo, since you'll probably work twice as fast, you take all of number two there." Meaning the other square where sod had been removed. "Hugh can work on the sod on number three, and Magnolia, you're on screen duty again."

"Fine by me." Miss Maggie rubbed her hands together. "I get to find the artifacts you all miss. Hugh, help me move the wheelbarrow over here beneath the tent. I want to be near the action. And we'll present a united front if we stay together."

Emmy showed Theo and me how to scrape the soil with the flat end of our picks, then trowel it into a five-gallon bucket. When the bucket was as full as could be comfortably carried—for me, not quite halfway—we were to lug it over to Miss Maggie for sifting. We had artifact bags, too—paper lunch bags labeled by test pit number, soil layer, date, and who was doing the excavating. Miss Maggie had duplicate bags, so none of the artifacts from Theo's pit or Hugh's sod would get mixed up with mine.

The thing that amazed me was how many artifacts we found. "Artifacts" by Miss Maggie's definition, I mean. I still had it stuck in my head that they should look like things taken from Egyptian tombs. Our stuff was what I'd call junk. Litter. And I never knew just how much of it was buried a few inches under my feet. Within the first half hour, my bag alone contained bits of glass, pieces of broken brick, a half dozen bent and rusted nails, two shards of red clay pottery, and one plastic button.

"Plow layers are like that," Emmy said, mistaking the basis for my incredulity. "One big jumble. You find eighteenth-century pottery over top of twentieth-century buttons. Can't date anything exactly. But we'll hold onto everything for now. What's that beside your ankle?"

I was kneeling, so I had to swing my feet around to see where she meant. A tiny wedge stuck out of the dirt, a stone at first glance, but then I saw the edge was too nicely rounded. Another nail, I thought. I used my trowel to pry it free and, picking it up, I rubbed the soil off with my thumb.

Not a nail. "A toy soldier," I said. "Or, wait . . . no, not a soldier. A cowboy."

Emmy took the little figure from me. "Tin. Twentieth-century, pre–World War II."

"Let me see that." Miss Maggie came over and Emmy handed her the find. "Well, I'll be. I remember the day my son Frank lost this little guy. Cried half the night about it."

That was the moment I got hooked, as I conjured up the image of a small boy playing on this spot. That's when I knew every piece of junk in my bag came with a story.

I admit I was relieved when Ross came out of our house empty-handed. I'd had this niggling fear that he'd stumble across something embarrassing of mine and bring it out for show-and-tell.

Then I realized I didn't have enough of a life to own anything embarrassing. Depressing thought.

The sergeant did claim one prize, though. After asking Theo and Hugh to step out of earshot, Ross questioned Miss Maggie and me about what Theo had worn the night before, then had Emmy confirm that he'd been wearing what appeared to be the same clothes when he'd first shown up at the lab—before the murder.

With a smile of triumph, Ross sent a trooper back inside for

Theo's white dress shirt. "We found some stains on the cuffs," he explained, when Miss Maggie began to harumph about it.

"Bloodstains?" I asked, uneasily remembering that Theo's sleeves had been rolled up to the elbow last night.

"Blood isn't the only evidence we look for. These stains might be gun residue."

Miss Maggie added another harumph for good measure. "Now why would an intelligent person like Theo roll his sleeves down and button his cuffs, just before shooting someone on a hot night?"

Ross ignored the question and, as he was leaving, he reiterated his earlier warning to Theo not to leave town—but this time in plain, clear English.

"Then I'd like to ask a favor, sir," Theo replied, with a respectfulness just this side of bootlicking. "There's a memorial service for Wyatt at his church in Rock Hill tomorrow morning. I'd like to go."

My heart went out to him, not only because of his request, but because he wanted to go so much, he was willing to give up his dignity and grovel for it.

Ross rubbed his chin like he was thinking it over, though I got the distinct impression of a Venus flytrap putting out a welcome mat. "I suppose I could give you a ride myself."

"No need," Miss Maggie piped in. "I was planning to go, too. Plenty of room in Pat's car for Theo. We'll meet you there, Sergeant."

Instead of being disappointed, Ross smiled—same Venus flytrap, now putting extra place settings on the table. "That's fine, Mrs. Shelby. I'll see you tomorrow morning, then, in Rock Hill."

We worked for another hour—all I dug up were more old nails. Then I went inside to refill the water bottles and figure out what to do for dinner. The kitchen felt too hot to even boil water for a pasta salad.

The sun tea jar still sat on the counter where we'd forgotten it in the afternoon's excitement. The tea didn't look hopeless—just a tad light. I put it up on the windowsill to finish steeping.

When the water bottles were replenished and back in the cooler, I checked the fridge. We had some leftover chicken, so tonight's special would be chicken salad. I'd chop a few tomatoes and put the whole concoction on a bed of green leaf lettuce. Watermelon for dessert. Or frozen yogurt. Or both.

Since Miss Maggie can't have real mayo and since the fat-free stuff has tons of non-mayo ingredients like modified food starch and corn syrup, I improvise. Back when my dad was recovering from his heart bypass, I used to puree fat-free ricotta down to the consistency of sour cream, add a few herbs, and—voila!—a tasty mayo substitute. Then one ricotta brand after another started slipping in non-cheese ingredients like xanthan gum (in my world, gum should be pink and made for blowing bubbles), so I've since switched to a plain nonfat yogurt base (thank God a few brands are still chaste). Tonight I mixed in honey and mustard.

The light supper went over well, and not only because of the heat. Most of us had jumpy stomachs—meaning Theo, Emmy, and me. Miss Maggie eats like a linebacker no matter what the circumstance. I guess surviving every major crisis of the twentieth century toughened her gastric lining. And Hugh, well, I bet his mom never once had to lay on the guilt trip about starving kids in China.

The reason I'm providing the menu is to show that I ate no peanut butter. Not even a dollop with my dish of chocolate frozen yogurt. And the *only* time I have truly weird dreams is when I eat peanut butter after, say, five P.M. But more on that later.

After one way-too-eventful day, the evening passed quietly.

Tense quiet, like the dead stillness in the eye of a hurricane. (How would someone from Pennsylvania know about that? I was at the Jersey shore when Gloria came up the coast, that's how.) All through the cleaning-up chores after supper, the extra hour and a half of plow layer excavation we got in before Emmy called it quits, and the bustle of wetting down the grids, covering them with traps, and putting the tools away, I felt like I was waiting for the eye-wall to hit.

Could be I was simply reacting to the slow exodus of our afternoon guests. By the time our supper was done, the forensic crew was gone, taking Billy and his truck with them. Brackin and Dwight went off together, probably in search of their own dinners. Other cops departed two by two, like they were headed for an ark designed to save law enforcement personnel from some approaching catastrophe. Maybe that's what put the image of "the calm before the storm" in my head.

I gave Hugh a ride down to his trailer to pick up some clothes and essentials. He'd decided to stay overnight at Miss Maggie's, so all us fair damsels could feel safe with a big strong man on the premises. He didn't say that last part aloud, but his attitude screamed "John Wayne." Even if I didn't agree with his motivation—none of us in that house fit the "fair damsel" mold, not even as a stunt double—I applauded the plan. For one thing, I wasn't about to let Hugh stay alone in his trailer with a possible sniper in the woods. Under more romantic circumstances, I might have volunteered to stay with him, but tonight "safety in numbers" seemed the wisest strategy.

Even so, with visions of bad guys behind every tree on the drive down the hill, I couldn't help slowing to a stop at the bridge. The upstream view of the creek was mostly blocked by Hugh's massive chest, so I leaned forward, hugging the steering wheel, for a better angle. Not that I could see much. The longest day of the year had been a mere two weeks ago, yet this evening the sun had already abandoned the forest canopy on this side of the hill. The dim woods seemed extra spooky—unnaturally hushed—and the air had that charged smell it gets right before a flash of lightning.

"See something?" Hugh asked, his voice tense, probably wondering if I'd spotted ghosts or gunmen.

"No." Something was there, though. I could feel it. Some kind of reverb from whatever had rattled the soul of those acres.

That, or my imagination was in overdrive again, keyed-up after too much chocolate yogurt. Shouldn't have had that extra scoop.

At the trailer, while Hugh grabbed a quick shower, I sat on the lumpy old sofa in the Lees' tiny living room, amid the twilight shadows, not wanting to give a sniper a lamp to shoot at. What seemed like a few seconds later, Hugh was suddenly leaning over me, shaking my shoulder, waking me. He smelled of soap and Old Spice, and some far corner of my brain flashed me a romantic-moment alert.

Unfortunately, the rest of my noggin was still in sleep mode and all I could manage was a confused, "Huh?"

"Come on, Sleeping Beauty," he said, straightening up and backing away to give me room to stand. "We've been gone thirty minutes already. Miss Maggie'll worry."

So the moment passed. *He* apparently hadn't been inspired by the opportunity.

Hugh followed me back to the house in his own car, giving me a chance to mope to myself. Did I look so unappealing while I was snoozing? Maybe I slept with my mouth open.

An inner voice reminded me about being patient and not pushing, and relishing my freedom while I could.

That was me, though. I didn't want *Hugh* to be patient.

At the bridge, I didn't slow down—it was too dark now for so much as a glance and I had other things on my mind, like if

I'd inherited my dad's snoring gene—but I fancied I heard distant thunder. Since it didn't repeat, I figured it was only my gut dealing with dinner.

Up the hill, where twilight was still on normal Eastern Daylight Time, one cop car remained, parked on the drive just beyond the forest, giving the two troopers inside a panoramic view of the house and side yard. I bumped onto the grass to get around them, stopping as I came even to ask through my open car windows if everything was okay.

The driver pulled the straw of a Wendy's Biggie from his lips to answer. "Got everything under control, ma'am. Just leave the porch lights on. If you need anything, we'll be here all night."

How nice. Our very own guards. So why did it feel like a stakeout?

Miss Maggie let us in, then closed and bolted the door after us. I knew before she said it that most of the downstairs was locked up as well. The hall was too stuffy—I could almost feel the day's heat radiating from the walls, with no place to go but into my pores.

The war room was cool by comparison. The windows there were open, though the blinds had been lowered with their slats angled, so a Peeping Tom outside would see nothing but ceiling. The TV was tuned to a baseball game, sound barely audible over the whoosh of all four of our electric fans, one each in front of the three windows, my little one in the center of the floor, blowing directly at the four recliners.

Five TV tray tables had been set up, one at each armchair, one at Miss Maggie's desk chair. On each table was an aluminum pie plate of water and what looked like a small cafeteria tray covered with paper towels. Emmy and Theo occupied the blue and tartan recliners respectively, each sitting forward, toothbrush in hand, scrubbing the dirt off the pottery shards we'd dug up today.

"Lab work," Emmy said as we approached. "Wash first, then I'll show you how to label each piece."

So we passed the time amicably sprucing up artifacts while Hugh and Theo alternately cursed the Braves for allowing the Diamondbacks to shut them out. Miss Maggie lamented that baseball hadn't been the same since the Senators left D.C.

You'd never guess we'd had our share of two murders that day. Just a cozy evening at home. Well, maybe more like one of those '70s sitcoms where the eccentric white family adopts the cool black dude. I suppose I'd been expecting more of a *Mod Squad* remake—one black, one white, one Italian, and a couple old ladies thrown in to draw the senior demographic away from *Murder, She Wrote* reruns.

My Head Got Wet With the Midnight Dew

No. 37, for the punishment of offenses by colored persons, the punishment shall be the same as provided by law for white persons who may commit like offenses.

—Bill introduced into the Virginia legislature, 1866

July 3, 1871—Freedom Holler

In the Holler, nobody's windows was glass, of course—just holes in the walls, each with a single shutter, hinged at the top, under the eaves. In fine weather, we prop the shutters wide open with a stick. When rain come, we let the shutters down and hook 'em. In our cabin, though, when the rainpour down hard, the water always find a way in, down the chimney, or through the north wall, where the boards fit together poorly. I'd have to quick get my pallet up off the floor to keep a dry bed.

That night I be lucky. Only a trickle of water come in, settling in a puddle by the door, so my usual spot didn't turn into a creekbed. Fact is, the skies wrung themselves dry in no more than the time it take Mama to tell me the story about Ananse trying to steal all the wisdom in the world 'cept he didn't have enough wisdom of his own to figure how to carry it.

But thunder rumbled low half the night through. When I wasn't dreaming of cannon shots or growling animals, the noise keep me right on the brink of sleep. First time I woke, I watched lightning fill the cracks 'round the shutters and under the door. Second time, the flashes fill up the whole cabin 'cause our door be open.

I reckoned Mama want to get a breeze in while the rain held off, and I start rolling over so I could sleep again, when I see Mama ain't on her pallet.

I blink the sleep out of my eyes and walk over to the door. After last night, I didn't much like the thought of her being outside by herself, even here in our cabin circle where help was near. And truth be told, I didn't much like being alone with the memory of that horseman in my head.

Lightning flash again, and I spied movement up on the church path. Not Mama, but Amos and Noah and some of the other menfolk, coming back to the cabins. What with the glove, and the sheets and horse being stole, then the storm, I'd clean forgot about Preacher likely calling a meeting and about my promise to him. Though I figured I ain't broke that promise 'cause Mama be the one who left, not me.

Noah see me as he cross this side of the kraal and he call soft-like, "What you doing awake, Mance? Get back to bed."

"You seen Mama up at the privy?" Our outhouse be halfway up the hill, just off the path he come down.

"Can't say I did, but this night's so black, she'd like to pass right by me without my noticing. Want me to go see for you?"

That's when Mama come 'round the side of our cabin, saying, "I'm here, Mance."

From the other side of the kraal, we hear a laugh so loud and coarse I knowed it come from Zeb Jackson, a black man who lived out here in the Holler 'til last year when he took up with Colonel Gilbert's cook. The Colonel make 'em marry good and proper, and now they live in the attic room next door to Colonel Gilbert's townhouse in exchange for Zeb mucking out the Colonel's stables. The Holler be quieter since Zeb left 'cause he always be coming from town all whiskeyed up, then he be loud and mean, and looking at Mama in a way I can tell she don't like.

Tonight, though, Zeb don't sound drunk, but the way he be laughing give me chills. "Middle of a stormy night, that outhouse seem miles away, don't it, Alma? I've visited that big tree back of your house myself on occasion."

"Get inside, Mance," Mama say, pushing me in ahead of her, then closing and latching the door behind us.

We heard Noah hiss at Zeb to get on home to his wife. "If the Colonel catches you out this late, he'll skin you for sure."

"Let him try and whip me." Zeb's laugh turned cold, like the bark of dog what been kicked too often. "He ain't *nobody's* master now. And I ain't nobody's slave. I's a *free* man. He lay a hand on me and I—"

"You so much as look the Colonel in the eye and they'll hang you," Noah say. "He could beat you half to death and who's gonna see justice done about it? Sheriff Cox? If you want to stay a free man, Zeb Jackson, you best watch your words in hearing of white folk. And you best sneak on up to your room tonight, and not let the night watchman catch you on the streets. Come on, I'll walk you down to the road."

When their voices got too far away to understand, Mama say, "I didn't have to go to the privy, Mance. Just needed some air. Got all stuffy in here with the windows shuttered."

Made more sense than her using the tree out back for

an outhouse. She be warning me all the time 'bout the poison ivy 'round that old maple. I reached over to hug her before going back to my pallet, which was when I felt how soaked through her skirt was. "How'd you get so wet, Mama?"

"Just 'cause the rain stopped don't mean the grass be dry already."

The grass 'longside the cabin be but high as my knee, though, and Mama be damp to the waist. I said as much, but she only answer, "Never you mind. Open that shutter for me so's I can wring out this skirt. Then get yourself back to sleep."

I done as she ask, all the while thinking how much higher the grass be up by them Rebel graves where our men have their meetings.

11

"Get up to bed, Pat," Miss Maggie said as my eyelids drooped for the umpteenth time, even though the mantel clock said it was only nine-thirty. "You'll bunk in with me tonight. Theo can have your bed. Hugh, you get the air mattress. And remember, everyone, stay away from the upstairs windows."

I thought she meant in case the sniper was still out there. Turned out, while Hugh and I were away, they'd booby-trapped all possible ports of entry on the second floor. In my room, pots and pans had been piled under each sill. In Miss Maggie's room, the stacks were books, piled smallest to largest so the slightest bump would topple them. The bathroom's sole window was protected by a tower of soap bars and T.P. rolls, with a full shampoo bottle on top.

Better than closing up the whole house, I supposed. We'd all have died from suffocation. And tonight a decent breeze had kicked in, blowing front to back.

I took a bath just warm enough to relax all the muscles I'd abused by diving facedown on the porch and by digging. I finished off with a minute of cold water from the shower. Rather than wake me up, the coolness was soothing and I almost fell asleep standing there.

Miss Maggie's water bed was an older variety, with no thermal pad on top. Without the heater on, it was perfect for summer sleeping, though that particular night, even after the day's adrenaline rushes, I was asleep before I felt the sheet under me. If the Idiot shot off cherry bombs that night, I didn't hear them.

The dream was the kind you can't at first separate from reality, mainly because it began with me waking up in Miss Maggie's bed. The room was dark—Miss Maggie had apparently not yet come upstairs. I rolled over to go back to sleep and saw Mance standing in the doorway, looking as he had in my other dream: pants with a drawstring waist, rolled to the knee, no shirt, scruffy bare feet. He held something in one hand, but I couldn't see what.

"You best come outside," he said. Seemed like a good idea at the time, so I followed him, not even bothering to slip a pair of shorts over my undies. Didn't matter—the house was deserted.

Outside, bright moonlight bathed the side yard. The grass wasn't dried out from the heat wave, but felt soft and cool under my bare soles. The entire yard had been sectioned off into grids and in every other one, the sod had been removed, creating a checkerboard effect. Though geographically impossible, the tarp covering Yorick's hole was now in the center.

I followed Mance over to the first row of grids. He showed me what he held—a Gumby doll made of a dark green clay. He gently set the doll in the middle of the grass on the corner square. Each square in that row and the one in front of it sprouted a similar Gumby doll. As I watched, they all grew to human height.

On the opposite side of the yard, two more rows of Gumbies grew also. They were light green, glow-in-the-dark.

"Checkers or chess?" Oddly enough, that was the only question I had.

Instead of an answer, Mance asked, "Whose side you on?"

Side? I did another Gumby scan. None wore a team insignia. "No preference. You?"

"Shouldn't ought to *be* sides. We all made of the same clay. But if I got to choose, I s'pose I be on the same side as Mary and the theologian."

Miss Maggie shook me awake right then. The room was bright—morning was well underway—and, predictably, she was already dressed, all duded up today in a pale yellow sundress and flat white sandals. "Rise and shine, Pat. If we're going to make that memorial service, you'll have to get up now."

I felt like I hadn't slept at all. Leaning on one elbow, I said, "Do we have time for me to tell you a dream?"

"Mance?"

I gave her the details while I still remembered them. Not that I thought the dream would fade from memory soon, if at all. Too vivid. Like I said, I'd had no peanut butter, so I couldn't blame digestive weirdness. Probably, after the events of the last two days, my subconscious simply decided that I needed the therapy of a fully animated Salvador Dali painting. Personally, I think insomnia would have done me more good.

But when I suggested that my own brain might have concocted the fantasy, Miss Maggie merely said, "Well, of course. That's why the dream was so bogged down in imagery. Mance was trying to tell you something and, subliminally, you filled in the blanks."

Whatever happened to a cigar being just a cigar?

"You probably came up with the checkerboard, because of our grid outside," Miss Maggie mused as she sat on the bed. The water beneath rolled my way to compensate. "Mance likely played with clay like any other kid, but the Gumby interpretation also has to be yours. As for the two different shades of green, well, with Billy Johnson's Protector ties being discussed yesterday—"

"—I had racial 'us-and-them' images on the brain. Okay, I admit that."

"As for the rest . . ." Miss Maggie reached for one of several Bibles she kept stacked on the bottom shelves of each nightstand, among them a King James, an American Baptist, and a Hebrew

Torah. She brought the Baptist tome onto her lap and paged through it. "For the life of me, I can't recall a passage anything like 'Mary and the theologian.' Can you, Pat?"

"I haven't cracked open the New Testament since college, Miss Maggie." Come to think of it, while working for Dawkins-Greenway, almost all the voluntary reading matter I'd had time for had been magazines in waiting rooms. "Do you think my subconscious came up with that one, too?"

"We won't know until we have time to look it up. After the service. Right now we'd better get a move on or we'll be late."

Four troopers arrived, not so much to relieve the night shift as to comb the woods for further evidence, but while conditions seemed fairly safe, Emmy decided to stay at the house and work on Yorick. Plus Dwight showed up in his digging clothes, back on "observer" duty. More like Brackin wanted a spy on hand to let him know what was going on with the troopers.

Hugh stayed, too, saying someone had to do the grunt work, though he announced this *after* I gave him some pancake makeup to cover the backs of his legs. I wished there'd been some way I could have stuck around—after all, Hugh would only be kidless another twenty-four hours—but Miss Maggie needed a chauffeur today and, as long as she was letting me sponge off her, I'd drive her wherever she wanted to go.

So, three of us squeezed into my Neon, Miss Maggie in the backseat and Theo beside me up front. He had on the black pants he'd been wearing Wednesday night, and Miss Maggie had lent him one of her son's short-sleeved dress shirts and a tie for the occasion. The shirt was a tad loose around the neck, and the tie—a conservative blue—was a tad wider than current fashion allowed, but Theo seemed grateful to get them.

To her own outfit, Miss Maggie had added a green pillbox hat with a touch of lace. "Not the standard mourning, I know," she'd said as she secured the hat with a lethal-looking, pearl-trimmed hatpin, "but I never wear black to a funeral. Always wear something green—the color of life. The years have taught me that much."

I wore my only cotton dress—a navy pinstripe that slimmed my hips a smidge. The hemline was long enough that I could get away with no pantyhose. In fact, I was thinking of abstaining from pantyhose for good, or at least until I had to conform to an office dress code again.

And that thought reminded me of the job at J. D.'s campaign office, which I still hadn't discussed with Miss Maggie. Well, the office was now closed for the weekend. No rush. And Miss Maggie might not want to talk about it with Theo in the car.

My procrastination served me well. As I turned right out of the drive, Miss Maggie started another conversation—if you could use that word for her giving Theo the third degree. Her approach was smooth. "You said you grew up in Rock Hill? Any relation to Beatitudes Clayborne?"

His answer seemed reluctant. "He's my father."

"You don't say. He was famous around here back during the late sixties. Though I guess you don't remember much of that."

"I was only four years old when Martin Luther King was assassinated."

"Must have been scary times for your family. Is your dad still preaching?"

"No." Theo must have realized how terse that sounded, but made it seem as if he didn't want to distract me while I was stopped at Route 3, waiting for a break in traffic. Whether he was being truly considerate or just stalling, I did need all my faculties for that left turn. Traffic was ten times worse than usual. I swear there must be thousands of drivers in the U.S. who only take their cars out on holiday weekends.

"He's retired now," Theo continued, after a woman in a yellow Volkswagen bug waved me across in front of her. "Still living in Rock Hill."

"You know," Miss Maggie said, "I always wondered how he came by the name Beatitudes. Is that some kind of family name?"

Theo seemed to relax at this turn of the dialogue. He actually laughed. "Weird names run in my family. Every kid for the last five generations has been christened with long, mouth-numbing labels. Dad's sister was named Song of Songs."

"What about you?" I said. "Theo seems pretty normal."

"That's why I made it my legal name the day I turned twenty-one. You would, too, if you were christened 'Theologian.' "

"Theologian! *Mio Dio!*" I gripped the steering wheel tighter to keep from driving off the road in my surprise.

"Oh, it could have been much worse," Theo said, mistaking the cause of my alarm. "That was only one of my dad's choices. Mom agreed to it because I could use Theo and not get teased at school. Dad wanted a name befitting a minister. He figured I'd go into the family business."

With the last sentence, Theo sobered abruptly and went taciturn on us for the rest of the drive down Route 20. Miss Maggie filled in the silence by playing tour guide, for my benefit, she said, since I hadn't yet been south of Locust Grove.

The drive took nearly an hour. I kept ending up behind slow battlefield tourists, then slow tourists heading for James and Dolley Madison's place (Miss Maggie pointed out Montpelier as we drove by and rattled off its history). Then came slow Barboursville Vineyard tourists, perhaps taking their time so as not to get their free tastings before the civilized hour of noon. Route 20 seemed to dogleg in every town, so I tended to ease off the accelerator as I looked for turns.

Before too many slow Monticello tourists could pull out in front of us, Theo came out of himself long enough to direct me onto the Rock Hill turnoff, a pleasantly deserted country road.

My air-conditioning had been cranked up full the whole way, but the hot sun had been beating in on the driver's side. At this point, I was freezing from the waist down and broiling from the waist up.

On a map, if you can find it at all, Rock Hill's a microdot about ten miles short of Charlottesville. "A group of freed slaves settled here and founded the town," Miss Maggie lectured from the backseat. "Good country for growing fruit, and the railroad here survived the war in better shape than in other parts of Virginia. So Rock Hill eked out a living, but the Appalachian foothills kept the town from growing very big."

We passed grapevines on our left, in straight rows that hugged the rolling land like naps of corduroy on a shapely derriere. On the right of us was an apple orchard. A handful of workers sweltered under the sun on both sides, mulching, pruning—doing whatever nursemaiding was necessary to coax the crops through this drought. Farmers couldn't afford a holiday.

Then all of a sudden the road was lined with quaint Victorian cottages. At the third cross street, on the far corner, was an equally quaint brick church—steep gables, thin casement windows with frosted glass. A waist-high black iron fence circled the churchyard and pigeons lined up on the ridge of the scallop-shingled roof.

Theo told me to hang a left and pull in behind the two cars in the driveway of the house next door—"the parsonage" he called it—another Victorian, larger than the town average and not at all quaint. Over the decades, all the whimsy of the original design had been sacrificed to function: modern windows, aluminum siding, asphalt roof. But between the house and church, along the fence, were a line of old, elegant gum trees shading a lovingly tended flower garden.

We were two minutes late. Theo didn't even wait for me to shift into park before he hopped out of the car, saying, "Excuse me. I need to talk to Shawna—Wyatt's sister—before the service starts." He vaulted the iron fence, sprinted between the grave-stones, and disappeared behind the church.

"Where's he going?" I asked, cutting the ignition.

Miss Maggie opened her door. "The sign out front says the pastor is the Reverend Shawna Avery, so I suppose he's headed for the sacristy, or whatever this congregation calls their minister's green room." She pulled herself upright as I walked around the car to her. "You could tell he's jumped that fence at least a hundred times. This was his father's church, you know. I can picture Theo growing up in this house."

We took the more accepted route, down the street to the church's front door, which faced the corner on a slant. The sign Miss Maggie had mentioned was one of those changeable letter boards in a glass case. ALL CHILDREN OF GOD CHURCH it read, with the pastor's name, service times, and a teaser for the upcoming Sunday sermon—in honor of the Fourth—INDEPENDENT OR FREE? WHICH ONE SEEKS GOD?

I pulled open one of the double doors and two heavenly sensations hit me at once: air-conditioning and music. I didn't recognize the hymn because my sacred repertoire is pretty much limited to Christmas carols and the Italian Catholic top ten—"Immaculate Mary," "Salve Regina," et cetera. But my hometown's multicultural, with at least one gospel concert in the park every summer, so I knew the style. This music had less organization and was obviously not rehearsed. I could pick out all the individual voices, each seeming to know slightly different versions of the tune. Or maybe each embellished the tune as their inner spirits saw fit. For all that, the sound was more beautiful, more soulful, than any hymns I'd heard before. These people weren't just singing together, they were sharing pain and love.

Miss Maggie had stopped right inside the door and I bumped into her. "Lord a'mighty," she said, too loud, then quickly lowered her voice. "Look here, Pat."

My eyes adjusted to the dim light of the vestibule. On the wall before us, between the doors leading into the sanctuary, was a painting—a portrait of a distinguished-looking black gentleman: sixtyish, wearing a brown suit from early in the century, with a starched collar and lapeled vest. He had a short crop of gray hair, round wire-rimmed glasses, a light complexion. The feature that really stood out, though, was the large mole over his right eyebrow. Even with a few age lines tacked on, I knew his face.

Mance.

"*Madonne*, it's him," was all I could get between my lips.

Miss Maggie rushed forward, squinting at the small letters on the brass plaque below the portrait. "What does it say, Pat?"

I joined her and read the etched words aloud, " 'Emancipation Clayborne. Founder of All Children of God Church.' "

"Clayborne," Miss Maggie repeated. "One of Theo's ancestors. And look, you can see the resemblance around the eyes and mouth. Well, no wonder Mance chose this week to come out of the woodwork."

"Mance came 'out of the woodwork' two nights *before* Theo showed up at our door," I reminded her, too stunned to do more than go into denial. "And what was it—nine, ten years ago when Beth Ann saw him? And both times he appeared as a little boy."

"Show me where it says a ghost has to come back the way he looked when he died."

I couldn't since, to the best of my knowledge, no written document existed that said *anything* provable about ghosts. Besides, my mind was on last night's dream. " ' . . . all made of the same clay . . . ' Do you think, Miss Maggie, that Mance was trying to tell me his last name?"

Before she could answer, a new song rang out of the church sanctuary, with a new voice leading it: Theo's.

"No time to talk now." She scurried toward the door on the left. "Let's get inside before we're any later."

12

The sanctuary was an octagon, with pews for perhaps two hundred. Today, no more than thirty sat in them, mostly women. Theo, in a blue choir robe, stood off to one side of the altar. Behind him, an elderly woman in a matching robe accompanied him on an old upright piano. The congregation was on their feet, singing along, swaying slowly, some with hands raised. The minister, in front of the altar in a black robe, palms toward heaven, was swaying, too, eyes tight shut as if to keep heartache at bay.

Miss Maggie led me into an empty pew, behind everyone else, but too far forward for my liking. I felt self-conscious. Not only was I one of the two non-blacks present, I was the *only* woman except the minister not wearing a hat. I was also too aware of my complete inhibition about singing, even when I knew a hymn, brought home to me all the more because Miss Maggie seemed to know all of the songs and belted them out shamelessly in a wobbly, but not half bad, alto.

Still, I couldn't blame my discomfort on anyone but myself. As we took our seats, the folks in that congregation smiled at us, handed us hymnals, in fact, went out of their way to make us feel welcome throughout the service.

I thought back to the Catholic parish I'd been raised in, to when the first Vietnamese immigrants had come to our church. No one had talked to them. No one had acknowledged their presence outside of rude stares and looks that said, "You don't belong here." Even our monsignor, when outside shaking hands after Mass, would snub them. Though, come to think of it, he always brushed off my family, too, his warmest handshakes being reserved for wealthy parishioners. Regardless, after three weeks, the Vietnamese stopped coming to our church. Righteous teenager that I was at the time, I'd condemned all the adults aloud while silently feeling ashamed that I hadn't so much as said "hi" to the newcomers myself.

Remembering that, I told myself to make up for it now. I smiled back, said "thank you," and when they began "Amazing Grace," I opened the hymnal and sang along, albeit less boisterously than Miss Maggie. But I still wished I had a hat, even though I hate wearing them. That Montella bad-hair thing again.

As the service went on, I found myself liking the minister—all the more as I watched her draw from what I suspected was every last bit of strength inside her. She not only saw to it that her brother was duly memorialized, she steered the emotions in that room away from shock and anger at the senseless murder of a young man, toward healing.

Shawna Avery was about my age, I guessed, though grief had etched lines around her eyes and mouth. She had a pretty face, the kind that ought to laugh often—the kind of wide, practical mouth more likely to say "Deal with it" than to let you feel sorry for yourself. She looked perfectly at home in a minister's robe, as if she'd always known what she wanted to be when she grew up. I envied her. Every time I used to don a business suit to go to work, I'd felt like I should take along a trick-or-treat bag.

Theo sang an unaccompanied solo—a gorgeous hymn that began "Give to the winds thy fears . . ." The melody seemed to play with the singer more than the other way around. I was thinking that even the stoniest heart would go all mushy hearing him, when I realized for the first time that Sergeant Ross hadn't shown up.

I waited until the service was over, after we'd all been invited over to the parsonage for lunch and everyone began heading for the side door, to tell Miss Maggie my observation.

"I was wondering about that myself," she said, urging me out into the aisle. "No Sergeant Ross, but I did see a white fella sitting in a car across the street when we came in. I doubt he's the meter maid. Especially since he looked kind of upset when Theo ran from the car."

I hung back a little from the rest of the congregation as we filed out of the door into the churchyard, where the heat swaddled us like Handiwrap with static cling. "Now that you mention it, I remember seeing him, too. But if he's a cop and he thought Theo was trying to escape, wouldn't he have chased him?"

"The fact that he didn't tells me he isn't the only policeman in the vicinity. Might be another one parked on the cross street who saw Theo go into church. Or—take a look at that clean-cut young man there ahead of us." She nudged her chin toward a black man with a military-style crewcut, who was wearing a dark suit and tie. "He hasn't given more than a nod and a howdjadoo to anyone. No one's called him by name or asked about his family. Could be he knows Wyatt from work or something like that, but since we left the church, he hasn't taken his gaze off Theo." She stopped abruptly. "Well, that clinches it."

Sometimes, I swear, Miss Maggie had more eyes than a housefly, all looking different ways at once. My attention was still focused on the proposed plainclothesman, my imagination filling in a shoulder holster beneath his suit jacket. I tried to see what nuance of him screamed "cop" to Miss Maggie. Turned out she didn't mean him at all. She touched my arm and redirected my eyes to a granite headstone off to her left.

"Clayborne," I read aloud, "Emancipation 1863 to 1938—*Mother of God.*" I'd suddenly realized what "clinches it" meant. "If he's buried here, he can't be—"

"—buried at our place," Miss Maggie concluded. "Emmy said

as much: the skull didn't belong to a full-grown man. I didn't want to discount the theory entirely—lots of men were, and still are, small. But the bone wasn't porous—no osteo-degeneration like you'd see in an elderly person, which was what Mance was when he died. So, I wonder who *our* skeleton is?"

"Someone Mance knew." I'd given up on denial. No getting around the fact that a man/boy who'd died more than sixty years ago had visited my REM sleep and shown me exactly where to dig.

"Let's ask Theo if he knows any old family legends," Miss Maggie suggested with another nudge of her chin toward the gate.

I looked up to see Theo, now divested of his choir robe, hands in his pants pockets, standing beside a grave in the back row, by the fence. Everyone else was on the garden path or parsonage porch, waiting their turn to pass through the front door—everyone, that is, except the supposed plainclothesman, who was watching Theo from the garden path.

"My mom," Theo said as we approached, as if needing to explain the stone before him. Like the other, it read CLAYBORNE. The name below was LUCY, and her dates were 1933–1967. Only thirty-four years old. Two years younger than me. A humbling thought.

"I should have brought some flowers," Theo said, though at the base of the stone was a cluster of white petunias, wilted in the heat, but alive and therefore probably watered daily.

"You must have been pretty young when she died," Miss Maggie commented.

"Not quite three. She was killed in a car accident." After a beat of silence, he turned toward the gate. "Let's go get some of that lunch before it's gone. Shawna said Aunt Song made her plum cobbler. That won't last long."

He was resolutely changing the subject, but I didn't mind—not only was I starving, I wanted to get out of the sun before more sweat surfaced on my dress.

We ambled after Theo, passing under the welcome shade of the gum trees. I noted that Officer Buzzcut, as I'd mentally named Theo's watchdog, was now nonchalantly leaning against one of the cars in the drive.

At the gate, Miss Maggie paused and said, "Let me ask you about the man who founded this church."

"The official founder or the real one?"

"Which one was Emancipation Clayborne?"

"Official founder. His son—my great-grandfather—was actually the first minister here. Saw to the building of the church and organized the congregation. But he credited his father with starting the Sunday meetings." Theo pushed open the gate, waving us through ahead of him. "From what I've heard, though, those gatherings were democratic—no minister and everyone took turns leading the prayers and hymns. More my kind of church."

"Was Emancipation born in Rock Hill?" Miss Maggie asked as we strolled the pansy-lined path to the house.

"No. He wandered around in his youth. Took a job in the vineyard here, met his future wife, and that made him finally settle down. Aunt Song knows more about him. Ask her. She keeps track of the family history."

He mounted the porch steps and was about to open the screen door for us, when one of his pants pockets began playing Bach's "Minuet in G." Taking out his cell phone, he said, "I told Emmy to call if she needs us to come back. Everyone else who'd call me is in this house."

My stomach rolled as my imagination came up with a reason for Emmy to call, namely, another massacre like yesterday's. I said a quick silent prayer for Emmy and Hugh—especially Hugh—to be all right.

Theo's expression changed from concern to exasperation. "Vicky, what are you doing at work on a holiday? . . . This isn't a good time. I'll call you back later . . . wait, slow down. . . ." His eyebrows drew together. "Okay, hold on." He took the phone from his ear and, loosening his tie, said to us, "Go on inside and eat. I'll be in soon."

I pulled the screen, but before I could turn the knob of the main door, it swung open to admit us.

"Come in quick," said the woman who'd been the organist. "Don't let the cool air out." Now, without her robe, I could see her black dress—vintage 1950s, short-sleeved, fringed with lace. Classy-looking. And she still wore her hat—black straw with a wide floppy brim and a white silk rose on one side. "I'm Theo's Aunt Song."

As I shut the door behind us, Miss Maggie introduced us, using proper Southern etiquette, which meant tacking a "Miss" before my name.

Aunt Song gave us a gracious nod. "Theo said you were kind enough to give him a ride down here today. Go help yourselves to some lunch." She gestured to Shawna, who was coming forward to greet us. "Bring Theo in out of the heat—he can take his call in your office. Then you can introduce our guests to everyone."

My nose had already determined the direction of the food. A blissful aroma emanated from the dining room and there we found the rest of the congregation loading their plates with fried chicken, Smithfield ham, deviled eggs, two kinds of potato salad, various casseroles, blueberry muffins, and a loaf of homemade bread. On the sideboard were desserts—pies, cakes, the infamous plum cobbler, and lots of other goodies. The sheer size of the feast—on a par with those thrown by my own family—made me feel right at home.

From comments like, "Sarah June, you make the best sweet-potato salad in all Virginia," I could tell that the myriad of drool-inducing foodstuffs represented a potluck meal. Shawna didn't have to introduce me—tasting all those offerings, in the company

of all those potential recipe sources, was my definition of net-
working.

At the end of an hour, I was stuffed to the seams and had
recipes for Sarah June's salad (yams with pineapple and pecans),
hoppin' John (rice cooked with black-eyed peas, ham, and hot
pepper), shoe leather (sort of homemade Fruit Roll-ups, made
out of dried apricots, peaches and raisins food-processed into
mash, then rolled out on a board coated with powdered sugar),
and a chocolate-strawberry upside-down cake that was sheer he-
donism. All this in exchange for Grandmom Montella's recipes
for tomato sauce and the ricotta filling for lasagna. United
Nations, take note: to bring cultures together all you have to do
is put a bunch of cooks in the same room.

Miss Maggie had been sitting in the opposite corner of the
living room, over by the door, with Aunt Song the whole time,
probably pumping her for Mance info. My new friends warned
me that the plum cobbler recipe was a Clayborne family secret.
"Song'll take it to her grave with her," Sarah June lamented.

Velma, the chocolate cake guru, disagreed. "I've heard her say
that when Theo gets married and settles down, she'll pass it on
to him."

"My family was like that." I sipped at my third cup of
raspberry-banana fruit punch. "Dad's sisters wouldn't have considered sharing the family cannoli recipe with him, but as soon
as he was married, they gave it to my mother, even though she
was half Sicilian."

"No, that's not it," Sarah June replied. "Song's just using it
as incentive. She knows Theo'll do most anything for that plum
cobbler."

"He didn't taste any yet today," said Dori, who'd made the
hoppin' John. "He and Shawna are still in her office."

Velma grinned wickedly and elbowed Dori's arm. "Working
on getting that cobbler recipe for good, I'll bet."

Sarah June wagged her head shrewdly. "He won't marry Shawna, for all they been sweet on each other half their lives. Not while she's wearing a preacher's collar. And she won't give it up for him."

"More like Theo's hiding out from—well, you know." Sarah June cast her eyes to the ceiling, which must have meant something to the others, for they all nodded, then turned apologetic glances at me, as if to say they'd share recipes, but nothing else.

Miss Maggie appeared at my side. "We ought to head home, Pat. I feel guilty leaving Emmy and Hugh with all the work while we're here having a nice lunch. Is Theo still on the phone?"

I volunteered to round him up. Velma directed me down the hall beside the stairs, to a room just off the kitchen, where Shawna had her office. The door was open, showing a tiny space made bright and cheery by a white Ikea-ish desk, matching filing cabinets, and a lavender rug. The desk was neatly arranged with only a beige two-line phone, a purple bin filled with papers, and a Far-Side day calendar. Shawna and Theo were MIA.

I heard men's voices in the kitchen, so I peeked in. This room was large, with a fascinating mix of modern appliances and banged-up, post–World War II metal cabinets. Three men sat at the table, talking about last night's Braves-Diamondbacks game, one saying how Wyatt should have seen it because he'd predicted Arizona would win by more than four runs. As eloquent a way as any to express grief.

Shawna was standing at the back door looking through its four-pane window. She'd seemed taller with the minister's robe on, but she was about my height. She wore black dress pants and a plain blouse, gray and sleeveless. Frills wouldn't have suited her.

"Excuse me," I said, "but where's Theo? Miss Maggie wants to get going and—"

"You'll have to wait 'til he brings my car back," said one of the men at the table.

"Your car?" I repeated dumbly.

Shawna had turned as I spoke, uncertainty and worry all over her face. Now she said, "I would have let him have mine, but I'm blocked in out front. Uncle Charles's Ford was in his garage next door, so—" She suddenly seemed to realize that logistics weren't what was causing my confusion. "Theo had to go talk to his boss."

"He drove in to work? Today?" I've known workaholics in my time, but Theo had seemed immune from the disease.

"He said he wouldn't be long." From the worry in her voice and the way she turned back to the window, I could tell he was already overdue.

I came to stand beside her so I could take in the view. The backyard was a square patch of lawn, straw-colored from the drought and surrounded by a high, squared-off hedge. This was the utilitarian part of the property—two Rubbermaid trash cans were set beside a four-foot wooden gate, and a clothesline ran from the gate post up to the door stoop. That made me wonder if the hedge had been a Victorian planting, so people wouldn't see the pastor's wet skivvies hanging there.

On either side of the yard was another wooden gate—one leading into the side garden, one to Uncle Charles's yard, where I could see the roof of the garage over the hedge.

"When did he leave?" I asked.

Shawna turned from the window again. "Right after he came inside."

The doorbell chimed, giving me hope. "Maybe that's him now."

"No, he'd never ring the bell." The sound made her more anxious. She seemed to be fighting some kind of indecision, and like frills, hesitation didn't look right on her.

Or maybe I just couldn't see anyone getting that worried over someone suddenly getting job-guilt. "He didn't go into work, did he?"

"I never said he did." With a sigh, she added, "Come into my office." Once there, she didn't close the door, but kept her voice lowered. "Theo said his boss knows something about Wyatt's murder. That's why he went."

There is a Balm in Gilead to Make the Wounded Whole

A white man may talk very well, but put him to work, and what will he say? He will say that hard work is not easy. He will say that it is hard for a man who has owned so many able-bodied Negroes to have the Yankees come and take them all away.

—Corporal Jackson Cherry, U.S. Colored Troops, in a letter to the *South Carolina Leader*, December 16, 1865

July 3, 1871—Stoke

Next day, after my chores, I walk into Stoke with Noah. I like going into town 'cause I can practice my reading on the signs, but I don't get there much, and never by myself. Mama say the white folk there want us to act like we still slaves, which, Mama say (since I be too young to remember), mean putting a look on my face like a well-broke dog what crawl on his belly and keep his head down and wag his tail when he hear Massa's voice. When I go into town, I s'posed to stay right beside the growed-up I be with, and don't talk 'less somebody ask me a question direct, then I got to answer polite and say "sir" or "miz." Which, Mama say, be the way I ought to talk anyway, to everybody all the time, white or colored.

Noah be going 'cause last night his roof leak again,

worse this time, and Ida say she want it fixed before another rain come. Since the sun be hiding behind clouds all morning, Ida say Noah better get the chore done today. Noah say he going into town for nails, until Ida point out that Preacher be scavenging good roof nails from the church. So Noah say he got to go into town anyway. If he got to split shingles, he need a sharp hatchet, which mean borrowing back his whetting stone from Zeb Jackson. Ida couldn't argue with that.

Noah ask me to go along 'cause Jordana tell him to fetch home more liniment for Uncle Henry. "I don't mind bringing Uncle Henry some comfort," Noah say to me as we walking down the road. "Just don't want to set foot into Caleb Fletcher's store. Seen enough of him back when I was a slave in his daddy's still house."

"You helped 'em make whiskey?"

Noah nodded. "Reckon that's why I got no taste for it now. The smell of it bring on memories best forgot. So do seeing Caleb Fletcher's face."

"Mama say he be bad as Charlie Harris before the war."

"Worse. Him and Massa Travis's youngest boy always coming down to the still house to get whiskey. And when they all on a drunk, they order us whipped for sport, then they go do what they please with our women. The war be a blessing in it took 'em away. Ought to have killed 'em both, but Caleb come back."

"Mama say he come back different. That's why he give her work and pay her any way he can."

Noah let out a laugh as bitter as green chokecherries. "He different all right. He come back poor. Had to sell all his daddy's land, which was worth next to nothing after both armies got through with it. Now ol' Caleb know what it like to have to work hard every day. But even if he done changed hisself into Abraham Lincoln, Mance, what good'll that do the whipping scars on my back? Tell me that."

The rest of the walk I think on what Noah say. By the time we get to town, I ain't keen on going into Mr. Fletcher's shop alone. "Mama won't like it," I tell him.

"Your mama don't have to know," Noah say. "All you got to do, Mance, is ask for two cents worth of the liniment he make up last time for Henry Jackson. Jes' don't be bold. If there be white folk inside, let them do their business first and wait 'til they leave before you say anything. Here, take the bottle and the coins Ida gave me. When you done, go 'round to the back alley and wait for me on the steps up to Zeb's place."

He left me where that alley come out to the street, so I only had to walk by two shops to get where I be going. I hear one white woman say to another as they pass me that the darkies shouldn't let their chil'un run wild, but I ain't running at all, right at that moment. I be standing in front of Mr. Fletcher's window, where he got hanging a big glass egg, filled with green liquid, clear and beautiful as it catch the sun. This be the first time I got a close-up look at the egg, but it look the same as always—still filled to the top—so I reckon the green liquid ain't for sale.

The door be open, so I climb up the one step and went inside, pausing just over the doorsill while my eyes blinked away the bright sunshine. The shop wasn't much bigger than the one room Mama and me live in, but it be filled up with dark wood cupboards, with bottles and jars of every size and color on the shelves. Running the width of the room was a counter, leaving only enough standing room on my side for maybe five customers.

Only one customer be in the shop, though, and I know her. "Mama!"

She turned, startled, from the counter where she been

talking to Mr. Fletcher. I ain't seen him close up before neither, but he didn't look much different than from 'cross the street like I seen him last. He be tall and all bones, with straight yellow hair, long on his neck and draped over half his forehead, and on his lip, too, making a straggly mustache. What surprise me about him was how he didn't look so old as I thought he be. No older'n Mama, anyway. Guess I s'posed he be old 'cause, when I seen him before, he be walking with a limp.

Mama look relieved to see me, but she put her hands on her hips and hissed, "What you be doing here, Emancipation Jackson? And by yourself when you be told—"

"Noah bring me." I explained how Noah be at Zeb's fetching his whetting stone while I come to buy Uncle Henry's liniment. "And I ain't by myself, Mama. You be here."

That made a smile tug at Mr. Fletcher's mouth, like he be laughing at me, though after his first glance in my direction, he quick shift his eyes to the door. I figure something I said be wrong. Preacher Moses's always telling me not to say "ain't." Maybe that be it, so I say, "I'm *not* here by myself, I mean."

"Last time I gave Henry Jackson some of the ache remedy I make up for Mrs. Burress," Mr. Fletcher say, his voice deep but tense and whispery, like he be afraid of hurting our ears with it. "How much of it do you want? Quick, before someone comes in."

White folk, he mean. Mama say most all the shops in town won't sell us colored nothing. Least, not when the other white folk looking on. "Two cents," I say, then with a glance at Mama, I remember what she tell me and add, "please, sir."

He start in to take bottles down from the shelf next to

him, but he hesitate. "You don't have a two-cent piece, do you?" He pointed to a sign on the wall behind his head. "Can you read that?"

"Yessuh. 'Two-cent p . . . pieces—' " I guessed that word from him just saying it, " '—are no longer a . . .' " I pause, wondering if the two "C"s that follow ought to sound like "K"s or "S"s.

" 'Accepted as tender,' " he finish for me. "Nobody wants them in change anymore. If I took them, I'd have to close up every few hours to cash them in at the bank."

"I ain't—I *don't* got a two-cent piece." Opening up my palm, I show him the four half-pennies I'm holding. "Seem silly to me, people not wanting coins, 'specially those be worth a whole two cents."

Mama give me a warning look and I add another "sir."

"I see you taught him manners, Miss Jackson," Mr. Fletcher say, as that half-smile peek out from under his mustache again, but he don't look at Mama or me when he speak. His eyes stay on what his fingers be doing. He take the glass stopper out of one bottle, and the scent that come my way be sweet—stronger than I remember Uncle Henry smelling last time he rub it on. Remind me of something besides Uncle Henry, too, but I can't recall what, so I ask, "What be that smell?"

"This?" Mr. Fletcher hold the bottle out so's I can sniff at it, and when I nod, he say, "It's called oil of wintergreen. This is what makes Henry's aches feel better. I guess his legs must be hurting bad for him to use up this rub so quickly," Mr. Fletcher add, seeming disturbed by the notion as he stir the wintergreen oil into a liquid from the other bottle. "Like I told Moses when he picked it up last time, shake this preparation each time you use it, and mix it with something like lard or soap. Then rub it in well."

Mama say, "We still got the instructions you wrote down, about how much to use and such."

"Good," Mr. Fletcher say. "Then you know not to let anyone drink this, and to keep it away from fire. It'll blaze up fast, with a blue flame that's sometimes hard to see. Easy to burn yourself bad."

A blue flame? All of a sudden I recollect where I smell a sweetness like that wintergreen oil—the other night, when the church first catch fire.

13

"Vicky?" How could she know anything about the shooting? In my experience, bosses like her had degrees in not knowing much of anything, and proudly wore their ignorance on their designer suit sleeves.

Shawna nodded. "That's the name he said. Vicky Gibson. Do you think—"

Miss Maggie, nibbling on a piece of shoe leather, came through the doorway. "Where's Theo, Pat? Because now we've got company at the front door asking for him. That nice-looking young man with the crewcut."

"The police?"

"Has a badge in his wallet. I doubt he got it with cereal box-tops." She licked the sugar off her thumb and forefinger.

"The shirt!" I exclaimed. "They must have found something incriminating on it."

Miss Maggie pshawed that idea. "I doubt they'd have those tests done already, not that I think they'll find anything but per-spiration and office ink. Besides, I asked the officer if he had a warrant and he said no, he just wants to talk to Theo, so—"

"But Theo's not here," I said. Between us, Shawna and I briefed her.

"Consarnit," Miss Maggie murmured. "I don't suppose he said *what* exactly Vicky knew."

Shawna leaned back against her desk as if she needed the support. "She wouldn't tell him on the phone. Too afraid someone would listen in."

I'd forgotten all about Theo's cellular. "He's still got his phone with him, right?"

"I've tried calling twice," Shawna said. "Fifteen minutes ago, I got voice mail on the first ring, meaning the line was busy. Five minutes ago, he didn't answer." She reached behind her for the phone, lifted the receiver and punched the redial button. After a few seconds, she said, "No answer again." She left a message on his voice mail instructing him to call ASAP, but she didn't sound optimistic.

"Maybe his battery died," I suggested as she hung up, to stem her worry—and my own.

"Or the hills around here could be blocking the signal," Miss Maggie put in.

"No," Shawna said. "They were supposed to meet at Morrison's, at the mall where my brother worked. Both Wyatt and Theo have called from there plenty of times with no connection problems."

Miss Maggie turned back to the doorway. "You didn't say you knew where he was headed. Come on. Only one thing to do."

"Go look for him?" I asked as Shawna and I trailed after her down the hall.

"Heavens, no. The troopers can find him faster than we can and—"

"Song!" A voice floated down the stairs beside us, sounding frail but urgent. I glanced up to see an elderly man leaning on the rail. He was tall and thin, stoop-shouldered, wearing a blue shirt under a brown cardigan that was buttoned crooked. "Song! Jackie's here. I saw her out the window. Song!"

"Aunt Song?" Shawna gave the older woman a pleading look, beckoning her over to us.

"I'll go up," Aunt Song said as she started climbing the stairs. "When he gets confused like this, you know he only listens to me anyway. You go talk to that officer outside. I'm coming, Bea. Calm yourself down."

The man backed away from the rail, as if to hide from the people down below, but he said, "Jackie's up the block, Song. Duke's with her. Come see," and he gestured excitedly toward the front bedroom.

"She called him Bea," Miss Maggie said to Shawna as we continued toward the front door. "Short for Beatitudes?"

Shawna nodded. "Theo's father. He had a mild stroke last year. He can take care of himself all right, but he can't handle social situations, which is why he stayed upstairs today. That's also why I took him in—being in a nursing home would kill him. But once in a while he gets confused. Thinks he's still pastor and that my father, Duke, is still alive." She'd stopped at the front door to finish talking and suddenly took a deep breath. "I'm stalling. Let's get this over with. I hope telling the police is the right thing to do."

As we opened the door, Officer Buzzcut's finger hovered over the bell as if his patience were about to run out. Beside him on the porch was his partner, the blond guy from the car across the street who I now nicknamed Officer Mustard-Stain-On-Shirt. He had a walkie-talkie to his lips, giving instructions to another trooper who was apparently around back. Waning patience aside, they didn't seem ready to storm the place, which confirmed Miss Maggie's hunch that this couldn't be about the shirt.

Miss Maggie pushed ahead of us and did all the talking. At first, Buzzcut and Mustard-Stain returned only frowns of skepticism, until the latter used his walkie-talkie to ask their lookout in the back alley if he'd seen a vehicle leave the garage next door. He had, over an hour ago—an old Ford sedan, vintage sixties, aqua blue.

Muttered epithets ensued, just this side of offensive. Miss Maggie was, after all, still standing there, prim and proper in her pillbox hat.

To make a long story short, the officers called Ross. A search was begun for Theo and, after it was ascertained that neither he nor Uncle Charles's Ford were at Morrison's, or anywhere in the vicinity of Fashion Square Mall, an APB was issued.

While all this was going on, no one would answer our questions about *why* they wanted Theo. "Sorry, ma'am, you can talk to the sergeant when he gets here," was all they'd say.

We decided to be sensible and wait inside. I phoned home to tell Hugh and Emmy we'd be late, giving them the sketchiest of details so Emmy wouldn't worry.

"Take your time," Hugh said, not sounding at all disappointed that we'd been delayed. "A young couple from the development showed up an hour ago. Said they heard about the dig in town and, since they had the day off because of the holiday, they thought they'd come over and offer to help. Emmy put 'em right to work."

"So you don't miss us? Is that what you're saying?" I wondered how "young" and how pretty the female element of the couple was.

"Sure I miss you. I need more of that makeup. Where'd you leave it?"

I sighed. "Under the sink in the downstairs bathroom." Saying my good-byes, I went to find Miss Maggie, who was picking at the dessert leftovers on the sideboard. First I gently suggested that her arteries would appreciate less chocolate cake and more fruit, then I relayed the news that we weren't needed home anytime soon.

"That couple probably just wanted to see where Billy got shot," Miss Maggie reasoned as she licked strawberry goo off her fingers. "I expect we'll get a few more ghouls before the end of the weekend. Though I'm glad Emmy's getting some workers out of it."

Ross only kept us waiting a half hour. As with the two officers, we entertained him on the front porch since the house was still full of mourners. To the critical eye, the sergeant was showing signs of wear. His belt buckle was a few millimeters off center and his hanky, as he wiped his head, had lost its perfect creases.

Shawna retold her story, ending with, "Now why is there an APB out for Theo? What's happened?"

"He's wanted in connection with a murder, Miss Avery." Simple as that, Ross's tone implied.

"He didn't kill my brother," Shawna said defensively. "Theo and Wyatt would have done anything for each other."

"And he *couldn't* have killed Billy Johnson," I put in.

Miss Maggie shushed the both of us by raising one hand and asking, "Whose murder do you mean, Sergeant?"

"A woman named Vicky Gibson." He paused to observe our reactions, all variations on the wide-eyes, dropped-jaws theme.

"Shot like the other two?" Miss Maggie asked.

Ross nodded. "In her car, just like Mr. Avery."

Shawna swung her head from side to side—either she was in denial or trying to clear her thoughts, or both. "Where? At the mall?"

"No." The sergeant unconsciously straightened his belt buckle. "Possibly Mr. Clayborne told you he was meeting her there so he'd have more time to get away."

"Theo wouldn't lie to me," Shawna replied, part protective, part confused, mostly sick with worry.

The door behind us opened and Aunt Song came out. "What's this Velma's telling me about Theo borrowing Charles's car and you looking for it? Why, that old Ford's parked right down on the next block. I saw it from my brother's window upstairs. That's what got Bea all riled—he must've seen Theo get out of it and imagined he was Duke Avery."

Shawna took off down the street and Ross barked an order for Buzzcut to go after her, "Don't let her touch that car!" To

Mustard-Stain, he said, "Get a forensics crew out here and I want every available unit. If Clayborne's still on foot, he couldn't have gone far." With that, Ross headed for his own auto.

Miss Maggie nudged me. "Go see what's up, Pat. I'll wait here in the shade."

It wasn't like her to let a little thing like heat stroke keep her from satisfying her curiosity, so I asked, "You feeling okay, Miss Maggie?" though, actually, she looked cooler than I felt. That's when I noticed that her eyes were sparkling with excitement, which usually meant her neurotransmitters were kicking around a new idea.

"Yes, yes, fine. Go, Pat, and bring back a full report."

I promised I would as I trotted off.

From a block away, and even with the big sycamore trees that lined the street partially blocking my view, I could tell that Charles Avery's Ford was a museum piece: an aqua four-door with big square lights and shiny chrome bumpers, door handles, and rearview mirror. At least thirty years old, but in immaculate condition.

Shawna was fast, even in heels, so Buzzcut didn't catch up with her until they were within ten yards of the vehicle. By the time I got close enough to read the "Custom 500" on the fender, she was promising not to add her fingerprints to any of the gleaming metal surfaces where the cops were probably hoping they'd find Vicky Gibson's prints.

Shawna's promise was specific for a reason. As soon as Buzzcut was off his guard, she snatched at the driver's side windshield wiper—or rather, at a piece of folded bright blue paper under the wiper. Buzzcut's epithets this time, since Miss Maggie and her hat weren't present, were much more graphic. Shawna was obviously being careful, though. She used only three fingers of one hand, even as she flipped open the paper to see the inside, so there wasn't much Buzzcut could do except warn her not to move her fingers around further or he'd arrest her for tampering with evidence.

I looked over her shoulder. The note was stationery-sized and, in a bold, black scrawl, it read:

Uncle Charles,
Sorry I couldn't put your car back in the garage, but under the seat you'll find something for gas. Tell Shawna not to worry.

Thanks, Theo

Besides bringing the car back as close as he dared and leaving an apologetic note, Theo had been conscientious enough to lock the doors. Uncle Charles had come down the street to see what the police intended to do to his Ford and, before anyone got any notions about breaking windows, asked me to go get his spare keys.

"My son Mike knows where they are," Uncle Charles said. "He's still at the parsonage, but he'll fetch 'em for you."

So I headed back to the house. Miss Maggie and Aunt Song had retired to the living room where they were amiably poring over old photo albums. In the opposite corner sat the remaining two men, having been kicked out of the kitchen by the rest of the women as the washing of dishes and Tupperwaring of leftovers commenced. I gave everybody a rundown of what was happening a block away and explained my mission.

The younger of the two men—maybe in his fifties, wearing a short-sleeved shirt and ivory pants—stood. "I'll bring the keys to him. Have a seat and cool off."

I must have looked as wilted as I felt. Expressing grateful thanks, I sank down next to Miss Maggie on the sofa.

She nudged me. "Pat, look at these pictures. Here's one of Theo and Wyatt. Can you tell which is which?"

In the photo, they were preteens and bundled up in winter coats, so I couldn't be sure of body build, but they sported matching mid-1970s Afros and their faces had similar bone structure. I took a guess, pointing to the slightly taller of the two. "Is that Theo?"

"No, that's Wyatt," Aunt Song said, turning the album pages. "Everyone mistook them for brothers. Here's a picture from their college graduation." She pointed to a faded Polaroid showing five people—Theo and Wyatt in their caps and gowns, with two older men and one woman.

Theo was easy to pick out this time, though I could see where strangers might have confused the two. But my attention was more focused on the older men in the photo. One was a sixtyish version of the man upstairs, and therefore Theo's father. The other man was at least a decade younger and, if looks alone counted, *could* have been Theo's father. I said as much.

"No danger of that," Aunt Song said with a laugh. "Duke Avery was in the Army at the time, stationed in Alabama. That's where Wyatt was born. Then they moved back here the next year. But that's why, when Bea gets mixed-up, he's always thinking that Theo's Duke."

"I guess Jackie was Duke's wife?" Miss Maggie asked, pointing to the woman beside him in the photo.

"Oh, no. Her name was Carole. Jackie was . . . well, just a student, that's all. One of those kids down at the university in Charlottesville who used to go on Civil Rights marches with Bea." Aunt Song turned the album pages once more. "Here's a better picture of Duke and Carole. That was taken on their last wedding anniversary together, five years ago. Duke died of a heart attack that year and two years later, breast cancer took Carole."

"Does Shawna have any other siblings?" I asked, thinking how I'd lost both my own parents in the same time period and my only brother in the Vietnam War.

Aunt Song looked at me as if I'd asked whether Shawna had

gills. "A month ago, I'd have said no." She glanced down at the anniversary photo again. "Duke and Carole at first thought they couldn't have children, so they adopted Shawna—she was only four months old. And no sooner had they brought her home then they found out Wyatt was on the way."

"Happens all the time," Miss Maggie commented.

Aunt Song agreed. "After Carole died, Shawna started searching for her birth mother. She hasn't located her yet, but just this past month, Shawna discovered she was put up for adoption along with a sister."

Miss Maggie had flipped backwards through the album as Aunt Song talked. One of the pictures caught my eye and I stopped her hand before she could turn the page.

"That's Theo when he was a tot," Aunt Song explained.

The photo she meant—a black-and-white square with a white border bearing the date "NOV 67"—showed an ultra-cute, knee-high Theo dressed in an oversized jacket and baggy, rolled-up pants, trying to see out from under a too-big Fedora. He stood on the parsonage's front porch, beside a homemade jack-o'-lantern.

However, the photo I was looking at, though it bore the same date, was of Bea Clayborne, standing on an outdoor platform, microphone in hand, speaking with energy. Behind him, to one side, stood a woman wearing a simple tan raincoat that emphasized the thinness of her face. She was holding Theo—he was resting his head on her shoulder, looking bored. What grabbed my attention was her expression. Her eyes—her whole body—seemed to project sadness.

"Is that Theo's mother?" I asked, pointing.

"Yes," Aunt Song said with a sigh. "Last picture we have of Lucy. She lost control of her car two weeks later and was killed. Thank goodness she didn't have Theo with her."

My gaze traveled from her face to her arms. She held her son tightly, as if to keep him from squirming. Maybe he had been a moment before the shutter opened. But I got the impression that Lucy Clayborne expected Theo to be snatched from her grasp.

We headed for home not long after. "Nothing further we can do here," Miss Maggie said, "and maybe Theo'll show up at Bell Run." She didn't sound like she believed it, though.

We stopped down the street to tell the sergeant and Shawna that we were going. From the latter, we learned that they'd not only found money for gasoline under the passenger seat, but also Theo's cell phone, dashing Ross's hopes of catching his quarry O. J. style.

When we were driving out of town, I voiced the question that had been bugging me all afternoon. "Why would Theo run like that if he isn't guilty?"

Beside me, Miss Maggie slowly slid the long pin out of her hat. "Because he finally realized what we should have suspected when Billy got shot." She carefully placed her hat on her lap and threaded the pin through the material once more. "Wyatt was driving Theo's car when he died, and they resembled each other enough that someone who didn't know them could mistake one for the other."

I got the urge to whack myself in the head for not thinking of it myself, but prudently kept my hands on the steering wheel. "So that's the idea you had when you stayed back at the house to look at photos. Theo was the intended victim Wednesday night. And yesterday, too, except Billy somehow got in the way."

"Seems like too much of a coincidence, what with the witness to Wyatt's murder showing up at our place that way. That first shot might have been meant for Billy."

The turn onto Route 20 stole my attention away from the conversation. Traffic had eased slightly in the heat of the afternoon, but was still bad enough that I finally gave up on making a left and hung a right instead, then swung around in a parking lot on the other side of the road. When we were finally heading north—with the sun beating in on my left arm—I refocused on Miss Maggie's deductions. "Do you think the *second* shot was meant for Theo?"

"Maybe. Thank the Lord he reacted fast and dove behind the truck. Take the next right up here, Pat."

I obeyed, thinking she was showing me a faster detour, until I glanced at the road sign. "Route 811?"

"I want to have a look at where Wyatt died."

The road was barely two cars wide and led uphill through a tract of tall grass, thickets, and scrawny trees. About a mile in, just before a meadow where high-tension wires crossed the road, we found a pile of wilted flowers beneath a simple metal cross on the shoulder. I pulled over next to it.

Miss Maggie squirmed in her seat to survey the area, but didn't get out. "No houses visible, and I only saw two driveways. This road's a shortcut over the ridge between Routes 20 and 15, though, by that time of night, I don't expect there were many cars back here. Drive on a little farther, Pat."

The grade became steeper and the woods thicker, with full-grown trees overhanging and shading the asphalt. We passed one more drive, then the woods on our right gave way to another, smaller clearing where a new house was being constructed. Four men were on the shady side of the building, putting up wood siding.

"Perfect," Miss Maggie said, and told me to stop. I parked behind two pickups in the drive and we made our way across deep, big-tire ruts in the bare red clay as we approached. The workers' pneumatic nail guns sounded an erratic rhythm of dull thuds, plus I could hear the buzz of a power tool and more traditional hammering from inside the house. The light breeze carried the heady odor of cedar sawdust.

One of the men—not much more than a teenager, actually, but with a friendly grin and sweaty tanned muscles across his bare, hairless chest—carried a piece of siding over to a portable workbench set up under a tree beside the first pickup. "You ladies lost?" In his central Virginia inflections, I thought I detected a hint of Hollywood tough guy. Ah, the influence of TV.

"Not at all," Miss Maggie said. "Tell me, were any of you working here on Wednesday evening? Say, around eight o'clock?"

That took him by surprise, but since Miss Maggie and I didn't fit his idea of anyone who'd pry for bad reasons—cops, gangsters, the IRS—he shrugged and said, "We all were. It's cooler working on the roof that time of night."

"I guess you heard about the man who was shot just down the road?" she ventured.

His eyeballs came forward in awed excitement. This plainly was his new favorite subject. "Aw, yeah. Spooky, happening so close like that. We heard the shot, too. Like a little firecracker. Or a cap gun, y'know? Anyway, that's what we figured, until the troopers came up here later asking if we'd seen any cars go by."

"Had you?"

"Seen cars?" Remembering the length of siding in his hands, he set it on the bench. "No. Not from the time we heard the shot. After the sun gets below the treetops 'round here, most drivers take the wider roads. The cops made us leave right away, but they wouldn't let us go out toward Route 20. We had to take 15 and double back on 33." He sounded disillusioned, as if he'd at last found himself in the action flick of his dreams and the police had failed to request his help.

Miss Maggie thanked him and we made our way back to my car. He'd never once seemed curious as to why we were asking. Maybe because, on TV, unlikely amateurs always end up investigating murders and that was his reality.

Miss Maggie handed me her hat while she buckled her seat belt. "Billy said that the SUV drove off up the road, but these workers didn't see any cars pass here. So where'd that Toyota go?"

"Down one of the driveways?" I passed the hat back to her,

fired up the ignition, and put the Neon in reverse. "No wonder the state troopers called in cops from all the surrounding counties. Must've been some manhunt."

"But they didn't find the car or the driver. Go back the way we came, Pat."

When we were moving down the road again, I said, "SUVs can drive off-road—"

"Only if you believe all the commercials. Some can, some can't. Depends on the axle height and size of the engine. If you're thinking that he cut overland to the next road, these woods are too thick. Likewise that scrub growth at the bottom of the hill."

"Except where the power lines cross the road."

"Pull over alongside 'em and let's have a look."

When I stopped the car, Miss Maggie again chose to do her snooping from the passenger seat. Just as well—too hot outside. "Look how trampled the grass is, Pat, on both sides of the road. The police must have done that the other night—and maybe more yesterday—looking for evidence."

I agreed. The first thirty yards or so in on either side looked as if a herd of rhinos had stampeded through. Beyond that, a service road crossed the meadow at the foot of the electrical towers. "That *must* be how he got away, Miss Maggie."

Miss Maggie turned to face front, her lips pursed in doubt. "You can see Wyatt's cross from here. If that's where he was found in Theo's car, then that's where Billy said he saw the SUV drive off. Billy should have *seen* it leave the road."

"Finding a dead body probably distracted him," I pointed out, thinking that in Billy's place, I'd have been too busy losing my supper to notice a little thing like which way the bad guy went.

"I suppose." She let out a perplexed sigh. "Let's go home, Pat. We have another mystery to solve there."

"You mean, who's buried in our yard?"

She nodded. "Maybe we'll have better luck."

14

On the drive home, Miss Maggie filled me in on what she'd learned of Clayborne family history from Aunt Song.

"Mance showed up in Rock Hill in 1889—let's see, that would put him in his late twenties. All he had with him were the clothes on his back, a sack of books, and the name 'Emancipation.' No last name and he wouldn't talk about his past at all. But he knew about farming, so they offered him a job in the vineyard. Since he could read and write, one family let him sleep in their barn in exchange for lessons. Pretty soon he was teaching everybody else in town. He fell in love with one of his students and, like Theo said, decided to settle down. Your left arm's getting sunburned, Pat."

I swung my sun visor over my head and tilted it down over my side window, but the shade didn't reach my forearm. "Sounds like Mance lived happily ever after, Miss Maggie."

"Maybe, but he wasn't Prince Charming. He had strong views—opinions a lot of people didn't cotton to. For one thing, he wouldn't hear of having a schoolhouse built or being hired permanently as the town's teacher. Said learning shouldn't be linked to one place or one person—that people should realize they can learn anywhere. He said they were all obligated to pass on what they learned. The Sunday meetings were an outgrowth of that."

"You said he only went by his first name. Where'd the name Clayborne come from?"

Even with my eyes glued to the road ahead—the town of Orange was coming up and I didn't want to miss the dogleg—I was aware of the grin she gave me in response. "Easy. His wife-to-be said she couldn't marry a man with no last name. He asked if she'd take the name Clayborne and she accepted. No one knows if that was his real name or not. I suspect he made it up—adopted it from his favorite saying."

"Favorite saying?"

"Another view that few folks—white or black—believed at that time. I'll wait until you stop for this next light."

"Why?"

When the car was at a standstill, Miss Maggie, still grinning, replied, "Because I didn't think you should be driving when you heard Mance's favorite saying. It was, 'All God's children are made of the same clay.' "

Oddly enough, I wasn't stunned. Maybe I'd had so many bombshells that day, my shock center was in overload. "So *that* part of my dream was definitely Mance. And 'theologian' was Mance, too, because I didn't know Theo's full name. So who's Mary?"

"There's only one Mary I know involved with this mess and you're looking at her."

I was so used to hearing her called Magnolia or Maggie that I'd forgotten Mary was her christened name.

"The most likely explanation," Miss Maggie continued, "is that your subconscious included me. Or maybe, since I've lived at Bell Run so long, Mance figures I've got squatter's rights where that grave's concerned."

"There's another possibility. Your grandfather—" The driver behind me leaned angrily on his horn—his way of pointing out that the light was now green. Back when I was working for corporate America, I would have responded with a picturesque Italian gesture in my rearview mirror—my way of pointing out what a *stronzo* he was. Now I simply shook my head, sadly but wisely, and pitied him as I lifted my foot from the brake.

"My grandfather?" Miss Maggie prompted. "What about him?"

"When I was in town yesterday, I had to go into the County Cafe a moment. That's where your grandfather's drugstore was, right?"

"Right." She said it slowly, like she was trying to see what difference it made. "Only thing left from his time is the shell of the building, though. Everything else has been renovated."

I told her about the ghost-scent.

"You smelled Ben-Gay?"

"Or mints. Something wintergreen. But only for a second."

"Wintergreen . . . now *that* brings back memories." Miss Maggie was silent a moment, reminiscing, I supposed. It turned out, the memory had a long way to travel. "I remember my grandmother smelling of wintergreen, 'specially on cold winter mornings when she first got up. That's 'cause at bedtime, she'd rub her achy knees with an arthritis remedy that contained wintergreen oil and her flannel nightgowns would soak it up."

"Also explains where you inherited your arthritis from."

"Oh, her whole side of the family suffered with it. Fact is, Granddaddy originally made up the remedy for Granny's Aunt Peg. But I don't recall his shop ever smelling of the stuff. Wintergreen's got a distinctive odor, but not as pungent as some of the other medicines he made up. One cough syrup I couldn't take unless I held my nose."

"If I'm experiencing Mance's memories, wintergreen must have some significance to him."

Miss Maggie agreed, with rising eagerness. "And it means Mance must have been in Granddaddy's shop at some point. My grandfather kept a record of every sale he made and I kept his books—"

"But what are the odds that a kid like Mance bought something? And besides, wouldn't we have to sift through thousands of transactions?" I was picturing decades' worth of old, dusty journals with faded handwriting and fragile pages. The proverbial needle in a whole warehouse of haystacks.

"*Tens* of thousands of transactions," Miss Maggie corrected, "and that's just during Mance's childhood. Good thing the first twelve years of those books are up on a web site."

"Web site?"

"That's what I was trying to tell you. The Stoke Historical Society stores Granddaddy's pharmaceutical paraphernalia for me and the County Library keeps his journals in their Special Collections room, but I wanted to make everything more accessible to researchers. Just a matter of matching up the right university with the right underwriter. So far, they've input up though 1878. We'll search for references to the word 'wintergreen.' See what turns up."

"What in tarnation's going on?"

"You're asking the wrong person, Miss Maggie," I said as I slowed to a stop.

As we'd come up Bell Run's drive, we spied a row of cars, pickups, and minivans parked along the shoulder to our right, between the woods and the house. All I could think was that there'd been another sniper attack and these were unmarked police vehicles. Yet the people in the side yard seemed more like sightseers than cops, and the youngster who jumped down from the lowest branch in the magnolia and ran toward us was a bit young even for a first-year trooper cadet.

Miss Maggie and I had both lowered our car windows on the

way through the forest, so we had no trouble hearing the kid's yell when he was twenty feet away. "Park at the end of the row. Don't block the drive." He used both hands to wave us on, as if directing a jumbo jet to its gate.

"Are all these people the ghouls you predicted, Miss Maggie?" I asked.

"Half the county?" She seemed more dazed than skeptical.

Ignoring the kid-cum-flight-technician, I took my usual parking spot, which wasn't easy since two older men were standing in the middle of it, talking, and seemed oblivious to my intentions until Miss Maggie hollered out her window, "Rudy? Hamilton? Mind taking your conversation over to the other side of the tree?"

"Not at all, Miz Shelby," and "Be happy to, Magnolia," were their responses, but instead, they surveyed my parking job, saying helpful things like, "Straighten your wheels," and "Don't go too far forward."

Miss Maggie was out before I'd shifted into park. I ran after her, taking my first good gander at the crowd. About half of them were in an orderly mob around Yorick's pit, and we could hear Emmy lecturing them about bones in general and why we had to proceed slowly.

Another faction was hard at work—a second tent had been set up along the edge of the grid closest to us, and the sod under its shade had been removed. The newcomers were scraping the plow layer. Hugh and Dwight were supervising.

Everyone else seemed to be milling around in the vicinity of the back porch. From what I could see—which wasn't much given all the bodies in the way—they were socializing as if attending a picnic. Come to think of it, I could have sworn I smelled hot dogs.

Hugh spied us and came jogging over. "Welcome to Bedlam. You two certainly took your good ol' time."

"You told us to," I argued.

"Yes, and I regretted it within the hour. Where's Theo?"

Miss Maggie waved away his question. "Long story. First tell me what all these folks are doing here."

"Look down behind Emmy's audience." He stepped closer to the house until he found the right vista and gestured to us to join him. "See who's manning the grill?"

A small charcoal grill had been placed in the shade beside the back porch rail. In front of it stood Sheriff Brackin, chest puffed out importantly while he munched a wiener. Someone must have told him to move, because he hastily shuffled to one side. Behind the grill, long-handled fork in one paw, the other clutching a woman's hand as a pro photographer preserved the moment, was the questionably Honorable J. Dudley Apperson.

I was howling mad. "You said he'd turn us into a photo-op, Miss Maggie, but I never thought he'd wait until we were away and—"

"It's worse than that," she said, sighing. "The woman whose hand J. D.'s clutching is Judge Cora Stevens, his opponent. Looks like we've become a political battlefield."

Hugh filled in the details. "J. D. started it. Not long after the first couple came, a half dozen more volunteers showed up, saying J. D. told them we needed help up here. Then he appeared with his tent, grill, and hot dogs. Cora got wind of it somehow and she brought over two coolers full of sodas and more workers. J. D. called in reinforcements, Cora did likewise, and here we are. But before you two get all hot under the collar and call for a mass exodus, you ought to know that the Bell Foundation has raked in some serious donations today from this impromptu doggie roast. Not to mention giving us so many volunteers, I had them sign up for rotating shifts over the next two weeks. By the way, I took the liberty of having all our workers sign liability wavers, so they can't sue the Bell Foundation if they get hurt."

Miss Maggie praised his initiative. I would have, too, if he hadn't already been grinning so smugly.

"Come on, Pat," Miss Maggie said. "Let's go freshen up so

we can greet our benefactors and thank our volunteers. And maybe we can steal that photographer away from the politicians for a little PR of our own."

"There she is! My new assistant."

Panning along with the grand gesture J. D. made with his oven mitt, the photographer turned toward me. His flash caught me square in the retinas.

I wanted to curse good and loud, but with everyone staring at me—especially all of our new financial backers—that didn't seem prudent. I'd forgotten all about J. D.'s job, excusable I thought, what with Theo and Mance and Vicky's murder jostling everything else out of my brain. For a beat of silence, all I could do was gawk at the congressman through the green spots in front of my eyes. He self-assuredly poked at half-burnt wieners with his long-handled fork, his toothy smile proclaiming me, and therefore this battleground, as his territory.

Time for some damage control. "J. D. offered me a part-time office job yesterday, Miss Maggie. Clerical stuff, ten hours a week, that's all. I told his office manager I wanted to think it over."

Before Miss Maggie could get a word in, Judge Cora said, "You can do better than that. Plenty of jobs down at the courthouse. They'd give you more hours, too. Maybe even full-time." Her smile was as toothy as J. D.'s, but with an aura of beauty-pageant contestant about it. The rest of her seemed a cultivated mishmash of Hillary Clinton hair, Geraldine Ferraro glasses, and the kind of clothes Christie Whitman would wear while promoting Jersey farm produce. Her message, of course, was, "I'll get you any job you want if you come over to my camp."

I had a sudden, frightening insight that the U.S. Capitol was in reality an internment facility for the pathetically power-addicted. We only had elections because, like all institutions designed to keep the abnormal off the streets, space was limited.

My imagination furnished secret, subterranean chambers, deep under the Rotunda, filled with two centuries worth of skeletons, all with toothy smiles.

Meanwhile, J. D. and Judge Cora bartered back and forth, each careful not to actually promise me anything definite. More spectators drifted away from Emmy's lecture to see what the hubbub was about, until I felt like I ought to be up on a stump, waiting for an auctioneer to yell, "Sold!"

Miss Maggie cleared her throat and everyone shut up. I was willing to bet most of the onlookers were former students, and that I'd just witnessed behavioral conditioning. Taking a step forward, Professor Shelby turned her head, making eye contact with, I swear, every single person present. "Since many of you were kind enough to give us your support today, the least I can do is tell y'all our new Foundation's plans for Bell Run, so you can hear what your money'll pay for. How 'bout we settle ourselves over on the porch and surrounding grass?"

The crowd obediently moved in that direction. Cora, either not wanting to be abandoned or realizing who present could sway votes, followed suit, leaving J. D. stuck at the stove with only Brackin for company. The sheriff, oblivious, dabbed a napkin at a ketchup stain on his shirt.

"Wow, Miss Maggie," I whispered, "you're good."

"Pat . . ." she began, all business.

"About the job, I—"

She impatiently waved away the topic. "We'll talk about that later. Right now, send Emmy's group over here, then give Emmy a quick rundown of what all happened today—and Hugh, if you can steal him away from the new test pits for a moment. But Emmy's worried, I can tell. She needs to know."

I agreed, even though breaking bad news to people was one of my least favorite pastimes. Moving Emmy's audience was no problem—their attention spans seemed ready for a channel change. And though Emmy could talk about bones and archaeology the rest of the day, as soon as we were alone, she asked about Theo. I called Hugh over and gave them the news in brief.

"Well, the fact that he brought the car back probably means he's not hurt," Emmy reasoned, consoling herself. "But Theo didn't run to save his own life. He isn't made that way. He ran to keep danger away from his family. And us." She sighed, then stepped into Yorick's pit, bending over to retrieve her trowel. "Nothing we can do to help Theo right now. He'd want us to keep digging."

"I'll go put on my work clothes," I said, glad of an excuse to get out of my dress.

"Take your time. I think we'll just put a tarp over our friend here 'til our visitors leave. Didn't get much done on him today, but I thought it more important to educate the public and get some funding. And I wanted to break in our new volunteers. That's why I set 'em to work over there to begin with, where they'd do the least damage. Go see if Magnolia needs you first. If not, I'll put you on pit number three."

I could tell from across the yard that Miss Maggie didn't need me. Expert storyteller that she was, she had her listeners mesmerized. I revised my assessment—these folks weren't behavior-conditioned. Miss Maggie was simply one of those beloved teachers who could make learning seductive. These people may have shown up today at J. D. and Cora's requests, but they really came to be students of Miss Maggie's again, and maybe to share the experience with their kids.

After exchanging my heat-wilted dress for a fresh T-shirt and shorts, I came back outside to find our new diggers standing in a clump under the tent closest to the woods. Emmy was giving another discourse, I guessed.

I came to stand beside Hugh and saw I was only partially right. In the corner pit, Emmy was on her knees, trowel in hand, scraping the sides of one corner as if making perfect ninety-degree angles in the dirt was her goal in life. And she sounded like she'd just discovered gold as she said, "This is definitely the top of a whole layer. Look." The point of her trowel traced over a thick, black line maybe a quarter inch above the floor of the pit.

"Charcoal," Hugh said in a low voice for my benefit. "That side of the pit was filled with bits of it."

I was disappointed. Someone's dumping ground for used briquettes. Big deal.

"Like I said before," Emmy continued, backing up slightly so she could etch the outline of a dark circle on the bottom of the pit, "this is a post hole. In other words, the post of a fence or building used to be here—a good-sized post, from the width of it. Put together with this layer of charcoal, we probably have here the remains of a wooden structure that burned."

I don't know what made me close my eyes at that moment, but the impulse was akin to pushing the playback button on an answering machine when I see the light flashing. Like I knew there'd be a message waiting for me.

Not a message, per se—another video clip. First, only flames—I could feel their heat on my face and the smell of smoke was strong enough that I held my breath. Then I could make out a silhouetted line of black men, women, and children, all of them trying to throw dirt on the fire. Too few had shovels. Others had hoes and axes to break up the ground. Some were using their bare hands. One of the children turned toward me. Glad to see me. Mance.

I felt a big hand on my shoulder and I opened my eyes. Hugh was looking down at me, troubled. Thank God, though, Emmy still had everyone else's attention and no one besides Hugh had noticed my little daydream.

I wiggled my eyebrows at him to stem his worry. He frowned to show he wasn't that easily conned. Maybe because my eyes were still watering from the smoke. Hugh left his hand on my shoulder, as if to hold me in the here and now. I should have enjoyed the sensation, but bouncing between eras tends to distract me.

Thing is, my vision hadn't told me much more than Emmy had already surmised, except that the fire had taken place while Mance was young, and that he'd been here at Bell Run at the time. What was he trying to tell me? Why did he always come back from the sweet by-and-by as a kid?

I thought back over what I'd just seen. Something didn't seem right—I mean, in addition to the now-familiar feelings of my own freakishness that accompany each of these episodes. Something important was staring me in the face. If only I could find some time alone to sit and think it out.

The World Can't Do Me No Harm

Dam Your Soul. . . . You have recommended a big Black
Nigger for Male agent on our nu rode . . . if he gets on
the rode . . . you will be taken on supprise and led out
by the Klan and learnt to stretch hemp.

—FROM A WARNING SENT BY PHILIP ISENBAUM,
JOHN BANKSTOWN, ESAU DAVES, AND OTHER MEMBERS
OF THE KU KLUX KLAN, 1871

July 3, 1871—Stoke

No sooner we be out of Mr. Fletcher's shop then I turn
'round to say, "Mama, I know where Uncle Henry lost his
liniment." My notion was that he brung it up to the
church at supper the other night—maybe to get Ida or
Jordana to mix it in some lard for him—and he spilled it
and forgot it, like he wont to do. That's why the fire be
so fierce.

But Mama only reach out toward me in alarm. "Mance,
watch—"

Too late. I backed into somebody and got pushed away
hard enough that I end up down on the sidewalk boards
with my palms and knees smarting from splinters.

I see Charlie Harris first, standing over me, cussing and
looking like he long to squash me with his boot the way he
might a garden snake that happened across his path at a bad
time. He work on occasion as a teamster, and he be dressed

as such now, with the smell of horse strong on his wool pants. Like always, he got on his army slouch hat. Mama say nobody s'posed to wear any part of Rebel uniforms, but ever since the Freedman agent go back to Washington, Charlie wear his hat all the time. Preacher Moses say men like the Harrises believe the South'll fight again, so they never give up soldiering completely. Mama say that hat just remind Charlie of the only time he ever feel important.

Like I say, Charlie be cussing me and looking like he be about to give me a taste of his boot leather. Mama come down on her knees beside me, asking pardon and saying, "Please don't let him hurt my Mance, Missuh Cox, sir. He didn't know Missuh Harris was there."

That's when I see Sheriff Cox behind me, his badge gleaming on the breast of his tan summer coat. He didn't seem mad at me like Charlie, but neither be he inclined to take my side. "Your boy should have been paying attention to where he was going."

"Yessuh, he should. But I'm to blame, hurrying him out of Mr. Fletcher's store like I did."

I didn't like hearing that, figuring Charlie might kick her instead, so I say, "No, Mama, you—"

"Hush, Mance."

"Let the boy talk," the sheriff say, hooking his hands around his lapels. "What've you got to say, boy?"

"Mama ain't to blame, sir. Just me."

Charlie laugh at that. "Why, he's calling his ma a liar. That right, boy? She a lying nigger?"

I stand up at that, mad enough to want to punch him. Mama put her arms 'round my waist to stop me.

"Bullying women and children now, Charlie?" That was Mr. Fletcher's voice and I turn to see him standing in his doorway, all his weight on the leg he don't limp on.

"Mind your own affairs, Fletcher," Charlie say.

"This *is* my affair. She's my cleaning woman, and I don't want her hurt so that she can't come do her work this evening."

Sheriff Cox step forward so he be between the two men. "What was her business with you now, Caleb?"

"She came to pick up a preparation for Mrs. Norton. Show him, Alma."

The bottle Mama take from her apron be Uncle Henry's liniment. She look at me, scared-like, while she do it, so I keep my mouth closed.

Sheriff Cox be satisfied with that, but he tell Mama, "Don't bring your boy to town with you next time, understand?"

"Yessuh, I won't," she say, getting to her feet and putting the bottle back in her apron.

"One more thing," the sheriff say, "Moses Jackson came down here yesterday and said that your church burned down. Is that true?"

Mama nod to say it was.

"He said the fire was lit by a man on horseback, but he couldn't identify him because both man and horse were covered with bedsheets. Is that right?"

Mama glance at me quick, then likewise at Mr. Fletcher, before looking back at the sheriff. "That's what Moses say. I be cleaning here at Mr. Fletcher's that night, so I got home after the fire got started."

"So you didn't see this rider?"

"No suh, I didn't." Mama keep a hand clamped hard on my shoulder, and I could tell she didn't want me to say what I seen.

Charlie laugh again. "Sounds more like Moses made up that horseman out of his head, just like he always does.

He keeps trying to make you believe the Klan is giving those niggers out in Darkie Hollow trouble."

"Doesn't matter," Sheriff Cox tell him. "There's nothing the law can do if no one saw the rider's face."

"Even if one of 'em did," Charlie say, "you need more proof than a darkie's say-so. 'Innocent until proven guilty'—that's what the law says."

"That it does. Well, good day to you Charlie, Caleb." The sheriff tip his hat to both of them, but not to me and Mama, and he mosey off down the sidewalk.

Mama shoo me ahead of her in the other direction, but we heard Charlie say good and loud behind us, "That church burning sounds like a bad omen to me. If I lived out there in Darkie Hollow, I'd pack up and leave before any more bad luck caught up with me."

15

When Miss Maggie was done her historical discourse/Foundation sales pitch, like any good teacher she dismissed her class. And they left. Oh, not in a big hurry, as if they couldn't wait to get out of school, but slowly, asking Miss Maggie a few final questions, taking one more look at the dig site. Showing actual interest in our project.

But they *did* leave, even Cora, taking with her what was left of her sodas—which, given the heat of the day, added up to three Mountain Dews and a Diet Coke. J. D., on the other hand, bequeathed the last of his burnt wieners to us for our supper, and said he'd pick his grill up tomorrow since it was too hot to move now. Cora had second thoughts about her sodas and ice chests—if J. D. was going to stake a claim, so was she. Miss Maggie averted the territorial war by cordially but firmly walking them to their cars. Brackin drove off right behind J. D.

Emmy let our volunteers go early, too, giving each a list of what to bring when they came to work again: heavy shoes, sunblock, bug repellent, something to kneel on, a water bottle, and a bag lunch. I was happy about that last one. Having to feed that crew each day would eat up our donations in no time.

Dwight helped us clean up the yards—not much litter, considering the size of the crowd—then he left, too, and we took a break of sorts. Hugh decided to cool down with a quick shower, and Emmy, notebook balanced on her knees, quietly sat on the grass beside the post-hole pit, diagramming it and making notes. I figured she probably needed a pick-me-up, so I fetched her a tall glass of iced tea, a ripe peach, and a handful of cheese chunks on a napkin, which she accepted with fervent gratitude.

Then, leaving my boots and socks under the front hall table so my feet could breathe again, I retired to the kitchen to contemplate what to do for supper. J. D.'s franks weren't an option— not that I have anything against hot dogs personally, but I was still mad at him and I'd made a resolution not to accept *anything* from J. D. from now on. Jobs included. Besides, with Miss Maggie's diet, I had to fix something else for her anyway. Might as well make a healthy meal for everyone while I was at it.

I found Miss Maggie sitting at the kitchen table, working her way through a banana. Two more glasses of iced tea had been poured, one of which she'd already half emptied. "I was so thirsty, I could've drained the Rapidan. Sit, Pat. You need some refreshment, too." She pushed the other glass toward me.

I sat opposite her and gulped a dose of the cold liquid, then, before she could bring up the subject of J. D., I filled her in on my latest vision.

"So Mance helped fight that fire," she mused. "You didn't see, or hear or smell, anything else?"

I shook my head. "The only sensations were the smoke and the heat of the flames. The building was past saving. That's all I know." Except something about that last psychic film clip nagged at me. Something obvious.

I figured Miss Maggie would ask me questions, dragging the truth to the surface like she always did, but she seemed stumped. Or maybe just too tired to think. With a sigh, she said, "What a long day," and we sipped tea without speaking for the next few moments.

The longer the silence stretched, the more I felt she wanted me to pick up the conversation, and my guilt built up, until I blurted out, "I didn't *ask* J. D. for the job, Miss Maggie." Then

I gushed on, telling her the whole episode, from my parking quandary through J. D. agreeing to a practically obscene hourly wage. "Of course, now I understand *why*," I concluded, my narrative becoming an angry tirade. "He just wants to use me to make it look like he has your endorsement. And I—"

"You never told him you'd take the job, right, Pat?"

"What? No. I wanted to discuss it with you first."

"But you didn't."

My fit of pique melted into embarrassment. "I meant to. We haven't had much time to talk since yesterday—"

"What with Mance and our skull outside and three murders to boot? Too true."

"And today, I completely forgot about the job, or I would have told you on the way home."

Miss Maggie took her banana skin over to the garbage container by the sink and washed her hands. "Your subconscious already had it pegged as a non-issue."

"You mean, I never intended to take the job anyway, because I knew instinctively that I couldn't work for J. D."

"No, not just J. D." She came back to the table, sat down, kicked her sandals off and wiggled her toes. "Admit it, Pat. All those other companies you've sent resumés to in the last month— could you picture yourself working at any of them? Not just in your fantasies, but in reality? Honestly?"

When I tried, I saw me behind a desk again, in a poorly lit cube completely cut off from sunlight, doing repetitive work that did nothing for the world except make a few people (none of whom were me) richer.

"Well, Pat?"

I realized my breathing had become shallow and I could feel my heartbeat in my throat. Fight-or-flight reaction, heavy on the flight. Good grief, she was right. I was a workaphobic. A new image swam before my eyes—me sponging off Miss Maggie and her estate the rest of my life. I'd end up like my Aunt Filippa, watching soaps and talk shows all day in a shabby housecoat and scruffy pink slippers. Although, instead of soaps, I'd watch the Food Channel.

Oddly enough, as frightening as this new mental picture was, it didn't come with a panic attack like the other. But I couldn't let Miss Maggie know that. "I guess I wasn't serious about job hunting before because I had my severance to tide me over while we got the Foundation off the ground. Now that we've got some patrons and volunteers, I'll be able to get a job and support myself, and help you with the bills—"

She let out one of her pshaws. "This isn't about money, Pat. It's about your sanity. Working for Dawkins-Greenway did a number on your self-esteem, and being unemployed is making it worse. You need to feel useful and independent."

"Both at the same time?" I asked, smiling as if making a joke. But I couldn't help thinking that "independence" was a total illusion. I had modes of dependency, that's all: Miss Maggie, Pennsylvania's State Unemployment Fund, and eventually, another employer. As for "useful"—that was something I felt when I did things for Miss Maggie that she couldn't do for herself. Or things that produced a tangible result. Like cooking.

Which reminded me, I had to decide what to do for supper.

"Yes, Miss Smarty-Pants, both," Miss Maggie said as I got up to assess the contents of the fridge. "And you need to get out more. Make some friends here in Virginia."

"I have friends. Besides you, there's Hugh and Beth Ann—"

"That's because they live right next door and Beth Ann spends half her time here. If they lived in town, would you make the effort?"

Okay, so maybe I didn't get out much. Bell Run had that effect me. It felt safe. But I'd never been an outgoing person. How could I be? For the last twelve years, I'd spent the bulk of my waking hours in a cube at Dawkins-Greenway. Sure, I'd had friends there—we'd do lunch together, or an occasional happy hour. We'd throw wedding and baby showers for each other. In the end, though, D-G's downsizing had taken those friendships away from me. I thought about my old cube mate, Denise, and remembered all the pranks we'd play on the dupes in the office. I missed Denise a lot.

"Pat, close the refrigerator door."

I pictured myself slamming it to let out some pent-up frustration. No, not in character. My gene pool was big on keeping frustrations bottled up. Of course, we were also big on stomach ulcers and hypertension. Then again, we'd never had to replace a broken door.

Grabbing the closest container on the top shelf, front—so as to prove I had a reason for having the fridge open—I shut the door and reverted to totally in-character behavior: whining. "Miss Maggie, I'm perfectly willing to go out tomorrow and be the most useful, independent, sociable person in Stoke County." Easy to say that when facing a weekend, and a holiday weekend at that, with a lot of businesses closed on Monday. "The catch here is that J. D. is the only person who's actually offered me a job."

She pursed her lips in thought—or, more likely, to keep herself from pointing out that I was transferring the blame. I already knew I was—at least J. D. came in handy for something.

Avoidance always worked better than whining. Time to change the subject to dinner. The container in my hand turned out to be a tub of nonfat sour cream. How appropriate. "For supper, I'm going to make a salmon dip," I decided aloud, crossing to the pantry to retrieve a can of salmon. "We can eat it on veggies and crackers."

Miss Maggie sat up straight, her nose in the air like a puppy waiting for table scraps. Food always made her forget everything else. "Mm. What are you putting in it besides sour cream?"

I'd come up with the recipe years ago while helping a cousin host a Tupperware party, but gave the impression I was being inspired on the spot. "I'll mince some onion, and—" I paused to contemplate the jars of dried herbs on the spice rack, "—chives and thyme, I think. You know, I'd kill for fresh herbs. All they have at the supermarket is parsley."

"Grow your own. You wanted a garden, didn't you?"

"Yeah, but now the yard—"

"Forget the yard. I've got stacks of flowerpots down in the cellar. You can grow herbs in pots, can't you?"

"Sure, I guess—"

The phone rang. "I'll get it. Don't do anything important until I get back."

If by "important" she meant opening the cans or mixing everything in my food processor, I couldn't anyway, because she brought the phone back into the kitchen with her, along with her laptop and reading glasses. Seemed rude to run noisy appliances while she was trying to hear the person on the other end of the fiber optics. In lieu of that, I fetched a small onion from the fridge.

"Heavens, no, Lizzie," Miss Maggie was saying as she set the laptop on the table and sat down in front of it. "I didn't expect you to close up shop and come out here today. Truth is, I didn't know anyone was coming. But it sure was nice to see your daughter again. The last time I laid eyes on her, she must have been in high school, and now she's got a toddler. . . ." Miss Maggie balanced the phone on her shoulder, uttering a sporadic "uh-huh" or "You don't say!" as she fired up the computer and set her glasses on her nose. Then, "Yes, well, we were all shocked about Billy yesterday. . . . No, the police seem convinced that the killer's long gone. . . ."

I'd just hacked the onion in half and lopped off one end, pushing it off the cutting board with the knife blade, when I realized that I hadn't seen any troopers since we'd arrived home from Rock Hill. They were convinced, all right—convinced Theo was their man. The onion fumes hit me, making my eyes sting. Pausing to muse while mincing an onion is *not* a great idea.

"That's one reason I had Cindy ask you to call," Miss Maggie continued. "My old memory's not what it used to be, Lizzie. Tell me, wasn't Rufus Gibson involved with the Protectors before he went into that nursing home last year?"

The name Gibson caught my attention. I stepped away from the cutting board so I could listen.

"High Puma? That's some kind of officer, I suppose? . . . Oh, like a vice president . . . Yes, yes, isn't it just like men to have to give themselves impressive titles. . . ." While she kept up her end of the conversation, Miss Maggie copied one of her recipe files and replaced the header with the words "Salmon Herb Dip." The multifacets of her mind amazed me. "Rufus has a son, doesn't he? . . . I remember his two daughters. Had 'em both as students. The son came along after I'd retired. Where's he living now? . . ."

More "uh-huh"s ensued, until I was tempted to run upstairs and listen in on the other phone. But then I'd have to waste time washing the onion off my hands.

"Did the son ever join the Protectors? . . . Yes, I know Billy's two boys are in it, but they're both still in Stoke, working in the family auto body shop. Never did go to college, not that anyone's surprised by *that*. . . ." A longer pause, then, "Isn't that always the way? They get so wound up in their careers these days— families take the backseat. . . . Well, I should say so! . . . No, really? Howard's moving to Richmond? What will you do for . . . You certainly *do* have your hands full . . ."

Disappointed, I went back to chopping onion.

"Well, I won't keep you, Lizzie. . . . Now that *would* be nice. Pat would get such a kick out of breakfast at your place. She's quite a cook herself, you know. . . ."

On hearing my name, I'd swung my head around. Miss Maggie was beaming at me, not as a proud parent, but as a shrink who's hit on a therapy for my socialization problems. She said good-bye to her crony and switched off the phone. "How much sour cream per can of salmon?"

"Equal parts. Wait. What's this about Rufus Gibson? Is he related to Vicky?"

"I don't know. Lizzie—that was Lizzie Adams who runs the Bluebell Bed and Breakfast in Stoke—she says Rufus's boy, Bradshaw, got his degree in engineering and he's living in Charlottesville, working for Sprint or Com-Dial, she thought. Gibson's a common name, but with Rufus being so active in the Protectors—"

"That *must* be the connection, Miss Maggie."

"One way to find out." Phone still in hand, Miss Maggie was on her feet and out of the room before I could ask how. I set down my knife and was about to rinse off my hands when I remembered that Hugh might yet be in the shower, so I ran after Miss Maggie as I was, hands up like a surgeon waiting for latex gloves.

I found her in the war room, at her PC, waiting for it to power up. "What are you doing?"

"Looking up Bradshaw Gibson's phone number." The PC finished its start-up routine and within seconds (the advantage of a cable modem), we were looking at AT&T's directory site. She typed in Gibson's name and "Charlottesville." Only one listing— good thing he had an unusual first name and didn't believe in unlisted numbers. Miss Maggie punched the digits into her handset and waited. A moment later she hung up. "Voice mail," she said. " 'Press one if you want to leave a message for Brad, press two for Vicky.' "

"So the Protectors *are* involved."

She nodded absently, then seemed to see me for the first time, which brought on a grin. "You'd better get back in the kitchen, Pat, before you forget you have onion on your hands and scratch your nose."

That, of course, made it itch. I bit my lip to give my brain a diversion.

"While I'm here," she continued, "I'll look up Granddaddy's

journal and print off what I can find on wintergreen. Write down your salmon dip recipe for me, will you?"

"Sure thing," I said and headed back to the kitchen, rubbing my itchy nose against my T-shirt sleeve.

I found Hugh seated at Miss Maggie's laptop, playing Minesweeper as he took a bite from one of J. D.'s burnt offerings. "Ugh," was my only comment.

"They look worse than they taste," Hugh said, not taking his eyes from the screen as he nimbly rotated the laptop's trackball with his middle finger. "Though this one's still cold in the center. Nothing a few seconds in the microwave can't fix." He abandoned his game to yank a napkin from the holder on the table, then crossed to the microwave.

"This *one*?" I repeated. "Out of how many?"

"In the last fifteen minutes? Or all afternoon?"

Like I said, I have nothing against hot dogs. In moderation. "Never mind. Better I don't know."

The microwave beeped and he retrieved his snack, now in a soggy roll. "Guess I worked up an appetite today."

"You won't have one left for dinner."

The grin he gave me said I'd do well to use two cans of salmon. "Do you need any help?" His glance traveled from the minced onion half on the cutting board to my hands, which I still held out away from my body, implying that I looked fairly helpless.

Tempted as I was to spell out exactly what I needed from him, I had a meal to get on the table, so I put him to work opening cans of salmon. When he passed that proficiency test, I gave him celery, carrots, zucchini, and red bell peppers to chop into dipable pieces. To my surprise, Hugh was a competent sous-chef, wielding a kitchen cleaver like the pros.

He caught me gaping. "I *have* been chief cook in the Lee household the last ten years."

I squeezed a third of a lemon into the salmon mixture with what I judged to be convincing nonchalance. "So you only eat hot dogs when you're out of balsamic vinegar? Oh, I *am* impressed."

"Ye of little faith. You'll have to come to supper sometime."

"When?" That was out of my mouth before I could stop it, and sounding anything but nonchalant. My imagination had immediately conjured up a romantic, candlelit, wine-accompanied dinner. Of course, a second later the left side of my brain filled in the realistic details: namely, a teenager named Beth Ann.

Before he could reply, Miss Maggie came into the room, all excited, her nose practically touching the computer printouts she read. "I found it. Mrs. Burress's Ache Remedy. Mrs. Burress was Granny's Aunt Peg. The original formula was one part oil of wintergreen to two parts alcohol."

"Yum," Hugh said. "Sounds like a recipe for a mint julep."

Miss Maggie shook her head. "Not that you'd ever want to drink. Granddaddy would have used wood alcohol, or rubbing alcohol, if it was around in the 1870s. He flat refused to put drinking alcohol in anything, even cough syrup. Wouldn't have it in his store at all. Too tempting for him."

"Your grandfather was an alcoholic, Miss Maggie?" I asked, reaching for a dish towel to wipe the lemon juice off my hands.

She nodded. "Pretty common during and after the war, especially in the South. And Granddaddy came from a long line of whiskey makers. His mother died when he was born and he was raised by a father who didn't see anything wrong with letting his son down all the home brew he could hold. Then in the army, Granddaddy used to volunteer for field hospital duty just so he could snitch their medicinal liquor. That's where he got interested in the pharmacist's trade. Smartest thing he ever did was stick to it and turn his back on distilling. Far as I know, he never once fell off the wagon. Not in my lifetime anyway."

Can't Hate Your Neighbor in Your Mind

De white race is so brazen. Dey come here an' run de Indians from dere own lan', but dey couldn't make dem slaves 'cause dey wouldn't stan' for it. Indians use to git up in trees an' shoot dem with poison arrow.

—FROM AN INTERVIEW WITH FORMER SLAVE SUSAN HAMILTON, 1930s

July 3, 1871—Stoke

Mama take my hand and pull me 'round to the back alley where we find Noah already sitting on Zeb's steps. He tell us Zeb be off to doing some chore or other, but that be as much as Mama let him say 'fore she give him a piece of her mind for making me go off alone here in town. Then she give Noah the bottle for Uncle Henry and tell him to get me off home right this minute.

"Ain't you s'posed to be washing clothes at the Colonel's farm today, Alma?" Noah ask, still sitting and not looking like he be in a hurry.

"I come into town to fetch something from the house for Miz Gilbert. You know she won't be pleased at how long it taking me, 'specially if I tell her it 'cause I find my son walking the streets by hisself."

Noah try to say how he be waiting for Zeb so he could get his whetting stone, but Mama won't hear a word of it, so he finally stand up and start walking, I think just to get away from her nagging.

Anyway, Noah and me end up going home without the whetting stone and without me having the chance to tell Mama about the blue flames. So, on our walk back, I tell Noah 'bout them instead, and how I think Uncle Henry's bottle got spilled by accident 'cause I smell the wintergreen oil when the flames first start.

Noah's jaw go all stiff like he be fighting mad. "That wasn't no accident, Mance. Most like that rider threw a bottle of this here liniment when he threw his torch, so as to make sure the fire catch. Which mean the horseman be Caleb Fletcher. And that don't surprise me one bit."

Mr. Fletcher, I knew, ain't got a horse of his own, and Mama say he just sleep on a pallet like us and don't use bedsheets either. So he be the same breed of white trash as the rider, I reckoned. And it made sense that he'd want to be on horseback, so none of us could see his limp and knowed it was him.

16

Hugh returned to veggie chopping. "Why are you looking up old ache remedies, Miss Maggie? Your arthritis been kicking up?"

She told Hugh about my olfactory phenomenon on the site of Granddaddy Fletcher's drug store. That got me one of his scowls, and his grip tightened on the cleaver in his hand. He didn't come across as scary, though, just paternal, like my Uncle Gaet looked the time my cousin Marcella and I used his golf clubs to play street hockey.

"So you see," Miss Maggie concluded, "the remedy itself doesn't matter. What's important is whether Mance ever smelled wintergreen on that spot."

"Mance?" Hugh resembled Uncle Gaet more than ever. I took the cleaver away from him. "What's he got to do with—"

She went on to tell him our discoveries at the All Children of God Church in Rock Hill, emphasizing the portrait of Mance showing the large mole on his forehead. "Remember how Beth Ann used to talk about that birthmark?"

"Yeah, but what—"

"All we need then," Miss Maggie went on, "is some kind of evidence—something to corroborate Beth Ann's and Pat's experiences—linking Mance to Stoke County or Bell Run." She waved her papers again, this time with purpose.

"You found something?" I rushed to look over her shoulder.

"That's what I've been trying to tell you." She set the printout on the table so both Hugh and I could see. On it was a list of rectangular boxes with the headings "Date," "Customer," "Description," and "Cost." A few of the entries were shaded gray, and Miss Maggie put her forefinger on one of these. It read "3 July 71—Emancipation Jackson—Burress Remedy, for Henry Jackson—2 cents."

"Jackson," Hugh read, a triumphant "ah-ha" in his tone. "You said his name was Clayborne, so this isn't the same man."

Miss Maggie rolled her eyes. "For the life of me, Fitzhugh Lee, I don't know how you got an A in my class. Before the war, who was the largest slaveholder in Stoke County?"

"Aw, Miss Maggie," Hugh whined. "You expect me to remember the answer to one of your test questions after almost thirty years?"

"You should remember *all* the answers, or what'd I waste the taxpayers' money for? The largest slaveholder hereabouts was Travis Jackson, so Jackson would have been a common surname among the freed slaves who settled the area."

Hugh tried to cut in with another protest, but Miss Maggie was ahead of him. "How do I know this particular Jackson was a freed slave—or the son of one—and not one of Travis's kin? Easy. Up through 1880, Granddaddy kept two sets of journals, one for sales to whites, one for blacks. This entry's shaded blue on the web site, meaning it came from the black journal."

"Why did he do that?" I asked, assuming some prejudice, but not seeing the point. Keeping separate books didn't have the same demeaning effect as, say, making someone use the back door. Then again, maybe Granddaddy Fletcher's shop didn't have a back door.

"I suspect Granddaddy didn't want his white clientele to find out he was selling to blacks," Miss Maggie replied. "At best, he could've lost the majority of his customers. At worst, he could have found himself entertaining the KKK."

She picked up her tea glass and swirled the ice-melt around

the bottom. "As I was saying, Jackson would have been a common surname, but freed slaves frequently gave up their masters' names in favor of something like Lincoln or Grant, or for a name that redefined the person. 'Sojourner Truth' is a prime example. Remember, Mance wasn't using a last name at all when he got to Rock Hill, and with his favorite saying, it's almost certain he adopted the name Clayborne."

She paused to gulp down the last mouthful in her glass. "Hugh, would you rather take the evidence we *do* have, along with Pat's and Beth Ann's experiences, and claim we're looking at a series of coincidences? History is like a pile of loose pottery shards. You take the ones that all have the same glaze pattern and fit them together. And you'll be able to see a bowl taking shape even with most of the pieces still missing."

Had I been the one to give that impassioned speech, Hugh would have had a comeback. With Miss Maggie, he conceded the contest.

She gave us a satisfied grin. "Now, what about that salmon dip?"

I rattled off the recipe for her as I put the finishing touches on the main course, then set the bowl of dip in the fridge for five minutes while I whipped up dessert. Keeping with the immersion theme, I mixed yogurt and marshmallow fluff as a fruit dip. I left Miss Maggie cleaning strawberries and Hugh chopping cantaloupe, and went into the war room to call out the window to Emmy.

She wasn't at the post-hole pit, or anywhere else that I could see. My slip-on tennies were in front of the blue recliner, where I'd kicked them off the night before, so I yanked them onto my feet and went outside to look for Emmy.

The basement door was already closed, but I checked there anyway. No luck. Given the events of the last two days, I don't think I could be blamed for the bit of panic in my voice as I hollered her name.

"Over here," I heard from where the drive entered the forest. I ran across the yard, over the brink of the hill. At first I didn't see her, but she said "Down here," and I spotted her more than halfway down the drive, where it curved to the left. She was sitting, so I thought she might have fallen and hurt herself. I ran toward her, my shoes crunching loudly on the gravel, emphasizing the silence around me. After two steps I had the urge to tiptoe, afraid of awakening the birds from their afternoon siestas. I'd noticed in the last month how Bell Run could grow eerily still on sultry days. Maybe the humid air muffled sound, like being underwater in a swimming pool.

Emmy wasn't hurt—I could tell that from twenty yards away. She sat cross-legged on the side of the road, gazing off into the forest to the right, a dreamy expression on her usually pragmatic face.

"I just wanted to tell you supper's ready," I said, feeling as if I were intruding. "What are you looking at?"

"The past."

A chill touched the back of my neck—her eyes were aimed slightly downhill, straight at the place where I'd seen the shacks by the creek. Maybe I wasn't the only one who'd seen them.

As I moved closer, she waved her hand, palm down, at the scene before her—a magician making a rabbit appear. "Look at this slope, Pat. Erase the vegetation in your mind. Can you see a sort of terrace right here beyond this bend in the drive?"

I hunkered down beside her, trying to get her perspective, then sat slightly behind her, so I could look past her arm. The land *did* seem to form a ledge here, little more than a yard wide. "I see it."

"Now try to follow that terrace along the slope, down toward the creek. It's eroded away in places, and if this had been a wet summer, the underbrush would be so overgrown, you wouldn't be able to make it out at all. But can you see it?"

"I think so."

The question in my tone—why did the shape of the hillside matter?—made her smile at me over her shoulder. "You're looking at part of the original road onto this property. Makes sense that there would have been one here, of course, with the Bell family grist mill downstream. Route 3 used to be a plank road between Fredericksburg and Germanna Ford. Bell's customers would have taken the plank road to this creek, then traveled along it to the mill."

Not a supernatural vision, after all. She'd simply read the bumps in the landscape.

"Another clue," Emmy went on, "is that none of the trees on this terrace are much more than a hundred years old. No ancient chestnut stumps like you see elsewhere in these woods. More brambles and underbrush than the rest of the slope. This road was used for a long time, and trampled enough that it took a while for nature to get a toehold again."

Since I'd come to Bell Run, I'd learned that the forest wasn't the same acre after acre, but could change character practically with each square foot. With Beth Ann's help, I'd begun to identify different trees and wildflowers. Now that Emmy mentioned it, I could see what she meant. Where the road had been grew tulip poplars, younger than the surrounding trees. And where the road approached the creek was a wider area of new growth. Right where I'd seen houses. "Down by the creek—was there a bigger clearing there?"

"You've got a good eye, Pat. Maybe that's where the mill race began and the road had to curve around behind it. Might also explain why the path then came uphill a bit, instead of staying along the creek."

"You mean the road didn't come uphill to . . . to get to the top?" Said like that, it sounded like the punch line of a chicken-crosses-the-road joke.

Emmy shook her head. "Don't be deceived by what you see now. Most of the drive is fairly new. Except right here—from this bend downhill to the next. Notice how this stretch is more sunken into the hillside than the rest? This is part of the original road—"

An explosion made us jump—a boom with a bass reverb that made the ground shake. I was on my feet, sprinting up toward the house, conscious only that the blast had come from that direction, when I heard a quick succession of other, quieter bangs.

Firecrackers. I slowed to a trot, though my heart was still trying for a land speed record.

When I reached the house, Miss Maggie was stepping off of the back porch, watching Hugh head down the trail that led to the Bell House ruin.

"Where's he going?" I asked. "It's only somebody shooting off fireworks. Probably kids."

"Yes, but they were close—on our property. You know how dry these woods are right now. One little spark and . . . Go help him check it out, Pat."

She didn't need to ask me twice. The thought of a fire destroying this beautiful forest sickened me.

I caught up with Hugh right where the trail came out from under the trees. The far side of the clearing was already veiled in late-afternoon shadows. There, the light colored the truncated brick walls of Bell House, where they weren't singed black, a sort of orange sherbet hue. On our side, where the sun was still bright, the bricks were their usual scruffy creamsicle shade.

The standing walls were surrounded by piles of brick rubble, and as we came even with the first mound, I smelled sulphur. Hugh pointed out the carcasses of freshly spent firecrackers halfway up the heap, saying with a sigh of relief, "At least whoever set them off had the sense to do it on the bricks and not down here on the grass."

He scanned the forest. For a better view, I clambered up the rubble pile until I could see over the wall, shading my eyes against the glare. No sign of anyone hiding in the trees, snickering at us.

"They must have heard us coming down the trail," Hugh said, waving me back down. "Come on. They're long gone."

"We shouldn't leave this trash here," I said, stooping to pick up what was left of the cardboard and plastic casings, still warm to the touch. "That'll only encourage the same kids to come back and do it again. Or maybe it was the Idiot from the development. But anyway—"

"What idiot?" Would it have killed him to help me? But no, he stood there, hands on hips, watching me work.

"The guy who's been shooting off firecrackers every night. You must have heard him. He was doing it before you and Beth Ann left for the shore."

"Well, he's not doing it anymore. That was Billy."

I paused mid-cleanup and, turning toward Hugh, sat down, casings still in one hand, so I could look him in the eye. Sort of. Even up here, I was a head shorter than he was. I could feel the heat of the sun-toasted bricks through my shorts. "Billy lived in the development? He didn't seem the upscale type."

"He bought a one-bedroom condo there after his divorce," Hugh replied. "Billy's idea of a 'swinging bachelor pad.' His words, not mine. I know he was the one shooting off firecrackers because when I delivered his mail last Saturday, he was bragging about it. Saw it as his solemn patriotic duty. He even gave me a few to set off on the Fourth."

I must have looked horrified, because Hugh rolled his eyes and added, "Just little ones. And I know how to be careful."

"What is it with men and things that go boom?"

"John Adams himself said that the Fourth ought to be celebrated with fireworks and—"

"He was a man, too. Though fire*works* are okay—the pretty kind that make you say ooh and aah and are handled strictly by professionals. Not the kind that can make everyone deaf and burn down your house and blow the hands off your loved ones—"

"Oh? Now I'm a loved one?" Hugh asked innocently, a gotcha-grin sneaking out from under his mustache. I suddenly realized that he hadn't been watching me work—he'd been enjoying the view of me in shorts, bent over right at ogle level.

My face must have turned scarlet—my skin felt hot enough to roast marshmallows. I couldn't quite hold in a laugh as I tried for a dignified, "I meant Beth Ann."

The mention of his daughter made him lose the grin. "Come on, let's go have supper. We'll clean up later."

I *hate* it when he gets sulky, and I said so. "What did I say this time?"

"Nothing."

"Not nothing. I say your daughter's name and—oh. She's supposed to come home tomorrow." And all of a sudden I remembered we'd been having a murder a day, one of which had taken place in our own front yard. Now *I* was worried silly about Beth Ann.

"No," Hugh said. "I called Rich and asked him to keep her there an extra day or two."

"She'll miss the fireworks tomorrow night."

"Rich'll take her to see Williamsburg's display. But she'll never forgive me for missing your cookout."

Cookout? I'd forgotten all about it. "We'll postpone it 'til she gets home. The main thing is, Beth Ann's safe for now. So what's your problem?"

He drew in a deep breath, as if intending to project his voice across the clearing. Instead, he spoke in almost a mumble. "My daughter can see ghosts."

"Ah." It came out sounding like I was Freud seeing a complex behind every word, when in truth I wasn't sure I saw anything at all. I quickly added, "She saw Mance nearly ten years ago, Hugh—"

"Not only Mance."

He meant the episode in May. Come to think of it, Beth Ann *had* seen more than I had, in the traditional ghost-sighting sense.

When I had visions, they felt like fantasies. That's what I'd call them if it weren't for Miss Maggie finding historical evidence to back them up. My dreams of Mance had felt like every other product of my REM sleep. With my eyes opened, the occult usually showed up as smells or sounds—not scary because I couldn't *see* what caused them. I realized a chunk of me was still in denial about my supernatural experiences simply because they didn't look like footage from *The Sixth Sense*. Even the one conventional ghost I *had* seen, my first week here at Bell Run—well, that was an ancestor of mine. Being Italian, I grew up expecting relatives to show up at odd times.

Hugh folded his arms across his chest, as if to remind me that I hadn't returned the conversational shuttlecock. I saw what was bothering him. It wasn't that he thought his daughter was a freak, no, he just couldn't protect her from what he couldn't see himself. He was using the murders as an excuse for Beth Ann to stay in Poquoson, but chances were he was also trying to keep her away from Mance.

And that made me feel guilty, as if I'd *invited* Mance to share my dreams this week. On the other hand, I couldn't believe Mance was dangerous. He'd grown up to have his portrait on a church wall, for Pete's sake, and he was patriarch to the Clayborne clan, which didn't seem to have a mean chromosome in its entire gene pool. Whether Sergeant Ross believed it or not.

In the end, all I could do was shrug and say, "If it worries you that much, talk to her about it."

Hugh's turn to look horrified. I swear, he must have gone to the same school of parenting as my mom, the alma mater of which states that nothing should be discussed with your progeny beyond whatever the said progeny was doing wrong at the time. Had I asked Mom about ghosts, the only talking would have been her reciting *Hail Marys* while she dribbled olive oil into a cup of water to see if I had the Evil Eye.

At that moment, I decided the bricks under me were too hot—and pointy—to sit on for much longer, so I pushed myself to my feet with my free hand. That's how I got something semi-mushy on my pinkie. My first reaction was "Oh, gross, bird poop," but then I noticed the stuff was a translucent pink. It felt silky, and formed an instant film on my skin.

"Is this what I think it is?" I stuck my hand out for Hugh's inspection.

He squinted at my fingertip, then rubbed his finger against mine, which felt pleasantly provocative, though he was only testing texture. "Wax," was his verdict. "Soft from being under the hot sun."

"That's what I thought." I turned back to where I'd been sitting. To one side was a slightly darker spot, maybe one inch round, with my pinkie print in it. Hardened dribbles of pastel pink clung to the front of that same brick. "Look at this. Whoever set off the firecrackers must have used a candle."

"Maybe." He drew out the word, unconvinced. I wasn't convinced either. Real men, I felt sure, would gravitate toward Zippo lighters, or whatever lit tobacco products happened to be hanging from their mouths at the time. Real kids emulating real men wouldn't use candles either. Besides, why bother? Other than the extra bit of distance a candle might provide. A safety feature real men would scoff at.

Hugh held his hand out to me. "We ought to get back. Miss Maggie'll be worried."

There were more casings to pick up, but I agreed about Miss Maggie being worried. So I put my hand in his and we walked back to the house.

Miss Maggie was where I'd left her, with Emmy at her side.

We reported what we'd found—next to nothing, as Hugh put it—and Miss Maggie let out a gargantuan sigh of relief.

"No harm done," I assured her. "Let's eat before the veggies and fruit get dried out." No one objected.

Emmy ran upstairs to wash up and change her sweaty T-shirt while the rest of us set the table and filled glasses with iced tea. She came down just as I placed the salmon beside Hugh's vegetable arrangement.

Emmy's expression was grim. "Guess what I found behind the shower curtain in the bathtub? Theo's gym bag. Unzipped, with the contents all jumbled. I know Theo refolded everything yesterday after the police were through."

"Sounds like we had a thief among our guests today," Miss Maggie said. "Pat, let's check our pocketbooks."

I followed her down the hall. Our handbags were still on the hall table and after a quick inspection, we decided nothing was missing. Or even disturbed.

"Must have happened before Pat and I got home," Miss Maggie deduced.

Hugh, meantime, had examined the desk drawer in the war room where he'd placed the Bell Foundation checks and came back to the hall a moment later. "I'm pretty sure they're all there."

Other than the TV, VCR, computer, and kitchen appliances—all of which a burglar couldn't have gotten out of the house with so many people around, we had nothing else worth stealing.

Emmy double-checked her stuff upstairs. "My purse is still on the bureau in the middle room, untouched. I think the thief only rummaged through Theo's bag."

"Maybe he was interrupted," I suggested.

"*Or,*" Miss Maggie said, "he was after something he knew—or thought—Theo had. Emmy, do you know if anything's missing from Theo's stuff?"

She shook her head. "I assume he has his wallet on him."

"Must have," I said. "He left gas money in the car. And he

had his cell phone, too. Maybe the person was after something that had to do with the murders—something incriminating that Theo had, but . . . but didn't know he had."

Emmy raised her eyebrows. "Who was here this afternoon who has a connection with any of the killings?"

I looked at Miss Maggie. "One of the Protectors?"

"A few of them were here," she replied. "They're all politically active and they're supporting J. D. in this election—mainly because they don't cotton to women holding public office."

"Hold on," Hugh said, butting in. "Are you forgetting our little pyrotechnic display? We all ran out of the house, remember? Anyone could have waltzed in the front door, gone upstairs, rummaged though Theo's bag, and left long before we came back inside."

17

We finally sat down to supper, after closing and locking the front door so we'd all feel a tad more secure while we ate and discussed recent developments.

"If Hugh's right," Miss Maggie mused, poking the air with a carrot stick, "could one person have lit the firecrackers *and* entered the house?"

"He'd have to be fast." Hugh had loaded his plate with a half dozen of each vegetable and a handful of Melba toast, and was arranging them as if the dish were an artist's palette. "He didn't take the most direct trail from the ruin to the house because *we* went that way. The next shortest route would be out to the office-complex parking lot, then down your drive."

Miss Maggie frowned as she dunked her carrot in the salmon goop. "I think Emmy and I would have seen someone coming from the parking lot. The post-office trail or front drive is more likely."

Emmy was meticulously spooning dip into a celery rut and spoke without looking up. "Pat and I were on the drive when we heard the bang, but I suppose someone could have been just around the bend, hoping we'd run toward the house, which we did."

The notion of a possible killer coming that close to us, not to mention creeping around our house afterward, made me reach for my fifth cracker. I'd get to the vegetables eventually, I assured my inner mom, after one more piece of starchy, crumbly comfort food to calm my nerves. I was craving salt, too, but with Miss Maggie's heart, all we kept around the house were rye Melba toast and low-sodium Triscuits.

"Either way," Hugh said, stacking up a Dagwood mini-sandwich between Melba toast slices, "one person couldn't have covered that much ground, even if he drove around from the parking lot to Bell Run Road. We're talking at least two people."

At least? I pictured us under siege, with a Protector behind every one of Bell Run's trees.

"Regardless how it was done," Miss Maggie said, "what were they after?"

We all munched in silence, stumped.

"What it *couldn't* be," Hugh said, eyeing his completed three-inch-tall sandwich, unsure how to eat it, "is evidence obviously related to the murders. The police would have taken anything like that away yesterday."

"It wouldn't be *obvious*," I said, resisting the temptation to, ala Beth Ann, use a "duh" for punctuation. "More like . . . you know how in spy movies, the bad guys are always after a micro-chip under the stamp on a crinkled envelope carried around by somebody clueless—like Jimmy Stewart?"

Hugh treated me to a patronizing smile. "I doubt spies, mi-crochips, and Jimmy Stewart have anything to do with this."

"What Pat's meant," Miss Maggie said, "was that Theo had something ordinary with him—something the police would over-look but that perhaps incriminates the killer."

"Right. And I don't hear you coming up with anything better, zucchini-boy." I swiped a slice of that particular veggie from the stockpile on his plate, but didn't get the chance to harass him further because the phone rang. "Save me some of the red pep-pers," I said as I headed for the war room.

Lynn Casey and, as usual, she didn't say hello or identify

herself. "Tell Magnolia I'll be right over to take those publicity photos for her."

I supposed that by now she'd heard about this afternoon's murder and Theo being AWOL. Probably wanted to interrogate us for yet another article. I was going to tell her that we'd already had a photographer out here this afternoon, then remembered that J. D. and/or Cora would be in all of those pictures, except for the one of me looking like a hunted rabbit. Maybe we could get a few posed shots sans politicians without telling her too much. "All right, but give us a half hour. We're eating dinner right now—"

"The sunlight won't wait. See you in ten minutes." She hung up before I could get another word in.

Back in the kitchen, the elves had been busy. On my plate were the last five slices of bell pepper, each with a generous dollop of dip (the bowl was now empty) and a circle of zucchini stuck in the center. I downed one canapé before passing on Lynn's message, then explained about her freelance work.

"For the *Register*, you say?" Miss Maggie frowned. "If she asks questions, let me do the talking. But I am glad you told her to come, Pat. You finish eating while we clean up. We'll have our dessert afterwards."

Hugh carried empty plates to the sink, then hastily excused himself. Time for more makeup, no doubt.

Eleven minutes later—after we'd all made ourselves more presentable—we reconvened in the side yard, just as the red pickup came up the drive. Lynn pulled over onto the grass and disembarked, her long hair pulled up into pigtails on top of her head and the tails of a sleeveless white blouse tied into a knot above her navel, though the effect was definitely *not* Maryann-from-*Gilligan's-Island*. I caught Hugh gawking at her legs, but instead of assuming an attitude of proper guilt, he grinned wickedly at me, wiggled his eyebrows, and went to help Lynn carry her camera bag, which was heavy enough that its wide nylon straps were strained to the max.

Miss Maggie gave Lynn a quick rundown of what we needed and how much our budget could stand.

"One Econo-Special coming right up," Lynn said as she scanned the house, forest, and last bit of sun, now stretching shadows of the back porch railing across to the very edge of the clearing. I got the feeling, as she scrunched up her nose in distaste, that the sunlight hadn't waited as long as she thought it would. She pointed a finger at Yorick's tent. "That has to go. And the tarp, of course."

While Miss Maggie and Emmy removed the latter, Lynn pitched in to help Hugh and me with the tent, during which she let drop that she was divorced and managed to glean from him his widower status.

I told myself that I wasn't jealous. Not in the least. Though I was awfully glad when Lynn at last took up her camera and got to work. And I had to admit (not grudgingly, of course, because that would imply that I'd been jealous and no way was I jealous)—that I was impressed by her expertise. Not that I know a thing about photography outside of the fuzzy, red-eyed shots my dad occasionally let me take with his Polaroid while I was growing up. But the way Lynn set up each photo—fully aware of her background, testing various angles, knowing when she needed extra light and from what direction (she had two nifty remote-control flashes that looked very sci-fi)—I labeled her an honest-to-goodness artist. And she obviously loved how she made her living, which made me drool with envy.

Envy, mind you. Not jealousy.

"Let me get one of all of you," Lynn suggested. "You'll want it for the Foundation archives."

So we gathered behind Yorick's hole, Hugh behind Emmy, me peeking over Miss Maggie's shoulder in a vain attempt (in more ways than one) to hide the Montella cellulite on my legs.

Lynn snapped three of that pose but didn't seem satisfied. "You should have a shot of the whole site, too. Maybe I could get it from one of your second-floor windows."

Miss Maggie agreed. "Pat'll take you upstairs."

"No, I want you all in this one." She had us each stand behind a different dug-up pit, with Miss Maggie center stage behind Yorick.

As Lynn took her Minolta and tripod inside to find a vantage point, it occurred to me that our pose was disturbingly reminiscent of the players on Mance's giant chessboard in my dream. Or worse yet, the ultra-hokey cover photos on Dawkins-Greenway annual reports.

Apparently our tableau looked lousy from the bathroom window, because Lynn—after moving the previous night's barricades out of the way, raising the screen, clearing off the sill, and setting up her tripod while we waited in place—called down, "Changed my mind. Just Magnolia." Which restored my faith in our photographer's aesthetic judgment.

When Lynn returned to the side yard, Miss Maggie thanked her, then echoed my thoughts. "Very impressive. Did you study photography privately with someone, Lynn? Or major in it in college?"

"I took a class in it," she replied, squatting down to repack her camera bag, "but I'm pretty much self-taught."

"You mean you weren't even an art major? You know so much about composition."

Surprisingly, Lynn blushed, pleased at the praise, but she kept her satirical smile firmly in place. "Political science major. Taught me how to put a good spin on what I see through the lens."

Miss Maggie raised her eyebrows. "I wouldn't have pegged you for political science. What school?"

Lynn zipped up her bag and stood before she answered, almost as if she couldn't decide what to say. In the end, though, she lightly tossed out, "UVA," then hastily changed the subject by saying, "I called the *Register*."

Here it comes, I thought. The third degree.

But Lynn merely said, "They're running an item in tomorrow's paper—about a fundraiser you had here today?"

"Impromptu," Miss Maggie said, "or I would have given you dibs, since you offered first. Though I expect that article will actually be more about the Apperson–Stevens race than us."

"Which explains why the *Register* wants a follow-up piece specifically about the Bell Foundation, for Monday's edition. If you can give me a press release or data sheet, I'll write something up to go with the photos."

I was about to say we had just such a thing in our computer— we'd created a summary of our purpose and goals for grant applications. Before I could offer to go print out a copy, Miss Maggie broke in with, "We'll bring it by your studio tomorrow morning."

"No. I'll come out to pick it up."

"Don't bother. Pat and I need to stop by the Historical Society anyway."

News to me—and I was surprised the Society would be open on a holiday—but I said nothing and everything was settled. Hugh carried Lynn's camera bag back to her truck for her (not that she asked him to) and she drove off, without one question about Theo or the murders. Maybe she'd already gotten the scoop elsewhere.

Since we had Yorick's pit open anyway, we decided to push off dessert an hour or two and get in some work in the cool (relatively speaking) of the evening. Miss Maggie went to change out of her sundress and I retrieved my work boots from the front hall.

Outside, I noticed for the first time just how much Hugh and Emmy had gotten done today before the hoards showed up. Pits one through four resembled a ten-foot square, one-foot deep, empty wading pool. Around the edges of its floor, the soil was reddish now instead of grayish—meaning the plow layer had been removed, except for a darker oblong in the center, not quite six by three feet. That, Emmy explained, was where someone had dug a hole and refilled it, mixing plow layer with subsoil. Since the oblong was about the right size for a grave, it bolstered our theories that a full skeleton lurked beneath the dirt here.

"We'll call this big spot Feature Number One," Emmy said, "and we'll excavate it three inches at a time, with trowels only. I'll take the head in pit one. Hugh, take the middle in pit two. Pat, you've got the feet. Magnolia, sifting duty. Go slowly and keep everything that's not dirt. Even stones until I can look at them."

She gave us small wooden stakes, three inches long and a half-inch in diameter, and showed us how to hammer them into the ground every six inches around the perimeter, until their tops were level with the floor of the pit. Using our trowels, we scraped away the soil between the stakes, working our way down the length of them. My imagination had us uncovering tomb artifacts on par with King Tut, but actually, we found nothing but splinters of burned wood and pockets of ash.

That was enough to excite Emmy, though. "This means there was a fire upwind of here not long before this person was buried. Certainly before another plowing was done, and before enough rain fell or wind blew to wash or blow this ash away. So our building fire over yonder can probably be dated by this grave and vice versa. This person may have even died in that fire. If any of the bones are charred, we'll know for sure."

Citing the firecracker incident, Hugh declared his intention of staying over again. I wondered if he was simply avoiding a night in a lonely trailer. His home might be small, but probably seemed pretty empty without Beth Ann there. Come to think of it, all of

Bell Run seemed subdued this week without her adolescent exuberance/hormonal mood swings.

Twilight was well underway by the time we all settled in the war room with our fruit, dip, another TV baseball game, and our various chores. Emily cleaned and sorted artifacts. Miss Maggie and I agreed that we needed to get thank-you notes out to all of this afternoon's donors. I got to work on the big PC, creating a mailing list for all the checks we'd received, while she snuggled into the tartan recliner—fruit and dip within arm's reach—and composed the mail-merge letter on her laptop.

Hugh split his time between making up a ledger of who gave what, running to and from the basement where he was doing a load of laundry, and scratching his legs while blaspheming my makeup. "I swear this stuff's giving me hives."

"Just pimples," I said. "Happens when you keep your pores clogged up all day."

"How do you women stand it?"

"Easy. We're the stronger sex." Actually, since leaving my job, I hadn't used makeup at all. I hated the way it felt on my face almost as much as I hated the way pantyhose felt on my legs. The same way I hated how high heels felt on my feet. With a noble lift of my chin, I decided, then and there, never again to be a slave to society's dumb fashion conventions.

On the other hand, was plain old unadorned me enough to attract Hugh's interest? Lynn wore makeup. Of course, she was also tall and svelte and oozing all the right pheromones. The flaw in my patience plan, I noted, was that it didn't take competition into account.

Before thoughts like that depressed me further, I started removing and sorting the checks in the desk drawer. Beneath them I found J. D.'s voter-registration form. "Who put this in here?" I said, holding it up.

"I did," Hugh said. "Cora brought it over for you today."

"You mean, now I've got two? Gee, back in Pennsylvania, they only ever let a person register once. Unless you're one of the 'vote early and often' crowd."

"Oh, we've always been progressive here in Virginia." Miss Maggie grinned mischievously as she seized the biggest strawberry on the plate and dunked it in the Fluff dip. "Put different names on each form and—"

Hugh shook his head. "She'd never get away with it. You still have to list a residence, and everyone in the county knows who lives here."

Miss Maggie chomped on her strawberry while she considered the problem. "She could put down an address in one of the developments, with a P.O. box for mail. Wouldn't have to be in a separate polling district, because the bogus voter could always cast an absentee ballot."

"Not that I want to spoil your plans, Miss Maggie," I said, "but I have yet to meet a politician in Virginia—or anywhere else, for that matter—who I'd *want* to vote for more than once."

"You're missing the point, Pat," she said, licking her fingertips. "We're talking corrupt politics here. *Want* has nothing to do with it. You'd sell that extra vote to the highest bidder."

"I suppose that would solve my job dilemma."

"Could be a whole new career for you." She couldn't hold back her mirth any longer and out came a loud cackle, which made the rest of us laugh along with her.

The remainder of the evening was much of the same type of banter, except when Hugh was cussing out the Braves again, or when I did likewise to the mail-merge program when it froze up the PC. There seemed to be an unspoken agreement that we needed a break from death and evil. Emmy was quiet all evening and retired early. Hugh stayed up just long enough after the game (final score: Braves, 2; Mets, 9) to catch the local forecast on the Weather Channel. Tomorrow would be a whole two or three degrees cooler. Chance of late-afternoon thunderstorms. They'd been saying that all week. What a tease.

I told Miss Maggie not to wait up. Although I knew the letters wouldn't see the inside of a mail truck until Monday, I figured I'd finish stuffing and sealing the envelopes before turning in. I felt restless. The day had been too long, with too many upsets. And too much marshmallow Fluff too close to bedtime.

But even after the letters were neatly stacked on the front hall table and I'd done a tour of the first floor, making sure everything was locked up, I was still too antsy to climb the stairs. I'd disturb the sleepers the way a breeze couldn't help waving a flag.

So I decided to try my regular nightly routine downstairs. By the dim light of only a small, shaded table lamp in the hall, I went back into the war room, wheeled the desk chair over to one of the front windows, raised the blind and sash, and sat down.

Not much of a view, given the porch and magnolia tree. A side window would have provided a less-obstructed vista, I know, but then I'd be overlooking the dig site—and Yorick's grave. I needed to relax, not be creeped out.

Then again, I couldn't see much anyway. No moon tonight. Or at least, if the moon was out, it was hiding behind a thick haze. I thought I could make out the drive, but that may have been more memory than optic nerve. The forest was the sort of absolute black that seemed to press against my eyeballs, making me blink and squint as much as bright sunlight.

So I used my other senses to explore. I breathed in the scent of the freshly turned earth from the side yard. Gardens smell like that, I reminded myself, when my imagination invoked open cemetery plots. Tonight, the air was still, too damp to move around, just shy of being a mist. Sticky against my skin. And, hearing-wise, the crickets were hosting a full-volume sing-along, with extra cicadas warming up in the wings.

I slouched down in the chair, closed my eyes, and let the forest harmonies wash over me, recalling similar sounds only two nights ago—before I'd heard about Wyatt Avery. Then I played back the beauty of Theo's song: *Sometimes I feel like a mourning dove....* Listening to that mental lullaby, my mind drifted into a half-sleep, floating on the docile roll of the melody, filling in my own words:

> *"Spread my wings and fly, fly, fly,*
> *Spread my wings and fly, fly."*

Suddenly I was wide awake, sitting upright. I could have sworn my mind hadn't concocted those lyrics, but that I'd *heard* them, in a faint but clear baritone. I strained my ears to listen, wishing for once that Bell Run's creatures would shut up.

Nothing but bug sounds. No singing. My imagination again.

Or—had it been another Mance dream? Another waking vision? Had I actually been asleep or not? I didn't know.

I gazed through the screen into the blackness. Was Mance out there waiting for me tonight? *Something* was, I was sure—if not Mance, then a slice of his past. Waiting for me. Waiting there all along, since I'd first glimpsed the cabins on the creekbank. Waiting tolerantly, politely, since my first impatient, self-centered, can't-you-see-I'm-too-busy-for-this reaction. Waiting silently, timidly—exactly the way a black person from 1870's Virginia would wait to speak with a white stranger.

Prejudice popped up in odd places. Here I'd been stereotyping ghosts, figuring they were all alike. *"Stupido,"* I called myself. Then, by way of apology, I closed my eyes again and, in a voice that more resembled my mother's than my own, I murmured, "I'll listen. Talk to me."

On the soles of my bare feet, I felt fine dry dirt, and wooden planks, worn to a silky smoothness where they weren't rough from rot or missing altogether. Dim moonlight poked through clouds. I saw a road, with rolling farmland on one side and a grassy slope dotted with scrubby thickets on the other. The shape of the land was familiar—I identified it as Route 3, less than a mile west of the Bell Run turnoff.

I wasn't alone. Looking up, I saw the profile of a face, thin and haggard, partially shrouded by blond hair and a mustache, both in need of a trim. His eyes shifted constantly, nervously, from the ground to sidelong glances at me, to quick looks over his shoulder or ahead. But those eyes were familiar, too—add a green spark to them, plug them into a ninety-one-year-old skull and, poof: Miss Maggie.

Looking at that face—looking out from someone else's eyes— brought a stampede of emotions: compassion, sorrow, anxiety, anguish, and an odd fusion of hatred and charity. Most of all, I felt fear—fear that fed on itself so that I could see no escape. How could I call myself free when I felt trapped?

DEATH WENT OUT TO THE SINNER'S HOUSE

Sunday morning, our citizens were shocked and disgusted by an exhibition John Scott . . . made on himself by escorting a negro girl down New Street.
—FROM *THE VALLEY VIRGINIAN*, APRIL 4, 1866

July 3, 1871—Freedom Holler

Like I say before, when Mama be coming home late, if the weather oblige, I climb the hill to watch for her. When I see her walking up the road from town, I sneak back to my pallet and pretend to sleep 'til I hear her come in.

The clouds held their rain all the rest of that day so, soon as our cabin circle be dark and quiet, I head up the hill as usual, like I be going to the outhouse, 'case anyone see me.

The moon be a fat half-wheel, working its slow way 'cross the sky toward Stoke, seeming to elbow the clouds out of its path as it go. That's how, when I got to my lookout, I could make out Mama's shape already coming up the road, and close, too—not more than half a furlong distant from my perch. 'Stead of going back to the cabin, though, I watched her, 'cause somebody be with her, a-hobbling in such a way that I knowed him for Caleb Fletcher.

Mama be walking fast and, by how she look around, I could tell she be scared. She don't seem scared of Mr.

Fletcher, though, 'cause when she ain't looking around, she be facing him and talking, and her manner be just like when she be telling me I can't do what I want. That make me curious. Black folk plain don't tell white folk what they can and can't do. Not ever.

On the slope below me, the grass be growed up high as my legs, and here and there be pricker bushes, big enough for me to hide behind. I figure I can make my way down nearer the road—maybe hear what Mama be saying as she walk by—and still have time to get back to the cabin 'fore she does.

So that's what I do, all crouched down so the grass hide me, and it work better than I 'spect, 'cause Mama stop in her tracks almost right below me and say, "Listen. Someone be up there."

I duck my head down quick, listening myself, but they stay where they be and Mr. Fletcher say, "It's nothing. An animal."

"You best leave me here. I'm obliged to you for seeing me home safe, Missuh Fletcher, but I got to go the rest of the way by myself, 'fore someone see us together."

"If what you told me about the church fire is true, you might still run into danger up ahead. I wish you and Mance weren't living out here, so far from town, Miss Jackson—"

"No, not 'Miz Jackson,'" Mama hiss, halfway 'tween angry and begging. "I ain't your equal. I'm your colored washerwoman, that's all. You call me 'Alma,' jes' like you did before the war. Jes' like all the other white folk call me."

Mr. Fletcher made a sound that could've been a grunt or a laugh, or both. "They call you worse than 'Alma.' I'm not like them. You're no longer a slave and I won't treat you—"

"Ain't I? Jes' 'cause no man can say he own me

like he do his horse don't mean I'm done being a slave. I got five masters now, 'stead o' one, and not one of them pays me what colored men get for less work, not even Missuh Reynolds, who pay the colored more'n anyone. What good be freedom if I can't give my son shoes again this winter?"

I heared Mama say words like that before, but I ain't never hear her so riled, even when she been complaining with Ida and Hattie and no men around. And she ain't never raised her voice to a white man like she doing now.

"You say we ought not be living out here," Mama go on, "but if the folks in the Holler didn't share what all they got, Mance and I be surely starved dead by now. Ain't a body in Stoke gonna hold out a hand to us that way."

"I would," Mr. Fletcher say, so soft I barely hear him. "I know I don't have much, but you and Mance could live in my back room, at least until the sheriff finds out who lit that fire—"

"In your back room?" Mama say, all wary like his words be a rabbit snare. "You looking to make me housekeeper of that big palace of yours, Caleb Fletcher? Or you got some other job in mind for me?"

"I wouldn't lay a hand on you, Alma, I swear. You know I haven't had drink in me these last two years, and I won't touch spirits ever again, I promise you. Let me put right some of the wrongs I've done. I could teach Mance how to clerk in a shop—or even how to be a pharmacist's assistant. Be a better life for him than working in fields."

Mama didn't answer that, and the fear hit me strong that she be weighing his offer. Without thinking at all, I go running toward her, yelling, "No, Mama, no. We can't leave here. I don't want to be no white man's clerk. Tell him no—"

She catch me by the shoulders and, looking back on it, I think she be too stunned right off to speak. But then she shake me hard, saying, "Hush, Mance! Hush, you hear me? You'll wake up everybody in the holler," and her tone be so urgent—just like it be when we meet Charlie Harris today—that I quick close my mouth and clung to her skirt.

To Mr. Fletcher, she say, "Get going. Run. 'Fore one of our men catch you here."

He already be backing away down the road. "Think about what I said, Alma. It's not safe here."

Mama shooed me off the planks, into the half-shadows of the thickets, then took me by the hand and pull me fast after her 'til we be under the trees near the path along the creek. That's when she stop and let her anger out. "What you doing out here this hour, Emancipation Jackson?"

I tell her how I was just watching for her—how I do that most nights that she work late 'cause I can't sleep lest I know when she be home. "We ain't gonna live in Stoke, are we, Mama?"

She sigh at that. "You seen what Stoke be like today, Mance. We can't live there."

"Then why's Mr. Fletcher say his house be safer than ours?"

Mama tug my hand to start me walking again—walking fast, like she ain't forgot 'bout being mad at me—and she don't answer 'til we be out on the path. "Caleb Fletcher think he can protect us is all. He think the Klan won't ride in town, and he think all the white folk gonna respect his servants, like they do Colonel Gilbert's. He don't see that all those folk be respecting is the Colonel's money. When a poor man put a colored woman under his roof, no one gonna believe she be there to do cleaning."

Thinking on that, I got a cold feeling in my gut. "Was he lying, Mama? Was Mr. Fletcher lying when he swore he wouldn't touch you?"

She sigh again and slow her stride. "No, Mance. He meant it. Caleb . . . well . . .'fore the war, he be a sinful man—sinful 'cause he be drunk all the time and liquor bring out the evil in most men. Now he know his soul need mending. You and me jest his project to keep hisself out o' hell." Her voice ain't riled no more, but her words come out harsh as lye soap. "And he too full o' his own virtue to see how folks'll talk."

Then she stop and look out on the crickwater beside us, all shimmery in the moonlight. "Missuh Norton been asking me, since spring planting, when you gonna come work in his fields. I been putting him off, hoping to find you other work. You can read some, better even than the Norton boys, and you got a sharp mind. Shouldn't ought to waste your thinking doing hard labor your whole life."

"Mama, if I go be a field hand, will we have enough money that you don't got to work at night no more?"

I see her mouth turn up into a smile. "No, Mance. They pay chil'un less'n women. Truth to tell, I been looking for more washing jobs, so I may end up working some other nights—"

"No, Mama—"

"Listen," she say, gentle-like, bending over to look me in the face. "Miz Reynolds tell me jes' today that she find out your brother James be sold again a year after Missuh Travis take him from me. That second master be down near Charlottesville, she think, and most his slaves still be working for him. When we got some money saved, Mance, we got to find James. If he be in a nice place, we all can live there. If not, I want to move up north—someplace you can learn a trade without white folk saying you can't."

She put her arm 'round my shoulders and we start in to walk again while I think on her words, but right away we hear voices ahead on the path. Loud voices, so it be easy to recognize them as coming from Noah, Amos, Moses and some o' the other menfolk.

They come toward us, walking fast, and soon we see they carrying shovels and buckets. When they see us, Noah slow down jes' long enough to explain, "Fire at Congressman Reynolds's place. Moses seen it from the hilltop."

18

I felt a queasy tightening of my stomach muscles, then the scene vanished and I was back in my chair. Before I opened my eyes, I was aware that my hand was being held, gently but firmly, as if perhaps I might need to pull myself up out of my (for want of a better word) trance.

Even if the bony joints weren't a clue, I knew the hand that held mine was Miss Maggie's. I opened my eyes and could just barely make out her silhouette standing beside me in the dark.

I gave her fingers a delicate squeeze. "I'm okay, Miss Maggie."

"If I thought you weren't, I'd have shaken you out of it two minutes ago when I found you here. What'd you see, Pat?"

"How late is it?" Yes, I was stalling—trying to decide what, if anything, I should tell her about her grandfather.

"Only about ten past midnight. Tell me what you saw, Pat, while it's fresh in your memory."

"I . . . it was like being shown a page of a story from the middle of a book, Miss Maggie. I don't—"

"That's what all history is. Don't try to make sense of it. Just give me the bare facts."

Facts? Not exactly the word I'd use in this situation. Still, I could tell Miss Maggie was getting impatient by how her grip had shrunk a centimeter in diameter—meant as encouragement, no doubt, but no longer cozy. So I haltingly related my experience.

Miss Maggie didn't let me get too far before she exclaimed, "Granddaddy? Escorting a black woman home?" Her tone was merely skeptical though, not outraged—questioning the historical accuracy of my yarn.

"He thought she was in danger. The church fire was set and he thought whoever did it might come back—"

"Doesn't matter." She let go of my hand and I heard her scratch her head. "A white man seen walking with a black woman . . . why, back then men were arrested for that in Virginia. In Stoke County, I suspect it was nearly a lynching offense. None of the whites would have cared if some racist was out terrorizing the blacks. Or if anyone did care, he'd keep quiet about it so as not to attract the attention of the Klan himself. What in the world was Granddaddy thinking?"

I told what Alma had said about Caleb trying to save his soul, adding, "Guilt can be a powerful motivator." The voice of experience—I'd been raised by an Italian mother, after all.

"Granddaddy was never much for religion," Miss Maggie murmured, as if picturing my reasoning on him and thinking it looked tight around the ego. "I suppose his conscience must have been bothering him. Only time he ever talked about what happened before the war was when he was warning us about the evils of drink. No details, though, just a lot of scary vagueness. Which worked for all of us except my brother Ed, who drank himself into an early grave. What else did you see?"

I told her the rest of it while Miss Maggie paced behind me. When I was done, she said, "You're right. A page from a book. There's a lot more to this story."

"I think she'll tell me more when she's ready."

The shuffling of Miss Maggie's footsteps stopped. *"She?"*

"That's what I should have realized this afternoon when I saw Mance fighting the fire. I was seeing him through someone else's eyes—someone he was glad to see. His mother. I'm pretty sure all my glimpses into the past this week have come from her."

"Maybe your dreams, too. We already know they've been full of symbolism—Mance might be just another symbol."

That disturbed me somehow. Mance was an innocent kid—sharing Dreamland with him was like visiting Aunt Lydia's when she was baby-sitting one of her grandchildren. Alma Jackson, on the other hand, came with a complex jumble of emotions fostered by a life of bondage and racial intolerance—emotions I'd only glimpsed tonight and couldn't pretend to fully understand. Did I want her fiddling around in my subconscious while I was most vulnerable? "What about Beth Ann's sightings of Mance?"

Miss Maggie placed her hands on my shoulders, making me jump. "A projection of his mother's memory, perhaps? What if Beth Ann only saw Mance in the evenings because that was when his mom remembered him best, after she came home from work each day."

Talking about ghosts in the dark right before bedtime was giving me the willies. Funny how my visions didn't spook me—not while they happened—but when I actually *thought* about them . . .

I let the weight of Miss Maggie's hands on my shoulders reassure me. "Time to go get some sleep." I meant her, of course—no way was I going to close my eyes tonight.

I woke up grinning. Yes, I'd slept, and well, too, after I got past that early stage of half-sleep where my brain hallucinated every object in the room into something sinister.

I was grinning because of a funny dream, though not a Mance dream, as I informed Miss Maggie, much to her disappointment. "I dreamt I was a spider. Not a real one—more like the kind in Garfield comics."

"Don't they always get squished?"

"Not this time. A big snake that had J. D.'s face was trying to eat me, but I outsmarted him and chopped him up like a stick of celery." Oh, I realized how Freud would have interpreted that symbolism. The dream had left me in too good a mood to care. I almost didn't mind being roused at seven-fifteen because we had volunteers showing up at eight.

We'd decided to take only half a holiday from the dig. For one thing, Hugh would be going back to work on Monday and Emmy wanted to use his brawn while she could. Plus four volunteers had offered to put in some morning hours before going off to picnics and pool parties.

Once everything was set up and Emmy had her workers sweating away, Miss Maggie said we should head into town, explaining, "I'd rather be absent from here this morning, while I know J. D. and Cora are busy with Stoke's Independence Day Parade. It doesn't actually start until ten, but I figure they'll be preening themselves in front of mirrors for a while beforehand."

As I waited for traffic at Route 3, I glanced down at my car radio. The clock read 8:44. "Is the Historical Society open this early?"

"Not open at all today," Miss Maggie said. "Got my own key. We'll have the place to ourselves."

Earlier, while I downed a bowl of Cheerios for breakfast, she and Emmy had discussed the possibility of finding some documented mention of the fire.

Emmy hadn't been optimistic. "Even if we're correct in dating the burial and fire to between 1864 and when your grandfather moved out here in 1875, that's still eleven years of newspapers to plow through, Magnolia."

Now, as we drove past the scene of my latest vision, Miss Maggie said, "Of course, we can't tell Emmy what you saw here last night."

"She'd think we're both nuts."

"Oh, I don't think so, but she needs to remain objective. And for the Bell Foundation to be taken seriously as a historic site, we need solid documented evidence. So, even though *we* know that the building was a church that burned a few nights before Congressman Reynolds was murdered—"

"What?!" Luckily, traffic was light enough that my momentary shock didn't result in more than a swerve on my part and one honked horn on the part of a Chevy Blazer. "I didn't hear anyone say he was murdered, only that there was a fire at his place."

"Octavius Reynolds was the first congressman for the thirteenth district after Virginia was readmitted to the union in 1870," Miss Maggie lectured, as if she expected me to let go of the wheel and take notes. "While he was serving his term, somebody murdered him and his whole family, then set his house on fire. I don't know the exact date, but that shouldn't be hard to find. So unless there was more than one fire at his place—"

"Who did it?" Somehow I was certain the same person had burned Mance's church, and I had this absurd feeling that, knowing who, I could stave off disaster.

"I don't think anyone was ever arrested for it, but everyone thought the Klan was responsible. Reynolds was black and—"

"Black?" I turned my car fan up a notch—the sun beating in through the rear window was heating up the car faster than the air conditioner was cooling it. "A black congressman? That soon after the war?"

Miss Maggie turned her air vents toward me. "Not surprising, really. At the time, something like forty-five percent of Virginia's voters were black, so naturally—"

"I thought blacks didn't get the vote until the twentieth century."

"When was the last time you read the Constitution, Pat?"

"The whole thing?" Actually, I couldn't remember ever reading it, but I knew parts of it. The preamble. I knew that. "We The People"—something.

"Remind me to print you out a copy when we get home."

Oh boy. I felt sure a quiz would follow.

For now, Miss Maggie gave me the Cliff Notes. "Article Fifteen, giving all men the right to vote regardless of race, was ratified early in 1870. That spring, the Force Acts were passed, saying the president could send in the military to enforce the amendment. But by the time Hayes got into office, some states had started making men pass literacy tests before they could register, while at the same time abolishing black schools. And they established poll taxes—unless you paid the tax, you weren't allowed to vote. Now this left out poor, uneducated whites, too, so they put in Grandfather Clauses, which said you could vote anyway, *if* your grandfather had been able to vote before the war."

"No president ever sent in the military?"

"Not only that, the Supreme Court upheld the state laws until 1962, when Congress finally passed Article Twenty-four, which said you couldn't keep anyone from voting in a federal election with any kind of tax. In 1965, the Voting Rights Act let the federal government take over voter registration."

"Took them long enough." I eased on my brake. Traffic was slowing up.

Miss Maggie agreed. "Of course, the other reason that men like Octavius Reynolds got into Congress was that former Confederate soldiers were required to take an oath of loyalty to America before they were allowed to vote again. Lots of them refused, decreasing the potential white voters. And the Fourteenth Amendment said no one who'd ever sworn to uphold the Constitution, then gone off to support the Insurrection, could ever hold office again, except by Act of Congress. That meant most of the South's former leaders couldn't run." She opened her window and looked out, around the brake lights in front of us. "They're detouring everyone because of the parade. Turn left at Elwood's road. I'll show you a back way."

When I was heading south, she resumed her lesson. "As I was saying, Reynolds was not only black, he'd married a white woman, which actually wasn't all that unusual. Poor white women didn't want the white men who'd lost everything in the war and were at the very bottom of the feeding chain. The richer white men wouldn't have them, so some of the poor women married black men who were better off. Turn right up here."

"Why wouldn't that have been as much a scandal as your grandfather walking a black woman home?"

"White men were supposed to behave differently. See the fork down at the bottom of the hill? Take the right branch." She waited until I'd done so. "Everyone figured blacks and women just didn't know any better. Double standard. Victorians were big on those. But, of course, none of the whites *liked* blacks and whites marrying and eventually Virginians passed a law prohibiting cohabitation. One man got around it by building his wife a separate house right beside his own. Keep going 'til the stop sign, then hang another right. That'll be Madison."

Ah, a street name I recognized—the other crosspiece of Stoke's main intersection. The southern end of Madison was lined with fat oak trees and, behind them, clapboard houses with porches, circa 1855 (per Miss Maggie—architecture-wise, I could tell a Greek temple from an igloo, but that was it). When this scenery gave way to older rowhouses and newer business buildings, she told me to find a parking spot.

I retrieved from the backseat two steno notebooks (with the press release info for Lynn folded inside one cover) and two mechanical pencils, and we walked the block and a half to Jefferson.

Catty-corner from there, in front of the Stoke Courthouse, a reviewing stand had been set up. Two women were taping red, white, and blue streamers to it while a young man tested a portable P.A. system, earning for himself the Most Prolonged and Piercing Feedback Award. A few parade-goers who'd already staked out shady vantage points with lawn chairs were holding their ears.

Miss Maggie led me around the corner onto Jefferson, past two neo-Williamsburg stores, to a graceful old brick house with half-circle transoms above the door and on the third-floor dormers. As we neared the door, I noticed letters carved into the bricks on either side, graffiti-like, but cut carefully in neat Times-Roman: "A.J.G. 63" and "P.W. NCar" and a few others so faint, I couldn't make them out.

Miss Maggie took advantage of a lull in the feedback to provide a footnote. "This place was used as a hospital after Chancellorsville and Wilderness. The soldiers chiseled their initials here and sometimes where they were from." She took a key chain from her shorts pocket. "Before the war, this was Bessie Morrow's Tavern, built in 1821. Stoke grew up around it."

The feedback resumed and we quickly let ourselves in. An old-building smell hit me—that unique bouquet created, I supposed, by the cool, damp atmosphere inside masonry walls mingling with aged wood and centuries of dust between the floorboards. Sunlight filtered in from the transom above, dimly illuminating a straight hallway which divided the downstairs in half. Display cases lined the walls, interrupted by two doorways on either side. The hallway ended in a U-shaped stairway with a landing at the back.

That's where Miss Maggie headed, saying, "This floor's a museum—the research areas are upstairs."

"What's this?" I asked, stopping before one tall display case. Inside hung a crystal egg—emerald green in color and long as a two-liter soda bottle—suspended from a fancy wrought-iron support, looking like a necklace pendant for King Kong. I didn't think I'd ever seen it before, but an oddly familiar feeling accompanied the sight of it.

Miss Maggie came to stand beside me. "That's Granddaddy's show globe. Pharmacists used to hang them in their shop windows to show medicine was available. Some independent drug stores still have them at their prescription counters. Granddaddy always put green water in the globe when the town was in good health. I remember the day he put red water in, back in 1918, after the first four people died of influenza. That was scary."

I did the math, figuring the man in my vision had been no more than thirty years old. Even so, he'd be in his seventies in 1918. "How long did your grandfather live, Miss Maggie?"

"He died the day after his ninety-third birthday. Nineteen thirty-eight. Come to think of it, that's the same year Mance died. *There's* an interesting coincidence for you."

I started walking toward the stairs again, not wanting to dwell on coincidences like that until I was back out in bright sunlight. "You come from a long-lived family."

She hooked her arm through mine and chuckled. "Now you know my secret. Pure genetics, and not clean living after all. I can go back to eating French fries and donuts."

"In your dreams."

Upstairs, the interior walls had been removed to make a large, cheery room. To one side were filing cabinets, drawers, book-shelves, and a card catalog. On the other side were long tables, a row of microfilm and fiche viewers, and a copier. In the center of the back wall, double glass doors led across an enclosed bridge to a new-looking, beige stucco addition, which Miss Maggie said contained the newspaper archives and Society offices.

"This area was set up, primarily, for genealogical research," she said, going over to the card catalog and sliding out the "R" drawer. "A good number of obits are on fiche. Reynolds ought to be there, since he was fairly prominent." She set the drawer on the closest table. "That's your job. Find his obit. Copy out what-ever looks important. After you get a date for his death, we can try the *Register* for the few days previous to see if there's a mention of the other fire."

Miss Maggie left me to it and shuffled off through the door to the addition. She returned, pushing a small library cart in front of her that carried a stack of maybe twenty newspapers. Set-tling herself at the table by the east window, she transferred her reading glasses from blouse breast pocket to nose, and began skimming through the papers.

My assignment wasn't all that difficult once I got the hang of the filing system. I had more trouble refreshing my memory on how a fiche viewer worked. The last time I'd operated one was back when I first started at Dawkins-Greenway, before PCs eliminated the need to store thick, eleven-by-seventeen mainframe reports. I kept forgetting that I had to move my hand *away* from the section I wanted to view—the exact opposite motion of a computer mouse.

But, at last, I read aloud, " 'Mr. Octavius Reynolds, a Negro who came to Stoke County from the North and who has for nearly one year been our Representative to Washington, was killed in the late hours of Monday last. Mrs. Reynolds and their four children also succumbed. The funeral will be held tomorrow morning at the Stoke African Church.' Four children. *Madonne*."

Miss Maggie came to look over my shoulder as I read. She tapped her finger to a date on the screen—July 6, 1871—which had been scribbled at the top of the clipping before it was fiched. "The day of the week'll be on the masthead for this issue, so we'll be able to tell what day 'Monday last' was. Anything before 1920 is on microfilm."

She showed me where to look—the reels were in flat drawers arranged chronologically. There were lots of gaps in the dates, but fortunately the last half of 1871 was present and accounted for. Then Miss Maggie had to show me how to thread and work a microfilm viewer before resuming her own project. Knowing now that the copies of the *Register* she scanned were post-1920, I asked what she was looking for.

"Anything about the Civil Rights protests in Charlottesville in the sixties. Theo's father in particular."

"Why? I mean, that can't possibly have anything to do with Wyatt's murder, could it?"

"I doubt it," she said distractedly, running a forefinger down one page and up another. "Did you find that issue yet?"

I took the hint and turned back to the film viewer. The *Register* was a daily then—Monday through Saturday—but each issue had no more than four pages. A moment later, I said, "July sixth was a Thursday. So Monday was the third." I got a chill down my spine as I realized my vision had occurred not only on the anniversary, but possibly at the exact time.

"Check that day and the Saturday before it." Miss Maggie closed the last newspaper, restacked them on the library cart and headed back to the addition. She was back two minutes later with another twenty or so *Registers*.

We each worked in silence for a while, me trying to dismiss my case of the willies as I browsed the cramped, small print for any reference to the church fire or the small ex-slave community at Bell Run. Miss Maggie was starting on her third stack of papers when I said, "Nothing. Should I get the reel with June on it?"

"First go forward a week from the third. Look for anything about the Reynolds' murders. That ties in somehow."

I found it under July Fourth. " 'It was reported to this office,' " I read aloud, " 'that the Octavius Reynolds family did not perish in the fire that consumed their home last night, but all had been smothered or strangled to death before the fire began, according to a witness who had gone into the burning house to save the occupants. The assassin is unknown at this printing, though Sheriff Cox told us that any rumors of the killer being a member of the Ku Klux Klan are entirely without foundation and, more likely, the slayings were done by a robber who set the fire to cover his escape—' "

"Sheriffs don't change much either," Miss Maggie said with a sigh.

"Wait, listen to this. 'We agree with Mr. Cox and would point out that, since most of the robbers in Stoke County these last years have turned out to be Freedmen, he need not look further than those coloreds living in the hollow east of the Reynolds' farm. A similar fire burned down their church Saturday night. As with the Reynolds' blaze, the flames were so intense, the glow could be seen from St. Anne's bell tower.' "

"Pay dirt," Miss Maggie exclaimed, thumping her palm onto the table for emphasis. "I have a copy of an old map at home showing where the Reynolds' place was—the first 'hollow' to the east is Bell Run. And if the fire was seen from Stoke, it had to have been on *top* of our hill, not down along the creek. Print it off, Pat. We'll show it to Emmy."

As the viewer was spitting out the page, Miss Maggie jumped to her feet. "Pat, come look at this." She spread the newspaper out flat on the table and pointed to a picture.

I went around behind her but, even before I got very close, I recognized two people in the photo. In the center was Theo's father, a younger version of the snapshot in Aunt Song's album. On either side of him, elbows linked as they marched down a street, were college students—some done up in the James Dean look, some in early hippie-chic. The other person I could identify was one of the latter, marching at Bea Clayborne's right hand, gazing at him as if he were a god. Her suede fringe and love beads hung perfectly from her tall, skinnier-but-still-svelte frame.

Lynn Casey.

Humble Yourself, the Bell's Done Rung

Hartwell Baker (colored) was assaulted by Patrick O'Nole who snapped a pistol at him several times, but as it did not explode he beat him with the butt of the pistol. Taken before a magistrate O'Nole was fined $1.

—Thomas P. Jackson, agent for
the Freedman's Bureau, 1867

July 4, 1871—Freedom Holler

"We *caught* him," I hear Noah saying, quiet but all disgusted, just as I be waking up. "Caught Caleb Fletcher, guilty as you please, coming out of the Reynolds' upstairs window—fixing on climbing down their big chestnut tree to make his escape—and when the sheriff come along, what's he do? Arrest Caleb? No, he don't."

I been sleeping on the floor in the Putnam's cabin, where all us young'uns was told to stay with Jordana and Uncle Henry while the rest of the growed-ups went to see what they could do to help the Reynolds. Every other child still be asleep—Uncle Henry, too, over on a pallet by the hearth—but I be closest to the open door. Jordana brushing past to go out be enough to rouse me. I peek 'round the door post. In the moonlight, look like most all the growed-ups—and Zeb Jackson with 'em—be standing out by the kraal, talking in whispers.

"Don't be a fool, Noah," Mama say. "If Missuh Fletcher done it, would he be telling the sheriff those folks was dead 'fore the fire start? We'd all be assuming they died in the fire, wouldn't we?"

"Mebbe they did," say Zeb. "Mebbe Caleb only say that 'cause he light that blaze hisself and *that's* what killed those folk."

"Jes' like Caleb burnt down our church Saturday night," Noah add. "Mance tell me today that, soon as the fire catch the other night, he smelled Uncle Henry's liniment. Now who else but Caleb could make up some of that potion and who else know how quick it take a flame?"

"Uncle Henry musta spilt it himself," Mama argue and Jordana agree, saying, "His bottle sure got empty in a hurry."

Ida shook her head. "We woulda all smelled it at supper, or when Moses was giving us our lesson after."

"I got to the Reynolds 'fore you all tonight," Zeb drawl out, taking a pause to spit down between his feet, "and Dinah, their housekeeper, tell me she got a whiff of something sweet right as she saw the flames in their front hall and run out the back."

I was wondering what Zeb be doing away from town so late, but Noah only say, "See, that prove Caleb be the one, 'less you thinking Uncle Henry carry his new batch of liniment down to the Reynolds and spill it there, too."

Mama turn to Hattie. "Is that bottle in Uncle Henry's room now?"

Jordana answer, "It be on the table right inside the cabin door. We mixed up some at supper and rub it on him after. What you thinking, Alma?"

Mama already be going 'round the kraal toward the Darden's cabin, and everybody forget 'bout whispering and call after her 'til Jordana shush them, saying they'd wake the babies. She mean all us chil'en, though only Adam Putnam be young enough for a baby.

Mama come out Hattie's door with the bottle we got at Mr. Fletcher's, and she hold it up to the moonlight, then shake it up next to her ear. She put the bottle in the cabin again and walk back, sounding puzzled as she say, "The bottle still be there, and near full, too."

"Well, what'd you 'spect?" Noah ask and most all echo him.

Amos spoke up for the first time. "You think Caleb be that fifth man come up here last time?" and Noah say it look that way.

"Sound to me—" Zeb give a low laugh as he talk, "—like it be fitting for ol' Caleb to meet up with those same ghosts what sent Jack Soyers packing to the Devil."

"No!" Mama cry, and all the other women protest along with her, saying the men is sure to get caught.

"One more white man get killed out this way," Jordana warn, "and Sheriff Cox'd string up the lot of you without waiting for a trial."

"Zeb ain't talking about killing," Noah say. "Jes' scare him some. Teach him a good lesson. Like we meant to scare Soyers. Ain't our fault his horse threw him right on his head. We all agreed last night that we didn't want no more killing. Tell them, Moses."

The preacher answer, his voice so soft I couldn't make out the words 'til everybody quiet their murmuring to hear him out. "Let's all get some sleep now. We'll decide what to do tomorrow."

19

"You knew." I sat in the closest chair, my brain more able to see connections when my knees were bent. "You knew last night when you asked Lynn where she'd gone to college."

Miss Maggie beamed. "I began to wonder about her ties to Beatitudes after she called on Thursday, when you said she asked about Theo's father and then acted like she was avoiding Theo."

"Yes, but when she said she was writing an article about Wyatt's murder—"

"Exactly. Lynn's a crime-scene photographer, Pat. She wouldn't be allowed to cover police stories. Conflict of interest."

"So she *was* avoiding Theo. Why? He couldn't possibly remember her. He was too young." I leaned forward to look at the newspaper's date. October 17, 1967.

"Just a toddler. But there's more to it, Pat. Read the caption."

Since I was still leaning forward, the print was easy to bring into focus. The caption named those in the photo. "No Lynn Caseys. No Lynns at all," I said excitedly, as my imagination toggled between putting her in the Witness Protection Program and making her a New-Age James Bond.

Miss Maggie, knowing I get carried away, underlined one name in the caption with an arthritic forefinger. "Her name was Jackie Turenne. 'Lynn' is probably short for Jacquelyn. And maybe she's been married since."

"She's divorced." But before I could be disappointed by her

conventional reasoning, I got excited again. "*Jackie!* That's who Theo's father said he saw yesterday."

She nodded. Her point all along. "He said that Jackie was with Duke. Think about that."

I felt my eyes stretch wide open. "You think Lynn was with Theo when he parked Uncle Charles's car."

"Explains how he got away, if she gave him a lift in her truck."

"Gave him a lift *where*? Do you think she's hiding him?"

"Why do you think I wanted an excuse to stop by her studio today?" Miss Maggie said. "Let's go ask her."

Easier said than done. By the time we'd put the Historical Society back the way we'd found it and locked the front door behind us, the parade had begun. Stoke's a small town, but when even fifty percent of its citizens decide to converge on one street, the sidewalks can be nearly as congested as downtown Philly right before Christmas. I couldn't see Jefferson Street, though I could hear a marching band going by, playing "Louie, Louie"—a spirited if anemic rendition. Half the brass section must have gone on vacation this week.

Miss Maggie and I politely muscled our way down the two blocks toward Lynn's studio, trying to avoid collisions with cotton-candy eaters. Everyone knew Miss Maggie, so she exchanged pleasantries as we went.

When we came to the County Cafe—open and doing a bang-up soda and bottled-water trade today—I wondered how we'd get across the street. Silly me. Miss Maggie grabbed my hand, squeezed through the multitudes, who amiably parted before her as soon as they got a glimpse of who was jostling them. Ten feet out from the curb, she waited for a strategic break in the parade. Three massive fire engines were rolling past, so I wholeheartedly approved of her discretion.

Now that I could see it, the parade made me a little homesick. Like my hometown, there was nothing glitzy here—no floats, no giant balloons, no piped-in music or choreography. Just scout troops, high-school bands, veterans, every vehicle in the county with a siren or National Guardsman at the wheel, and all the local bigshots, sporting Styrofoam-straw hats and being chauffeured in shined-up convertibles with American flags duct-taped to the fenders.

Before I could get too nostalgic, Miss Maggie was hurrying me across the macadam in front of a troupe of young baton twirlers. Back home, the mothers carrying the banner probably would have uttered a few choice words concerning our rudeness. Here, they both smiled and asked Miz Shelby how she was.

While Miss Maggie was saying howdy, I glanced ahead, figuring one of us ought to be watching where we were going. That's when I saw Sergeant Ross standing up on Lynn Casey's top step, scowling down at us over the heads of the onlookers.

Miss Maggie saw him the next instant, as well as the trooper who stood behind him in the studio's open doorway. "*That* can't be a good omen. Come on, Pat." She doubled her pace and the crowd made way for us in self-defense.

"Fancy meeting you here, Sergeant," Miss Maggie said, putting one foot up on the bottom step, as if resting up for the big climb.

"And yourself, Mrs. Shelby. Come into town for the parade?"

"Just running some errands before the day gets too hot. If you'll excuse us, we have business inside." She ascended another step, in case he was having problems sorting out her intention.

He spread his feet apart and crossed his arms on his chest, showing *his* intention. "Miss Casey isn't here."

"And you are? Is she dead, too?" Miss Maggie was done playing charades with him—she wanted answers.

She'd had to raise her voice for the last question, over strains of "Go Tell Aunt Rhody" played by a passing bagpiper. Curious spectators within earshot turned toward us. Ross scowled again and told us to come inside.

He closed the door behind us, leaving the trooper outside on guard. The air inside was hot and stuffy but, to my relief, didn't smell like anyone had died there. Officer Buzzcut came forward, today in uniform. "Nothing in the back rooms or upstairs, Sarge, and no basement."

"She have an office?" Ross asked.

"Only this desk and some filing cabinets in her darkroom."

"Start there. I'll be done here in a minute."

When Buzzcut retreated through the doorway to the back, Miss Maggie turned her teacher look up full-volume, aimed at the sergeant, letting him know she wasn't going to ask her question again and that she was out of patience.

"Miss Casey is under arrest," he said. "And I'm only telling you that so you can squelch the rumors you just started outside."

I was thankful not to have to deal with another victim, of course—especially not someone I knew, even if she *had* flirted with Hugh last night. But arrested? I jumped to the obvious conclusion. "Lynn's the murderer?"

Ross took a deep breath, giving the impression that he had better things to do than correct my conclusions. Then, apparently, more potential rumors swam before his eyes, because he replied, "She was arrested for breaking and entering."

"Where?" asked Miss Maggie.

"That's all you need to know, ladies. Good day." He reached past us for the door.

"Wait," I said, stalling, "we have information for you."

The sergeant froze, eyebrows rising. Miss Maggie's eyebrows went the opposite way, into an expression of warning.

"Lynn was out at our place last night," I blurted out.

Ross straightened up, warily. "Why should that matter?"

I was wondering myself, but then the analytical part of my brain caught up with my intuition. "You arrested her last night, didn't you? Not this morning?"

He went from wary to highly suspicious. "How exactly would you know that?"

"Because it's hot in here. I'm guessing she shut down the air conditioner yesterday after business hours before she came out to Bell Run. Then she went . . . wherever you arrested her, without coming back here, or she would have at least opened some windows." That sounded pretty flimsy to my ears, but I couldn't tell him my real reasoning.

"And what was Miss Casey doing at your house?"

"Taking pictures," Miss Maggie said. "Publicity photos for the Bell Foundation."

Ross rubbed his chin pensively. "Was she alone in your house at any time last night?"

Miss Maggie's eyes met mine, both of us remembering how Lynn had gone upstairs by herself. "Let me guess," I said. "She had something of Theo's on her."

Ross didn't answer, which was confirmation enough, so I asked myself what Lynn could have had. Emmy had returned Theo's gym bag to the back room before supper, and said it held nothing but clothes. Had Lynn swiped a change of undies for Theo? Not worth the risk, and besides, I didn't think she'd had time to go into the back room. The only thing of Theo's in the bathroom was his shaving kit, doubtless the standard razor and toiletries—

"Stupido!" I whacked myself on the forehead. "Theo's ID card. I saw it clipped to his pants when he arrived Wednesday night. He must have forgotten he was still wearing it in the rush to borrow Wyatt's van and pack, so he stowed it in his shaving kit for safekeeping, where he'd be more likely to see it Monday when he got up for work again."

Miss Maggie jumped to the chase. "And why would Lynn *want* Theo's ID?"

"Because it probably unlocks all the doors at his office building."

"Where Vicky Gibson also worked."

"So Lynn was arrested for breaking into Vee-TAC."

"Is that right, Sergeant?"

Ross gaped at the two of us as if he'd witnessed a nuclear reaction too late to don his safety suit. Then his training kicked in and he put his game face back on. "How do you know Mr. Clayborne put his ID into his shaving kit?"

"She deduced it, of course," Miss Maggie said. "We both remember seeing the card on Theo Wednesday, Sergeant. If you found it on Lynn last night, where else could she have gotten it?"

"Assuming we *did* find it on Miss Casey—" Ross smiled at his clever phrasing, as if we couldn't recognize the admission it was, "—perhaps Mr. Clayborne gave it to her."

Did that mean Ross knew they'd left Rock Hill together? Had Lynn told him where Theo was? Were troopers out picking him up right now? My stomach rolled uneasily with each possibility.

"If so," Miss Maggie said, "then Lynn met up with Theo *after* she left Bell Run. Otherwise, she wouldn't have come out to our place first, not if she already had the ID."

Ross couldn't argue with her logic. Or at least, he chose not to. Personally, I could see one huge loophole in it—that Lynn came because Theo told her where the ID was.

The sergeant asked us more questions, like what time Lynn left us last night and if she'd alluded to her planned raid on V-TAC. Instead of returning the favor when we asked what Lynn was doing at Theo's office, he dismissed us again. This time we went.

"Oh, good, the parade's over," Miss Maggie said when we were outside the door. She pointed to Dwight driving his patrol car, acting not only as parade caboose, but as shepherd to a line of bumper-to-bumper traffic as the westbound lane of Route 3 was reopened. Instead of trying to cross midstream this time, she nudged me into the flow of the crowd walking toward Madison, most of them apparently headed for the parade's terminus to claim a family member from the ranks of the marchers.

I figured her plan was to cross the street in front of the courthouse, at The Light (Stoke only had one, unless you counted the yellow/red flasher that dangled over Jefferson between the entrances to the Little League field and Food Lion strip mall), but Miss Maggie turned right at the first street.

"Might as well pay one more social call while we're in town," she said. "The Protectors clubhouse is down this next alley, behind Johnson's Auto Body. With the parade and all, we'll probably find someone there now."

The alley was typical of commercial zoning—all asphalt, building walls, and Dumpsters. The only shade was where utility poles made short diagonal stripes on the ground. The sun's heat radiated from every surface, making me wish I'd worn a hat—and had one of our freezer cold packs under my T-shirt.

Fortunately, we didn't have to go far. Johnson's Auto Body was on the next street parallel to Jefferson. Their parking lot stretched through between the buildings and the triple doors of the garage faced the lot. Vehicles in various stages of body work and repainting were visible toward the front of the property, but closer to us were parked eight SUVs and pickups, almost as big as Billy's. Fords, Chevys, Dodges, GMCs. No Toyotas.

Tacked onto the alley end of the Johnson garage was a wooden lean-to addition, maybe fifteen feet square. The walls were exterior-grade plywood, painted white, with a row of foot-high windows tucked up under the eave. A small air conditioner, built into the same wall, was rattling loudly. On the near corner was a plain metal door and on that, cheap black-on-gold stick-on letters spelled out "America's Sovereign Protectors."

The structure looked solid and built to code, but something about it reminded me of the "fort" our next-door neighbor's sons constructed out of old lumber the summer I turned nine. Their sign had said, "No girls allowed," so naturally, I had to check it out as soon as they went off to the shore with their parents. All I'd found inside were Green Hornet comic books and baseball trading cards, the latter all bent from pitching against the wall.

Not that anyone knew then what a '75 Mike Schmidt would be worth.

Miss Maggie marched up to the Protector's door and walked in without knocking. I heard the words, "We've got more than enough for a two-thirds quorum," and "No, let's wait for—" then silence. Stepping in far enough to shut the door behind me, I surveyed the dozen men present, all staring at us like we'd caught them in their birthday suits. Not that I would have blamed them, considering how inefficient their air conditioner was. But no, they were all dressed—many in uniforms of some sort from having been in the parade: veterans, firemen, scoutmasters, and Civil War reenactors. And all clutched sweating bottles of Coors.

The faces were young and old, literally, with no one between, say, twenty-five and fifty. I recognized the senior citizen who bagged groceries at Food Lion and the recent high-school grad who manned the cashier's booth at the Mobil station.

The room was fairly plain—bare cement under our feet, un-painted drywall, stained from condensation where it met the floor. The men sat on folding chairs except for one, who stood before them between two flags: American and Confederate Battle. In the corner to his left, an old refrigerator was humming louder than the air conditioner. On the fridge door, held in place by Johnson Auto Body magnets, an NRA poster was the room's only artwork.

The guy up front—a chubby fiftyish man wearing yellow seer-sucker pants and a white polo—recovered first. "Miz Shelby?" His tone mixed "Can I help you?" with "You must be completely senile busting in here like that." And maybe a hint of "I've been scared of you since the eighth grade."

I know Miss Maggie heard all the nuances, too, but she merely said, in her teacher voice so as to be heard over the appliance noises, "Thought I'd stop by and personally thank you fellas for coming out to my place yesterday and supporting the Bell Foun-dation."

They all seemed to remember their manners at once, their folding chairs squeaking against the floor as everyone stood. A few of the older men put their beer bottles behind their backs in what might have been sheer reflex. I wondered how many times Miss Maggie had caught them drinking on school property.

"Especially," she continued, "with all the tragedy that's hit your organization this week—Billy's death, and I hear Rufus lost his daughter-in-law yesterday."

A group nod ensued.

"And I feel particularly bad about Billy being killed right outside my front door," she concluded.

"Now, Miz Shelby," the spokesman said, "we all know you aren't to blame."

"Yeah," said another, "you didn't know that colored boy was up to no good when you took him in . . ."

". . . he had you completely fooled . . ."

". . . you couldn't tell he'd go after Vicky Gibson next . . ."

And suddenly they were all talking, trying to assure Miss Maggie she was in no way responsible while at the same time making it clear *someone* was, for letting that (fill in the politically incorrect racial adjective of your choice) boy loose in Stoke County. More than one set of eyes focused on the only non-WASP Yankee in the room—namely me. I nervously slid over a step, behind Miss Maggie.

Seersucker-Man took a swig of his Coors, then held his other palm up to quiet the crowd. "Rest easy, Miz Shelby, we'll make sure that boy's caught."

"Caught and put on death row," someone up front shouted.

"Here, here," said another, and about half the room drank to the notion.

"Well, sorry I can't stay longer," Miss Maggie said with a farewell wave. "Keep out of trouble, boys."

They all took that as a joke and their laughter accompanied our departure.

"Let's go back out to Jefferson," Miss Maggie suggested, fanning herself when we were out under the sun once more. "More shade. I should have thought to bring hats."

I agreed, casting a worried glance in her direction as we began retracing our steps. She usually barely noticed the heat. Then again, our little Protector encounter had likely raised her blood pressure.

"They were about to have a formal meeting, Pat," Miss Maggie said. "Called only yesterday, I'll bet." She pursed her lips in thought. "They were waiting for someone. Of course, Rufus wasn't there, and neither were Billy's two sons, but I counted five empty chairs. I wonder who else—"

We both heard a car coming down the alley behind us. Turning, I saw a brown sheriff's sedan. It pulled into the Johnson lot amid the pickups and SUVs. As soon as the engine cut off, Dwight was out of it, hurrying toward the clubhouse door without a glance in our direction. He disappeared inside without knocking or donning his hat.

"What do you think, Pat?" Miss Maggie asked. "Is that an official police call, or just a man late to a meeting?"

I made Miss Maggie stop in at Tom's Sweet Tooth on Jefferson where I treated us to ice-cream cones (Blueberry Ripple, the non-fat flavor of the month), mainly so I wouldn't feel guilty asking for big cups of ice water. Then I made her sit there in the air-conditioning while she slurped.

I lapped at my own cone slowly, my stomach feeling woozy either from the heat or realization that Dwight was almost certainly a Protector. Sure, his choice of words Thursday morning should have been a red flag, and yet I couldn't picture him wearing a robe and burning crosses. Come to think of it, *none* of the men in that clubhouse seemed to fit that mold, even now that I'd heard their rhetoric.

I said as much to Miss Maggie, in a low voice, though the customers from the parade seemed to be thinning out, leaving us alone in the little seating area.

"Careful, Pat. Robes and burning crosses are stereotypes, too."

She was right. I was letting my mind grasp at images I'd seen on TV. "What I mean is, the Protectors all looked so harmless. Scoutmasters and firemen, for Pete's sake." Not to mention beer bellies and balding pates.

"That's who they are, Pat." She reached for her water and sipped through her straw. "Little League coaches and busboys. Fathers. Left to themselves, most of them *would* be harmless, which is exactly why they're so susceptible to this kind of hate. How many men *like* to feel harmless?"

I saw her point. "No one I know. Not many women either, for that matter. Even the ones who act meek like getting their own way."

"We all prefer to think we're masters of our own destinies." Miss Maggie bit into her cone, sending a creamy blue and white rivulet over her thumb, which she licked off. "People want to feel in control. When they aren't, it's human nature to find someone else to blame. All those men need is a scapegoat to rally 'round to go from harmless to dangerous."

"You think they'd get violent?"

"Don't think they aren't capable of it. They're born followers, Pat. A strong leader could make them do anything. Even without a leader—primed by enough beer and years of watching action movies, Lord knows what scheme they might come up with on their own." She yanked two napkins from the holder, passed one to me and used the other to dab around her mouth. "But danger doesn't have to be violent. Bigotry spreads. We base our friendships on it; we pass it down to our children. All hate needs is an excuse. Nazi Germany's a prime example."

"That couldn't happen in this day and age," I protested.

"Don't kid yourself. Oh, it's become unfashionable to be

openly intolerant, and it's become all too easy to hide behind political correctness. But we're all prejudiced to some degree, Pat—we make assumptions about anything that's not part of our own experiences. And too many people these days simply repeat assumptions they hear on TV. We've become lazy about our biases, or dishonest, and that's why we're vulnerable."

I agreed with the theory, but my mind kept steering back to our specific case. "What about Dwight? He shouldn't be allowed to belong to a group like that."

"Listen to yourself, Pat. That's as intolerant as anything the Protectors believe. Dwight's a citizen, too, guaranteed the basic right to meet with his friends to complain about the world." The last morsel of cone disappeared between her lips, beating her personal best speed for ice-cream consumption. "Besides, whether he's in a group or not won't change his beliefs."

"Then he shouldn't be allowed to be a deputy. With his job, he needs to be fair to everyone."

"And I remember folks saying John Kennedy shouldn't be President simply because he was Catholic. Mind you, I think the Protectors are dead wrong, but they have a right to believe anything they want, as long as they don't interfere with the rights of others." Miss Maggie wiped her fingers on the condensation of her water cup, then dried them with her napkin. "Eat while you walk, Pat. We need to get back."

I dumped the rest of my ice cream in the trash on the way out. When we were once more headed toward Madison, drinking water as we went, she continued. "Dwight *is* a special case, though. He's sworn to uphold the Constitution. If he does anything in violation of that oath, he'll lose his job, and he'd never get another where that oath was involved."

"In other words, he can meet and kvetch with the Protectors all he wants, but he has to be careful what action he takes."

"Right. If he spends his free time, say, putting up campaign posters for J. D., that's fine. He's acting within the system of government. But if he somehow discourages one black person from voting, or even if he *knows* other Protectors plan to keep minority voters from the polls, that would be a violation."

We came out from under the shade, where the trees ended before the courthouse. The reviewing stand was abandoned except for the same two women, now removing the streamers they'd put up earlier, and the same young man, now packing up the sound system. We walked around behind the stand and crossed both streets.

"Dwight might actually be a good influence in that meeting," Miss Maggie said. "He'd naturally dampen any action liable to get him in trouble. Presuming, of course, that the murders aren't some kind of Protector conspiracy and he's already up to his ears in it."

"You don't think he's one of the murderers, do you? He can't be. We're his alibi every time." But as soon as the words were out of my mouth, I realized that if Wyatt had been killed around eight, Dwight had more than enough time to come up to Bell Run afterwards. And when Billy was shot, maybe there'd been time for Dwight to leave his patrol car just out of sight, creep into the woods, fire at Billy and Theo, then dash back so he could look like he was riding to the rescue. I couldn't remember—time had seemed to stand still in those minutes.

Anyway, for Vicky's murder, Dwight had been at Bell Run all day, helping with the dig. Hadn't he? I made a mental note to ask Hugh.

20

"Miss Maggie? Okay if I make a quick stop at the post office?" I hit my turn signal in anticipation of the left onto Bell Run Road.

"Won't be anything in our box today. No mail 'cause of the holiday."

"I know. Actually, I want to take a look around the outside of the trailers."

"For?"

I made the turn before answering. "Last night, just before my vision, I sort of half-dozed and dreamt I heard singing. Only now, I don't think it was a dream."

She sat up as straight as her shoulder belt allowed. "You heard Theo?"

"I think so. Now that we know it's possible he left Rock Hill with Lynn, I've been wondering if she dropped him off in the woods yesterday, before she came up to the house."

"Why?"

"All I know is, I heard him singing." I passed our drive. A groundhog was nosing around a patch of chicory at the forest's edge. "Lynn was probably supposed to pick Theo up later."

"Instead he got stranded here all night, likely with no water, and in this heat, he'd get dehydrated fast. That's why you're checking the trailer. Only water nearby that Theo could drink would be from our hose—risky, somebody might see him or hear the water running—or Hugh's outside faucet. With the post office window closed for the weekend and Hugh staying at our house, that's the safe bet."

I pulled onto the gravel in front of the post office. Not another car in sight. We got out and hurried around the side to Hugh's private entrance. At the corner of the trailer, half hidden by an overgrown azalea, a steel pipe came up out of the ground, capped by a faucet. A cluster of rocks beneath protected the ground from erosion. The rocks were wet and the ground on the downhill side was muddy. Someone had used the water recently.

Miss Maggie scooted around the azaleas, to where she could see both trails leading into the forest, one to our place, one to the river. "Theo?" she called, just loud enough to be heard this side of the creek. "Pat and I are alone, so if you're there, show yourself."

The only thing that showed itself was a startled squirrel who ran out from under a bramble and hightailed it, literally, up the nearest tree. Of course, Theo might not have stayed nearby. In his place, I'd be within eyeshot of the house, trying to figure out how to sneak in and grab a snack.

"He'll come back eventually for more water," I said. "We could leave him a note."

"No!" The voice was way too low for Miss Maggie's, and it came from the other side of the honeysuckle-and-morning-glory thicket at the head of the river trail.

"Stay where you are," Miss Maggie said. We ducked behind the shrubs and there was Theo, shirtless, sweaty, and needing a shave. His pants and torso were covered with powdery dirt and clumps of dry mud fringed his dress shoes. Between his appearance and the way he jumped at every sound, he more closely resembled a runaway slave than a computer programmer in the twenty-first century.

"Don't put anything in writing," he said. "I've already caused you enough trouble."

Miss Maggie merely nudged her chin toward his long black

pants and oxfords, saying, "You must be dying of the heat in those things."

Theo looked down at himself and his little half-smile surfaced. "I thought about taking them off, but if I got caught wearing nothing besides my briefs, Aunt Song would die of mortification."

"You must be starving," I put in. In a crisis, I always fall back on the Montella family motto: "Food first."

"We'll get him something later," Miss Maggie said with a dismissive wave. "You came here with Lynn Casey?"

Theo nodded. "She followed us to Rock Hill yesterday, then followed me out to the mall. Wanted to talk to me alone. I didn't remember her at first, but she used to be my baby-sitter thirty-odd years ago."

"Baby-sitter?" I exclaimed.

"That's right. Just as she was telling me who she was, her police scanner came on, saying I was wanted for yet another murder. Jackie convinced me not to turn myself in until she found out who'd been killed and why I was suspected. I insisted on returning Uncle Charles's car, so she followed me back to Rock Hill, then took me to her studio in Stoke. She made a few phone calls and found out the victim was my boss. Which explains why Vicky never showed up at the mall."

"Any idea who'd want to kill her? Or why?" Miss Maggie asked.

"Not who." Theo crinkled up his eyebrows in thought. "As to why, Vicky said she knew something about Wyatt's murder— that's why I was supposed to meet her. I have an idea it involved something she was up to at work. Something illegal, I mean. We acquire a lot of databases and, on occasion, they contain confidential information. As soon as we extract the address and marketing data, we delete the original feed, but if we're backed up, and we usually are, the confidential info can sit on our server for a day or two. I found a file of that data on Vicky's hard drive last Wednesday while I was troubleshooting her PC."

I asked what kind of information.

"See, that's just it," Theo replied. "The file included credit card, bank card, and Social Security numbers, but the feed was old—from almost two years ago—and it was a 'recently deceased' database, so most of those accounts should be closed by now."

Financial info? Were we way off thinking the Protectors were involved when Vicky may have only been, say, trying to transfer forgotten money out of old bank accounts?

"Did Vicky know you'd found that file?" Miss Maggie asked.

"I asked her about it." Theo paused to shoo a fly off his shoulder. "She'd gone to get a soda while I was at her desk and when she came back, I had the file up on the screen. First she said she didn't recall what she'd needed it for, which I thought was odd because the last access date was only a week ago Thursday. But I pointed out that it was taking up a big chunk of drive space and ought to be deleted. That's when she suddenly remembered she'd used it for one of Bob's projects—he's the VP for our section. She wanted to ask him first if he'd need the data anymore. I said okay and I left work a half hour later."

"And Wyatt was killed that very night," Miss Maggie mused, "possibly in your place."

"That's what I think," Theo said, "though Vicky couldn't have done it—had to be someone who doesn't know me."

Miss Maggie nodded. "At least one other person was in on the scheme with her. Someone with a Protector connection, because I'd bet my last nickel that Billy wasn't a chance witness Wednesday night." She turned back to Theo. "I don't suppose you know that Lynn Casey was arrested?"

He let out a frustrated sigh. "That explains why she never came back to get me last night."

"I presume you told her where to find your work ID?" Miss Maggie asked.

Theo nodded. "We figured there might be more evidence on Vicky's PC, or in her office somewhere, but I couldn't go because all the guards know me—they'd call the police right away. Jackie was going to claim she was a new hire if anyone stopped her, or simply someone trying to return an ID she found. It seemed worth the risk."

"She must not have uncovered any evidence," Miss Maggie said, "because the cops are still looking for you. Good thing you hid out here while she was at V-TAC. What put that in your head?"

For the first time, Theo looked away, saying "um" twice, before a sheepish smile played with his lip muscles. "You're not going to believe that part."

"Try us." The challenge of a teacher who wants to hear a plausible excuse for missing homework.

"I, uh—" Theo rubbed his hands together nervously, "—I was actually only looking for a ghost."

My jaw hit the ground, but Miss Maggie merely asked, "A little boy or a woman?"

Theo's turn to be startled. "You have more than one ghost?"

"Heavens, yes." Miss Maggie chuckled. "Odds are Bell Run's got at least a half dozen. Though I've never seen one myself." She couldn't hide her disappointment. Not that she tried. "How'd you hear about them?"

"Easy. I saw one. Wednesday night, as I was driving through the forest up to your house—" he gestured over towards the drive, "—I thought I saw a woman run across the road, just beyond the headlight beams. I asked Emmy if she saw her and she said no, but thought it was probably a deer. Later, when we were all standing around the pit looking at the skull, I saw her again. She ran out of the forest, toward us, then stood there looking up as if something horrible was happening right in front of her. Then she faded and was gone. That's when I knew she was a ghost. I could see her clearly—as if some kind of light were shining on her— but none of you noticed, although we were all more or less facing that way."

"That's why you wanted to sleep outside," I said. "You wanted another glimpse of her."

Theo shrugged. "That, and . . . since I was the only one who saw her, and since she was black, I wondered if she was trying to tell me something."

"Likely," Miss Maggie said. "She's your great-great-great grandmother. Emancipation's mom."

Theo went beyond startled this time. He was speechless.

"Too long a yarn to tell you right now. Have you seen her again since?"

"No . . . but I did dream about her last night." Then abruptly, he laughed. "I dreamt she told me an Ananse story. My grandfather used to tell them to me. He said Emancipation taught them to him. Maybe that was her way of saying she was family."

Miss Maggie laughed too, saying to me, "Ananse stories are folk tales from West Africa, Pat. Get this—Ananse's a spider."

"A spider." Like me in my own dream. "By any chance, did her story have a snake in it?"

"Sure," Theo said, "a big python. One of my favorite tales. Ananse feeds the snake a big meal and gets him in a good mood, then says he'd like to measure the python because he's never seen such a long snake before. So the python lies alongside a log and allows himself to be tied to it at even intervals—"

"But instead of counting the intervals, the spider chops him up, right?"

He was nodding when we heard a car pull onto the gravel. We all froze, then Miss Maggie peeked carefully around the thicket. "The Morgans' car," she whispered. "Probably just checking their mailbox." Jack and Penny Morgan both worked in Richmond but had a house on the Rapidan where they spent their weekends. When we heard whichever Morgan climb the post office steps and go inside, Miss Maggie said, "We shouldn't stay here anyway. I wish we could hide you up at the house, Theo—"

"No. Like I said, I've given you enough trouble. I'll be okay out here. I was an Eagle Scout."

"Well, we'll get you some food and more comfortable clothes, anyway. Pat, you haven't watered the flowers out at the cemetery since Thursday, have you?"

"I forgot all about them."

"Good. Gives us an excuse to walk out there." She gave Theo directions for following the river trail up to the cemetery and, as soon as the Morgans were gone, we headed back to the house.

"What do you think it means, Miss Maggie?" I asked as I turned onto our drive. "Why would Alma send me the same dream as Theo?"

She mulled it over until we bumped over the bridge. "Maybe she just wanted to make you both laugh."

While Miss Maggie kept Emmy and Hugh busy, giving them the lowdown on what we found out at the Historical Society, plus all the gossip about Lynn being arrested and Dwight probably being a Protector, I dashed upstairs with a plastic grocery bag. Into it went Theo's work boots and assorted clothes from his bag. From the closet, I took the Little Playmate cooler that I'd used to pack my lunch in back when I was a desk jockey (most of my co-workers brought frozen dinners—I brought serious leftovers from whatever I'd cooked the night before).

Downstairs, I threw a small jar of peanut butter, a bottle of water, a third of a loaf of bread, a quarter pound of sliced turkey, a few pieces of fruit, and a set of utensils into the cooler. Then I took up the cooler and bags, and crept out the back door.

Miss Maggie still had everyone occupied in the side yard. I trotted into the forest until I couldn't be seen from the house, and left the bag hanging from a low-limbed tree with the cooler underneath, praying that no forest creature would nose into them before I returned.

I was ten steps short of the back porch when I heard Miss Maggie yell good and loud, "If you're going inside, Hugh, tell Pat I'll be in directly." Our prearranged warning. I dashed through the door, careful not to let it slam, grabbed an empty gallon jug, and began filling it at the sink, trying all the while to catch my breath as I listened for Hugh's footsteps—forgetting that his footsteps were inaudible to normal human ears.

"Aha, here you are." His voice sounded right behind me and I jumped, splashing water onto the counter as I spun around.

I gulped my heart back into my chest cavity and turned back to the sink to shut off the tap and wipe my spill. "You need to be belled."

Hugh leaned one elbow on the counter and put on his best evil leer, which wasn't evil at all, but comically roguish. And damned sexy. "You need to be kept guessing."

"Yeah?" It was all I could do not to laugh. Or jump his bones. I was in the mood for both, simultaneously. "Guessing about what?"

A perfect cue, I thought. This was where we were supposed to look into each other's eyes, realize we couldn't fight destiny, and let our lips drift together, setting off the most explosive Fourth of July fireworks of both our lives.

Miss Maggie charged through the back door, carrying another empty jug. "Here, Pat, refill this for the cooler outside. Then we can get going."

"Going where?" Hugh asked, without a trace of disappointment in his tone. Apparently I'd been the only one mentally lighting fuses.

Sighing, I reached around him to take the jug. "Out to the family plot. I haven't watered the flowers there since noon Thursday. Figured I'd better do it now before the day gets too hot." It was already over ninety degrees out there—how much hotter could it get?

He turned to Miss Maggie. "I'll go with her. I can carry more water than you."

Had he ever volunteered before? No. Not even the day I'd planted the geraniums and had needed extra hands to help carry them and water and tools. Now, the one time I *couldn't* be alone with him, he decides to earn a merit badge.

"Emmy needs you," Miss Maggie said, "especially without Dwight here. We'll be right back. Take that jug from Pat and bring it outside with you."

He obeyed. Miss Maggie had that effect on people. Even Hugh.

As we walked toward the forest, the sun actually went in, if only for a moment. I looked up to see a smattering of fluffy clouds across the sky. "Think it'll rain, Miss Maggie?"

"They said possible thunderstorms—still, those clouds don't look that mean. Not yet, anyway."

"What will Theo do if it storms?" We were far enough away from the house that we couldn't be overheard, but I lowered my voice anyway.

"Oh, I think we can make sure the cellar door stays unlatched for a night, don't you?"

I agreed.

We found the clothes and food undisturbed. After some juggling to figure out how we could carry the bag, cooler, and three water jugs (any less would have aroused Hugh's suspicions), we decided we couldn't, and left one jug under a tree before trudging off down the path. A muggy breeze had kicked up, rustling the tree branches above. As we passed through the clearing around the Bell House ruin, the sun went in again, longer this time. A robin swooped down from his perch atop the brick wall, crossing the path to the safety of the underbrush.

"By the way," Miss Maggie said as we reentered the forest, "I asked Emmy if Dwight was here all day yesterday. He wasn't. Like Thursday, he went home for lunch. Unlike Thursday, he was away an extra hour. Said his kitchen faucet had sprung a leak and he'd fixed it. Came back about the same time J. D. and his entourage showed up—two-fifteen, two-thirty."

"You think Dwight killed Vicky?"

"All I'm saying is, he doesn't have an alibi, unless one of his neighbors saw him come and go. His wife wouldn't have been home—she works for the Park Service. Fridays, she's at the Fredericksburg Visitor Center. Not likely she'd have taken off on one of the busiest days of the season."

I mulled over this development until we reached our destination. The cemetery felt different today—not its usual tranquil mood. Of course, part of that impression might have come from the geraniums, which all looked morbidly dehydrated. I set down my load on the wall, uncapped one jug, and went to work while Miss Maggie called softly, "Allee, allee in free!"

Theo emerged from the cover of the river trailhead, wary, but apparently anxious for whatever supplies we'd brought. As he hopped over the low wall, the feeling I had intensified. Everything—the trees, grass, even the air—seemed fidgety.

Suspecting this was Alma wanting my attention, I mentally told her I'd be happy to oblige once we were alone. To Theo I said, "Eat the turkey in the cooler first. The meat'll go bad in no time with this heat."

A blast of cold air hit the back of my head. Very funny, I thought.

"The water bottle will come in handy," Theo said, glancing inside the cooler. "I've been wasting too much water sticking my head under Hugh's faucet every time I need a drink. Let me get going, before anyone sees you with me."

Miss Maggie gave him instructions for ducking into our cellar in case of lightning or rain. All the while, I felt as if someone were pulling at my shirt tails, someone getting more anxious as Theo talked about leaving.

"Wait," I said. "Theo, do you see Alma right now?"

From beneath raised eyebrows, he scanned the clearing. "No."

"Is she here, Pat?" That was Miss Maggie, hopeful as a puppy begging for a Milk Bone.

"I think so." To Theo's look of incredulity, I said simply, "Don't ask."

"Maybe she's ready to tell you the rest," Miss Maggie suggested. "Close your eyes."

I did. Like before, I couldn't focus properly. I felt like I was watching the old TV my parents had kept in the kitchen (so Mom could see Oprah while she cooked dinner)—you'd have to bend the rabbit-ear antenna every which way, then you couldn't let go of the aerial or the picture would go all fuzzy again. I guess it was that association that made me say, "Theo, give me your hands."

After a moment of stunned silence, he said, "What are you, some kind of medium?"

"I'm a large." I could usually do more with a straight line like his, but good stand-up isn't easy with your eyes closed. "Just play along."

I heard Miss Maggie urge him on, then his big, warm hands took mine, and almost immediately I found myself in Stoke, watching yet another parade.

Got a Little Book With Pages Three and Every Page Spells Liberty

The arm of the Federal government is long, but it is far too short to protect the rights of individuals in the interior of distant states.

—Frederick Douglas, 1866

July 4, 1871—Stoke

Next morning be the Fourth of July and Preacher Moses say we all ought to go into Stoke as usual, to watch the parade and let Joe Putnam run in the colored's foot race 'cause he got a chance of winning this year. Mama and Jordana be against it, after the trouble the night before, but Preacher say us not going would give those whites what done it the notion that they be keeping us in our place. He say then we see more trouble.

So we all head to town, 'cept for Jordana who stayed behind to tend little Adam, since he be too small to come, and Uncle Henry, since he ain't up for the walk. Jordana say she seen enough Fourth of Julys in her life already. She say the only celebration she waiting on now be Judgment Day.

The African Church be one block up from Jefferson Street, but they got a long, high wall behind the churchyard, and all us chil'un, and even some of the growed-ups, climb up top so's we can look down over Shifflett's

Livery and watch the parade. Mostly I like seeing the red fire company wagon, and Tucker's Marshall Band in their green uniforms, shiny brass instruments catching the sun. They be playing "Dixie" as they go by. Just like she do every year, Hattie say it be the only song they know, and like every year, we all laugh. We watch the veterans go by, dressed in their Sunday best with yellow ribbons hanging from their coat lapels, none of them looking like I figure soldiers ought to look.

Lilla be sitting on my left and I tell her, "Preacher say the parades up North all got real soldiers marching in 'em, all in fancy uniform, with color guards, and mounted Zouaves, and they got teams of eight horses each pulling big cannons."

"If I never see a soldier or cannon again," Mama say, "it won't be too soon. We had our share during the war."

"You be glad enough if President Grant send troops to get rid of the Klan," Ida say. Nobody argue with that.

Lilla ask her mama where her daddy got to and Ida say, "He be off talking with the men, that's all."

"I seen 'em go 'round the side of the church," Hattie say. "Probably somebody brung a jug of corn shine. Zeb Jackson, I bet."

"Zeb be with 'em," Ida say, "but Noah say they be meeting so as to plan what to do about Caleb Fletcher."

I feel Mama get all tense against my right arm. "What they want to do to him?" she ask.

"Jes' scare him. Give him some o' his own back." Ida lean around back of Lilla so she could talk quiet. "They talking 'bout getting grain sacks to put over their heads, like they done with Jack Soyers, so Caleb can't tell who be ambushing him."

"Jack Soyers end up dead," Mama whisper behind my head.

"Only 'cause his horse throwed him. Ain't one of us felt bad about that, did we?"

"We woulda if any of the men got hung for it."

"Well, Caleb don't own a horse, so he can't get throwed. But even if he up and die from a fit, you can't tell me he don't deserve it, after what he done to them Reynolds chil'un."

"He didn't do *nothing* to them. Somebody else kill that family. I know 'cause . . .'cause I seen Caleb walking behind me last night, all the way out the plank road, 'til I turn off on our path. He didn't have time to get back to the Reynolds' place and kill all of 'em—the fire be already started when I met our men going that way."

Ida wrinkle up her nose like she smelling day-ol' chicken skins. "Why you ain't say nothing last night?"

"Too upset, I guess."

"Yeah? Or you jes' thinking to get square with Caleb for all he done to you while we was slaves?"

Mama look down at her bare toes. "That be long ago. Best left in the past."

Ida straighten up, shaking her head. "I can't forget that easy, Alma—the way him and young Travis come and use us whenever they be drinking. Then Caleb make you his own private whore. You wasn't allowed to talk to any of us, remember? And they took Jim from you almost soon as he be born. You forgive that?"

"No!" Mama's voice come out louder than she plan and she quick change to a whisper, but I can still hear anger in it. "Never said I could forgive. Not any of it. Not ever."

"Well, sister, that be reason enough to let the men give him his comeuppance tonight."

"Tonight!" Mama exclaim.

Ida lean over again. "Reckoned it be best—the town

picnic in Clarke's Grove and the mayor's dinner at the hotel be keeping most of Stoke off the roads. 'Cept for them few drunken fools what always be out shooting off their guns on the Fourth."

"I got to stop 'em." Mama hop down from the wall.

Ida catch her wrist 'fore she could run off. "Think about it, Alma. Even if Caleb ain't guilty of murder, he done evil in his time. And why he be coming out our way last night, following you, if not bent on more mischief?"

"You want Noah to get hung?"

Ida give a sigh. "No, but I don't wanna end up like the Reynolds neither. Our men's jes' protecting us. Who else is gonna if they don't?"

21

The scene faded slowly and I was once more aware of Theo's hands, twice as sweaty as before, clutching mine. I opened my eyes and saw him standing there with his own peepers shut, above a frown of puzzlement, and below beads of perspiration on his brow that glittered in the sunlight.

"Theo?" I hazarded.

His eyelids popped wide open. "What *was* that?"

"What was what?"

"A dream, I guess. I was at a parade . . ." He went on to tell me exactly what I'd just witnessed.

I let him know I'd seen the same movie. "Not a dream, but don't ask me what." If I had to be a freak, though, it was nice to have company.

"Caleb Fletcher," he murmured. "I remember hearing that name before."

"Miss Maggie's grandfather. She must have mentioned him—"

"No. Something about Emancipation. Aunt Song would know."

So I turned toward Miss Maggie, who wasn't where I'd seen her last but over by the cemetery entrance. That's when I saw who was standing beside her. Hugh. Looking like he'd swallowed a box of tacks. One of his fists was wrapped around the handle of that third jug we'd abandoned in the forest.

He was staring at my hands, which is when I realized I was

still holding on to Theo. The latter abruptly came out of his time-travel lag, released my hands, and bounded for the cemetery wall.

"Wait, Theo," Miss Maggie called. "Hugh won't tell anyone you're here. Come back and get your things."

He obeyed her, the way a squirrel grabs at acorns when he sees a dog tied across the yard. I turned to Hugh and asked him what he was doing here.

"You said you'd be right back. Pardon me for getting worried. I'll just get back to work." He did an about-face, remembered the jug he carried, handed it to Miss Maggie, then strode off down the trail.

He was cranky, no doubt about that.

I took the jug from Miss Maggie and emptied it around the plants as she quizzed both me and Theo about what we'd seen. Our details were the same, down to the color of the band uniforms.

Theo left us and we began retracing our steps to the house. Miss Maggie was pensive, probably churning over the specifics of this latest vision, but I wanted to know what Hugh had seen, and thought I'd better ask now before I saw him again.

"Oh, not much," Miss Maggie replied. "He only showed up right before you two came out of it, and you didn't talk or move or anything."

"Is he mad because we didn't tell him about Theo?"

"He'll use it as his excuse, I'm sure, though he knows I'd never force him to be an accessory."

"What did he say when you asked him not to tell anyone Theo was here?"

"I didn't ask him anything of the sort." Miss Maggie ducked under a low branch. "That was Hugh's decision. He knows Theo's innocent. And I think he considers Theo a potential buddy—they must have bonded over baseball the other night. Though what either of them sees in the Braves is beyond me."

Buddy? It hit me that if Hugh had friends, I hadn't met or

heard about any of them. Wondering if his social circle was smaller than even mine, I asked Miss Maggie.

"Hugh's downright gregarious to all his mail customers, but close friends?" She shook her head. "He was never one for socializing in the usual guy hangouts and, being a single parent, when he does go out, it's usually to places like Beth Ann's school band concerts. And he's too shy to pick up the phone and—"

"Shy? Hugh?"

"Yes, Hugh. Especially around you." We were still walking single file, Miss Maggie in front, but I could see her ribs shaking and knew she was silently giggling.

"Around me." I made it a statement, so as to more effectively show my skepticism.

"You get that poor boy absolutely tongue-tied." She spun around suddenly, her green eyes dancing. "Why do you think he came home early this week?"

"His sunburn—"

"Sunburn, my foot. Another excuse. He figured maybe he'd get to spend some time with you without Beth Ann chaperoning him constantly." She resumed walking, into the clearing around Bell House.

"Then why, when we went down to his trailer together on Thursday, didn't he . . . uh . . . say anything?" I almost said "do anything," and I was thinking exactly what I would have liked him to do. I felt my face go crimson.

"Of course he didn't. You didn't either, did you?"

"No, but—"

"The problem with you two is, you live too near each other. He's your neighbor and your mailman, and you've got a nice little camaraderie between you to boot. You're both afraid of rocking the boat and ruining everything."

Put that way, my sane plan of patience sounded like sheer cowardice. A little inner voice told me to take a good look in the mirror. "Did Hugh tell you that?"

"Didn't have to. If he weren't half-besotted, would he have reacted the way he did when he saw you with Theo today?"

"That wasn't jealousy, Miss Maggie. It's this ghost business." I told her about the conversation Hugh and I had the day before, about Beth Ann. "Odds are, he'll never let me near his daughter again." So much for our nice little camaraderie.

Miss Maggie turned again, her eyes no longer dancing but puzzled. "What's he got against ghosts? They're only dead people. Half the folks I've ever known are dead. See, Pat, there's another prejudice for you."

"Don't worry about lunch yet," Miss Maggie said as we deposited our empty jugs on the kitchen counter. "We'll wait for the volunteers to leave, then we'll just have tuna sandwiches. Something I want to do first. Get us some glasses of iced tea and meet me in the war room."

By the time I joined her, she'd fired up her PC, had her reading glasses on the brink of her nose, and was looking up the phone number for the All Children of God parsonage. Handing her one drink, I fetched the phone for her from the side windowsill. She downed a long swig before dialing.

"Shawna?" Miss Maggie identified herself. "Any news about Theo yet?" She made sympathetic noises into the phone for a while, before saying, "Listen, I need Aunt Song's phone number. Do you have it? I have another question for her about Clayborne family history. She's there? Great. Put her on."

More sympathetic comments and noises, then, "Yes, I do have a question. And if you don't mind, Song, I'd like to put you on my speaker so Pat can listen in." We lost a minute locating the speaker under the stacks of printouts on her desk but, finally, she switched it on. "Can you hear us?"

"Just a bit louder, Magnolia," said Aunt Song. "My hearing isn't what it used to be."

Miss Maggie moved closer to the mike. "What I wanted to tell you is that I've found a mention of someone named Emancipation living near Stoke in 1871. His last name was Jackson and he bought some liniment from the pharmacist here—name of Caleb Fletcher."

"Caleb Fletcher? You don't say. He was a pharmacist?"

I could tell that Miss Maggie wanted to do handstands at the recognition in Aunt Song's voice, but merely clutched the speaker tighter. "You've heard of him?"

"If he's the same Caleb Fletcher who kept up a correspondence with my great-grandfather, I have letters from him."

"Letters!" both Miss Maggie and I exclaimed.

"Only two—that's what my mother found in Emancipation's room after he died. Both of them dated 1938, but they sound as if those two had been writing each other for a while. I remember my mother sending a note to Mr. Fletcher, to inform him of my great-grandfather's death, but he never wrote back to her."

"Caleb died in April of that year," Miss Maggie said.

"That explains it. Emancipation died in May."

I couldn't stand the suspense any longer. "What do the letters say?"

"Oh, not much," Aunt Song replied. "I don't have them with me—they're back at my house—but I remember in the last one, Mr. Fletcher thought he knew someone related to Tobias Avery— Duke Avery's great-great-grandfather. That's one reason I kept them. That, and I was always curious as to who Caleb Fletcher was and how Great-grandpapa knew him."

"I can tell you *who* he was," Miss Maggie said. "He was my granddaddy."

"You don't say! Small world, Magnolia."

"Listen, Song. Can I get a copy of those letters? I think I might be able to find out more about Emancipation."

Aunt Song agreed eagerly. After some brainstorming about

method of delivery, Aunt Song said she'd bring the letters to church tomorrow and fax them to us from Shawna's office.

"Wow," I said as she hung up. "Letters from your grand-father."

"Primary sources, Pat. Heretofore unknown historical documents. From a source I can personally verify. Written proof that Emancipation knew at least one person in Stoke." She sipped her tea thoughtfully. "I hope they can give us a few more clues about what happened here."

She seemed to be trying to distance herself from this particular history. For objectivity? Or because she was afraid of finding out something bad about her grandfather?

"Not," she continued, "that I don't trust your revelations."

"But we can't put them on grant applications."

"Exactly." Another sip. "Was it clearer today, Pat? The vision, I mean, while holding Theo's hands."

I leaned against the arm of the blue recliner. "Like someone suddenly hooked me up to cable. I could practically smell the valve oil on the euphoniums as the band marched by." Actually, I only knew the word "euphonium" from watching my *Music Man* video ten times and had no idea if any of the unfamiliar brass instruments in Mance's parade fit the bill. Descriptive license.

Miss Maggie didn't question my musical education. "Unfortunately, we can't bank on Theo being around when Alma's ready with the next chapter. You do realize, Pat, that Alma's the most likely candidate for our skeleton?"

I nodded. I hadn't wanted to think about it. Even though my rational mind told me that, ghost or not, Alma Jackson had been dead for a long time, I didn't want to think about *how* she'd died, any more than I wanted to speculate on the inevitable demise of anyone I knew. The irony here was that I, social derelict that I was, seemed to have no trouble striking up close acquaintances among the departed.

Car doors slammed outside. Miss Maggie jumped up and hurried over to the window. "The volunteers are beginning their exodus. We should go thank them all." She bustled out and I followed her, catching the screen door before it could bang behind her.

Afterwards, while Hugh and Emmy washed up, I went to the kitchen to slap together four tuna sandwiches. Miss Maggie's converted me to her method: putting just a dab of mayo (fat-free, of course) on the bread instead of a glob mixed with the tuna. Less partially hydrogenated fats that way. Hugh came in as I was washing a tomato. Without a word, he slid a knife from the drawer, took the tomato, and began slicing it. The cranky look was off his face, but he wasn't smiling either.

I was wondering if I should apologize, and what for exactly, when Emmy walked in and I lost my chance. I put her to work washing fresh cherries for our fruit du jour, and went off to find Miss Maggie.

She was on the front porch, phone to her ear, saying goodbye to someone. "Sergeant Ross," she said after disconnecting. "I wanted to let him know about that database on Vicky's PC. I made it sound as if Theo had mentioned it before he went AWOL and we only just remembered. Lunch ready?"

I told her it was and she said, "Let's picnic out here. The breeze is picking up. Feels good in the shade."

So I brought out the troops. Emmy and I sat in the rockers, Miss Maggie leaned against the railing between us, and Hugh settled on the top porch step.

"Let me ask you a question, Emmy," Miss Maggie said, after making half her sandwich disappear. "You knew Theo's father, didn't you?"

"A little," she replied. "He was on the anthropology faculty at

UVA my first two years there. Part-time—taught a course in early American religions."

Miss Maggie spit a cherry pit toward the magnolia tree. "He left because of some kind of scandal, right?"

"That was the justification." Emmy broke off a corner of her sandwich. "The university wasn't crazy about him instigating student protest marches. They jumped on the first excuse that came along to ask for his resignation. Though it was his own fault for giving them the out."

"Which was?"

"The usual. He had an affair with a student."

My eyes met Miss Maggie's. Hers warned me not to say a word. "Did you know her?"

Emmy popped the sandwich bit into her mouth, shaking her head as she chewed. "I'm not sure I ever heard who it was. Someone from his band of protesters. Not many of them were anthropology majors, so I probably didn't know her anyway."

Miss Maggie let the subject drop. Or maybe she just wanted to work on the other half of her sandwich a moment. In the meantime, Hugh spoke up.

"Rich called while you were . . . at the cemetery." The last phrase seemed to taste sour in his mouth. "Long story short, I have to go pick up Beth Ann tomorrow. So Emmy and I thought we'd work the rest of today instead."

Miss Maggie gave her approval. "As long as we finish in time to go see the fireworks in town tonight. July Fourth only comes once a year." Like I said, a big chunk of her had never grown up.

"Shouldn't be a problem," Emmy said, reaching for a cherry. "We need to finish excavating the bones by tomorrow, or Monday at the latest. She's starting to get moldy."

"She?" Miss Maggie and I said in unison.

Emmy nodded. "I saw enough of the pelvis this morning to be sure."

Miss Maggie leaned forward. "What else can you tell about her, Emmy?"

"Just that Theo's idea about a black cemetery has some merit. She would have been considered black in her time."

"Considered?" I echoed.

"Her skull shape is generally Negroid, but with some Caucasoid features."

"In other words," Miss Maggie said, "she had some white blood in her. No news there. Sally Hemmings wasn't the only slave to have a child by her master."

But Emmy couldn't tell us much more. Not how Alma died. Not yet. So we finished up our lunch, cleaned up, and headed back out to the side yard.

Another three inches of soil had been cleared from the head and middle sections of Feature One. Now, all but the bottom of the skull was visible, and I could see half the ribs, resting flat as if they'd fallen domino-style, and the pelvis, shoulder blades, thigh bones, and bits of vertebrae peeking through the dirt. All of them were brown and seemed two-dimensional, I supposed from the weight of the ground over more than a century.

Emmy put Hugh on the lower legs this time, because he could remove that dirt faster. I was handed a dental pick and told to peel back the soil around the ribs. Emmy took the skull again. Miss Maggie sifted. The weather cooperated, breeze settling in for the duration, clouds giving us more and more shade as the day went on.

And so we passed the time—Miss Maggie and Emmy chattering about history, Hugh being . . . not sulky, but quieter than usual, and me? I thought being in such intimate contact with Alma's bones would bring on more visions. Nada. Maybe she took the afternoon off for the holiday.

So instead, I stole peeks at Hugh, to see if he was stealing peeks at me. If he was, I didn't catch him. No earth-shattering discoveries that afternoon, archaeological or otherwise.

Feeling the need to actually *cook* something for supper, even if it only meant boiling water, I whipped up a bowl of my special cold *pasta fagiol'*—a pasta salad of small shells tossed with cooked lentils, bell peppers, black olives, onions, and Italian dressing. Watermelon for dessert.

While we were all in a contented mood from dinner, Miss Maggie insisted on us all going to see the fireworks. Hugh didn't seem thrilled, blaming his sunburn. He hadn't put on the makeup today, to keep his skin from breaking out further, but I supposed being embarrassed in front of a half dozen volunteers isn't the same as being embarrassed in front of the whole town. Miss Maggie told him to wear long pants if he had to, he was coming.

Her plans were fine by me—I needed time away from Bell Run that had nothing to do with murder, past or present. At her direction, we all swiped on a layer of bug goop, then loaded a couple of folding chairs and a blanket into the trunk of my car, which could carry four people more comfortably than Hugh's Ford Escort.

After a stop at Hugh's trailer so he could don a pair of chinos (no sign of Theo, thank God), we headed for town. The display was to take place at Stoke's Little League field, and was scheduled to start at eight-thirty. "First they have a little pageant of sorts," Miss Maggie explained. " 'The Star-Spangled Banner,' then the local bigwigs all have to say something, and the high-school marching band usually plays last season's halftime show. They shoot off the fireworks soon as it's dark enough."

At the flashing traffic light on Jefferson, a sheriff's cruiser was blocking the Little League entrance and Deputy Brenda was standing on the yellow line, waving everyone into the Food Lion lot. I parked and we joined the stream of folks crossing the street. We passed through a smaller lot, apparently reserved tonight for dignitaries' cars—I spied J. D.'s beige Caddy not far from the entrance. Then came a grassy embankment, no more than about a twenty-foot drop, but wider than the two baseball fields at the bottom. All along its length, people were marking small territories with ground covers and coolers.

The two ballfields were arranged outfield backing outfield, home plates in the far corners. Each had real dugouts, a big score-board, an announcer's booth, and night game lights, which were on. Good thing. With all the clouds, twilight had begun early. Lightning bugs were already out, hovering, drifting, blinking their little yellow butt-lights on and off.

At the base of the slope on the far left was a low building clearly marked "Restrooms" at one end and "Snacks" at the other. A service road circled the whole complex, apparently with egress out to Jefferson off to the right, because a fire truck and ambulance stood over on that side, at the ready.

"You can see our priorities, Pat," Miss Maggie commented with a sigh. "Tax money for kids comes here instead of into the schools."

Hugh, who'd been bringing up the rear, called up to the front, "Where do you want to sit, Miss Maggie?"

She studied the terrain. Inside the service road, right below us, two pieces of four-by-eight plywood had been laid down to define an impromptu square stage. On it was a double row of chairs occupied by suits. J. D. was seated front and center, Judge Cora in the back row, end. Brackin was there, too, sweating in his dress uniform, standing off to one side with his cell phone to his ear. I could see two pyrotechnic gurus doing a last-minute inspection of their mortars along the opposite side of the field. The high-school band was lining up along the right ballfield's third-base foul line.

"Let's sit closer than usual," Miss Maggie said at last.

"You'll have to climb back up the hill," Hugh warned her. "That's why we always sit up here."

"I know, but my eyes are just as old as my heart and my legs.

If I have to, I'll ask for a lift in the fire truck. Always wanted a ride in one. Or worse comes to worse, Hugh, you could carry me." She threw him a grin to show she was kidding, and started moving downhill. "Only thing we won't be able to see well will be the marching band, and with half of them on vacation, their formations won't be too precise anyway."

At the bottom of the slope we had our choice of spots, since everyone else preferred the vista from above, or perhaps wanted to keep a safe distance from the politicians. Miss Maggie chose the very front, middle, right across the service road from J. D., explaining, "They'll move all this stuff after the folks sitting here blow off a little hot air, so they won't be in the way of the fireworks."

As Hugh set up the chairs for Miss Maggie and Emmy, I shook open the blanket, seeing advantages to sitting on it, once it got dark and loud booms made me snuggle closer to the nearest male.

I sat down, but sprang up a moment later. "The grass is wet. It's coming straight through the blanket."

"They must have hosed down the ground because of the drought," Miss Maggie said. "Smart. Any of those sparks come back down, dry as this grass is . . . Well, you can stand for a minute or so, Pat. Then maybe Hugh'll let you sit in his lap."

Hugh either hated that idea or, like me, didn't relish the thought of getting his pants wet, because he said, "I'll go stand over by the snack bar and watch from there. If you fold the blanket a few times, the water shouldn't come through."

Was he being chivalrous? Or didn't he want me to tag along? As he walked away, my musing was cut off by the marching band drums (none of whom were on vacation), who struck up a loud roll. One of the suits (the mayor, I found out later) yelled into a cordless mike, "Please join in singing our National Anthem."

By the end of the first line, everyone was on their feet and short little me had lost sight of Hugh. I turned back to Miss Maggie but, even if I could have brought myself to be totally disrespectful, she was having way too much fun belting out the high notes for me to interrupt her. So I sang along, down an octave, facing the flag, which had been marched onto the field by a living history color guard wearing, interestingly enough, Confederate uniforms.

After a too-drawn-out "home of the brave"—after somebody behind me shouted "Play ball!"—I told Miss Maggie I was going to the snack bar, too.

"I thought you might. No need to rush back. But if you think of it, bring me a box of Cracker Jacks."

Everyone sat down, settling in for the boring part as the mayor introduced the VIPs. I took off down the service road at a fast walk, trying not to attract attention. That's when I spied Hugh, walking with purpose toward a familiar figure—emphasis on figure—leaning casually against the side of the snack bar, her thumbs hooked into the pockets of tight black jeans. Lynn.

22

I froze, thinking I must be mistaken. The glow of the field lights didn't stretch much beyond the dugouts, but the shadows around the snack bar weren't quite deep enough to play tricks on my eyes. No one else looked like that—long hair, untethered and draped over a loose tunic top, the hem of which stopped strategically right above the firm butt of her pants.

What was Lynn doing here? She couldn't be out on bail already, could she? On a holiday weekend? And she wasn't acting like an escaped convict.

Someone tapped my shoulder. "Pat? Sorry, you have to move."

I turned to face Dwight, uniformed and in his official hands-on-gun-belt stance. My mind was still on Lynn and I absently glanced around my feet to see if I'd stopped beside a fire hydrant.

"You have to move," he repeated. "You're blocking the view for these folks." He waved a hand at the spectators beside us. "They can't see J. D."

That's when I realized that the drone coming through the P.A. system was now J. D.'s voice. "In the immortal words of Tom Jefferson," he was saying, " 'When in the course of human events'—well, the course of human events has surely brought us here tonight. And George Washington said . . ."

I did a scan of the people whose view I was blocking. Even in the fast-fading light, I could tell that no one seemed particularly broken up about not being able to see the congressman. The women and children were preoccupied with each other. Most of the men in that section I recognized as Protectors, and they were giving me the same once-over I'd gotten this morning in their clubhouse, when they were looking for someone to blame.

I got a bad feeling, seeing them all seated together, even though they were with their families. Nonsense, I told myself, why *shouldn't* they be here? Most of the rest of the town was. I saw other people I knew. There was Elwood Walsh with, I supposed, his wife. Further up the hill, I spotted J. D.'s office manager, Kiesha.

"Sorry," I said to Dwight, wondering what he'd been told about Miss Maggie's and my visit to the clubhouse. I backed away, still glancing up the slope, watching all those Protectors' eyes follow me. Stepping up my pace, I turned back toward the snack bar.

Hugh and Lynn were gone.

Still walking, I surveyed the hillside once more. It was now too dark to identify anyone farther away than, say, thirty yards, but I figured Hugh's silhouette against the steel gray sky would be unmistakable. No luck. I glanced back toward our blanket. Miss Maggie and Emmy had their heads together, discussing something, but Hugh hadn't joined them.

At the snack bar, I stopped where I'd seen him last, as if, like a bloodhound, I could pick up his scent. I did a circuit of the building—he wasn't behind it or ordering sodas at the snack window. Lynn wasn't in the ubiquitous line in the women's room, nor at the sinks. No hems of black jeans showed below the stall doors either. I asked a preteen coming out of the men's room if he'd seen a red-haired giant inside. He shook his head.

My stomach was tense—some instinct was telling me to find Hugh and soon. I paused to make my brain analyze the feeling. Jealousy? Not enough to worry like this. Oh, I didn't *like* the thought of Hugh being with Lynn, but more because she was somehow mixed up in the murders. Because she'd lied—or at least been misleading—about her involvement.

But she *couldn't* be the murderer, could she? She'd been with Theo yesterday and hadn't tried to kill him. She'd even gone to V-TAC to find evidence to clear him.

Then, abruptly, everything Theo said came together. I had a clear idea what that evidence might be, along with a short list of who would murder for it. And I knew why my guts were telling me to find Hugh pronto.

"Hey, lady." The preteen was back, with two clones of himself. "My friend Stu here says he saw that guy you're looking for."

Stu's hand came out of the pocket of his baggy shorts so he could gesture. "Big guy? Red hair and mustache?"

"That's him."

"He went that way—" the arm flung out, indicating the service road, away from the crowd, toward the closest dugout, "—with a *very* sexy lady." His eyebrows did the mambo, expressing what he wouldn't say aloud, and his two friends made "woo-woo" sounds.

Thanking him, I hurried down the road. Stu called after me, "Hey, you his wife?" I ignored him.

Glancing over at the field, I saw a line of grammar school-age kids filing onto the stage, each clutching a sheet of paper as if it were a wild animal likely to escape on the evening breeze. The mayor said, "We'll now have the reading of the Declaration of Independence by Mrs. Alsop's fourth grade," and each child began reading a line or two, starting with "In Congress, July 4, 1776."

Good, I thought. Gave me more time. I figured Hugh was probably safe, at least until the band took the field.

I stepped into the shadows behind the dugout. The structure was painted forest green and the road was black macadam, probably newly repaved this season. Nothing reflected light. To my left was a wooded area—I heard the trickle of a creek. Through the trees, I could see dim house lights, too far distant to do me any good. The only way I knew I was on the road and not the grass was by the feel of the surface under my sneakers. Every time a lightning bug blinked on in front of my eyes, I jumped.

But I *could* see the announcer's booth ahead, since it was two stories high and one side was illuminated by the lights. White siding, windows facing the field, louvered vents in the side wall, top and bottom. I walked toward it, squinting through the shadows for any sign of Hugh or Lynn.

I strained my ears, but heard nothing except the Declaration and the mass whisperings of the crowd. As if to fill the void, the boom of a cherry bomb sounded, at least two blocks away, but close enough to do a job on my nerves.

Stepping onto the grass, I made for the break between the dugout and the booth, the only landscape feature resembling a hiding place. When I got there, though, instead of an alcove, I found a narrow entrance to the bleachers behind the diamond, with light peeking around the dugout wall. From there, across the double field, I could see the band silently filing into their starting positions. I'd try the announcer's booth, I decided, and look down the length of service road behind the fields before heading back.

I felt my way along the vinyl-sided wall of the booth. Over the P.A. I heard, "We mutually pledge to each other our Lives, our Fortunes, and our Sacred Honor," followed by enthusiastic clapping and cheering from the audience.

I found the entrance to the booth on the side facing the service road. The plain white door was pushed halfway open.

"Hello?" I said, diplomatically sticking my head inside. Warm, stuffy air hit me in the face. Light from the field streamed through the big windows on the second floor. I saw a landing under those windows, with stairs leading up on my left. A couple of stools and a table sat under the windows, but apparently announcers had to bring their own sound equipment. Or it was stored elsewhere. The interior walls were unfinished wood framing, but everything was painted white, so the light filtering down from above was enough to show that no one was there.

In the quiet after the applause, I heard a rustling noise behind me, but before I could turn my head, a big sweaty hand clamped over my mouth, pulling me back against a shirt dampened by the body heat radiating through it. I felt something hard and about the size of a nine-volt battery push into my side around kidney level. Something else, like a big pillow, cushioned my right buttock.

"Inside." Said in a hiss, but still recognizable as the person heading my short list. My stomach did a reverse flip with a full twist. The word was a direction—I was immediately hustled forward until we were both over the threshold. My assailant must have used a foot to shut the door.

Outside, I heard the band begin to play, I think, *Star Wars*. Hard to tell with the trumpets missing.

"I'm going to take my hand away. No one will hear you scream over the music. If you do anyway, I'll shoot you. Understand?"

Which confirmed my guess about the object burnishing my ribs. I nodded.

Not only did he remove his hand—he shoved me toward the opposite wall. I turned to face him and that's when I had my first shock.

The man in front of the door had longish blond hair under a navy blue baseball cap, riding low over lightly tinted glasses. His blond mustache looked like a collage of poodle clippings. He wore an extra-large black tee and work gloves, and a dark green trash bag was dangling from the bottom two fingers of his gun hand. The gun itself was smaller than I expected.

I recovered my voice. "J. D.?"

He shrugged. "Not much of a disguise, I know. I could only hide so much under my clothes tonight, but it got me out of the men's room unnoticed—if you carry a trash bag, everyone figures you for a janitor and doesn't give you a second look." He dropped the bag on the floor. "Now, tell me what you know."

"Know?"

One of J. D.'s Post-it Note expressions surfaced: disbelief. "No games, Miss Montallo. You arranged this meeting. If you intend to blackmail me, let's hear what you know."

Well, that explained what Lynn was doing here—she'd probably arranged the rendezvous, but J. D. didn't know who he was supposed to meet. Okay, one ace up my sleeve, but I didn't see how it could help. Stall, I told myself. "I know you meant to kill Theo, not his friend Wyatt."

That brought on a scowl of resentment. "A black man got out of that Honda and went into the mall, and a black man who looked like him came back out. I've been paying for that little switch of theirs ever since."

"And Billy covered for you by pretending to be a witness. You shot him because he knew you killed Wyatt."

J. D. grinned indulgently. "There you're wrong. Billy believed the road-rage story—I told him *I'd* witnessed it, but couldn't report it to the police because I'd been on my way to meet with a campaign contributor who needed to remain anonymous. Didn't want the newspapers saying I'd been down in that neck of the woods. Billy was only too glad to help out."

"So why'd you kill him?"

Sweat had begun to run down the sides of J. D.'s face and neck. Pushing his hat back, he swiped the glove of his free hand across his brow. "I stopped in at Billy's the next day, after I saw you in town. When he heard about the switched cars, he got it into his head that Theo must be guilty, just because he was black. Billy was bent on changing his story and blowing my whole setup. All I wanted was a simple road-rage explanation with an untraceable vehicle."

Another swipe with his glove, this time around the back of

his neck. His wig was probably acting like a thermal cap. "Anyway, I told him he couldn't accuse anyone unless he had proof, so he came up with this cockamamie scheme of confronting Theo and making him confess."

"Which is how you got Billy to come over to Bell Run," I said.

"Practically his idea. All I had to do was convince him that he should bait Theo alone while I hid in the woods and observed."

The band began a new song. I couldn't place it, but J. D. cocked his head to listen, then said, "*Titanic*. Saw that movie four times."

Probably just to watch people drown. "You used a different gun on Billy." I left the comment hanging, in want of an explanation.

J. D. obliged. "I got rid of the twenty-two Wednesday night. The forty-five was what I always kept in my car. 'Course, I had to get rid of that gun, too. Damn shame. I liked that firearm. Perfect balance, beautiful action. But I didn't have time to fetch another one from home."

Another one? J. D. obviously collected guns the way my Aunt Floss collected souvenir salt and pepper shakers. Though I doubt the little number in his hand had "Niagara Falls" etched into the grip.

"What else, Miss Montallo? Come on, we don't have much time."

Time? That's when it occurred to me how nicely the fireworks would cover gunshots. "You met Vicky Gibson through her father-in-law, probably when the Protectors worked on your last election campaign two years ago."

"Yes. Go on."

"She must have told you about a project V-TAC was doing for another politician—a get-out-the-vote mailing, with preprinted voter-registration forms. At the same time, Vicky was working on another mailing, sent to families all around the country who'd recently experienced a death. That database contained Social Security numbers. One of you got the idea to take dead people from other states and register them to vote in Virginia. In your district."

"Vicky's brainstorm," J. D. said.

"Then what? Absentee ballots for those names?"

"Applications can be submitted ten months in advance. She sent a few a week, from different post offices. Then, she sent in the ballots themselves."

"That's what put you over the top last time, isn't it, J. D.?"

He put on a Ronald Reagan golly-gee expression. "Way I see it, if I'm going to spend more money than my opponent anyway, some of it ought to guarantee me votes."

I spied a little brown spider crawling up the door frame and recalled my dream. J. D. certainly was as vain as the snake, but I didn't think he'd let me strap him to a log and chop him up. I went on, "Vicky was doing the same thing for you this year. Easier, now that those voters are established. She kept the 'deceased' database on her PC because she needed the names, dates of birth, and Social Security numbers. There must have been other files, too—say, linking the names to bogus Virginia addresses. After Theo mentioned the one database, Vicky couldn't be sure what else he'd seen, so she called you. Though I doubt she expected you to go right out and kill him."

"That's where I have to correct you." J. D. wiped his brow again. "Vicky said she was sure Theo was going to talk to their boss about the file the next morning. Said if she went down, she was taking me with her. She may not have used those exact words, but she wanted me to do something drastic. . . . Oh, listen, the last song."

Titanic had ended and the band was beginning its finale (the theme from *Shaft*), signaling the probable approach of my own finale. "So Vicky only got scared yesterday, after she heard about Billy. Then she tried to back out."

"She didn't get scared," J. D. said. "She got greedy. I'd been paying her generously for her services, but yesterday she asked for more. No, *demanded* more. Blackmail, pure and simple. Just like you."

Now I was confused. "But she was going to meet Theo, to tell him about Wyatt."

"No. She only called Theo to set up the meeting, then I went in her place."

"Except that Lynn Casey was with Theo when you arrived."

Another scowl, beyond resentment, into rancor. "And after he drove away from the mall, she stayed right behind him. I couldn't keep following him because I needed to get to Bell Run."

"To establish your alibi?" I ventured.

J. D. laughed, but didn't stop scowling—an ugly combination, especially with his fake mustache drooping in the heat. "No one suspected me. What I wanted was a way into V-TAC. Vicky had forgotten her ID or I would have taken hers. I knew Theo's wasn't in his apartment—I'd searched there on Thursday afternoon to make sure he didn't have any other evidence that could hurt me. So I took the chance he'd brought his ID to Bell Run with him."

"When did you go through his bag? During your doggie roast or after you set off the firecrackers and got us all out of the house?"

This time, I got a broad smile. "You don't know? Then the firecrackers worked. I went through his things during the afternoon, but somebody came up the stairs while I was in the bathroom and I had to hide the bag behind the shower curtain. I reckoned, when you found it, you'd know someone at the party was responsible, and Magnolia was already looking at me funny, wondering why I kept showing up. So I staged that little diversion afterwards to muddle the issue. Fitting send off for Billy—he gave me the firecrackers in the first place. I used a birthday candle and a pack of matches as a delayed fuse. Bet I was back in Stoke before it went off."

That's when the music stopped. I needed a plan, quick. As soon as the band got off the field, they'd turn off the lights and—

They'd turn off the lights. No town would spend tax bucks for a fireworks display, then ruin it by leaving the field lights on. And those lights were the only thing illuminating the booth. Until the fireworks themselves, that is. Which meant a few seconds, minimum, of total darkness.

23

J. D. had to know the lights would go out, I told myself. No one was that shortsighted. Then again, it only just occurred to me. Plus, if J. D. were big on thinking things out, he wouldn't have botched Theo's murder, or told Billy about the car switch, or killed Vicky before making sure all the evidence at V-TAC had been destroyed. Outside the drums began their exit cadence.

"What proof do you have?" he asked.

Proof? Oh, right, blackmailers were supposed to have incriminating letters or photos. "You left something of yours at one of the crime scenes." True enough—he'd never come back for his grill.

His eyes narrowed as he tried to remember. "Doesn't matter. So you picked up something of mine. I could say I lost it at Bell Run during the doggie roast."

"I didn't pick anything up. It's where you left it, and I know it has your fingerprints all over it."

"Tell me what it is." J. D. made that a threat, taking two steps toward me and extending his gun arm.

I resisted the urge to back away, scurrying instead to one side in pretended fear (okay, maybe only half-pretended fear), to give myself a less-obstructed path to the door. "No. If I tell you, you'll know exactly where you left it and you won't need me anymore."

The drum cadence ended with a flourish.

"I'm supposed to take your word for this?" he asked incredulously. "How do I know you aren't bluffing?"

"How else would I have figured out you were the murderer, J. D.? You were clever enough to cover your tracks otherwise."

I thought for sure he'd smell the b.s. in that, but no, his conceit got in the way (Ananse was right—I vowed, if I lived past this night, never to kill a spider again). J. D. nodded slowly as, I supposed, he mentally revisited all his tracks, making sure nothing was showing. The perfect moment for him to disregard me, it turned out, because that's when the lights went out.

I half expected him to panic and pull the trigger. He didn't. Even so, I didn't wait for his reaction, but lunged for the door, fumbling for what seemed like an eternity until I felt the knob in my hand. I was through the opening by the time J. D. uttered his first curse, and around the corner of the booth, headed for the field, by the time I heard sounds of pursuit.

I wasn't even halfway across the infield when a *phoomph* sounded ahead of me, and a column of luminous smoke climbed skyward, erupting into a red starburst with a boom so loud it set off three car alarms in the parking lot. A simultaneous *pop* sounded behind me, and on the pitcher's mound a few feet ahead, a cloud of dirt mushroomed as the bullet hit. Veering, I heard another shot, accompanied this time by a loud grunt. That bullet went wider, uprooting a divot between the mound and third base. More grunts, then curses, in stereo. I glanced over my shoulder.

J. D. was flat on his face beside the dugout, having been tackled by Hugh, who was hugging him around the waist. J. D. was trying desperately to stretch forward, to reach the gun on the ground in front of him.

Picturing him grabbing the weapon and turning it on Hugh, I did a one-eighty and charged. J. D. and Hugh looked up at me just as another rocket lit up the field. Hugh's face registered shock, J. D.'s, horror. The latter made a last, frenzied jab at his gun, missed, then covered his head with his arms.

Much as I wanted to kick him, I put my foot to better use, placing it behind the grip of the gun and gingerly pushing the firearm another five feet beyond J. D.'s reach.

A bright light blazed on in the gap between dugout and bleachers, blinding me. I put my hand up to block the glare. Behind the light were Dwight and Brackin, coming toward us, guns drawn.

"Come away from there, Miss Montella," Brackin said, assuming his normal Police-Line-Do-Not-Cross attitude. "We'll take it from here."

"Dennis, glad to see you," J. D. blustered, albeit anemically because he couldn't get a full breath with Hugh on top of him.

"Stuff it, J. D.," came Miss Maggie's voice from behind the sheriff. "Dwight, tell the congressman about his right to remain silent. Maybe that'll shut him up for once."

Problem was, the lawmen weren't willing to arrest J. D. without giving him a chance to explain (mind you, they didn't ask *me* for an explanation). And Hugh wasn't willing to release his quarry unhandcuffed. So for a few minutes we were at a stalemate, with J. D. assuring everyone that this was all a misunderstanding, and me shrieking things like, "Misunderstanding? He tried to kill me!" Meanwhile, the pyro-mavens realized they were being up-staged and paused their presentation. The lights came up, giving us an audience, which only encouraged J. D., though, in his disguise, no one in the crowd recognized him.

We'd still be there arguing if Ross hadn't shown up. His maroon sedan, followed by three state cruisers, sirens on full blast, skirted the emergency vehicles at the entrance and tore down the service road in back of the fields, screeching to a halt next to the booth. The spectators cheered, thinking this part of the show.

The sergeant had no problem barking out orders for J. D. to be arrested, cuffed, and stowed in the back of a squad car.

Hugh stood up and brushed off the shins of his chinos, then walked over to me. "You okay?"

I nodded, even though my legs and stomach were both feeling rubbery as I watched Ross drop J. D.'s gun in an evidence bag.

"Well, I'm not." Hugh put an arm around my shoulders and steered me toward Miss Maggie. "I pulled every muscle in my back. And there's no way I'll get the grass stains out of these pants."

His grousing brought me out of my shock, as I'm sure it was meant to. I smacked him on the stomach with the back of my fingers, peeved-Italian style. "Where *were* you? I was looking for you when—"

"I know, I know." He got a short reprieve while Miss Maggie hugged both of us. "I was on the other side of the announcer's booth, with her." He pointed to Lynn, sauntering out of the shadows toward us. "We were waiting for J. D. to go into the booth. You weren't supposed to be there."

"The plan," Lynn said, "was for me to follow J. D. inside, where I'd get him to confess while Sergeant Ross listened in through this." She raised the hem of her tunic, until we could all see a mini cell phone, fastened between her bosom and belly button with cloth medical tape.

"Her plan, not mine," Ross said as he walked by us. To Lynn, he said, "I told you when you called that I was twenty minutes away."

"You could have sent someone else." She waved a hand to indicate the troopers at his beck and call.

"Without proof? On one of our busiest nights of the year?"

Lynn turned to Hugh. "See? This kind of ass-backward thinking is why I asked you to be my insurance tonight."

"Insurance?" I asked.

"He was supposed stay outside, around the side, and listen through the vent in the wall, in case I needed rescuing." Lynn smiled at Hugh as if he were her pet St. Bernard.

"You would have put him in danger," I protested.

"And you didn't?"

"Ladies, ladies," Ross said. "Argue later. I need to take your statements so I know what all to charge J. D. with."

"You must have some notion, Sergeant," Miss Maggie said, "if you checked into everything I suggested to you on the phone this afternoon."

Ross glanced toward the cruiser where J. D. was incarcerated. "Unfortunately, Mrs. Shelby, Vicky Gibson seems to have 'accidently' formatted her computer hard drive before she was killed. I intend to check out the voter registers Monday—"

"But you've got diddlysquat for now. Rats."

"I wouldn't say that. Vicky had periodically deposited large sums of cash. J. D.'s campaign fund showed payments of similar amounts to a consultant named Smith. And we have Miss Casey's statement that she saw J. D. going into Theo's apartment building on Thursday afternoon."

"Dressed as a delivery man," Lynn said. "Brown ponytail, goatee. The man's got a fake-hair fetish." Then she seemed to realize that we hadn't all turned toward her to get a description of J. D.'s disguise, but were wondering why she'd been at Theo's apartment. "Pat gave me the idea to go talk to his neighbors—see if I could dig up an alibi for him for Wyatt's murder. No luck."

At that point, one of the fireworks guys came over to ask if they should pack up. Ross decided to let them finish their show, then dismiss the crowd. Miss Maggie sent Dwight over to fetch Emmy and the blanket and chairs, so we could all be comfortable, which we were, since the grass here was dry. I even felt big-hearted enough to offer Lynn a corner of the blanket. She declined, preferring to flirt with one of the troopers instead.

When the field lights came on again, Ross took statements from me and Hugh, and then Miss Maggie, who explained how she'd sent Brackin after J. D. when he left the speakers' platform. The sheriff lost the congressman at the restroom, so Miss Maggie led the search herself, finding Hugh and me by interrogating the same preteens. By the time Ross was finished with us, the crowd was gone, hastened by flashes of lightning in the western sky and low rumbles of thunder.

Ross, feeling charitable, had one of his troopers give us a ride back to my car—not exactly the fire truck Miss Maggie had hoped for, though he did let her play with the siren.

On the way home, Miss Maggie told us why she'd suspected J. D. "He kept popping up. I saw him more these past few days than I have since he showed up regularly in my detention room. I assumed he was trying to use the Foundation's project for free publicity, but really, it wasn't close enough to the election for that kind of effort. After Theo's bag was searched, I thought, if the thief was one of our visitors yesterday, well, who arranged for those visitors to be there in the first place? Then today, when Theo mentioned what was in Vicky's database, it fell into place. Oh, she *could* have been stuffing the ballot box for the Protectors, because of strong political beliefs, but big money is usually the better motivator and J. D. would have paid her well. Plus, he had the most convincing motive."

Hugh grunted his agreement. "Salary, benefits, perks, not to mention lobbyists wining and dining him, and—"

"Symptoms," I said. "His motive was his power addiction."

Miss Maggie concurred. "He's one of those people we talked about this morning. One of the harmless who becomes dangerous."

A bright streak of lightning lit up the whole car. I counted the seconds to the thunder. Four, compared to seven the last time. Getting closer.

At the house, as the first drops of rain hit the car. Hugh and Emmy hurried inside, I stopped Miss Maggie on the porch. "If Theo's in the cellar, I want to—" there was no other way to say it, "—to have a séance." Alma had been patient all night, as if giving me a chance to get Theo out of trouble. Or perhaps she was shying away from the next part of her story. Time to coax it out of her.

Miss Maggie nodded. "Do you want me to keep Emmy and Hugh upstairs out of the way?"

"No. I won't do it behind Hugh's back this time. Not only that, but—your grandfather's involved somehow. I want you to sit in."

The light from the front hall was enough for me to see her eyes open wide. The shadow of a moth on the screen made a dark spot on her forehead that reminded me of Mance. "All right. I'll talk to Emmy and—" A bolt of lightning silhouetted the tops of the trees, accompanied by an almost-simultaneous crash of thunder. "Quick, get inside. Let's see if Theo's downstairs."

He was—in the dark, huddled over by the outer steps, with the cooler and bag of clothes, looking forlornly homeless. It took some doing to assure him he'd been cleared.

When Miss Maggie and I brought him upstairs, Emmy was overjoyed to see him, scolding him to keep herself from breaking down and crying. "You've been here in the woods the whole time? I wasted a ton of worry on you, Theo Clayborne."

Then, too impatient to wait, I asked him, "Are you up for another visit to your great-great-great-grandmother?"

He grew solemn and nodded. "I doubt she'll let me sleep tonight if I don't. I saw her again, just before I came inside. Running through the woods, like last time." He looked down at himself, now dressed in his shorts and work boots, but no less scruffy than when we'd seen him this afternoon. His five o'clock shadow had crossed the international date line. "Let me wash up first. If I'm going to see a grandmother, I want to be clean behind the ears."

Theo went upstairs. Miss Maggie took Emmy into the war room to brief her on the upcoming spook summons. That left me alone in the hall with Hugh, who looked like I'd taken away his favorite toy.

"Come into the kitchen," I said, entering that room myself and switching on the light. I'd heard once, on a cable documentary about spiritualism, that mediums never eat before séances. None of them must be Italian because, in my family, we eat before everything. And after. Right now, I needed a chocolate fix.

Hugh stopped in the doorway. "I should get home. I've got a long drive tomorrow."

That took me by surprise. Of course, with the danger gone, he had no reason to spend the night. No excuse, anyway.

"Wait 'til the storm passes." On cue, thunder boomed and the lights flickered. Rain lashed loudly against the kitchen windows. Good thing we hadn't left them open.

From the freezer I retrieved the tub of Neapolitan frozen yogurt, and from the stainless drawer, two spoons, one of which I held out to him. He hesitated, but seeing that I intended to stand there until he took it, he finally came forward. Setting the container on the counter—strategically, so he had to inch closer to me to help himself—I spooned out some chocolate and let it melt on my tongue.

"Here's the deal," I said as I scooped out another dose. "Once Beth Ann gets home, I'm giving up this ghost stuff for good. In fact, the word 'ghost' will be gone from my vocabulary. Swear to God."

Hugh had a spoonful of strawberry almost to his lips. He stuck it back in the tub. "You mean that?"

"What part of 'Swear to God' don't you understand? If it weren't for Miss Maggie, I'd give it up tonight." Miss Maggie *and* Theo, and needing to finish what I'd begun, and being consumed with curiosity. Hugh didn't need to know all that. I downed a third mouthful of yogurt. "In return, for starters, I want dinner."

His eyebrows went up. "For starters?"

"Yeah. Depends how good dinner is."

That got me one of his pseudo-evil leers. Another thunder clap—the loudest of all, making me jump—got me his arm around my waist. I decided my patience and freedom-relishing were expendable. Tossing my spoon on the counter, I put my hands on his shoulders.

His leer mutated into revelation, but he merely said, "Watch, any second now, Miss Maggie'll bust in here."

"Bound to."

But she didn't bust in. Instead, she yelled from the front hall, "Come on, Pat. Theo's ready."

"We'll be right there," I yelled back, but neither of us moved.

"Dinner," Hugh said decisively. "Monday night. And we'll maroon Miss Maggie and Beth Ann here with a couple of videos. Okay?"

"Long videos."

Another flash and boom and the lights flickered off completely, as if Someone Upstairs was telling us to shut up and kiss. Who was I to ignore divine intervention?

"Pat had trouble finding the flashlight," Hugh said smoothly as we entered the war room and Miss Maggie asked what took us so long. It was true. I hadn't yet had occasion to use the kitchen flashlight. Hugh knew where it was, but he'd been, well, busy.

Miss Maggie waved the explanation aside, having more important things on her mind. "What do you think, Pat? The kitchen chairs?"

Oh, sure, I was the resident expert in what chairs to use for invoking the dead. "Why not?" I said, and sent Theo and Hugh to fetch three, because I wanted only Miss Maggie and Theo in the circle with me.

Once set up, everyone took seats—Hugh and Emmy perched anxiously on two of the recliners (Hugh wanted to pace, but I wouldn't let him). Miss Maggie, Theo, and I joined hands and closed our eyes.

And nothing happened.

"Pat?" Miss Maggie said, after I'd been looking at the insides of my eyelids for an eon, feeling foolish.

"Not yet," I said, thinking I should have known. Every other time I'd tried to go after a vision, with no provocation from the Other Side, this is what happened. "Theo?"

No answer. His hand held mine in a snug grip. I could hear him breathing evenly. "Theo?" I opened my eyes and a flash of lightning coming through the side window lit up his face: bearded, since he hadn't shaved yet, but serene. Like he was in a deep sleep. Or someplace far, far away. Is that what I looked like when I went under?

I closed my eyes again and this time, instead of reaching out to Alma with my mind, I reached no further than Theo, as if he were a satellite dish for Afterlife Direct TV. That's when the thunder and lightning and rain beating against the windows faded.

ALL MY TRIALS, LORD, SOON BE OVER

I had crossed the line of which I had so long been dreaming. I was free; but there was no one to welcome me to the land of freedom.

—HARRIET TUBMAN

July 4, 1871

By the time Mama go 'round to the side of the church, Noah and Zeb be already gone—off hunting up burlap sacks. Amos stay behind, saying they be on a fool's chore and he had his fill of such nonsense the night he seen Jack Soyers with his neck broke. Preacher Moses stay behind, too, but Joe Putnam go with 'em and that make Ida mad. Joe miss the colored boys race. Homer Brown from Stoke won it for the third year in a row.

Mama tell Preacher what she say to Ida—'bout Mr. Fletcher being on the road last night, so ain't possible he killed the Reynolds—and how Noah and Zeb got to be stopped. Preacher say not to worry, that he gonna go find them. Even if he can't, he gonna send word to Caleb, telling him to stay off the plank road tonight, no matter what he hear 'bout someone needing medicine out our way.

After the parade, there be baseball games for any man or boy who want to play, then the African Church

307

preacher bring out big watermelons and we all eat some. I spit out the seeds farther than Lilla.

But Noah, Zeb, Joe, and now Preacher still be missing. Mama and Ida say we ought to get home 'fore dark, in case there be trouble like at the Reynolds, 'cause Jordana, Uncle Henry, and little Adam be alone.

"But Mama," I say, "we gonna miss the Roman candles."

"We'll go up the top of the hill, Mance," she say. "I bet we can see 'em from there."

So we leave town and have our supper on Church Hill, and when it get dark, we watch toward Stoke. The Roman candles wasn't high enough, but we seen five rockets shoot up over St. Anne's church steeple. We hear shots, too, somewhere 'tween us and town. Preacher come back then, but he ain't found Noah and Joe and he be surprised they still gone.

Wasn't 'til later, when Mama and me was in our cabin and she was telling me a story 'fore I go to sleep, that we hear somebody running up the path from the town road. Running and yelling, so we both run out on the doorstep to see what the fuss be about. Ida be outside already, 'cause she know the voice be her Joe's.

He stop in front of her, holding his side, breathing hard, looking like he seen the Yankee ghosts down on Orange Turnpike. "Mama, we got to get away from here. The Harris brothers be coming, and Sheriff Cox with them. Gonna burn us out, they say."

"Where's your Pa?"

"He coming behind me. Told me to run ahead and tell you to pack up what we could carry. The sheriff catch Zeb and they taking him back to jail—that's how we got time to warn everybody—but they say they coming out to burn our homes and arrest all our menfolk. They say we set torch to our own church and to the Reynolds' place, and kill Miz Reynolds 'cause she be white. They gonna hang any man they catch."

Noah come while Joe be talking and he said it all true. Him, Zeb, and Joe be lying in wait for Caleb, 'cept he never came. 'Stead, Charlie Harris happen by, so they jump out to ambush him, only it be a trick. Three men on horseback, all done up in white sheets, come out of nowhere. "Jes' like last harvest time," Noah say. "Only this time all of them speak. That last man be Sheriff Cox, so it won't do us no good to ask for justice. Quick, Ida. Grab what you can. Me and Amos'll carry Uncle Henry on his chair."

Mama pull me inside and make me roll my one shirt and her good shift inside our old quilt. She put what food we got in her sewing bag. All the while I hear the men shouting back and forth 'bout where we ought to go.

"They gonna be on the road," Noah say, "maybe follow it up all the way to Salem Church looking for us."

"We oughta head north," Amos say.

Preacher agree. "We can ford the river below the graveyard. It's not that deep right now. We can carry the children on our backs."

So we all head back up the hill, taking whatever was light and fit in our arms. Uncle Henry balance the small iron kettle on his lap, which be the only pot we take. Jordana brung her hoe and a sack full of collards, beans, corn, and seeds, saying she can grow food any place there be water and wasn't the first home she be put out of. Joe put a tether on the she-goat and lead her along, carrying her when she get mulish. We can't take the chickens, so we let 'em go free.

Up at the Rebel graves, as everyone start down the trail to the river, Mama hold me back. "Wait here, Mance."

She run over to stop Jordana and whisper in her ear. Jordana all of a sudden be hugging her and saying, "You sure, child?" and giving her food from her sack. Mama whisper something more, and Jordana nod and say, "You be careful, too."

Mama come back to me, and set down her bundle so's she can put her hands on my shoulders. "Listen, Mance," she say softly. "We ain't going with them. We going south to find your brother."

"By ourselves, Mama?"

"We gonna be fine. All we got to do is get across the road and follow Flat Run."

She gather up her things as she talk, but 'fore we can move, Preacher call from the top of the trail, "Come on, Alma. Everyone else is already halfway across." I can hear water splashing soft below.

"I ain't going, Moses."

"Not going." Preacher say it like he knowed it all along. He walk toward us, out of the shadows, carrying his sack of clothes and books. "I guess you think you're headed back to Caleb."

"No, Moses—"

"It won't do you any good. Caleb's dead."

"Dead?" Mama repeat, dazed-like.

"Burned with his store tonight, so you've got no place to go but with us."

"Not true," say another voice, back behind the trees. Mr. Fletcher hisself limp out, wearing no jacket or tie. His shirt be torn, and moonlight shone off a white bandage he got wrapped 'round his head, except one spot on the cloth be ugly dark with blood. But he be alive as me, and holding a shovel at the ready, like it be a club. "Moses tried to kill me tonight, but he only hit me hard enough to stun me for a moment, and he didn't know I keep a homemade fire extinguisher handy in the store. With all the July Fourth revellers on the streets, he couldn't stay around to make sure his flame did its work."

"So I was right," Mama say. "I knew that glove Mance found meant a black man burned our church. Only reason to wear a fancy glove like that be to hide something like a scar—and no white man I know got one on his hands—or to cover up skin color. Why, Moses? Why you set torch to your own church?"

"I didn't mean to burn the whole building. Caleb's tonic went up faster than I thought it would." Preacher glance over his shoulder, down at the river, like he worried the others'll hear him, but water ain't splashing no more, so I guess they's gone. "I chose the church, Alma, because nobody would be inside. And because I knew Mance would be up on the hill, watching for you to come home. He'd see a man on horseback, dressed like the Harrises were the last time they came out here, and his description would plant the idea in everyone's mind that a white man was responsible. When Congressman Reynolds's house burned the same way—"

"But it didn't," Mama say. "Uncle Henry's bottle be full when I saw it."

"Full of water, Alma."

"The Reynolds?" I say, not believing my ears. "You kill the Reynolds, Preacher? All 'em? Even the chil'un?"

He take a deep breath. "Remember our lesson the other night, Mance? Our talk about how the whites weren't content to enslave our race? How they've diluted our blood with their own? Made us weak? You and I, Mance, we're both weak because of it. Mr. Reynolds was so weak, he took a white woman into his bed. Just like all the white men that took our women. Am I right, Caleb? You're as weak as they come."

Mr. Fletcher didn't answer, though he lower his shovel 'til his arms be hanging straight down.

Preacher Moses turn back to me. "God never meant for coloreds and whites to cohabit, Mance. It's wrong. All I did was stop Mr. Reynolds. And I tried to stop Caleb tonight, from making your mother do wrong again."

"Moses, you fool," Mama say. "We ain't going to live with Caleb. We be going south to look for my other boy, Jim."

"Is that right, Alma? Are you done being Massa Caleb's woman?"

'Fore she could speak, we all hear horses galloping fast up the plank road, though Preacher keep talking like he didn't care. "First I wasn't supposed to look at you because you were a fieldhand and I was a house servant. Then they moved you to the house, but only because young Travis's friend, Caleb Fletcher, had taken a fancy to you. After that, if any of us so much as glanced at you, Travis and Caleb had us whipped. Did you know that, Alma?"

"I knew, Moses," Mama say soft. "Nothing I could do."

We hear commotion down in the holler—shouting, and horses trampling the brush.

"Nothing you could do *then*." Preacher come a step closer. "What about now? You took a job from him, Alma, after what he did to you."

"I got to feed and clothe my son, Moses." Mama spit that out, her voice an angry whisper now. "All I be is a colored woman. I got no almighty vote. Black men turn down jobs for the same wages I bring home. I can't be particular who I work for."

"No?" Preacher say, "Then what about that story you came up with today, saying Caleb was on the road behind you, when I saw you walking together last night with my own eyes?"

There come more loud crashing from the holler, and through the trees, I see flames shoot up—our homes getting burnt. Mama and Mr. Fletcher look over there, too, and that's when Preacher catch us all unawares.

I hear Mama cry out and see Preacher charging at Mr. Fletcher. In Preacher's hand, something gleam in the moonlight: his skinning knife.

"Moses, no," Mama say, and she go darting after him, grabbing at his shirt. He send his elbow back into her face and she go down hard.

"Mama!" I run to her, dropping to my knees.

"I be fine," she manage to say, though one side of her jaw be crooked and blood be coming out her mouth. "Run now. Hide yourself."

But I don't listen 'cause I ain't gonna leave her. She get to her feet, watching Preacher and Mr. Fletcher circle each other, the latter using his shovel mostly like a shield. Sometimes he get in a good swing so Preacher got to jump back. Mr. Fletcher's bad leg, though, it be slowing him down. And he be calling over to us, "Alma, get Mance away while you can," and such, 'stead o' keeping his mind on the fight.

That be his undoing. When he glance in our direction, Preacher's free hand grab the shovel up under the metal, making Mr. Fletcher stumble and land on his knees, his neck right in line with the next slash of Preacher's blade.

Mama lunge, clutching Preacher's wrist, throwing all her weight away from Mr. Fletcher. Preacher, swinging his shoulders toward her, lose his balance. They fall together, Mama on the bottom.

Preacher let go of the shovel as he fall. Mr. Fletcher

jump to his feet, sweeping it over his shoulder and down onto Preacher's head with an awful thud. Preacher make a gurgling sound in his throat and lie still.

Mr. Fletcher roll him off Mama. "It's all right now, Alma. He's dead."

"No," she say in a coarse whisper. "He put his knife in me, Caleb. I be dead, too. Mance, honey, where are you? Come close . . ."

24

Miss Maggie skipped church the next morning and let me sleep late. I deduced this from the bright sunlight streaming through the bedroom windows, open wide to receive a dry, cool breeze that smelled exhilaratingly fresh.

When I reached for my watch on the nightstand to confirm my deduction, my hand encountered a picture postcard of a pretty pink flower called a Virginia rose. I knew that because the name was printed in one corner, under the words "Chesapeake Bay." Flipping the card over, I saw, in an awkward cursive, with circles dotting the "i"s:

Pat,
There's a whole bush of these wild roses in back of my uncle's shore house. Wish you were here to go swimming and biking with us.

Love, Beth Ann

Under that, in an almost illegible scrawl: "Me, too. Hugh."

And over below my address, in small, neat printing: "Hugh, this was in our box by mistake. P. Morgan."

Postmarked last Monday. Better late than never. I reread the "Me, too," a few times before heading for the shower, which is when I remembered that Hugh would be halfway to Poquoson already. He'd bring Beth Ann home this evening and, as promised, I'd start saying no to ghosts.

I hadn't dreamt of Alma or Mance, or even of spiders last night. I thought I would. My latest vision had ended when Alma died. Theo said he'd seen no more than I had. Miss Maggie, much to her disappointment, had remained in the here and now. According to her, Theo and I neither moved nor said a word. Hugh had pronounced our séance duller than televised chess. Emmy, while amazed that Theo and I could concoct the same story, was understandably skeptical.

So I still didn't know what happened to Mance after Alma died—or to Miss Maggie's grandfather, for that matter. Then again, Alma wouldn't know either. The whole business felt unsettled.

I dressed and headed downstairs, only to meet Theo coming up, two steps at a time, singing "Oh, What A Beautiful Morning." He grinned through his warbling, but didn't slow down.

Miss Maggie's and Emmy's voices came out of the war room, the latter exclaiming, "I wouldn't have believed it if I hadn't found it myself!"

"Found what?" I asked as I entered.

"Tell her, Emmy," Miss Maggie said.

"I went out first thing this morning," Emmy said. "Figured if there was an ounce of truth to what you two said you saw, I might find a knife scrape on one of the ribs."

"And you found one?"

"Hell, no. I found the blade itself, a quarter inch below the bottom left rib."

"Another piece of solid evidence," I said, not feeling very excited about it. "But we'll never have enough to be able to prove who she was."

Miss Maggie pshawed. "Don't give up yet, Pat. Read this first. Start here. Read it aloud. I want to hear it again."

She held out a paper for me to take, pointing to a spot halfway down the page. The handwriting was neat, though cramped and blurred by a fax transmission, so I read slowly. " 'I've grown too old to tend Alma's grave. Squirrels ate half the tulip bulbs on it, and the ones that came up this year are all overgrown with wild mint and clover.' "

"The only place I know that Granddaddy planted tulips," Miss Maggie said, "was right where those bones are now, and I recall the weeds that last year. What you're holding, by the way, is his next-to-last letter to Mance."

I was too busy reading the rest of it to myself to hear her. "I won't be cheating the devil much longer," Caleb had written. "I wanted to tell you—well, I just wish things had been different from the start. Though I guess, if they had been, I never would have known you. That night we buried Alma, I said I was going back to town and get drunk. You reminded me of the promise I'd made to her, never to touch spirits again. I've kept that promise and it's time I thanked you for it."

I felt tears well up in my eyes, but Miss Maggie said, "Don't get all choked up yet. It gets better. Here's page two. Read the paragraph that starts 'Much as I wanted. . . .' "

" 'Much as I wanted you to stay with me,' " I read aloud, " 'you were right to leave Stoke and pursue Alma's last wish. I was always sorry it never worked out for you. Odd, though, you mentioning a neighbor named Avery. I seem to recall Jim's last master being an Avery, though like as not, your brother changed his name since—' "

"Stop there," Miss Maggie said, swapping papers with me one more time. "Now, here's Granddaddy's last letter. He was pretty sick at the time—you can see that the handwriting's shakier—but he thought this important enough to post without us knowing it."

" 'Dear Mance,' " I read, struggling over the script, " 'By the time you get this, I expect to be dead. I had to tell you, though, of one piece of luck. Ask that neighbor of yours if he knows a

Tobias Avery. If he does and you can find him, Alma will finally rest easy, and so will I.' "

"Madonne," I murmured, as I realized what it meant.

Miss Maggie grinned. "You're thinking what I'm thinking—that Alma's last wish was that Mance find his brother. Song told me this last letter was unopened when her mother found it—Mance had been too sick to read it. Never knew his brother lived right next door all those years."

"If Jim Jackson became Tobias Avery," I mused, "then Theo and Wyatt were cousins."

She nodded. "There *was* a family resemblance, remember. If the family wants to be absolutely sure, they can have a DNA test done. The 'Y' chromosomes ought to match perfectly."

"No, Magnolia," said Emmy. "That would mean Mance and his brother had the same father, not the same mother."

"Same mother *and* father." Miss Maggie slapped her thigh for emphasis. "And I'm willing to volunteer the DNA of any or all my brothers' sons and grandsons to prove it." She turned to me. "Pat, when we were talking about Granddaddy the other night, you said guilt's a powerful motivator. Well, blood's a thousand times more potent."

"If you're right, Miss Maggie, then you and Theo are cousins, too."

"You ask me," Emmy said, "the whole story's turning into a Shakespeare comedy. Next thing you know, Magnolia'll say she's my long-lost twin."

"Did you tell Theo?" I asked. I could still hear him upstairs, singing his way through the entire score from *Oklahoma!* "No, you couldn't have, or he wouldn't be in such a good mood."

"Smarty-pants. Yes, I told him. His mood stems from the fact that Shawna's driving up here after her service, to give Theo a lift back to his apartment."

"Oh, that's right. His weekend's up today." I was bummed.

"He'll be back," Emmy said. "He and Hugh already have a

date to watch a Braves game together the Saturday night after the All-Star break."

It'd taken me two months to get a real date with Hugh. Theo landed a Saturday night after only three days. Sheesh.

Ten minutes later, when Shawna walked in, Theo picked her up and spun her around. "Do you know how glad I am that you're adopted?"

"What?" she gasped.

"Because if there were any chance of us being cousins—even fourth or fifth cousins—I'd feel funny asking you to marry me."

Her mouth hung open for a moment, then she said, "Was that a proposal? I thought you minded me being a minister."

"Not if you don't mind me being an anthropologist. I'm giving notice at V-TAC next week. Emmy said she'll give me field-work credit for this dig and—"

"What about your music?"

"You never heard of an anthropologist who sings for weddings and funerals?"

For an answer, she kissed him.

Before they got too maudlin, Emmy asked them for a ride to Charlottesville, so she could pick up her car and some other things from home. Shawna agreed, but was anxious to get going, so Miss Maggie and I shooed them on their way, saying we'd cover the pits and put away the tools. Then, for the first time since Wednesday night, we found ourselves alone at Bell Run.

I slipped my feet into my tennies and we went around to the side yard. Small tree branches and bits of bark littered the ground today, and one tent—J. D.'s appropriately—had blown over in the storm. The grass was wet, soaking quickly through the canvas toes of my shoes. As we pulled the tarp over Alma's remains, I asked what would happen to her.

"Theo's already given Emmy the Clayborne family's permission to move Alma to UVA for testing," Miss Maggie said. "They'll be able to learn a lot from her—about the nutrition, lifestyle, and general health of freed slaves—that sort of thing. After the testing, we all agreed that she ought to go back to Rock Hill, to be buried with her two sons."

"Good, that's exactly what Alma's wanted all along." I got a teacher look—one that asked if I'd been doing extra credit without telling her. I tried to explain. "When we were in Rock Hill, you said the ghost came out of the woodwork this week because Theo showed up at our door. That's backwards. Alma came back on the anniversary of her death—but this was the *first* anniversary that one of her descendants was in a position to come to Bell Run if human remains were found."

"You're saying that because Theo was Emmy's assistant . . ."

"Right—but even if he'd been one of our volunteers, or one of Brackin's deputies, or anyone else who'd become involved, or if, instead of Theo, Wyatt were in the same position—"

"Oh." A lightbulb went on in Miss Maggie's eyes. "You're saying that, to get one of her family here, she sent Mance into your dreams to tell you where to dig."

I nodded. "When Theo arrived, she started haunting him as soon as he crossed the creek. He even said he wondered if she had a message for him."

"Did she tell you this, Pat?"

"No." I did a quick internal scan, to find out why I was so sure. "Maybe sharing her experiences—and her feelings—so much the last few days . . . I guess she did tell me, indirectly."

Miss Maggie stepped out of the pit, then turned to look back at it. "When this dig's over, what would you think if, instead of planting vegetables, we put a tulip garden here?"

I said I loved the idea.

As we were mounting the porch steps, Lynn's red pickup came out of the woods. She took the turnaround clockwise, so she could lean out of her truck cab to talk. "I've got a petition here, trying to get my name into consideration for the congressional race. Someone has to run against Cora this fall. Oh, it won't be me—

the party bosses'll no doubt pick a clone of J. D.—but if I get enough signatures, maybe I can shake up the system some."

Miss Maggie snatched the petition and pen from her hands, signing it even without her reading glasses.

While I was adding my John Hancock, Lynn said, "I'm not supposed to know this, but Ross already did a ballistics test on that twenty-two J. D. had last night. Same gun that killed Vicky. He got lazy about disposing of weapons."

"Good," Miss Maggie said. "Got him for one murder, at least. Admirable how you threw yourself into this investigation, Lynn. You can stop feeling guilty about Theo's mother now."

She grinned, even laughed quietly, but her manner was pure resignation. "You're shrewd, Magnolia."

"I'm right, too. Lucy Clayborne's death had nothing to do with your affair with her husband."

"Sure it did." Lynn took back the petition. "Lucy walked in on us that night. She was more than a tad upset when she drove off."

Miss Maggie pursed her lips. "You know, Bea had a stroke last year. An old friend sitting with him now and then might help bring back his confidence."

"Like I said, Magnolia. You're shrewd." Lynn put her truck in gear and drove away without a good-bye.

"Must be my Italian blood," I said as I held the screen door for Miss Maggie. "All this guilt flying around makes me hungry."

"Get your car keys, Pat. I'm taking us to Sunday brunch at the Bluebell."

Bad enough that she paid for groceries. I hated that I couldn't treat her to a meal out once in a while. Tomorrow, I told myself, first thing, I'd go job hunting.

The Bluebell was a quaint, American Gothic bed-and-breakfast. The waiting line for tables was out the door—a good sign at any eatery—but when Miss Maggie walked in, the staff made a fuss that rivaled the restaurant scene in *Hello, Dolly*. She waved off the special attention, telling them to take care of their other customers first, that we'd take a turn around the garden while we waited. The proprietress herself, Lizzie Adams—quaint, too, in an artistic-people-person kind of way—came out to be our guide.

"The garden's small," she said, opening a white picket gate off the back patio, "but I like to use fresh herbs in the summer, and put my own flowers on the tables and in the rooms. Though lately, with the drought and heat, everything's dying. Even last night's rain doesn't seem to have helped much."

She had a kitchen plot that made me drool with envy—chives, dill, oregano, basil, you name it. But the plants looked limp, and only the most established shrubs were flowering.

"The ground's gotten so hard," I said, "the rain must have run off without soaking in. Probably all you need to do is break up the dirt around the roots, then make sure you give everything a good watering—every day for the herbs. Maybe a dose of Miracle Grow after about a week."

Lizzie smiled. "She's hired, Magnolia."

"Hired?" That was me, puzzled.

"My gardener retired and moved to Richmond," Lizzie explained. "I've been looking for someone to take over. Of course, it's just part-time—not much money. Though I know I wasn't Howard's only customer."

I raised my eyebrows at Miss Maggie, who was grinning from ear to ear, not even trying to look like she hadn't planned this.

"Pat," she said, "you can go back to one of those office cubicles you hate so much or, at least for the next few months, you can spend some time outside, nurturing living things. Which sounds like more fun to you? Decide quick. I'm starved."

No brainer. I took the job where I could best use my pantyhose—to tie back vines.

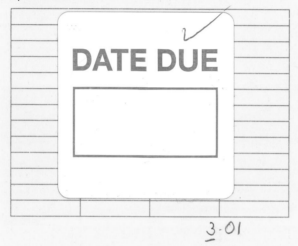

DATE DUE

3·01

001692   9776156